KU-671-424

The
Dying Day

Vaseem Khan

HODDER

First published in Great Britain in 2021 by Hodder & Stoughton
An Hachette UK company

This paperback edition published in 2022

3

Copyright © Vaseem Khan 2021

The right of Vaseem Khan to be identified as the Author
of the Work has been asserted by him in accordance with
the Copyright, Designs and Patents Act 1988.

All rights reserved. No part of this publication may be reproduced, stored
in a retrieval system, or transmitted, in any form or by any means without
the prior written permission of the publisher, nor be otherwise circulated in
any form of binding or cover other than that in which it is published and
without a similar condition being imposed on the subsequent purchaser.

All characters in this publication are fictitious and any resemblance
to real persons, living or dead, is purely coincidental.

A CIP catalogue record for this title is available from the British Library

Paperback ISBN 978 1 529 34109 6

Typeset in Adobe Caslon by Hewer Text UK Ltd, Edinburgh
Printed and bound in Great Britain by Clays Ltd, Elcograf S.p.A.

Hodder & Stoughton policy is to use papers that are natural, renewable
and recyclable products and made from wood grown in sustainable
forests. The logging and manufacturing processes are expected to
conform to the environmental regulations of the country of origin.

Hodder & Stoughton Ltd
Carmelite House
50 Victoria Embankment
London EC4Y 0DZ

www.hodder.co.uk

This book is dedicated to all those who love a good puzzle. And, so ... If you can tell me which Indian artefact/structure the below riddle refers to, your name shall go into a lucky draw. The winner will receive a free box of FIVE hand-curated crime fiction bestsellers from my publisher. If you're not sure of the answer, enter anyway! I'll pick a second name at random to use in a short story featuring the characters in the series.

A spectral presence, at water's edge,
That grief hath raised, by sovereign's pledge,
Twixt walls of snow, lie lovers' past,
Neath stony Crown, by masons cast.

To enter the competition, please visit my
website: www.vaseemkhan.com

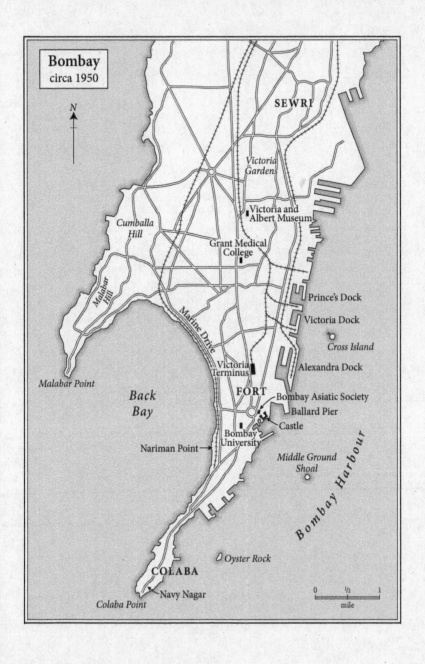

Bombay
circa 1950

N

SEWRI

Victoria Gardens

Victoria and
Albert Museum

*Cumballa
Hill*

Grant Medical
College

*Malabar
Hill*

Prince's Dock

Victoria Dock

Cross Island

Marine Drive

Alexandra Dock

Malabar Point

*Back
Bay*

Victoria
Terminus

FORT

Bombay Asiatic Society

Ballard Pier

Castle

Bombay
University

Nariman Point →

*Middle Ground
Shoal*

Bombay Harbour

Oyster Rock

COLABA

→ Navy Nagar

Colaba Point

0   ½   1
mile

I

The dog watched her as she toiled up the steps. Thirty steps, shimmering in the late morning sun. At the summit a security guard was attempting to shoo away a limbless beggar strategically positioned at the base of one of the portico's Doric columns. She wondered how he'd made it up the steps.

The guard raised his lathi but then caught sight of her out of the corner of his eye. Something in her expression stayed his hand. Or perhaps it was her khaki uniform and the revolver at her hip. His milky eyes widened. Like many in the city, he had yet to absorb the fact that there was now a living, breathing female police inspector among them. At times, she felt like a mythical creature, a mermaid or a fabulous Garuda bird.

She watched as he melted back towards the Society's foyer.

The dog twitched its ears, lolling on its forepaws. There was something knowing in its gaze, world-weary and cynical.

Persis turned back to look for her colleague. Birla had stopped a dozen steps below to wipe his forehead with a handkerchief, his dark, pockmarked face shiny with sweat. Behind him the vista opened out on to Colaba Causeway and the Horniman Circle Gardens. The road was alive with traffic: cars, trucks, bicycles, a red double-decker bus, the side of its upper deck pasted with an advert for Pond's talcum powder. Tongas ferried passengers at a leisurely pace while handcartwallahs moved load around the city. Below the steps a row of wizened men sat on the pavement beneath black umbrellas selling everything from fruit to wooden dolls.

Birla caught up with her. 'It's just a missing book,' he muttered. 'Why does it need two of us?'

Not bothering to answer, she turned and headed into the building. The beggar salaamed her as she walked past and she realised that his arm had been hidden under his ragged shirt while he feigned disability.

The Bombay Branch of the Royal Asiatic Society of Great Britain and Ireland had been around in one form or another since 1804, when James Mackintosh, a chief justice of the Bombay High Court, had established a literary group in the city. In the century and a half since, the Society had evolved into both an impressive storehouse of rare books and manuscripts, and a hub of intellectual endeavour, serving, for a time, as Bombay's Town Hall. The building itself had been fashioned from stone transported from England. Despite the British having been shown the door more than two years earlier, the place continued to exude a sense of its colonial upbringing.

Persis had visited on infrequent occasion. Her father, Sam Wadia, sometimes came across books that, in good conscience, he could not sell on in the family enterprise. His donations to the Society were always gratefully received, even if the bill that accompanied them was not.

The Darbar Hall was as she last remembered. Whitewashed walls, dark wooden flooring, cast-iron pillars topped by ornate capitals, and Gothic chandeliers in which pigeons routinely roosted. Light flooded in from lead-lined windows to illuminate a succession of marble busts of the great and the good. Mainly white men, but the odd Indian had snuck into the parade. Steel cabinets hugged the walls, jammed with books. Ceiling fans affixed to the tops of the pillars served only to stir the heat from one end of the room to the other.

They introduced themselves to a portly man with a scrappy moustache lurking at a counter. He held up a finger as if testing the wind, then vanished through a side door, returning swiftly, with a white woman in tow.

She was tall, late-middle-aged, slightly stooped, with intense blue eyes and grey hair worked into a bun behind her head. Her features were patrician and put Persis in mind of the stone vultures that adorned the façade of her father's bookshop. She was dressed in a starched suit, in formal grey, with an A-line skirt, flaring out from broad hips to just under the knees. The cut and cloth were expensive. Sensible shoes.

Something in her expression reminded Persis of a picture of Agatha Christie that she'd recently seen in the *Times of India*.

She introduced herself.

'Yes, I recognise you.' The woman regarded her with a steady, unblinking gaze, like that of a stuffed bird.

Persis wondered if, like many who had read of her recent exploits, she was assessing whether the young woman before her could really have merited such praise. For many, she was a publicity stunt, a trick dreamed up by post-independence liberals aimed at portraying an India thundering towards the future now that it had thrown off the British yoke.

'My name is Neve Forrester. I'm the Society's president. Please come with me.'

They followed her through the hall towards a wrought-iron Regency staircase leading down to the basement levels, Forrester's heels clacking loudly on the iron steps. Persis recalled that she'd briefly met the woman once before, years ago, with her father, not that she expected the Englishwoman to remember.

Forrester spoke without glancing back. 'How much have you been told?'

The question returned Persis to Malabar House, an hour earlier, when she'd been summoned to Roshan Seth's office. The SP, usually morose, seemed agitated. 'I've just got off the line with Shukla. He's asked us to handle a tricky situation. Apparently, those oddballs at the Asiatic Society have a problem.'

She'd considered Seth's words. Any matter that warranted the involvement of Additional Commissioner of Police Amit Shukla could not be dismissed as trivial. When Seth explained, she almost burst out laughing.

'I was told you've lost a book,' she now said.

Forrester stopped, turned, and held her with another low-lidded look.

Persis wished she could rephrase her words. She, better than most, understood the value of a book.

'I felt it best not to reveal the exact nature of our loss,' said Forrester eventually. 'It's a politically sensitive matter.'

Politically sensitive. That explained much, including why Shukla had diverted the call to Malabar House. In spite of Persis's recent success in investigating the murder of a senior British diplomat, the fact remained that the small force at Malabar House was considered a standing joke by the rest of the state's police apparatus. A handful of misfit cops in bad odour, stuffed into the basement of a corporate building that had stray dogs in the lobby and a dearth of air conditioning below the first floor. Persis had been parked there because no one knew where else to put her. Such was the antipathy she'd faced following her passing of the Indian Police Service exams that, for a while, it seemed her career would be stillborn.

But recent events had changed all that.

For better or worse, she'd arrived in the national psyche.

'We are a treasure house, Inspector,' continued Forrester. 'Stored within these walls are priceless artefacts: books, coins, manuscripts, records. It would be a mistake to dismiss the importance of our work.' She turned and continued down the staircase.

Birla rolled his eyes, then shuffled off behind her.

They arrived in the basement and passed through a reading room: tiled floors and reading lamps, the familiar, comforting smell of old volumes. Here the bookcases were polished Burma teak. Plush reading chairs and sprung sofas were dotted around the place, some occupied; an elderly white man dozed in a leather wing chair.

They arrived at a dark wood door, manned by a guard sitting on a wooden stool. An engraved plaque was bolted above the door, bearing a Latin inscription – AN VERITAS, AN NIHIL – below it, the English translation: *The Truth, or Nothing*.

The guard leaped to his feet as Forrester loomed into view.

'Our Special Collections room,' said the Englishwoman. 'We call it the Crypt.'

They found themselves in a large, well-lit room, double-heighted, with a sunken floor.

Around the room were numerous glass cases and steel cupboards. A series of long, polished tables ran through the centre of the room with reading aids – magnifying glasses, manuscript blocks, spring callipers – laid out along their length. Anglepoise lamps were positioned at regular intervals. The air was ripe with the rich, solid smell of learning.

A marble counter was set on the room's eastern side behind which lurked an Indian male. Persis could see a steel door behind the counter but other than that there were no doors or windows save the one they'd entered through.

Neve Forrester waited for them to finish taking in the scene. 'We have almost one hundred thousand artefacts at the Society but here is where we house our most valuable treasures. A five-tola coin from Emperor Akbar's reign; a wooden bowl reputed to belong to Gautama Buddha himself; ancient maps from around the world, manuscripts so old they are written on palm leaves. We have in this room a Shakespeare *First Folio* dated 1623 – there are only about two hundred known copies in the world; we have a copy of both volumes of *A Voyage Towards the South Pole and Round the World* by James Cook, and a two-hundred-year-old *History of the World* by Sir Walter Raleigh.' Her eyes gleamed. 'But our most priceless artefact is a copy of Dante Alighieri's *La Divina Commedia – The Divine Comedy* – one of the two oldest copies in the world. It's been dated back more than six hundred years. And now that manuscript is missing.'

Birla gave a small puff of annoyance. 'How valuable can an old book really be?'

Forrester's gaze threatened to annihilate the sub-inspector where he stood. Persis didn't need an answer.

She recalled now the last time the manuscript had made headlines.

It had been put on display just after the war when a noted Dante scholar from the London branch of the Società Dante Alighieri had arrived in the city to deliver a lecture. The talk had ended in chaos – rioters, in the grip of independence fervour, had attacked the Society. They'd stopped short of torching the place or looting its treasures, but the British expert had had to be smuggled out by a rear entrance and whisked back to the airport, his ardour for Dante forgotten in his desire to flee the manifest perils of the subcontinent.

In the aftermath, the newspapers had rehashed the old rumour that Benito Mussolini had offered one million dollars to the Indian government for the manuscript back in the 1930s, a staggering sum. The offer had been quietly refused. Mussolini was no longer around to make another offer, having been hung by the heels in Milan at the end of the war, though the new Italian government continued to insist that the ancient manuscript be returned to its homeland.

She understood now why Forrester had described the loss of the manuscript as politically sensitive.

'Tell me what happened.'

Forrester pursed her lips, her expression grave. 'Almost two years ago the Society hired a new Curator of Manuscripts. A scholar by the name of John Healy. Have you heard of him?'

Persis shook her head.

'John Healy is something of a celebrity in the world of palaeography. He studied at Cambridge before securing a research position there. He made his name working on thirteenth-century manuscripts ascribed to a monk known as "the Tremulous Hand of Worcester". This particular scholar is believed to have sat at Worcester Priory – in England – and worked on numerous manuscripts, annotating them in a distinctive fashion: the notes – or glosses – that he produced are leftward leaning and written in a "shaky" hand. John produced the definitive work on the Hand's extensive career, even conjecturing as to his identity – something that had remained a mystery till then. The work brought him worldwide attention in the scholarly community, and he seemed set for a stellar academic career.

'And then the war intervened. John was a patriot. He signed up to fight and somehow ended up on the front lines. He was captured in North Africa and spent almost a year in a prisoner of war camp. Following the war, he returned to England a hero, and shortly thereafter resumed his career.' She paused. 'You can imagine our delight when he contacted us in the winter of 1947 to express an interest in coming to Bombay. He wanted to spend some time working with our copy of *The Divine Comedy*. I discussed it with the board and persuaded them to offer him the role of Curator of Manuscripts – the previous curator had recently passed away. I never expected him to accept. But he came out here, stayed for a month, and decided it was to his liking. I was delighted when he agreed to take up the position.'

'What was his interest in *The Divine Comedy*?'

'John is one of the world's foremost Dante scholars. It became an obsession for him after the war. He was producing a new English translation. John was a linguistic historian, among his other talents.'

'He worked *here*?' Persis indicated the room around them.

'Yes. We do not permit *The Divine Comedy* manuscript to leave the Crypt – unless it's for a public exhibition. But we haven't had one of those since that unfortunate incident in '46.'

'When did you realise it was missing?'

Her eyes clouded over. 'Frankly, it was John's absence we noted first. He failed to come into work yesterday. This was unusual, to say the least. John is a workaholic and rarely deviates from his routine. Each morning he's here at the opening of our doors – at precisely seven a.m. He's never late and he takes only one day off a week – Sunday.

'Nevertheless, we did not try to contact him. He was more than entitled to time off and I had no wish to intrude on his privacy. But when he failed to show up again this morning, I decided to call his home. No answer. I became worried and so I sent one of the peons around. There appeared to be no one there.' She stopped. 'I'm not a naturally suspicious person, Inspector, and, heaven knows, John has never given us any reason to doubt him. But when you're responsible for such treasures as I am, one cannot help but be overcautious. I asked Mr Pillai, our strongroom librarian, to check on *The Divine Comedy* manuscript. That was when we discovered it was missing.'

Missing. The word tolled in Persis's mind. A priceless manuscript and a famous British scholar. Both *missing*. It defied the odds that the two were unconnected.

'Let's assume for a moment that John took the manuscript—'

'I'm not making that accusation,' interrupted Forrester. 'Not yet.'

'I understand. But let's assume, for the purposes of conjecture, that he did. How would he have been able to get it out of here?'

'Follow me.' She led them to the marble counter Persis had noted earlier. A red ledger was chained to the counter.

'Anyone wishing to examine one of our rarer artefacts must present an authorised requisition here. To Mr Pillai.' Forrester indicated the nervous-looking Indian behind the counter. The small man, balding and bespectacled, nodded at her. With his liquid eyes and sad expression, he put her in mind of a depressed lemur. 'Mr Pillai notes the request in the ledger, then goes into the strongroom behind him' – she indicated the steel door behind the counter – 'and returns with the artefact. The individual may then examine the work within the confines of the Crypt before returning it to Mr Pillai.'

'Who authorises these requisitions?'

'Two members of the board must sign a requisition. For longer-term researchers such as John – who was also a staff member – we naturally provide an ongoing approval.'

Persis turned to Pillai. 'I assume Healy came here the day before yesterday and took out the manuscript?'

'Yes, madam.' The short man spoke with the clipped manner of a Dravidian from the deep south.

'At what time did he return it?'

'At nine p.m. Our official closing time. I noted it in the register.'

'And you saw it? With your own eyes?'

Pillai's expression became queasy. He glanced fearfully at Forrester. 'I – I thought so.'

'Please explain.'

9

He stepped backwards to the steel vault door behind him, unlocked it, went inside, and returned swiftly with a carved wooden box roughly eighteen inches on a side and four in height. He set the box down on the counter, then said, '*The Divine Comedy* manuscript is kept inside this box. Each night when Professor Healy returns the box to me, I check inside.'

He removed a key from his pocket, unlocked the box, lifted the lid, and turned the box around. Inside was a large volume, wrapped in red silk.

'This is what I saw when he returned it. Naturally, I assumed it was *The Divine Comedy*.'

Persis looked at Forrester. 'May I?'

The Englishwoman nodded.

Persis lifted out the volume, set it down on the counter, then unwrapped it from its cape of red cloth. She had handled old volumes before – in her father's bookshop – and was careful with her movements.

What lay before her was a copy of the King James Bible, beautifully bound in polished black leather. She knew the book – her father sold them in the bookshop.

She looked at Pillai. 'I take it you didn't check beneath the red silk?'

He shook his head wretchedly.

'Tell me, did Healy have a bag with him, or a satchel?'

'Yes. He always carried a leather bag with him. It contained his notebooks.'

'So, in theory, all he had to do was swap the manuscript for the Bible, put the manuscript in his bag, and walk out of the door with it.'

'The whole thing wouldn't have taken more than a few seconds,' remarked Birla behind her. She'd almost forgotten he was there.

'Was anyone else present at the time he left here?'

'No,' said Pillai.

'Did anyone requisition the manuscript yesterday, when Healy was absent?'

Forrester replied, 'Only one other person currently has permission to view *The Divine Comedy*. An Italian scholar named Franco Belzoni; he wasn't here yesterday.'

'I'll need his details.' Persis turned back to Pillai. 'Was anyone other than you working the counter yesterday or this morning?'

'No.'

'Does anyone else have access to the strongroom?'

'No.' He hung his head, his misery complete.

'Mr Pillai has worked here for thirty years,' said Forrester sharply. 'He has nothing to do with this.'

Persis refrained from replying. She was early in her career but knew enough to know that suspicion was a democratic beast. It devoured anyone and everyone in the vicinity of a crime. '*Why* would Healy take the manuscript? Assuming it was him?'

'A question I cannot answer,' replied Forrester. 'Yes, the manuscript is incredibly valuable, but John was a scholar. To him the value of such a work cannot be measured in monetary terms.'

Birla snorted. 'You have a very flowery view of academics,' he said, earning a glare from the Englishwoman.

'Have you searched his home?' asked Persis.

'I don't have a key to his residence,' said Forrester. 'Besides, it wouldn't be right for *me* to break down his door and ransack his home.' It was clear from her tone that this was precisely what she expected Persis to now do.

'I'll need a list of his colleagues, friends, and other acquaintances. Anyone he may have associated with.'

'I shall draw one up immediately. Though his circle was very small. He was a guarded man, completely focused on his work.'

Persis looked down at the Bible. She wondered where Healy had purchased the volume. It was a Blackletter edition – a faithful rendering of the 1611 King James Bible using the same Blackletter font and English grammar employed in the original and printed in the sixteen-inch 'pulpit folio' format. A collector's item. Presumably, any number of bookshops in the city sold it.

Her fingertips brushed over the leather binding, the gold lettering reflecting the overhead lighting. On an impulse, she lifted the cover and looked inside the flyleaf.

She was surprised to find writing on the normally blank page.

What's in a name?
Akoloutheo Aletheia

Below this was a signature and a date: 6 February 1950.

The day before yesterday.

'Is this Healy's signature?'

Forrester peered at the page. 'Yes.' She seemed shocked. Persis guessed she hadn't bothered to look inside the Bible.

'The 6th was the last day he was here,' continued Persis. 'The day, presumably, that he stole the manuscript. Why would he leave this inscription behind? . . . Akoloutheo Aletheia.' The words felt strange on her tongue. 'Do you have any idea what this means?'

'It's ancient Greek,' replied Forrester, still hypnotised by the page. 'My Greek is rusty, but I believe "akoloutheo" means "to follow", and "aletheia" means "truth".'

'Follow the truth,' whispered Persis. It had the ring of an incantation.

What was Healy attempting to communicate? She was certain he was trying to tell them something. But why? And what did the first sentence have to do with the second? *What's in a name?* It sounded familiar, but she couldn't place it.

'I'll need to take this,' she said. She nodded at Birla who wrapped the Bible back in its silk covering and then tucked it under his arm.

A thought occurred to her. 'Do you have a photograph of Healy?'

'Follow me,' said Forrester.

She led them back up to the Darbar Hall, to a large notice-board propped on an easel. A collage of flyers and notices were pinned to the board. She pointed at an old newspaper cutting. The headline read: 'Famed British academic to take up position at Bombay Asiatic Society.' Beneath the headline was a photograph of Forrester and a cluster of elderly board members, both white and native. In the very midst of them stood a tall blond white man, wearing a tailored suit and eyeglasses. He looked frankly back at the photographer, unsmiling. There was something reserved in his gaze, Persis thought.

'How old was he?'

'I believe he was in his late thirties. Possibly thirty-eight or thirty-nine.'

He looks older than his years, she thought. 'Where does he live?'

2

Healy's home was a short drive away, on a leafy road not far from the Flora Fountain. Passing through the congested junction within which the fountain stood, at the top of Mile Long Road, Persis couldn't help but notice the idle ranks of black-and-yellow taxis, their drivers milling around, smoking, chatting, a few arguing with irate passengers brandishing suitcases. The impact of Nehru's social reforms had yet to trickle down to the lowest rungs of Indian society. The taxi drivers had decided to force the state government's hands by waging a two-day strike, all but bringing the city to a standstill.

An overcrowded tram rattled by as she swung the jeep around the fountain, a solid-looking structure topped by a magnificent statue of the Roman goddess Flora. Not that many Indians knew or cared. The Hindu pantheon contained a multiplicity of deities. No one had time for anyone else's gods.

She parked beneath the branches of a banyan tree and checked her watch. Where was he?

Exiting from the jeep, she waited for Birla and Neve Forrester to join her.

Forrester led them across the road to an unassuming, single-storey, whitewashed bungalow with a red mansard roof.

No security guard at the gate, Persis noted.

Forrester sensed her unspoken question. 'John refused to take on any staff. No chauffeur, no cook, no cleaner, and no security guard. As I said, he is an intensely private man.'

Madness, she thought. It was unusual for a westerner not to employ servants. It had been one of the principal comforts of empire. Indian labour was so cheap that even the poorest of Brits found themselves elevated to the status of gentry, with the arrogance and manners to match.

The front door was locked. Persis knocked, not expecting an answer. When none came, she stepped back. 'Go ahead,' she said, nodding at Birla.

The sub-inspector stepped forward, hefting the crowbar he'd taken from the jeep.

Moments later, the door swung back like a broken jaw.

Persis checked her watch again. She looked back at the road. She'd made the call just before leaving the Society. He should have been here by no—

A car came churning up the path, skidding to a halt behind her jeep.

A tall, dark-haired white man scrambled out from the vehicle, all legs and flailing arms. He spotted her and grinned broadly, the smile lighting up his handsome features. He waved vigorously with one hand – the other was weighed down by a brown leather doctor's case.

He crossed the road in a few long strides, the sun glinting off his spectacles.

'Hello!' he said as he came alongside, flashing green eyes at Persis. Turning to Neve Forrester, he stuck out a hand. 'Archie Blackfinch.'

Forrester ignored his hand and looked to Persis for an explanation.

'Archie – Mr Blackfinch – is a forensic criminalist with the Metropolitan Police. He's currently stationed in Bombay, working with our own police service. I thought his skills would be useful in examining Healy's home.'

Blackfinch set down his bag, opened it, and removed several pairs of white gloves. 'Please put these on,' he said. 'Try not to touch anything.'

Forrester's expression made it clear exactly what she thought of being given orders by a man younger than her by some decades. She snatched the gloves from the Englishman and pulled them on with ill grace.

'Wait outside,' said Persis to Birla, before turning and entering the home.

The first thing she noticed was how small and bare the place was, more a hermit's cave than the residence of a bachelor. There were only four rooms: a living space, a kitchen, a bathroom and toilet, and a bedroom. In the kitchen was a stove and oven, a sink, and a General Electric fridge. She opened the fridge – it was empty save for a lump of hard cheese, bread, a half-eaten tin of sardines, a couple of eggs, and a bottle of milk.

She twisted off the lid, took a sniff, then almost retched. Rancid.

In the bathroom, she found basic male toiletries: a razor, a bar of shaving soap, towels, toothpaste, a toothbrush, toilet water. The bedroom was equally bare: a single bed – without a mosquito net – a bedside table and lamp, and a wardrobe, inside which she discovered three men's suits in various shades of grey, three pairs of brogues, half a dozen shirts, and a selection of undergarments. The fabrics were neither cheap nor expensive.

She searched the clothing, but found nothing, not even a scrap of paper or the wrapper of a boiled sweet.

In a bedside drawer, she found a half-empty bottle of red-and-blue tablets. The bottle was labelled Tuinal.

She paused for a second to look up at a wooden Cross on the wall. Christ the Redeemer. The Cross was positioned opposite the bed, Jesus looking down forlornly at the bed's headpiece. A large, ornate ormolu dressing mirror was affixed to the wall below the Cross, scratched and spotted with age.

She glanced again at the Cross. It seemed incongruous in the bare room. She wondered if Healy had installed it.

'Is he a religious man?' she asked Forrester, back in the living room.

'Not that I'm aware of,' replied the Englishwoman. 'He certainly made no mention of being a churchgoer. In my experience, practising Catholics cannot stop wringing their hands about their faith.'

'He's Catholic?'

'Yes. He comes from Irish stock, though he was born and raised in England.'

'He lives alone?'

'I would have thought that was obvious.'

'I meant does he have a partner? A female companion?'

'I'm afraid I'm not in the habit of keeping track of my colleagues' personal arrangements.'

'Looks like a bachelor to me,' said Blackfinch behind her. He'd removed a camera and tripod set-up from his bag and was screwing a flashbulb to the top of the camera. 'This place lacks a woman's warmth.'

He gave Persis a smile. Against her will, she found herself flushing. Her relationship with the Englishman had become complicated. They'd met on her first case, just weeks earlier, the murder of a British diplomat in the city. Blackfinch had been invaluable during the investigation.

Something unspoken had passed between them, a mutual attraction.

And then she'd shot him.

She turned away, concealing her awkwardness by striding to the waist-high bookcase in the corner of the room, dropping to her haunches, and examining the half a dozen volumes. An English-to-Hindi dictionary; Jules Verne's *Twenty Thousand Leagues Under the Sea*; *The Hobbit* by Tolkien; a translation of selected works by Rumi, the thirteenth-century Persian poet and scholar; a torn copy of Fitzgerald's *The Great Gatsby*. What looked like a new Lewis Carroll: *Through the Looking-Glass*.

She knew these books, had read them growing up in her father's bookstore. But here, they seemed lifeless, discarded.

She stood and took in the room. It was as empty as the rest of the home. An oxhide sofa, a claw-footed coffee table, a depressing painting of a grim foreign landscape on the wall, the bookcase, a sideboard on which stood a telephone ... and that was it. Not even a radio or a gramophone.

What did Healy do here? Unless he was fond of staring at the walls, there was literally nothing *to* do. Perhaps this explained his desire to spend every waking minute at the Society.

'Monkish,' observed Blackfinch, startling her out of her thoughts.

'He's a man of simple tastes,' countered Forrester. 'There's something to be said for a restrained appetite in this age of excess.'

'There's no sign of the manuscript,' said Persis. It had taken little time to search the place thoroughly. There was no hiding place worth the name. 'There's also no sign of Healy's bag, the one Pillai mentioned.'

'Do you think he's left the city?' asked Forrester.

'Why would he leave his clothes behind?' It was a weak argument. A man with a manuscript worth a million dollars need not worry about taking his wardrobe with him.

She realised what it was that was bothering her.

There were no personal effects here.

No family photographs to remind Healy of home, no gewgaws, none of the junk that people tended to accrete over time. He had lived here for over two years and yet, aside from a handful of worn garments hanging in his wardrobe, it was as if he'd never been here at all.

Loneliness. That was what seeped from the walls; the scent of loneliness, as strong as Mercurochrome.

'It's not inconceivable that he borrowed the volume, then met with an accident,' said Forrester. The explanation sounded disbelieving even as it left her mouth.

'It won't take long to check the city's hospitals,' replied Persis automatically. She'd already arrived at the conclusion that Healy wasn't coming back. But if he *had* intended to vanish, why write that enigmatic message in the Bible he'd left behind?

What's in a name? Follow the truth.

Whose truth? And follow it to what end?

'What was your impression of Healy?'

Forrester thought about the question. 'He was – is – a reserved man. Guarded. When he spoke, it was with appropriate thought. Not the gregarious type; he preferred his own company, by and large.'

'Did he engage with others at the Society?'

'Not really. Our scholars tend to be solitary animals. As Curator of Manuscripts, John was, of course, consulted on all matters regarding the purchase or donation of new items to our collection. His expertise as a palaeographer was unquestioned.'

'What exactly does a palaeographer do?' asked Blackfinch, who had returned to the room after photographing the rest of the house.

'How can I put this in layman's terms?' said Forrester, not bothering to hide her condescension. 'Palaeography is the study and decipherment of ancient writing. Palaeographers bring old documents to life so that we might learn from them. For instance, the world's libraries are full of medieval manuscripts, but without palaeographers, medieval history would remain a blank to us. Even Shakespeare would be an unreadable morass. Language evolves over time. Dialects, writing systems, alphabets, the meanings of individual words. Compare *Beowulf* to modern English.'

'You seem very passionate about the subject.'

'I'm a palaeographer by training,' said Forrester. 'I was unable to practise due to an unfortunate marriage.'

This surprised Persis. Neve Forrester did not seem the type of woman to allow a man to dictate her fate. 'There's nothing more to be learned here,' she said. 'I'll need that list of acquaintances as soon as you can get it to me.'

Outside the home, Persis examined the neighbouring buildings. One was an abandoned old house, similar in form to Healy's. The doors and windows were boarded up. A dead end.

On the other side were the premises of a corporate enterprise. She spoke briefly to a guard sitting inside the gate.

'Do you know the man who lives next door? The white man?'

The guard scratched thoughtfully under his armpit, gawping at her uniform. 'I've seen him, madam. I don't *know* him.'

'Did you see him yesterday? Or this morning?'

He thought about it, then shook his head.

'When was the last time you saw him?'

'The day before yesterday. He left his house in the morning.'

'Did he leave by car?'

'No, madam. He always walks.'

3

Persis was greeted outside the fire temple by Krishna, her father's driver, cook, manservant, and all-round dogsbody. Krishna had been a fixture in the Wadia household since Persis had been a child. Following the death of her mother, Krishna had served as a sort of nanny, helping her father to raise the seven-year-old girl he'd suddenly found in his sole care.

Not that either of them had been any good at it.

It was fortunate that her mother's younger sister, Aunt Nussie, had been on hand to steady the ship. Nussie's well-meaning efforts had been hindered by the ongoing animosity between her and Sam Wadia, an antipathy that stemmed from the fact that her father had eloped with her mother. As Nussie had been at pains to explain to her, Persis's mother – Sanaz – and Nussie herself hailed from grander Parsee stock than her father. Sanaz had married below her station.

Persis wondered why her aunt was mystified that Sam held such a low opinion of her.

She left Krishna leaning against her father's Ambassador, and walked past the enormous door statues, a pair of winged, human-headed bulls – the *lamassu* – and entered the temple. Stepping briskly through the outer courtyard and into the main hall, she encountered the familiar scent of burning sandalwood.

Inside the hall, a congregation milled about, some seated, some chatting in corners.

A pair of priests in white moved among the mourners, offering words of advice and consolation.

She spotted her father, sitting in the corner of the hall in his wheelchair, head bent into conversation with Dr Shaukat Aziz, one of his oldest friends.

She wondered briefly how Aziz had managed to get into the temple. Entry into agiaries was generally prohibited to non-Parsees. The fire here had been continuously lit for over a century, symbolic of Ahura Mazda's eternal flame, transported from Persia, original home of the Zoroastrian faith, before Muslim persecution had sent them eastwards to the subcontinent.

She made her way to Sam, then dropped into a seat beside him. He broke off from his discussion with Aziz and glared at her. 'The least you could have done is change out of your uniform.'

'I'm still on duty, Papa.'

'Boman was your uncle. You'll probably turn up at *my* death ceremony wearing a swimsuit.'

She refrained from pointing out that Boman Mistry was her father's third cousin, once removed. She remembered him as a greying moustache occasionally floating in and out of her childhood. In truth, she'd thought he'd died years earlier, not ten days ago. By now the vultures at the Towers of Silence where his body had been left to desiccate would have had their fill. Boman had not been a tall man; the vultures would have made short work of him.

The joke brought a grim smile to her lips.

'What are you laughing at? You think death is funny?'

'Acta est fabula, plaudite!' said Aziz. 'The play is over, applaud! Emperor Augustus's last words.'

Sam shot him a venomous look. 'Why don't you keep your homilies to yourself? If they find out I smuggled you in under false pretences they'll ban me from setting foot in here again.'

'I'm only here to ensure your well-being,' said Aziz, unruffled. 'It's not my fault you had a stroke.'

Sam reddened. 'For the last time, it wasn't a stroke.'

'When a man goes red in the face and keels over, drooling at the mouth, I don't call it constipation and offer him a laxative. I took a Hippocratic oath.'

'I'm in great shape. Physically and mentally. Which is more than I can say for you. You're losing brain cells just sitting there.'

'Attacking me isn't the answer. You've been under a great deal of stress lately.'

'I'm about as stressed as a goldfish.'

'Actually, goldfish die of stress all the time.'

Persis tuned the pair of them out. The two men had been jousting for more years than she could remember. She was glad that Aziz was here. Her father's recent health issues had frightened her, at first, but she felt confident that Aziz would get to the bottom of it.

Her thoughts returned to the case.

When Seth had sent her to the Asiatic Society, she hadn't expected much in the way of intrigue. But now she found herself drawn into the case, not just by the circumstances of Healy's disappearance, but by the facts to hand. Her mind looped back to the strange note in the Bible he'd left behind in place of the stolen manuscript. Why bother with the note at all? And where was Healy now? Why would a renowned scholar destroy his reputation by committing such a crime?

She found it difficult to believe that Healy was motivated by monetary gain. The academics that frequented her father's bookshop had always struck her as otherworldly, lost to the abstractions of their scholarly endeavours. There was no doubting the immense value of the stolen volume, but she was certain – on no more evidence than her own instinct – that something else lay behind Healy's curious behaviour.

'I'm going to say a few words,' said Sam.

She watched as he trundled his wheelchair to the front of the congregation, waiting for the mob to settle down. 'Like me, many of you knew Boman. I've heard many of you talk eloquently today about how smart he was, how generous, how accomplished; a good family man, a pillar of our community.' Sam paused, looked down at his feet, then back up again. 'Well, not me. The man was a liar, a cheat, and a scoundrel. The only reason I came here today was to make sure he's remembered as he was and not as a bunch of snivelling hypocrites would like him to be.'

'Oh dear,' said Aziz beside her.

Persis sighed. This was going to take longer than she had thought.

4

A brass band was playing on John Adams Street, bludgeoning passers-by with a cacophony of trombone, tuba, trumpet, and French horn. A man dressed in Congress white stood beside the entrance to Malabar House handing out leaflets.

She looked up at the building's façade, certain that the plaster must be crumbling and the gargoyles lining the edge of the roof would have fled.

Malabar House was the corporate headquarters of one of the country's leading business houses, a four-storey Edwardian affair, fronted by red Malad stone and large casement windows set behind balustraded balconies. In the seven months since she'd graduated from the academy, it had become her second home. Sharing the building with corporate worker ants had proved to be a minor inconvenience. In many ways, the police presence at Malabar House was all but invisible. Few knew of the station's existence; the cases that arrived at their door, such as they were, tended to be referred via other units in the service.

She walked through the arcaded front entrance, and then down into the basement where the station had been given a temporary home.

The place, a maze of battered steel filing cabinets and old desks, was all but deserted.

She saw Sub-Inspector George Fernandes hunched over his desk. A big man with a head like a medicine ball and a thick moustache, he spotted her and quickly turned back to the report he was typing one-fingered on an ancient Remington. She brushed angrily past him – the mere sight of Fernandes these days caused a throbbing at her temples.

On her desk, she discovered the Bible they'd taken from the Society. Birla had left it there inside an evidence envelope, together with a note detailing his activities since returning from Healy's home. The note told her that Archie Blackfinch had dusted the Bible for fingerprints and would report back in due course.

At the far end of the office she knocked on Seth's door and was summoned inside.

The superintendent was smoking behind his desk, a glass of Scotch balanced precariously on the edge. She coughed in the cloud of lung-searing smoke and glared at him.

Seth ignored her for a moment as if savouring the calm before the storm.

A man of intellect and no small talent, the SP had once been groomed for the top, a rising star in the Indian Imperial Police. But the advent of independence had seen his ambitions collide headfirst with the sympathies of those seeking to redress the imbalances of British India. Men like Roshan Seth had, in the eyes of many, performed their duties a little too zealously under their former colonial masters.

Seth found himself sidelined to Malabar House, a temporary crime branch unit, supposedly established to handle the overflow of cases from the state's Criminal Investigation Department, the much-maligned CID.

Seth knew the truth, of course.

Like a limping horse, he'd been put out to pasture until it was time to send him onwards to the glue factory where he might be shot and put to some use.

There were moments when he seemed inclined to do the job himself.

He stirred in his chair, waved his glass at her. 'So, what have those queer ducks at the Society been up to?'

She quickly briefed him on the case, the missing copy of Dante's masterpiece, John Healy's disappearance. When she mentioned the manuscript's value, Seth straightened, taking the cigarette from his lips. 'A million dollars?'

His tone was disbelieving.

'That was almost two decades ago. Who knows what it's worth now.'

'But who would you even sell it to? Something that famous, you could never let it surface publicly again.'

'Apparently, there are private collectors willing to pay a fortune for a manuscript this rare.'

'The Italians will have a fit when they find out. Now I understand why Shukla gave us the case. That man has a sixth sense for trouble.' His finger tapped the side of the glass. 'So, what next?'

'We need to talk to the local fences. It's highly unlikely Healy will try to get rid of the volume in Bombay, but we'll check anyway. Birla's already called the hospitals, the Juhu aerodrome, RAF Santacruz, and the major train stations. Healy's description has been circulated.'

'Do you have a photograph?'

She took out the cutting she'd taken from the bulletin board at the Asiatic Society and showed it to him. Seth grimaced, his lower lip curling into a pout. 'Miserable-looking bastard.'

Persis refrained from comment. For a man who'd once venerated the British, Seth's bitterness knew no bounds. He wasn't alone.

Post-independence India was not shaping up as the utopia many had dreamed of. The British had departed, and that was only right and proper, but Prime Minister Nehru's planned agrarian reforms had set the cat among the pigeons. Noble houses and feudal landlords were fighting tooth and nail to prevent legislation that would effectively strip them of their ancestral wealth and parcel it out to the peasantry that had, until now – with the blessings of the British – remained steadfastly beneath their boot-heels.

Nehru's dreams for a better India had collided sharply with the iceberg of entrenched reality.

She couldn't help but feel that Gandhi's assassination had changed the course of her nation's political future. Nehru endeavoured to forge a country based on Gandhian ideals, but lacked his late comrade's force of personality.

Or perhaps cult was a better word.

That was how her father had always described Gandhi's followers. Caught up in the zeal of the Quit India movement, she hadn't understood what he'd meant then, but the cracks in the façade of the new republic were gradually becoming clear to one and all.

Seth handed the cutting back to her. 'I suppose you'd better get on with it. And try to keep a low profile. The longer we can keep a lid on this, the better. Once word gets out, we'll be under siege; you realise that, don't you?'

She understood. Her last investigation had engendered national headlines; there was little doubt that the present case would also send shock waves around the country, though for different reasons. Given all the treasures that had been looted from the subcontinent over the centuries, it would be bad form to so tamely surrender a priceless European artefact. In the space of a heartbeat, the case had gone from an art theft to a matter of national honour.

'Sir, where is everyone?'

'If you mean Oberoi, he's extended his leave. Apparently, he's managed to twist an ankle while skiing.'

Persis refrained from smiling. Hemant Oberoi, the other full inspector in the unit, had made his antipathy clear from the moment she'd set foot in Malabar House. The scion of a wealthy family, he was the epitome of arrogance, a man who expected life's red carpet to be rolled out for him at every juncture. A badly judged affair had derailed his career and he now found himself treading water at Malabar House with those he considered beneath him in every way.

The arrival of a woman had been the final straw.

'As for the others ...' Seth lit another cigarette. 'They're out on crowd control. In case you've forgotten, Bombay is still hosting the National Games. Birla and Haq are at Brabourne Stadium.'

The National Games had been foisted on to the city by the state of Bengal, on the far side of the country, still recovering from the horrors of Partition.

Sawn in half by the Radcliffe Line, the state had seen horrendous rioting that had accompanied the migration of Hindus and Muslims between West Bengal and the newly created East Pakistan. More than two years later, the region remained turbulent; memories of the Calcutta killings – the communal bloodshed unleashed by Mohammed Ali Jinnah's call for 'direct action' during his push for a Muslim homeland – lingered in the state psyche.

The ongoing administrative turmoil meant that Bengal had begged off organising the National Games, foisting them on to Maharashtra, with Bombay, as the state capital, the natural venue. After all, the port metro was still the nation's entertainment capital; thousands of Europeans lingered in India's 'city of jazz'.

She returned to her desk, studiously ignoring Fernandes, who continued his grim, mono-fingered typing. Slipping out the Bible from its envelope, she ran her fingers over the plush binding, then opened it to the flyleaf.

What's in a name?
Akoloutheo Aletheia

Follow the truth. There was no earthly reason for Healy to leave this message. To sign it and to date it. With each passing moment, she became certain that he had done so deliberately. Which meant that he wished for the message to be found, read, and acted upon.

The question was: were they smart enough to understand its meaning?

She dragged her own typewriter to the centre of the desk and inserted a sheet of carbon paper, then spent the next couple of hours typing up an FIR, a first incident report. Her notes were extensive – it was a habit she'd picked up during her teenage years, recording the minutiae of daily life in a set of cloth-bound journals taken from her father's bookshop. The journals had been a way of combating the loneliness of growing up without siblings, without a mother – her father had never remarried – and with few friends.

By the time she looked up again, it was past seven. She was about to pack up for the day when Seth's door opened and he beckoned her inside.

'Another case came in. With Oberoi out of action and you leading the Healy case, I'm giving it to Fernandes. I want you to supervise him.'

She stiffened. 'I won't work with Fernandes.'

'Won't?' Seth smiled nastily. 'And here's me thinking these stars on my shoulder meant *I* was in charge.'

'You know what he did. You really expect me to just . . . *forget*?'

Seth picked up a silver pen, rolled it around in his fingers. 'Fernandes is a good officer. He made a mistake and ended up here. He was offered a way out and he took it.'

During the investigation into the death of Sir James Herriot it had become clear that a member of the team was leaking information to the newspapers, deliberately fuelling an unflattering portrait of Persis's handling of the investigation. She'd suspected

Hemant Oberoi, but, to her horror, had discovered that it had been Fernandes, a man she'd admired.

'Integrity is a movable feast,' muttered Seth. His eyes were hollow and she wondered if he was thinking about his own situation. 'Fernandes did what he thought was right. For himself, for his family. And he's hardly alone in his prejudice against women on the force.'

'That doesn't make it right.'

'Persis, look around you. None of us are here because it was *right*. What cannot be cured must be endured.'

She glared at him, but it was pointless. Seth was right. What was life at Malabar House, last way station on the road to obscurity, but an exercise in endurance?

'What's the case?'

'A woman's been found dead. On the tracks near Sandhurst Road station.'

'That's by the Dongri police *thana*. Why aren't they handling it?'

'Because our victim is a white woman. The station-in-charge at Dongri doesn't want the case. Fortunately for him, he's distantly related to our beloved commissioner. He pulled some strings and voila! Another grenade lands in my lap.' He ran a hand through his thinning hair, his slim moustache crinkling in distaste. 'Take Fernandes and check it out. For the avoidance of doubt: I'm not asking, I'm telling.'

5

Fernandes had taken the news that they'd be working together with wide-eyed shock. He'd listened to Seth's instructions in silence, then turned and walked stiffly back to his desk, swept up his peaked cap, checked his revolver, and headed upstairs to the lobby.

They'd taken Persis's jeep. The silence between them was as dry as tinder; a single word and Persis felt the very air might combust. The truth was that she was astonished that George Fernandes remained at Malabar House. Following the Herriot case, she had lodged a formal complaint against him. An officer who had compromised an investigation by talking to the press? She'd expected the man to be hauled over the coals. Yet, somehow, he'd escaped censure.

She couldn't understand it; Seth had remained tight-lipped on the matter.

She *expected* to work with officers who despised her because she was a woman intruding on what they believed was their exclusive domain. But Fernandes had seemed different, an officer of integrity, consigned to Malabar House only because he had inadvertently shot an innocent bystander while chasing down a known criminal.

They arrived at the scene to discover a pair of constables, one tall, one short, standing at the base of a bridge shelling peanuts and chatting to a trio of women in revealing saris and an excess of make-up. Persis recalled that the red-light district at Kamathipura was close by. A single dull street lamp lit the darkness, a cloud of insects dancing around the light fixture.

She looked up at the bridge, an iron construction that ran over a double set of rails. The bridge lay close to the Prince's Dock, a kilometre to the east. She imagined that workers from the dock would pass this way, using the footbridge to cross the tracks.

'You two!' The constables turned from their discussion to gawp at her uniform.

Eventually, they walked over. Behind them, the three prostitutes melted away.

'Where's the body?'

The constables stared at her as if she was mad. Both men swivelled their necks towards the hulking figure of Fernandes.

'What the hell are you looking at him for?'

Their heads snapped around.

'Madam,' the taller of the two ventured, 'the body is further along the track.'

'Then what are you doing *here*?'

'There's no light there.'

A man walked across the bridge behind the pair, lighting a cigarette as he went.

'This is what you call guarding the body? How many people could have trampled through the scene while you've been standing here?'

He exchanged glances with his partner, but did not dare reply.

'Take me to her.'

The tracks veered around a corner and into darkness. Ballast crunched under their boots.

'Did you stop the trains?'

'No, madam.'

They arrived at the scene, a flat, open area, undeveloped, dry grass and scrub stretching into a rustling darkness on either side. A dirt path ran parallel to the tracks.

She came upon the body almost without realising.

The woman – what remained of her – was small, slender, lying on her front just clear of the nearmost track. Her face lay on its side, partially covered by raven hair. Her lower legs had been cut off at the knees. Of the missing limbs, there was no sign.

Persis stared down at the scene, overcome by a strange light-headedness. It was more than the sight of a mutilated corpse – she'd seen plenty of those during the Partition years, discovering, to her own surprise, that she had no weakness of constitution that made the sight of death unpalatable.

It was the dress. A short-sleeved navy polka-dot tea dress, rucked up just above the knees.

A scab of memory. She was transported back to her childhood, a year after her mother had passed, wandering into Sanaz's room, opening her wardrobe. Her father, still coming to terms with his wife's death, had refused to throw out her clothes – in the wardrobe Persis had found a selection of fashionable dresses. There had been one, a navy, polka-dotted dress, that had taken her fancy. She'd slipped it off its hanger, put it on. Hopelessly large for her, but, as she'd flapped around inside it, pretending to be her mother, the memory had become a needle note of unhappiness.

The dress rustled.

There was no breeze.

Horror gripped her and she stepped forward, reached down and shook the woman's right leg, what remained of it. A rat appeared from under the dress, lean and dark against the flesh of her thigh.

Persis staggered back, stifling a cry. The rat ran for cover.

She waited until her pulse had steadied. 'Was this how you found her?'

'Yes, madam,' said the taller constable.

'Where are the lower halves of her legs?'

The constables exchanged glances. 'We don't know, madam.'

Her fingers itched. She wanted to slap them both, as hard as she could.

'Spread out. Find them.'

It didn't take long.

'Madam!' The shorter of the constables waved her over. He pointed with his lathi into the scrub, about thirty metres from the tracks.

They lay in the grass, pale calves shimmering in the weak moonlight, feet shod in black-heeled sandals. The feet were shapely, the toes painted red.

She must have lain across the tracks, Persis thought. Waited for the train to run her over. Had she changed her mind at the last instant, attempted to crawl out of the way? That would explain why she had been severed at the knees, rather than higher up the body.

But if she wanted to kill herself, why not just step in front of the speeding train?

Bombay's railways were a magnet for suicides. Every officer in the city knew that.

That's why suicides received so little attention.

But a white woman taking her own life in this way? That was rare enough to make it a bureaucratic headache.

A train horn sounded in the distance; a dull vibration hummed along the tracks.

Persis returned to the body. 'We have to move her further away.' She stepped forward, but Fernandes got there first.

'I'll do it.'

She watched as he stood over her, put his hands beneath her armpits, then lifted her bodily upwards, swinging her around like a rag doll – she could not have weighed half as much as him – stepping away from the tracks, and then gently placing her on the ground, this time on her back.

Something slithered away in the grass.

Persis dropped to her haunches, pushed the straggle of hair out of the woman's face.

She was beautiful, that much was apparent. Red lipstick smeared her mouth. She looked like a starlet. Or a model. The sort of woman that graced the fashion magazines her father ordered in for bored housewives.

'Did you search the body?' she asked the constables who had gravitated back to the corpse.

'No, madam. We were told not to touch anything.'

She wished that Blackfinch was here. She could send one of the officers back to their station to call for him, but by the time he got here, who knew how many more trains would have thundered through, further wrecking the scene.

'Who found the body?'

'A dock worker. He was on his way home. He practically tripped over the woman and decided to report it at the station.'

'He found nothing else?'

The constable smirked. 'If he had, he wouldn't tell us.'

She thought for a moment. 'Wait here.'

She jogged back to the jeep, returning swiftly. She handed out gloves and torches. If there was one thing she'd learned from Archie Blackfinch, it was to be prepared. The constables looked at the items as if she'd handed them sticks of lit dynamite.

'Put the gloves on. We're going to carry out a fingertip search.'

'A search of what?' said the smaller of the two.

She reined in the urge to hurl abuse at him. Instead, she explained what she wanted them to do. As she did so, the tracks began to vibrate steadily, then clack loudly. Before they knew it, the train was upon them, rounding the curve in a thunder of noise and light. They waited as it roared by.

Spreading out, they went over the ground on their knees. Fernandes had looked dubious at the suggestion but had decided not to argue, lowering himself painstakingly to the earth with the rest of them.

'Madam!'

She got to her feet and walked over to the taller constable. He held something in his palm.

It was an enamelled brooch, about three centimetres tall, round and topped with a red and gold crown. At the centre was the somewhat spoiled image of what looked like a sword, superimposed on a crossbow, with a blazing red sun behind. Around this motif were words in gold that she couldn't make out – the brooch had suffered damage. Below the circular section was a banner on which were two further words, in black, this time just about legible: VERUM EXQUIRO.

She turned it over. Around the edge of the reverse: *H.W. Miller Ltd, B'Ham.*

The brooch felt heavy in her palm, something made of more than base metal.

'You can't be sure it's hers,' said Fernandes, appearing at her shoulder.

'Who else could have dropped something like this out here?' She gazed into the surrounding darkness. The night swelled around her. 'How did she get here?'

'She could have come on foot. Taken a cab to the main road and then just walked out here.'

It was possible. 'Why here?' she whispered, to herself.

'What?'

She refused to look at him. 'Why did she come *here* to kill herself? Why not throw herself into the sea? Why out here?'

Fernandes had no answer. In the darkness, she saw a pair of eyes glittering. The dog barked; another responded.

'We have to get her to the mortuary.' She sent one of the constables off to the Dongri station to organise a mortuary van.

They returned to the woman.

Fernandes dropped to his haunches, reached out for the body.

'What are you doing?'

'I'm searching her.'

She realised that this should have been her first act. She hid her anger by raising her voice. 'Don't touch her. I'll do it.'

Fernandes stared at her. She sensed his rage, but then he stood up and stepped away.

She completed the search quickly. 'Nothing,' she said. 'No wallet. No ID. No suicide note.' Her mind whirred. 'How did she get out here without a wallet? How did she pay the cab?'

'Maybe she carried just enough cash. Or told him to keep the change. She wasn't going to need money where she was headed.'

She glanced sharply up at him, but he was staring down at the body.

'She doesn't look like a woman dressed to kill herself. She looks like a woman ready to go out.'

'How many women have you known that killed themselves?' he said.

She felt herself flush and was glad of the darkness. She pushed herself to her feet. 'Our first priority is to find out who she is.'

She stared down at her. Such beauty! What could have pushed a woman like this into taking her own life? How desolate her end seemed. How meaningless.

It bothered her how the constables had abandoned the body.

Partition had shattered her illusions. For years, it had been the British who'd been held up as the epitome of evil – no Indian could behave with the unthinking cruelty that distinguished the white man. But the murderous sectarian violence that had marked the riots had amply demonstrated how her own countrymen could value human life just as cheaply.

Who was she? Who had she been?

Bombay. The city of dreams. But dreams soured. While the city went on, regardless, indifferent. The struggle for independence was fading into the past; Bombay was once again the city of good times. The bars and clubs were booming and the movie industry was churning out films, a healing gloss over the recent horrors that had wracked the nation and still simmered below the surface.

Open wounds in some parts of the country.

On the way back to Malabar House, she sensed that Fernandes wanted to say something. *Needed* to say it. The tension became unbearable.

Finally, he spoke, without looking at her. 'You said "our".'

'What?'

'*Our* first priority is to find out who she is.'

'So?'

'Seth asked *me* to lead this investigation.'

She sucked in a deep breath. 'Under *my* supervision.'

'For me to run the investigation, *I* must give the orders.'

'Leading an investigation isn't about giving orders.'

An angry silence huddled between them like an unwanted child.

They remained this way until she dropped him back outside Malabar House. She watched him as he walked stiffly away towards the rickshaw stand on the corner.

As he slipped into the rickshaw, her eye alighted on a black Studebaker parked across the road. The silhouette of a man in the driver's seat. She couldn't make out his features, but the profile . . . something about him . . . Recognition reared up inside her. It couldn't be.

She stepped out from the jeep, began to walk towards the car, her heart suddenly pounding against her ribcage. But before she could get within a dozen yards, the Studebaker started up, pulled into traffic, and powered away along the road.

She stood there, momentarily unmoored, her blood humming. It couldn't have been him. It was just a trick of the light.

She took a deep breath, spun on her heels, and walked back to the jeep.

6

Sam was sat by the window, fingering notes on the Steinway. Akbar, her overfed grey Persian cat, sat atop the piano, looking vaguely traumatised. Back at home now, Persis had showered, changed into pyjamas, then returned to the living room to find her father had arrived from the bookshop below.

'You're late,' said Sam.

She walked over and kissed him on the cheek. 'And *you* are incorrigible. I'm surprised you got out of the agiary alive.'

He grunted, then wheeled his chair over to the dining table. 'Krishna!' he bellowed, startling the potbellied manservant up from the sofa where he'd been comfortably dozing.

Krishna staggered to the kitchen area, helped himself to a glass of water from the sink, then began clattering about with pots and pans.

The door rang. Persis answered and was immediately smothered in a hug by Aunt Nussie. A cloud of Chanel parfum invaded her nose. 'Persis! How lovely to see you!'

Aunt Nussie had been away. A week in Pondicherry with friends. Contrary to all that was holy, Persis realised that she'd *missed* the woman.

Usually, she saw more of her mother's younger sister than she would have preferred – Nussie made it a point to invite herself over for dinner two, sometimes three, times a week. She had long ago taken it upon herself to manage her only niece's *feminine* affairs, as she put it, believing Sam incompetent in such matters, not without reason.

Persis appreciated her aunt's efforts, but the past few years had been distinguished by Nussie's ham-handed attempts to marry her off to her cousin, Nussie's only son, Darius. Recent events had made that an untenable proposition – Persis had managed to insult Darius, sending him scurrying back to Calcutta where he was busy climbing the ladder at a prominent managing agency. It was not that Darius was unhandsome or lacking in intelligence; marriage was simply a matter that could not be further from her thoughts.

She hated hurting her aunt's feelings, but there was as much chance of her wedding her cousin as there was of her father joining the circus.

Nussie bundled into the apartment, flapping shopping bags at them. 'Gifts!' she announced. 'How are you, Sam?'

Sam gave her a surly look, then belched.

'Charming, as ever,' said Nussie. She rummaged in a bag and took out a black slip of cloth, a vision of satin and lace. 'For you, Persis. They call this a step-in teddy. It's all the rage in Paris, by all accounts.'

'And why precisely would she want to wear something like *that*?' growled Sam.

'Maybe not now, but in due course. When she marries.'

'She'll marry when she's good and ready.'

'Did I say she was getting married today?'

Sam looked set to launch into another of his diatribes, but was prevented from doing so by Krishna slapping a plate on to the table under his nose.

Persis ate quickly and in silence – lamb dhansak and rice – tuning out her aunt as she launched into an exhaustive recounting of her adventures in the south. Her father watched her from under thick eyebrows. 'Is there a race on?' he said. 'How about telling us about your day?'

She apologised. It was a habit they'd fallen into. Each evening they would eat together and she would apprise Sam of her working day. He would listen in silence, occasionally bursting in with opinions and critique, usually of the dolts he believed she worked with.

She briefly outlined the investigation that had begun that day at the Asiatic Society. She decided not to mention the mutilated woman on the railway tracks.

'I've met Forrester before,' said Sam when she'd finished. 'She and her cronies think the Society is some sort of British citadel; a place where they can halt time, keep everything the way it was. Hah.'

'She seemed pleasant enough.'

'More fool you,' he muttered. 'Did you know that in the beginning the Society wouldn't admit Indians? They soon learned you couldn't study India without speaking to the bloody natives.'

Sam's opinions of the British had changed with the advent of the independence movement. Having grown up holding the British in the highest esteem, once it became apparent that the arch colonialists would do anything to hold on to power, he had, like millions of his contemporaries, flocked to Gandhi's banner. His revolutionary fervour had infected Persis at an early age. Later, as an adult, she too would live through years of protest and rebellion, spurred on, in no small part, by the death of her mother.

A disturbance had broken out at a rally Sam and his pregnant wife had been attending. In fleeing, Sam had crashed their car, killing Sanaz and losing the use of his own legs in the process.

For two decades, Sam had kept the truth from her, allowing her to believe that the British had been directly responsible for her mother's death. When he'd finally come clean, it had proved anticlimactic. Too much time had elapsed. She could no longer summon up the ghost of her mother at will, as she had been able to in her youth. Sanaz was now a memory, one that continued to haunt her father, but only flickered at the edges of her own consciousness.

She told them about the Bible John Healy had left behind, the inscription he'd written inside. 'The Greek words mean "follow the truth". I can't work out what the first part is. *What's in a name?* It sounds familiar but I can't place it.'

Sam's brow crunched. They both stared into the distance, wrestling with the problem.

'That?' said Nussie, focused on her plate. 'It's from Shakespeare.'

Sam looked at her incredulously. '*You* know what that means?'

She patted a napkin around her mouth. 'Don't sound so condescending. Frankly, I'm surprised *you* don't. I thought you ran a bookshop.'

Sam glared at her. Persis could see that her aunt was savouring the moment. She put a hand on Nussie's arm. 'Tell me.'

'Well, it's from *Romeo and Juliet.*' She cleared her throat. '"'Tis but thy name that is my enemy; thou art thyself, though not a Montague. What's Montague? It is nor hand, nor foot, nor arm, nor face, nor any other part belonging to a man. O, be some other name! What's in a name? That which we call a rose by any other name would smell as sweet."' She beamed. 'I played Juliet in our college production.'

Persis vaguely recalled the quote now. She'd read Shakespeare diligently as a teen but *Romeo and Juliet* had never been one of her favourites.

She considered the play. What could it possibly have to do with anything? The quote referred to Juliet's dilemma; namely, that had Romeo been named anything other than Montague, their romance might have proceeded without hindrance.

Why would Healy write this above the two Greek words? *Akoloutheo Aletheia.* Follow the truth. The two lines had to be related in some way . . .

'While we're on the subject of romance,' continued Nussie, not looking at Persis, 'I don't suppose you bumped into any eligible young men at the agiary?'

'For God's sake,' spluttered Sam. 'She didn't go to the man's death ceremony to find a husband.'

Nussie set down her napkin. 'She'll be twenty-eight years old next month. She refuses to be set up with anyone, refuses to come to any of the parties I organise. What should I do?'

'Have you tried minding your own business?'

Nussie coloured. 'She's my only niece. I owe it to Sanaz.' She turned to Persis. 'If you won't let *me* find you someone, then find someone suitable yourself.'

Someone suitable? Unbidden, Persis's thoughts flashed to Archie Blackfinch. She could not think of someone *less* suitable in her aunt's eyes than the handsome, awkward Englishman. Nussie was a modern woman, by Indian standards, but for a Parsee to marry an Englishman . . . unthinkable.

'An unmarried woman is like a garden in need of a gardener,' continued Nussie.

Persis pulled off her napkin and stood up. 'I'm going downstairs to find a copy of *Romeo and Juliet*.'

'You see what you've done?' growled Sam.

She leaned down and kissed Nussie on the forehead, then turned and walked on to the landing. From here, she took the rear stairs down into the bookshop.

A ghostly radiance filled the shop, lamplight falling in through the shop's bay windows from the street outside. Her father – and his father before him – had never bothered with shutters. During the various riots that had convulsed the city, the glass façade had been shattered more than once. Sam refused to hide behind a wall of steel, telling her that it would ruin the shop's look: Doric columns in yellow sandstone, an ornamental frieze displaying muscular scenes from Zoroastrian mythology, and a pair of stone vultures perched high on plinths.

She wandered through the maze of shelves – order was something else her father had never bothered to instil in the shop. *He* knew where everything was, and that was all that mattered.

Somehow it worked.

The store had a longstanding and loyal clientele. Even in the war years, it had continued to do a brisk trade. For Persis, it had been a haven, a place to hide from the troubles of finding her way in the world. Growing up a single child, motherless, hampered by an independent-minded, prickly persona, it was inevitable that friends would be few and far between. Loneliness had become a way of life.

Her mind flashed back to Healy's spartan home. *There* was a man who understood loneliness.

She made her way to the *Classics* section and walked her fingers along the shelves, eventually pulling out a copy of *The Complete Works of Shakespeare*, published by Oxford University Press.

She walked to the front of the shop and sat at her father's counter. Akbar had followed her down, and now curled up by the door, staring up at her with his ghostly green eyes.

She turned to *Romeo and Juliet*, found the relevant passage – Act 2, Scene 2 – and spent some time going over it. But nothing new leaped out at her. If there was a hidden message that Healy was pointing to, it eluded her.

Finally, she rose, and returned the book to the shelf.

Another thought struck her. She walked now to the shop's military books section.

She quickly found what she was looking for: *Military Badges of the British Empire: From the Boer War to WW2*.

She returned to the counter and placed the large volume atop it.

Closing her eyes, she summoned up an image of the brooch they had found by the body of the woman on the tracks. Three centimetres in height. A sword, a crossbow, a blazing sun. And on top: a red and gold crown. It was this that had given her the idea.

She had seen plenty of such crowns at the Anglo school she'd attended – the school badge had included one, set above a Latin quotation. She recalled a girl in her house, Felicity, whose father had served in the British air force. He'd been killed in action and Felicity had worn a military brooch for weeks afterwards, until her mother had decided to pull her out of the school and return to England.

Persis found what she was looking for towards the very end of the volume.

There it was, a pristine colour illustration of the badge on the brooch, beside it a brief description:

> *Royal Air Force Wyton station Pathfinder Airfield badge, the centre depicting a blazing sun surmounted by a bow pointed down and sword pointed upwards with the Latin motto 'Verum Exquiro' – Seek the Truth. Wyton Airfield has been in military use since 1916, firstly by the Royal Flying Corps, and later by its successor, the Royal Air Force. Various units served at Wyton during World War One and, more recently, World War Two.*

Seek the truth. *Verum Exquiro*. She was struck by the synchronicity of the words, how they chimed with the words Healy had left behind.

Follow the truth.

She wasn't sure how this new information took her any further forward. Her instincts told her that the woman from the tracks hadn't served in the RAF at Wyton, though she couldn't be sure.

How else might she have come into possession of the brooch? Might it be a lover's gift? Persis had heard of such 'sweetheart brooches'. She hadn't noted a wedding band or engagement ring, but those might easily have vanished in the dead of night. She reminded herself to speak with the man who'd found the body.

An image of Fernandes reared up before her. *Seth asked* me *to lead this investigation.*

She stamped on her anger.

Perhaps the brooch was a memento mori, a keepsake of one now departed. More importantly, how could it help them to identify the woman?

A bicycle rattled by in the alley outside. Akbar scrabbled to his feet, hissed through the glass.

Persis picked up the phone on her father's counter and dialled. 'Hello?'

'It's me,' she said.

'Persis!' Blackfinch's enthusiasm radiated from the receiver like the greeting of a wet dog.

'I need your help.'

Quickly, she described the gruesome discovery on the tracks. 'Can you fingerprint her? See if she's in the records anywhere?'

'Consider it done.'

'Also ... can you call Bhoomi and ask him to conduct the autopsy tomorrow?'

Raj Bhoomi was Bombay's chief pathologist, and a friend of Archie Blackfinch's.

'What's the rush?'

'Can you do it?'

She imagined him frowning. 'That was rather curt. Something about this has got under your skin.'

He was right, of course. In the short while they'd known each other, they had become attuned to each other's thoughts. After a silence, he said, 'I'll call Raj. He owes me a favour. On another note ... might I request the pleasure of your company at dinner tomorrow?'

She hesitated.

It was not that sharing a meal with the Englishman was an unattractive proposition; it was more the confusion that his presence engendered.

Her priorities were clear, to *her*, if to no one else.

The mantle of being India's first female police detective was one that she wore lightly. But the advancement of her own career, that was a different matter. She had no wish to become embroiled in a romantic liaison, particularly one that might colour the image that others held of her. Until now, she hadn't cared how she was perceived, but in the past month she had become – as others continually pointed out to her – a symbol, a woman whose actions provoked both plaudits and censure at a national level. To begin an affair with an Englishman ... it was inconceivable. She would instantly be cast as one of *those* Indian women, the kind that had served as mistresses to their Anglo masters, even as their countrymen suffered.

On the other hand, there were *professional* matters that she needed to discuss with Blackfinch. The Englishman was as socially adept as a camel but there was no doubting his intelligence or his extensive knowledge of the forensic sciences.

'Yes. That would be fine.'

'Excellent. Shall we say eight o'clock at the Wayside?'

'Very well.'

Back in her bed, with Akbar curled under the cotton sheets, her mind lingered on the woman from the tracks.

Who was she? What existential angst had brought her to death's door at such a young age?

The grim thought followed her into a fitful sleep.

7

An hour into the morning a peon arrived at Malabar House bearing an envelope from the Asiatic Society. Opening it, Persis discovered a sheet of paper inscribed with a list of John Healy's acquaintances. The list was short and written in a flowing hand; at the bottom a complicated scribble marked Forrester's signature.

Persis picked out the three names that Forrester had marked with an asterisk – these were the ones that Healy appeared particularly close to, though Forrester had given no indication as to the nature of the relationship.

> Franco Belzoni
> Erin Lockhart
> James Ingram

She called Birla over.

'I want you to do two things. First, make a tour of the local fences, the ones that handle high-ticket items. After that, pay each of these people a visit.' She pointed at the names on Forrester's list that hadn't been marked with an asterisk.

'What am I asking them?'

'I want their impressions of Healy. Anything they can tell us, anything that might shed light on why he may have done this. Don't mention the manuscript for now. Just tell them he's missing and the family is worried.'

She watched Birla walk back to his desk, then picked up the phone.

Fifteen minutes later, she'd made appointments to meet with Belzoni and Lockhart. Ingram had proved harder to track down.

Seconds after she returned the receiver to its cradle, the phone rang. It was Blackfinch.

He had visited the morgue that morning to take fingerprint cards of the woman from the tracks. He hoped to have an answer for her by the time they met for dinner. At the morgue, he'd also taken the opportunity to confirm with the pathologist that the post-mortem would be expedited. It would take place later that day, at three p.m.

She thanked him and put down the phone.

Glancing over at Fernandes's desk, she noted that he hadn't been around all morning. Unusual. Fernandes might be a back-stabbing, treacherous cad, but she couldn't deny his commitment. He was rarely late or absent and seemed to live for his work.

As if summoned into the centre of a pentagram by the mere evoking of his name, the big policeman appeared, striding into the office towards his desk, taking off his cap and wiping a forearm across his sweaty brow.

'Where have you been?' she said, automatically.

Fernandes turned and stared at her. 'I went to interview the man who found the body on the tracks.'

Her shoulders straightened. 'And?'

'He claims he took nothing from her. He didn't even touch her. There was no point. She was dead and a white woman. He simply went on his way; but then his conscience got the better of him so he reported her to the Dongri station.'

'Do you believe him?'

'Yes.'

She paused. 'The brooch we found belongs to a British Royal Air Force unit.'

'How does that help us?'

'I'm not sure yet.' She hesitated. 'I know a military historian. He's a friend of my father's. I'll give you his details. Take the brooch to him and see what he says.'

'We could just put her face in the newspaper.'

'No.' She stopped. She didn't want to tell him that the same thought had occurred to her and she'd dismissed it. She didn't want to risk alerting . . . who? There was no evidence of foul play. Family, then. She wouldn't wish a loved one to discover a death as gruesome as this via a salacious headline.

His moustache twitched. 'It's my call. As the lead investigator.'

Anger flared at her temples, but she clamped her mouth shut. They stared at each other, until Fernandes sat down. 'Very well. Let's follow up what we have. For now.'

'The post-mortem is scheduled for three p.m. at the Grant Medical College.'

'So soon?' His voice radiated surprise.

Bombay's post-Partition growth spurt meant there were more people in the city than the infrastructure could handle. Nehru's reforms were promising an economic miracle; in the meantime, the instability created by the withdrawal of the British, and the nationwide shortages caused by the economic troubles left in their wake, drew the poor to the city of dreams, an endless procession of the weary and the hopeful. But overcrowding and scarcity led to conflict. And conflict led to hostility.

The murder rate in the city had spiked, overloading the handful of qualified pathologists at Raj Bhoomi's disposal. It was rare for a post-mortem to be conducted within a week, let alone a day.

She pulled open a drawer and took out the Bible that Healy had left behind.

Turning to the flyleaf, she considered again the inscription: *What's in a name? Akoloutheo Aletheia.* There had to be a connection between the two lines, otherwise why place them together? The impression of Healy that she'd formed was that of a deliberate man. Why use ancient Greek? Why not simply write 'follow the truth' in plain English?

She recalled something Forrester had said at their first meeting about how language evolved over time; how the meanings of individual words could change.

An idea flashed a fin.

She stood, tucked the Bible under her arm, and headed for the door.

She found Neve Forrester in the Society's basement, in a room labelled *Conservation and Restoration*. She stood, breathing down the neck of a slim Indian man half her age who was seated at a table, wearing white gloves and gently tweezering apart the pages of a manuscript that was either incredibly old or had seen better days. Sweat shone on his brow; every few seconds, a nervous twitch passed through his arm. Persis got the impression that his anxiety was at least partly induced by the hawk-like presence of Forrester.

'May I speak with you a moment?'

Forrester stepped away. 'How can I help you, Inspector?'

'Is there anyone here who is an expert on ancient Greek?' Quickly, she explained her conjecture.

Forrester's pale eyes rested on her. 'You're not satisfied with my translation.' It was a statement, rather than a question.

'I'm exploring all options.'

Forrester turned on her heel. 'Follow me.'

A short walk later they were back in the Special Collections room. This time there was a white man working at one of the tables, a manuscript open before him as he scratched in a notebook laid flat on the table.

Forrester walked over to him. 'Albert, may I have a moment?'

The man ignored her. He was old, Persis saw, with a round, beery face, hoary stubble, and wisps of white hair around the edges of a liver-spotted cranium. His fingers, like his body, were short and thick. Pince-nez glasses were balanced precariously on the end of a drinker's nose.

He finished his sentence, set down his pen, and looked up at Forrester. Persis sensed an unspoken hostility between the pair.

The Englishwoman turned to Persis. 'May I introduce Professor Albert Grant, our resident classicist.'

Persis introduced herself and quickly explained what she was looking for. 'Can you help?'

Grant pulled off his spectacles and waved them at the manuscript before him. 'Do you know what this is?' He did not wait for an answer. 'It's one of the world's oldest books on Greek grammar. Dated 1495. I daresay I am *amply* qualified to assist.'

Persis bit back a retort. Grant was like many successful men that she had recently met, puffed up with a sense of his own importance.

She dug out her notebook and showed him the inscription Healy had left behind.

What's in a name? Akoloutheo Aletheia.

'I'm told that this second statement means "follow the truth". I was wondering if there might be another meaning, one that might link to the first sentence?'

Grant studied the line for a moment, then sat back and laced his fingers over his stomach. 'It's a question of subtlety. The word *aletheia*, in its original Greek sense, means "unconcealedness", a philosophical notion sometimes equated with truth, though this is not, strictly speaking, correct.' He glanced at Forrester. 'The philosopher Martin Heidegger equated its meaning more closely to the notion of "disclosure", the idea that matters become intelligible to us only when interpreted as part of a greater whole.'

Persis considered his words, but nothing seemed clearer. 'Anything else?'

His face fell. He looked away, back to his manuscript, as if dismissing her. 'Of course, if we wish to be prosaic, then the word *aletheia* has also been employed as a name, an all too common one. In Greek mythology, Aletheia was a female daemon of truthfulness and sincerity. Can you guess the modern derivation of the name?'

'No.'

'Alice,' said Grant emphatically. 'Your line might be interpreted as "follow Alice". Or, to be more precise, "follow in the footsteps of Alice".'

Persis allowed this conjecture to flow around her mind. She felt certain now that Healy's first line – *What's in a name?* – had been intended to lead them to decipher his Greek words as "follow Alice". But who was Alice?

'Did Healy have an acquaintance by the name of Alice?'

'You received the list I sent you?' asked Forrester.

'Yes.'

'Was there an Alice on it?'

'No.'

'Then you have your answer.'

Persis flushed. 'Is there anyone else at the Society named Alice?'

'No.'

She continued to examine the problem as Forrester led her back out.

On the portico steps the Englishwoman spoke. 'Inspector, I'm not certain that I impressed upon you just how imperative it is that we recover the Dante manuscript. Perhaps you received the impression that the political fallout was my main source of concern. Nothing could be further from the truth. My responsibility is to this institution. We rely on donations to survive. To lose one of the world's great treasures would be a scandal I fear may mortally wound us. The Society is more than the sum of its parts. It is in this building that Queen Victoria's 1858 proclamation took place, abolishing the East India Company and transferring administration of the country to the crown. It is here that a portion of Gandhi's ashes were kept so that his devotees could pay their last respects. The Asiatic Society is, in and of itself, living history.'

Persis turned her gaze to the Horniman Gardens, deserted at this hour.

By the evening the gardens would be alive with office workers, smoking, chatting, courting, taking a moment to recover from the tribulations of the day before heading home. Not long ago, a band had played there in the cool of the night. With independence, the band members, a jazz quartet from the American south, had returned home.

Forrester's words resonated with her own growing feelings about the case. That it was about more than a lost manuscript. The Society was a link to the past, a tangible thread that connected the India of her ancestors to the India that was now taking shape under Nehru's stewardship. Healy's theft felt like a betrayal of that legacy.

Her thoughts fell again to his parting missive. Follow Alice ... But which Alice? Her mind wandered around Healy's home, the nearly empty fridge, the spartan bedroom, the living room with its bookca—

The thought came like a thunderclap. The bookcase.

She turned to Forrester. 'I'll bear your words in mind. Thank you for your assistance.'

*　　*　　*

Fifteen minutes later, she broke the police seal that Birla had set over John Healy's front door. Walking straight to the bookcase in the living room, she bent down and picked out the copy of Lewis Carroll's *Through the Looking-Glass*.

The book was new, a recent purchase. She opened it to the flyleaf. Healy had signed and dated it on the day he'd vanished.

Follow Alice. Follow in the footsteps of Alice.

She walked into the bedroom and stood before the large ormolu mirror. Then, stretching her arms across its expanse, she lifted it from its fittings and laid it down on the bed.

She looked at the wall. Nothing.

Disappointed, she hesitated a moment, then turned back to the mirror. She saw that it had a thin plywood backing.

She went to the kitchen, rummaged in the drawers, and returned with a knife.

Quickly, she levered her way under the rim, then popped out the backing. Turning it around, she found what she was looking for.

Written there, in inch-high letters, was a message:

> *Sundered from Alba's hearth he came;*
> *To beauty's bay, seeking Sinan's fame;*
> *Enjoined to begg, his labours Empire's pride;*
> *His infernal porta, a King denied;*
> *'Neath Cross and dome, his resting place;*
> *Together we await in fey embrace.*

8

The meeting with Franco Belzoni was due to take place at midday, at the Victoria and Albert Museum. It took Persis half an hour to drive the seven kilometres north to the site, through unusually difficult traffic. Ongoing protests were clogging up the city's arteries; she was forced to wait as a gang of striking mill workers added to the daily havoc outside the Victoria Terminus railway station. The workers had chanced on the clever idea of bringing along a herd of cows. These now formed a perimeter around the chanting labourers, preventing the police from getting rough. It was one thing beating down those demanding their rights in the new India, quite another laying hands on avatars of god.

She left the jeep outside the museum and entered through the front door into the central hall, with its soaring, patterned ceiling, parquet flooring, and grand gallery. Visitors were greeted by an unsmiling bust of Queen Victoria and an equally unsmiling host sat behind a marble counter. Persis introduced herself and was duly led through the museum, her guide taking it upon himself to provide a running commentary, as if a string had been pulled and he could no more stop his recitation than a clockwork soldier could stop the movement of its mechanical limbs.

The Victoria and Albert was the city's oldest museum, established to commemorate the transfer of power from the East India Company to the British crown and to serve as an expression of the loyalty of Bombay's merchants to the new Raj. As such, many of its older exhibits came from a temporary 'economic museum' once housed at the barracks of the Bombay Fort. During the 1857 rebellion the fort had been requisitioned to barrack British troops on their way to Calcutta; to make room, most of the exhibits had been unceremoniously thrown into the street. Those that hadn't suffered terminal damage had been relocated to the V&A, and the lush botanical gardens within which it sat.

She found Belzoni waiting for her in a small office on the upper floor, overlooking the gardens. The Italian rose as she entered, proffering a hand.

'Dr Franco Belzoni. You must be Ispettrice Wadia.'

He was of middling height, younger than she had anticipated – no more than thirty – with thick black hair, quick, dark eyes, and a strong jaw. He was dressed conservatively in a suit, though the jacket had been discarded, and the tie was hanging loose at the neck.

She couldn't blame him.

It was early in the year but the daytime heat had already become stifling. If this kept up, the city would parch – the monsoon was a good four months away.

A ceiling fan blew the smell of sweat and carbolic soap towards her.

'May I offer you coffee?' Belzoni's copper skin glowed against the whiteness of his shirt. As did his teeth.

'No. Thank you.'

'Please, have a seat.' He waved at the table before them, then realised that it was covered in books and a selection of Mughal miniature paintings. '*Mi scusi,*' he said, and then clapped at a peon lurking in the corner. The man leaped to action; in short order, the table was cleared. 'I was invited here today to present a talk,' explained Belzoni, slipping into a seat. 'I requested an office for our meeting and this is what was available.' He leaned over the table. 'Tell me, how may I help you?'

Quickly, she explained the situation to him.

Belzoni listened intently, his eyes darkening as it became apparent that *La Divina Commedia* was missing.

'*Impossibile!*' he finally managed. For an instant, he was too stunned to say anything more. He stood and began to pace, muttering under his breath.

'I'm told you knew Healy well.'

He spun around. 'Me? No. I knew *of* him, *sì*, but I only met him three weeks ago, when I arrived in Bombay.'

'Why *are* you here?'

'For the manuscript, of course. I am an art historian by training, but I have a passion for rare manuscripts. I am employed by the University of Bologna. Three years ago, the oldest known complete copy of the Hebrew Torah was discovered in the library there, a parchment scroll wrongly catalogued as belonging to the seventeenth century. The scroll has now been authenticated to the late 1100s. I was one of those who worked on the authentication.

'I am currently working on a catalogue of all extant copies of *La Divina Commedia*. Of course, there are no surviving copies in Dante's own hand, but at least four hundred copies from the fourteenth century are known to exist. Many are in the possession of private collectors. The copy here at the Asiatic Society is *molto importante* because of its age.'

'Is it true that Mussolini once offered a million dollars for it?'

Belzoni flashed a rueful smile. 'It is true that Il Duce was obsessed by Dante. But then, so are many Italians. He is the man who gave us the Italian we now speak. *The Divine Comedy* is not just one of the great works of world literature; in Italy, it established the Tuscan dialect as our national language.'

'You've studied it for a long time?'

'All my life.'

'Tell me, who might be interested in the manuscript? I mean, someone who would go to any lengths to possess it.'

He waved his hands around as if conducting an invisible symphony. 'There are unscrupulous collectors everywhere – the trade in rare manuscripts is very lucrative. I once held in my hands a stolen copy of *De revolutionibus orbium coelestium* by Copernicus, the book that redefined our place in the cosmos. The collector had paid thirty thousand dollars for it. In his private vault, we found another of the rarest manuscripts in the world, a 1455 Gutenberg Bible, one of only forty-nine that still exist. The Gutenberg Bible was one of the first books created using mass-printed movable type, the technique Johannes Gutenberg invented.

'Rare manuscripts are not simply valuable artefacts. They are our connection to our past, the building blocks by which humanity has ascended the steps towards enlightenment.' His eyes shone. 'Can you imagine what it would be like to return to the past and walk through the halls of the Great Library of Alexandria? To hold in my hands the *original* works of Socrates, Plato, Aristotle, men who have shaped human thought for two thousand years?' He sighed. 'Of course, not everyone holds knowledge in such esteem. Sometimes, illuminated manuscripts are butchered – the engravings they contain are cut out and traded in the art market, piece by piece.' A shudder passed through him. 'I will do one thing for you. During my career, I have come across many international dealers who might be able to traffic the *Divine Comedy* manuscript. I will contact them discreetly and find out if they have heard anything.'

'You expect honesty from them?'

'They are fiercely competitive. If one has it, the others will not hesitate to volunteer his name.'

She nodded unenthusiastically. If the manuscript had already found its way into the hands of such a dealer, then the case had already moved beyond her purview.

His dark eyes lingered on her. 'It is unusual, *sì*, a *poliziotta* in your country? A woman, I mean?'

'Is it usual in Italy?'

He conceded the point. 'Our *polizia* is very, how you say, *cosa di maschi* – a male thing.'

'When I put on my uniform I forget that I'm a woman,' said Persis. 'All that matters is the task at hand.'

'*Le chiedo scusa.* I did not mean to cause offence.'

'I'm not offended. Just ... tired of the question. Sometimes I feel like a zoo animal, a rare exhibit. Maybe as rare as one of your manuscripts.'

He nodded sympathetically, but said nothing.

'How did you end up here?' she asked. 'I mean, after the war ...'

'Ah. I was wondering how long before you mention the war. Mussolini and our Pope, together they have ruined Italy's reputation. All I can say is that not all of us wore the *Camicia Nera*.'

'Did you know of Healy before you arrived here?'

'Yes, of course. His reputation as a scholar is excellent. I contacted the Society and asked for permission to view the manuscript. When they informed me that Healy was working on a new translation of *La Divina Commedia*, I was delighted.'

'What did you make of him? I mean, what kind of man was he?'

The question seemed to surprise him. 'A very private man. I am Italian. We are like Indians. We live for food, family, and conversation. But Healy ...'

'Did you get to know him well?'

'I don't think I got to know him at all.'

'Looking back, is there anything that he said or did that might offer a clue as to why he may have taken the manuscript or where?'

He shook his head. 'I can think of nothing.'

She pulled her notebook from her pocket. 'I discovered this written on the back of a mirror in his home. Does it mean anything to you?'

She waited as he scanned the odd inscription.

'What makes you think this has anything to do with Healy?'

'It was written in his hand.' She leaned forward. 'I believe that Healy has left behind clues. I believe he *wants* us to find him.'

'Why would a man steal one of the most valuable historical artefacts in the world and then leave a trail for those following him? It makes no sense.' He waved the notebook at her. 'These words make no sense.'

She sat back, disappointed. 'Are you planning to return to Italy?'

'I cannot. My work with the manuscript is not yet complete. And now I cannot leave the country while it is missing.' He stood. 'You must find it, Inspector. *Rapidamente.* This has the makings of a political disaster.'

9

As disasters went, the recent death of the city's chief pathologist, Dr John Galt, had struck Persis as particularly tragic, more so given that his replacement was a man who could not have differed more – in look and temperament – from the patrician Englishman.

She arrived at the Grant Medical College in good time for the scheduled post-mortem, making her way quickly into the interior of the depressingly bleak building – it always put her in mind of some ogre's keep with its multiple turrets and austere façade. She recalled reading somewhere that entrance exams had once included a test based on Milton's *Paradise Lost*. She'd often wondered how mastery of a novel about the fall of man might be a reasonable examination of someone's ability to carry out surgical procedures on the college's hapless early victims. On the plus side, the college *had* decreed that admittance would not be decided on the basis of caste or creed.

Only women, of course, were barred from applying.

A plaque outside the mortuary declared that the very first autopsy had been conducted there in 1882. She wondered briefly who that unfortunate individual had been and whether his misfortune had extended beyond death to having a man as incompetent as Raj Bhoomi hacking away at his cadaver.

Perhaps she was being unfair.

In the short while that she'd known him, Bhoomi had proved a more than able pathologist. It was his manner that set her teeth on edge.

She found him in the autopsy suite on the first floor, examining a corkboard on to which had been pinned a series of photographs of women.

He heard her enter and turned, a small man, bulbous-nosed, peering at her through round-framed spectacles. She saw that he'd tidied up his moustache. The last time she'd seen it, it had resembled a spider that had crawled under his nose and died there. An odd smell emanated from him ... She realised, with a faint horror, that it was some sort of aftershave, as powerful as a gas leak.

'What do you think?' He turned back to the board and waved at the photographs.

She looked at the women, the sad faces, the glassy-eyed stares. The pictures had been taken during life, but now, transformed by death and the macabre environment of the morgue, they reminded her of shades, wavering between this world and the next.

'It's ... terrible,' she said. What else was there to say?

Bhoomi looked confused. 'What is?'

She waved at the women. 'Their misfortune.'

He coloured, his back stiffening. 'Inspector, I must say I find that rather insulting.'

It was her turn to look confused. 'I don't follow.'

'Well, I would hardly label the prospect of encountering me a *misfortune*.'

'And *I* would have thought that anyone who ends up here must be unfortunate indeed.'

They stared at each other. Then Bhoomi said, gently, 'Inspector, these women are not dead. They're prospective brides. My mother is attempting to arrange my marriage.'

An apology stumbled around her mouth. She was saved from having to force it out by the arrival of George Fernandes.

The sub-inspector bundled into the anteroom, led in by a heavy smell of sweat.

Persis introduced the pair, then they followed Bhoomi into the autopsy room, the acrid smell of formaldehyde cancelling out all other odours. On consideration, she preferred it.

'I have afternoon tea scheduled with one of my potential brides-to-be,' remarked Bhoomi as he pulled on a bottle-green apron and gloves. 'Do you think I should tell her what sort of medicine I practise?'

'No,' said Persis.

Bhoomi shrugged. 'I shall trust your judgement. I'm rather inexperienced in such matters.'

He moved to an autopsy table upon which lay a body covered by a white sheet.

Pulling off the sheet, he revealed the truncated cadaver of the woman from the railway tracks. The lower parts of her legs were placed beside the body, making a ghoulish tableau.

She heard Fernandes cough uncomfortably beside her. She doubted he had attended the autopsies of many white females. For that matter, neither had she. The sight of the dead woman, her pale flesh made paler by the overhead lighting, filled her with a sudden sense of desolation.

They waited as Bhoomi's assistant set up a camera and took photographs of the body, back and front. Bhoomi then painstakingly examined the woman's outer clothing, blackened by soot from the railway sleepers, before cutting off her dress and bagging it. The naked cadaver was now photographed, followed by measurements of the body's limbs, scribbled into a notebook.

Next the pathologist went over the body in fine detail, using his fingertips.

Having completed his observations, he went to his bank of instruments.

They waited in respectful silence as he carried out the autopsy, opening up the body with a practised hand, removing the internal organs, weighing and bagging them, and then turning to the head. Making an incision behind one ear, he drew his scalpel across the crown, then peeled back the scalp.

In moments, the brain was exposed, scooped out, weighed, examined, and set aside.

After a while, Persis became aware that Fernandes kept shifting from one foot to the other. She angled her head and saw that sweat glimmered at his temples, even though it was relatively cool in the autopsy suite.

Strange, she thought; she had never pegged the gruff, taciturn Fernandes as lacking the stomach for this sort of thing.

Then again, she hadn't pegged him for a misogynist either.

The thought angered her and she returned her attention to Bhoomi.

Time crawled on, until finally the pathologist stepped away. His boots clacked on the tiles as he walked to the sink and ran water over his gloves.

When he returned, he rattled off a summary of his findings.

'This woman did not die on the railway tracks. What I mean is that the cause of death wasn't the result of trauma and blood loss occasioned by the severing of her limbs. She was dead before she was laid out on those tracks.'

'Laid out?' echoed Fernandes.

'Yes. This woman died from ligature strangulation. Technically speaking, death was the result of compression of the windpipe leading to asphyxia and cerebral hypoxaemia. Her injuries bear this out. The hyoid bone has been fractured, the tongue and larynx are enlarged, and there is conjunctival and facial petechial haemorrhaging.' He flashed a grim look. 'Judging from the lack of rope fibres and the width of the ligature markings around her throat, I think some sort of wire was used.'

'Couldn't the bruises have come from a suicide attempt?' Persis asked.

'If she'd tried to hang herself, the ligature marks would exhibit a raised imprint, pointing in an upward direction as gravity pulled the body downwards.' He shook his head. 'I'm afraid this poor girl was murdered. Brutally. And then her body was dumped on the tracks. My guess is the perpetrator laid her out with her neck on the rails, in the hope that the train would disguise his crime.'

Fernandes looked quizzical. 'Then how is it that the train ran over her at the knees?'

'Did you notice her dress?' said Bhoomi, taking off his spectacles and wiping them with a handkerchief. 'It was torn at the shoulders. I found bite marks on her clavicles and rear deltoids. Tell me, were there any stray dogs in the vicinity?'

Persis's thoughts flashed back to a pair of eyes glittering in the darkness, and a wolf-like baying. 'Yes.'

'My guess is that they tried to drag her off the tracks – take her someplace where they might eat undisturbed. They only partly succeeded before the train came along.'

They contemplated this grisly image as he returned his spectacles to his nose.

'Is there anything you can tell us that might help us establish her identity?' asked Persis.

'By my estimate, this woman was aged anywhere from twenty-three to late twenties. I'm sorry I can't be more accurate but, with nothing else to go on, morphological determination of age is notoriously difficult. What I *can* say is that the five vertebrae of the sacrum are fused into a single unit – and that usually happens by the age of twenty-three, hence my lower limit. She was in good physical shape, but had suffered physical trauma in the past. There is evidence of scarring on her back, and a series of cut marks on the inner part of her left thigh. I've seen such marks before. My guess is they're self-inflicted.

'On her left breast, there's a burn scar. Faint traces of a tattoo are visible through it – not enough to make out what it is, but enough to tell me she may have tried to get rid of it by scarring herself.' He grimaced. 'There's another five-inch horizontal mark just above the pubic mound. At some point this woman had a C-section – a caesarean birth. This was a woman with a troubled past.'

'An abusive partner?' mused Persis.

'Quite possibly.'

'This is pure speculation, of course,' continued the pathologist, 'but she may have exhibited emotional or mental instability. The cut marks on her thigh might be evidence of self-harm. In which case, being a westerner, she may have visited with a medical professional. You may want to check around. There aren't many psychiatrists in the city. We've always been rather backwards in our thinking about such matters on the subcontinent, tending to believe that mental distress is caused by divine curses, bad karma, and the like. It was only during the Raj that we got our first luna-tic asylums – the British established them to lock up soldiers slowly going out of their minds with heat, dysentery, and malaria.' He paused. 'Thankfully, things have changed in recent years. In fact, a colleague of mine runs a diploma in psychological medicine here at the college. You might want to check with him.' He stopped again. 'There's one other possibility. Having examined the woman's sexual organs, I can state that she was very active in that area. In fact, unusually so. Not that I'm suggesting there is any usual frequency . . .' He tailed off, and coughed.

Persis wondered why men found it so uncomfortable to discuss such matters around her when they seemed perfectly content to be obnoxiously direct about her career.

Bhoomi pushed his spectacles up his nose. 'I once performed post-mortems on dozens of women who had perished in a gas leak in Calcutta. Brothel workers. This woman exhibits very similar characteristics of long-term trauma to her sexual organs.'

'Are you saying she was a night worker?' Fernandes seemed astonished.

'It's a possibility. I can't be certain. She might just have been in a sexually aggressive relationship,' said Bhoomi.

Persis turned to leave, then remembered something. 'By the way, do you know what Tuinal tablets are for? It's for another case.'

'They're sleeping tablets – sedative-hypnotics that use a barbiturate base. Very new. They're manufactured in America by Eli Lilly.'

Back outside, she compared notes with Fernandes. He had been to see Augustus Silva, a military historian who frequented her father's bookshop. Silva worked at Bombay University, where he taught courses on India's military past.

'Silva confirmed what you already told me,' said Fernandes. 'He phoned someone in England, a colleague of his. He gave him a description of the woman, asked him to check if anyone like that had ever worked at RAF Wyton.'

She looked away, at a beggar beseeching a man entering the gate. The beggar was on a trolley. She wondered if it was the same one she'd encountered at the Asiatic Society.

'I'm going to call him back and give him an updated description,' continued Fernandes. 'The photographs that Bhoomi took will be ready soon. I'll take him those too. Or, at least, one of her face.'

She nodded, unable to fault his suggestions.

Privately, she continued to doubt that the woman had ever worked at RAF Wyton. She knew that all sorts of women had made it into the British war effort but if Bhoomi's conjecture was correct and she was an escort working in Bombay, it would make such a scenario highly implausible.

She dwelt momentarily on the notion of a prostitute murder. Such crimes were by no means uncommon in a city as congested as Bombay, but the murder of a *white* escort? She couldn't recall such a case.

Erin Lockhart had requested a meeting at her residence, back at the southern tip of the city, a grand bungalow just yards from the Church of St John the Evangelist, better known in Bombay as the Afghan Church. The British had raised the church to commemorate the dead of the First Afghan War and the terrible retreat from Kabul in 1842 that had cost the lives of some sixteen thousand British soldiers and their families, forced to slog through the winter snows of the Hindu Kush in a doomed attempt to reach Jalalabad. Such was the shock of the debacle that the Governor-General of India at the time, Lord Auckland, had suffered a stroke upon hearing the news.

Lockhart's bungalow was in the Navy Nagar cantonment, an area that housed senior personnel from the Indian Navy. A checkpoint had been established during the war and Persis was forced to present her credentials before entering.

The whitewashed bungalow glittered in the late afternoon sun, a navy pennant flapping from a red-tiled roof in a gentle breeze rolling in off the sea.

She found Lockhart on a wide, lush lawn that sloped down towards a rocky beach. Palm trees made regimented lines either side of the lawn, and a white picket fence marked its furthest boundary. A small white dog yapped after a ball.

The maid that had let her in returned to the porch as Lockhart stood in the sunlight examining an object set on a table before her – a spinning wheel, faded and cracked.

'What do you think?'

Persis examined the wheel. 'It's seen better days.'

'Wrong,' said Lockhart. 'As each day passes, this particular wheel *gains* value. It belonged to one Mohandas K. Gandhi.'

Like most Indians, Persis knew the story.

In 1932, Gandhi had been imprisoned by the British in Pune. During his incarceration, he had decided to begin making his own thread with a *charkha*, a portable spinning wheel. What started as a means of passing the time soon became a symbol of the resistance, with Gandhi encouraging his countrymen to make their own cloth instead of buying British cotton.

Now, the wheel was part and parcel of the Mahatma's legacy.

'Erin Lockhart,' said the woman, sticking out a hand.

'Persis Wadia.'

The American's grip was firmer than she had expected, her hands rougher than her groomed appearance implied. Lockhart was a small woman, but clearly in good physical condition. She wore a sleeveless white blouse above khaki-brown slacks. Her arms were lean, the muscles of her shoulders sharply defined. Her blonde hair was almost white, contrasting with her tanned face and a splash of red lipstick.

'I've just bought this from Gandhi's estate,' she said. 'If I told you how much it cost, you'd probably faint.'

'I never faint.'

Lockhart's dark eyes rested on Persis's face. 'No. I don't suppose you do. You wouldn't get far as India's first lady cop if you did, I suppose.' She smiled. 'May I offer you something to drink?'

They sat on the porch, drinks in hand – a gin and tonic for Lockhart, a lime soda for Persis. Quickly, she brought the American up to speed. 'I'm told you were close to Healy?'

'I was and I wasn't,' she replied, cryptically. Persis waited. 'If you must know, I was sleeping with the man. I suppose that makes us

73

close. But if you want me to tell you what was going on inside his head, I'm afraid I can't help you.'

Persis shifted in her chair. There had been no mention so far of Healy engaged in a personal relationship.

'We kept it quiet,' said Lockhart, as if reading her thoughts. 'Or rather, John preferred to keep his private life to himself.'

'How did you meet?'

'At an Asiatic Society talk he gave three months ago. He was quite the most uncomfortable man I've ever met. Monosyllabic, no social graces. But the talk was fantastic. He led us through the priories of medieval England in a way I've never seen anyone else do. When he spoke about his passion, he was a different person.'

Persis sipped at her soda. 'What are you doing in India?'

'I work for the Smithsonian.' She threw the name out there in typically American fashion, as if there was no possibility that Persis might not have heard of it. Fortunately, she knew quite a bit about the great museum, gleaned mainly from a book she'd discovered in her father's shop as a teenager: *Explorations and Field-work of the Smithsonian Institution in 1937*.

The volume had captured her imagination with its account of archaeological and anthropological expeditions to all corners of the globe, in search of treasures to be taken back to the self-proclaimed 'world's greatest storehouse of knowledge'.

'I'm working as part of a mission to catalogue India's journey to independence,' continued Lockhart. 'We're putting on a big exhibition next year and I'm out here to source exhibits.'

'Do you think a spinning wheel can really tell you the truth of what we had to do to achieve our freedom?'

Lockhart tapped the side of her glass. 'I sense hostility. Do you think we're paying lip service to your struggle? Nothing could be further from the truth. America fought for its own independence from the British. Granted the scale and the history are different,

74

but please don't believe that I'm some sort of amateur explorer here to steal your soul with my picture box.' She smiled but there was ice behind it. 'Look, you want the truth? It's simple. History needs to be preserved or it decays. In the hands of unscrupulous historians, it becomes malleable. How much of the past that we take for granted is *actually* true? How much has been exaggerated, distorted, shaped to meet the ends of its chroniclers? I'm here because I want to capture this important moment in *your* nation's history. And yes, if that means taking some of your cultural treasures back with me to a place where I know they'll be looked after and valued, then so be it.' She raised a hand to still Persis's protest. 'Before you get on your high horse, take a look around. India's cultural monuments are crumbling out of neglect. The British did little to preserve them, and the Indian government has bigger fish to fry.'

Persis bit back an automatic retort. The truth was that Lockhart was right. In the new India, the preservation of history was low on the government's list of priorities.

She tacked back to the case. 'When was the last time you saw Healy?'

'That would be four days ago. We had dinner.'

'No contact in four days?'

'We're not joined at the hip, Inspector. We're both busy people. We see each other when the need arises, for dinner, a drink. We're attracted to each other and we act on that impulse whenever we get the itch. But we certainly aren't mooning around every second we're apart.'

'Did he mention anything about the manuscript?'

'Do you mean did he tell me about his master plan to steal one of the world's most valuable art treasures? No.'

Persis flushed. The woman was acid-tongued. She resisted the urge to return in kind. She'd been working hard to rein in her naturally combative tendencies. A good detective needed guile, not anger.

She took out her notebook and showed Lockhart the inscription she had found in his bedroom.

'You found this behind the mirror?' Lockhart seemed perturbed. 'I've spent nights in that room. I hated that mirror. And the Cross above it. Did you notice that? It's almost as if John put it up there to annoy me. I mean, I'm not religious, but no one wants to think of Christ looking down on them while they're in the throes of passion.'

'Have you any idea what it means?'

She watched Lockhart's lips as she read out the inscription. *'Sundered from Alba's hearth he came; To beauty's bay, seeking Sinan's fame; Enjoined to begg, his labours Empire's pride; His infernal porta, a King denied; 'Neath Cross and dome, his resting place; Together we await in fey embrace.'* Her eyes rested on the page. 'It's a riddle. John loved them. Riddles, crosswords, literary puzzles.'

'Why would he leave this behind?'

Lockhart's eyes quickened. 'It's a treasure hunt.'

'Please expand.'

'I think John has hidden the manuscript and this is his way of leading us to it.'

'Why would he do that?' She decided not to mention that she had arrived at a similar conjecture.

'That I can't tell you. He must have had his reasons.' She took up the notebook again. 'Did you copy this out exactly as he left it?'

'Yes. Why?'

Her eyebrows bent into a frown. '"Beg" is spelled wrong. *Enjoined to* begg. John would never make a mistake like that.'

Persis absorbed this, then moved on. 'Is there anything you can tell me at all that might help?'

She considered this. 'John was a complicated man. You know he suffered terribly in the war? He was in a POW camp for a long time. I think they tortured him. Not just physically, but mentally. He'd wake up in the middle of the night, bathed in sweat, crying out. He refused to talk about it, but I knew. Nightmares, the sort that never leave you no matter how far you run.'

'Is that what you think he was doing in India? Running?'

'It would explain a lot. I mean, no disrespect to your country, but a scholar of John's standing . . .? He could have walked into any institution in the world. He didn't need to come to Bombay to translate *The Divine Comedy*. There are other copies.'

Persis thought back to the tablets they'd found in Healy's bedside drawer. This backed up Lockhart's account that Healy was having trouble sleeping.

'There's one other thing. Possibly nothing.' The American hesitated then plunged on. 'About a week ago John had a row with a colleague. At the Society. It was over the manuscript.'

'Who?'

'A guy named Belzoni. Italian. Have you met him yet?'

'What did they argue about?'

'Belzoni wanted more access to the book; he's working on some sort of catalogue. As Curator of Manuscripts, John was in charge and he barely let Belzoni near it.'

'Why?'

'He wouldn't say. But I think Belzoni got John's back up when he started talking about India having a moral responsibility to return the volume to Italy. John isn't fond of Italians – it was in Italy that he spent all that time in prison. He didn't like the word "moral" in an Italian's mouth, I guess.'

Persis thought back to her meeting with Belzoni. The Italian had failed to mention a tiff with Healy. Why?

'Does he have any other acquaintances that you think I should speak to?'

'As I said John was an intensely private man.'

'Any other lady friends?'

She raised her chin. 'That was very direct. No, Inspector, I don't think John was sleeping with anyone else. He wasn't that sort of man. We may not have been lovesick teenagers but we were a pair. I didn't step out on him and, as far as I know, he didn't step out on me.'

11

'I'd rather poke knitting needles into my eyes. With all due respect.'

Seth glared at her from behind his desk, then walked around to the near wall and stood with his back turned, looking up at a print of the Mughal emperor Akbar on elephant-back. 'Do you know what the punishment was for insubordination in the Mughal empire?'

She waited, taking refuge in silence.

'The emperor would order a public gathering. He'd call for his favourite elephant, have his guards force the offending subject's head down on to a stone plinth, and then instruct the beast to crush the man's skull underfoot.' He turned back to her. 'When I say to you that it is my wish that you work with these women, I mean that I expect you to do it.'

The trouble had started on her return to Malabar House.

She'd noticed a pair of youngish women emerging from Seth's office. The SP had a complaisant grin pasted across his face, one at complete odds with his usual demeanour. He'd shown the women to the station's interview room, then beckoned Persis into his office.

She'd given him an update on both the Healy case and the investigation into the death of the woman from the railway tracks.

'Murder?' he'd said glumly as she detailed the pathologist's conclusions.

The murder of whites in Bombay was now a rarity and one that instantly attracted press – and political – attention. With independence, a line had been drawn under the colonial era. Any foreigners that remained in the country were generally deemed worthy of ally status – India and her former rulers were now partners in the new world order, no longer master and subject. Throttling one's allies was usually considered beyond the pale. 'Well, I suppose we'll have to follow it up. Is Fernandes behaving himself?'

She'd stifled the urge to speak ill of her fellow officer, instead presenting a factual account of how the case had progressed. Seth absorbed the information, then said, 'It sounds like you have a plan. Now, what about Healy? What are your next steps?' He explained that he'd received a call from ADC Amit Shukla. 'Delhi has been on the line to him. The Italians have thrown their pasta at the wall. Apparently, Nehru is climbing his own walls, up at Viceroy's House.'

'Rashtrapati Bhavan.'

'What?'

'They renamed it on Republic Day. Have you forgotten already?'

She showed him the inscription Healy had left behind, and described her meetings with Belzoni and Lockhart. Seth could make nothing of the strange riddle.

'It's always the quiet ones you have to watch out for,' he'd sighed. 'Stealing the manuscript I can understand, but why play games? Why kick a man in the balls when you've already shot him through the heart?'

She'd refrained from comment. Seth's language became increasingly colourful in direct proportion to his agitation and the amount of whisky he'd consumed.

'I think he wants us to find the manuscript,' she offered. 'I think he's hidden it somewhere.'

'I ask again: why?'

But that was the question to which there was yet no answer.

Seth had leaned back in his chair. 'I have another task for you. Did you notice those two women I was talking to when you came in?' Her antennae began to send out warning signals. 'They're from the Margaret Cousins College of Domestic Science. It's some sort of institute aimed at progressing women's rights. As if we didn't have enough trouble on that score.' He gave her a pointed look. 'They would like you to come to their institute and deliver a lecture. Apparently, you're quite the celebrity down there.'

'A lecture?' she echoed.

'Yes. A talk. Tell them about your life. Your experiences as a policewoman. Very straightforward.'

She stared ahead, rigid-backed, radiating refusal. 'I don't think so. Sir.'

He frowned. 'There's nothing to it. It's a couple of hours of your time.'

'If there's nothing to it, why don't you send someone else? Better yet, go yourself. I'm sure they'd appreciate a man of your experience.'

'These women have the ear of the chief minister's daughter, Persis. Refusing them is not an option.'

'I'd rather poke knitting needles into my eyes. With all due respect.'

That was when Seth had gotten up and made his speech about Mughal elephants.

He stared at her now until she was forced to look at him. 'How can you expect me to do this? Now? Didn't you just say how important the Healy case was?'

'I'll tell you what my old boss told me when I made a similar complaint early in my career: life is a balancing act. Learn to juggle.'

*   *   *

The women stood to greet her as she entered the interview room. They made an odd couple, one tall and thin, the other short and round. Side by side, they resembled the number ten made flesh. Both were dressed boldly, the taller one in a cream, two-piece, collarless suit with round blue buttons and a peacock brooch on the lapel, the other in an embroidered white kurta over a long rainbow skirt with high-heeled, lace-up Oxfords.

'Inspector Wadia,' said the taller one, extending a hand. 'How lovely to finally meet you. My name is Jenny Pinto. This is my colleague Scheherazade Mirza. We represent the Margaret Cousins College of Domestic Science. We were hoping that you might spare some time for a chat.'

'I'm really rather busy at present.'

'Of course. I imagine being at the vanguard of a movement can be quite trying.' Pinto smiled. She had a wide forehead and small eyes, magnified somewhat by the spectacles that sat on her aquiline nose. Her hair was cut short and styled into fashionable bangs.

'Movement?' Persis frowned.

'Our nation's first female police inspector. A movement of one is still a movement.' She smiled. 'Even the monsoon begins with a single raindrop.'

'I'm not exactly clear what you want from me.' She knew that she was being curt, but she had no more wish to be held up as a symbol by women as she did by men.

The shorter woman, Mirza, stepped forward. She had catlike eyes, heavily lined with kohl, and a sulky mouth. She wore a surfeit of bangles, and her hair was piled up into a beehive. 'We're presuming that you're familiar with the All India Women's Conference?' Her voice was singsong, the voice of a koel. 'This year our college has been chosen to host the conference's annual gathering. Over one thousand women will be in attendance, from around the country. We were hoping you would speak at the event.'

'Why me?'

'We feel your unique experiences will provide both positive encouragement and an inspirational message.'

'I'm not a professional speaker.'

Pinto smiled. 'Sometimes actions speak louder than words, Inspector.'

Persis flapped around for a lifeline. 'I wouldn't know what to say.'

'We can help you to prepare a suitable talk,' persisted Mirza.

Silence reigned. 'Surely there must be someone else,' Persis finally managed. Her throat had become dry.

'Not unless you know of another female police inspector in the country?' Pinto smiled again.

She felt a fluttering inside her chest, like a bird had become trapped in there; she realised that it was panic.

'Superintendent Seth assured us of your cooperation,' said Pinto.

'Though we're certain you need little persuasion,' added Mirza.

They advanced on her, in a pincer movement.

She recognised the futility of further protest. 'Very well.'

After the pair had left, she returned to her desk and forced herself to focus on the work at hand. Pinto had handed her a card and invited her to the college for a look around and to further discuss the talk.

She flung the card on to the desk.

Birla arrived, flapping his shirt as he stood beneath the ceiling fan. Saddlebags of sweat were visible under his arms. He barked at the peon, Gopal, to fetch him a glass of water.

Once he had slaked his thirst, he wandered over to her, notebook in hand.

'So ... the fences were a bust. None of them claim to have heard anything about a valuable manuscript on the market. Not so much as a peep.'

'Do you believe them?'

He shrugged. 'They lie and cheat for a living. For what it's worth, they seemed genuinely mystified. I also managed to talk to all the names you gave me. They had surprisingly little to say. John Healy was an acquaintance, nothing more. Not one of them used the word friend, or expressed any great distress at his disappearance.'

'And you didn't mention the manuscript?'

'No. I stuck to the script, namely that he'd vanished without telling anyone and his family was concerned about him. Not that you're going to be able to keep a lid on this for much longer. Anyway, one thing they all agreed on: the man was a loner.'

She gave him an update on her findings since they'd last discussed the investigation.

He peered at her notebook, at the strange riddle Healy had left inside his bedroom mirror. 'Means nothing to me. But it does make you wonder what he's up to.'

'Lockhart agrees that he's leaving us a trail leading to the manuscript.'

'That's very gracious of him. It would have been simpler if he didn't steal it in the first place.'

As Birla walked back to his desk, she focused again on the enigmatic riddle. Her mind snagged on a couple of the lines. Firstly: *To beauty's bay, seeking Sinan's fame.*

Sinan. The name was familiar.

She closed her eyes and cast a net into her memory ... Ah. There it was.

Sinan might be a reference to Mimar Sinan, the Ottoman architect from the sixteenth century who had served Turkish sultans such as Suleiman the Magnificent. Sinan had designed hundreds of well-known buildings, including the Süleymaniye Mosque in Istanbul. He was often compared to Michelangelo.

Indeed, it was said that Michelangelo and Leonardo da Vinci had met Sinan on visits to Istanbul in the early 1500s.

Her memory dredged up one further detail.

Sinan had a connection to India, too.

He had helped design the Taj Mahal.

Her eyes tracked to the first part of that sentence: *To beauty's bay.* Anyone who had lived in Bombay for any length of time knew that the city's name came from the original Portuguese *bom bahia* meaning 'beautiful bay'. It seemed a small leap to believe that this is what Healy had meant. Coupled with the first sentence, *Sundered from Alba's hearth he came,* she conjectured that Healy's riddle was referring to a man who came from a place associated with someone called Alba *to* Bombay in search of fame – Sinan's fame . . . the fame of an architect.

But then what did *enjoined to begg* imply? 'Enjoined' meant 'forced into'. Did this mean that the architect had fallen on hard times, that he'd been forced into beggary? If so, he wouldn't be the first man to arrive in India in search of fortune only to discover the opposite.

She continued along the passage: *his labours Empire's pride.* These words seemed to imply that Healy's mysterious architect had been prominent in the Raj. Unless the reference was to another empire – the vastness of the subcontinent had seen many civilisations come and go. The Dravidians in the south; the Aryans in the north; the Cholas, the Chaulakyas, the Mauryans, the Mughals . . . the list went on.

She scanned the remaining lines. *His infernal porta, a King denied; 'Neath Cross and dome, his resting place; Together we await in fey embrace.*

What did infernal porta mean? Her mind drifted back to the Latin class at the Cathedral Girls School where she had studied. It had never been her best subject, but she had a hazy recollection that *porta* meant gate. And *infernal*? Wasn't that something to do with hell? So might the line be read as a 'gate to hell'?

She frowned.

That made no sense. What architect could possibly have built a 'gate to hell'? The following line also made little sense. *'Neath Cross and dome, his resting place*. If Healy was talking about a grave, then did he mean the grave of the architect? But then, how could it be 'Cross' *and* 'dome', one a Christian symbol, the other a Muslim one?

The final line gave her some hope. She chose to believe that the 'we' in this sentence included Healy, a suggestion that if she could find his mysterious architect she might find the Englishman too.

She worked the problem for another half an hour, but could make no further headway.

By the time she left the office, she was already fifteen minutes late for her dinner appointment.

12

The maître d', a beanpole dressed in a black and white tuxedo and sporting a prominent widow's peak that gave him the aspect of a vampire, looked at her in the same way a Catholic priest might look at a scimitar-waving Muslim that had just wandered into church. 'Is there a problem, madam?'

'Problem?' The source of his consternation finally dawned on her. She hadn't had time to return home and change out of her uniform. 'I'm here to—' She stopped. 'I have a meeting with a Mr Blackfinch. I believe there's a reservation.'

She was led through to the rear of the fashionable restaurant.

The Wayside Inn, Colaba, had a longstanding reputation.

Situated at the Kala Ghoda roundabout, at the centre of which pranced the black equestrian statue of the Prince of Wales Edward VII, rumour had it that none other than Dr Bhimrao Ambedkar had dined here daily, drafting much of the new republic's constitution during the late forties.

She recognised a few faces – actors and actresses, a couple of prominent businessmen.

Heads turned as she walked past. Unbidden, a warmth crept into her cheeks.

Blackfinch rose to greet her. His expression stalled momentarily as he saw that she was still in uniform, but then the warmth of his smile returned. 'Late as usual.'

'What?' She frowned. 'I'm never late.'

He raised an eyebrow.

'Rarely,' she said. 'Rarely late. And only when unavoidable.'

'Well, you're here now and that's all that matters.' His enthusiasm was both welcome and disturbing. She realised that he'd made a special effort. He was immaculately turned out in a double-breasted herringbone suit, a striped shirt and a well-matched tie – for once, knotted perfectly. His smooth cheeks gleamed in the overhead lighting, and his thatch of dark hair had been Brylcreemed back, giving him the neatness of an otter. He looked at her through black-framed spectacles, his green eyes crinkling with good humour. A waft of aftershave floated across the table.

She took off her cap and set it down, suddenly feeling acutely out of place.

'Do you mind if I visit the washroom?'

'I've waited this long,' he said, picking up his whisky tumbler.

In the washroom, she daubed a handkerchief under the tap and wiped the sweat from her face and neck. She stared at herself. The large, dark eyes, the strong nose, the high cheekbones. Thick black hair that she kept back in a bun or braided into a single plait. She had been told many times that she closely resembled her mother, a society beauty in her day. She'd certainly never lacked for male admirers. But her focus had always been elsewhere, much to Aunt Nussie's chagrin.

The past drove a kick into her ear.

There *had* been one. A fellow Parsee who'd worked his way under her skin, a smooth-talking charmer with pedigree, charisma, and a sharpness of wit that had beguiled her. One night she'd given herself to him. Had she known that he'd vanish shortly after and only contact her again by way of a card inviting her to his wedding, she'd never have made that mistake.

She was left feeling foolish, an ingénue hoodwinked by a womanising charlatan.

Later, the rage had come.

Her mind flashed back to the Studebaker she'd seen parked outside Malabar House, the shadowy outline in the driving seat . . . It couldn't be. That snake had moved to Delhi, to live with his wealthy in-laws. He hadn't been seen in Bombay for years.

Returning to the table, she saw that Blackfinch's tumbler had been refilled. Another Black Dog, of which he was inordinately fond. He'd loosened his tie and his cheeks glowed.

Her thoughts lingered on the oddness of their relationship.

The attraction that had sprung up between them had been unexpected; she'd expended considerable energy denying it.

The barriers had broken down when Blackfinch had accompanied her to Punjab in pursuit of the Herriot investigation. She'd learned about his background – years as a chemical engineer in the war, then working with the Metropolitan Police Service as a forensic scientist, and finally, receiving an invitation to come to post-Partition India and supervise the setting up of a forensic science lab in Bombay. He'd told her about his family – a brother named Pythagoras – Blackfinch's own given name was Archimedes – and an ex-wife. She'd learned also of that curious quirk in his character that made him detail-oriented in a way she'd rarely encountered; it also gave him a social awkwardness that was second only to her own.

She had no idea how to characterise the current state of their relationship.

They'd dined together several times, and attended a couple of functions in the wake of their success on the Herriot case. Something had undoubtedly passed between them. But were they *together*?

More worryingly, did Blackfinch *think* that they were or that that was a possibility?

She couldn't be sure.

Neither of them had said anything, skirting around the issue like moths around a flame.

They fell into conversation.

Blackfinch updated her on his attempts to set up his forensics lab. He was busy training a batch of young men in the dark arts of crime scene analysis.

'Men?'

He blinked. 'Well. Yes. All the students are male.'

'Why?'

'Why what?'

'Why are they all male?'

'Ah. Well, all the candidates for the programme were male.'

'And why was that?'

'I don't follow.'

'Did you make any attempt to recruit women?'

His mouth opened, then closed again. 'I wasn't really involved with the recruitment side of things.'

'I thought you were in charge.'

He coloured.

She let him wriggle on the hook for a few moments, then asked him about his family.

'Thad lost a couple of cows at the weekend.' She recalled that his brother went by his middle name, Thaddeus, and that he was a farmer. Blackfinch showed her a letter from his young nieces. It detailed an adventurous tale of sheepdogs and fairy princesses.

She glanced at it. 'They've spelled "ogre" incorrectly.'

'They're children, Persis.'

'That's no reason not to correct them.'

They ordered, then chatted for a while, waiting for their food to arrive. She watched Blackfinch fiddle with his cutlery, lining up each piece of silverware with exacting precision beside his plate. It was funny how one became used to such oddities, she thought, the idiosyncrasies that distinguished one person from another.

Their order arrived and they carried on talking, working their way around to her twin investigations.

'Your Jane Doe from the train tracks is going to remain a mystery, I'm afraid,' said Blackfinch, fencing at the risotto on his plate with a fork. 'I had the chaps over at fingerprint records compare her card with everything on file. She's not in the system. I hadn't expected her to be. There aren't that many female convicts.' He smiled. 'You could try the Foreigners Registration Office. All foreigners in the country on a long-term basis are required to report to their local registration officer on arrival. As per the Registration of Foreigners Act, 1939. I had to do it myself.'

She kicked herself for not having thought of this.

Picking at her sautéed salmon, she next brought him up to speed on the Healy investigation, finishing by reading out to him from her notebook the riddle he had left behind. 'I think the first few lines refer to a man who came to Bombay to become an architect, possibly for the Raj.'

'That doesn't really narrow it down,' said Blackfinch.

The British expansion in India, led by the East India Company, had been a gold rush. With the building of the railways, the country opened up to settlers from all over the empire. Architects had flooded to the new frontier, a place where labour was cheap, marble was plentiful, and the freedom to think big almost a requirement. India's cities were a testament to the extravagance of its colonial draughtsmen.

'Can I have a look at that?' He reached for her notebook and peered at the page. 'I'm afraid this means nothing to me. Riddles have never been my strong suit. Sorry.' He beamed at her. 'You look well. The grubby uniform really suits you.'

'I didn't have time to change.'

'It's not a problem. Really. I think you look magnificent.'

An awkward silence descended between them, broken by a loud laugh from a nearby table. 'I've been seeing a bit of the city,' continued Blackfinch. 'Been here more than a year and haven't really gotten to know the place yet.'

Another orphaned silence huddled on the table, waiting for one of them to speak.

'I don't suppose—' He stopped, then seemed to gather himself. 'I don't suppose you'd like to come out for a jaunt on the weekend?'

'A jaunt?'

'I was thinking of visiting the Elephanta Caves. Out on the island. I've been told they're well worth a look.'

She stared at him. The idea was tempting. A day away from work, from the routine of Malabar House, a day in the company of a man she actually liked . . .

'No,' she said. 'The investigation into Healy's disappearance is pressing. I can't take the time.'

'Ah. Of course.' He stared resolutely down at his glass. 'It would only be half a morning. On Sunday.'

'No.'

His shoulders fell a little. 'Persis . . . I wonder . . .'

She waited.

'Have I done something to upset you?'

It was her turn to hesitate. 'No.'

'Right.' He still couldn't meet her gaze. 'It's just that – I thought we were getting along . . .'

'We are getting along. We work very well together.'

'That's not what I meant.' He looked as if he would say more, but then gave up, lifting his tumbler and slugging it back.

Blood rushed to her cheeks. The awkwardness between them became unbearable. It was a relief when the waiter arrived to take their dessert order.

The rest of the meal passed in relative silence. Towards the end Blackfinch said, 'There *was* one other thing I noticed when we went over Healy's place. I got the distinct impression that it had already been searched. Nothing I could put my finger on; it's just that he struck me as a meticulously ordered man and there were things that seemed to have been moved and then not returned to their proper place.'

'How would you know?'

'As I said, it was just a feeling. My mind gravitates to such details. I can't help it.'

Who else would have searched Healy's home? Certainly no one from the Society. And, according to the testimony she had so far, he hardly knew anyone else in the city.

The word rose unbidden to the front of her mind: conspirators.

It stood to reason. Stealing the Dante manuscript was no small enterprise. To smuggle it out of the country; to find a willing buyer; to evade capture. Surely Healy would have needed accomplices?

But why would they have searched his bungalow? If they were conspirators, then Healy would have gone straight to them after the theft. Unless . . . perhaps Healy, having taken the manuscript, had decided to strike out on his own. In which case, she wasn't the only one in Bombay looking for the vanished academic.

And if Healy *had* double-crossed criminal elements, she doubted they'd look kindly upon him once they caught up with him.

She considered the trail of clues he'd left behind.

Might this be an elaborate ruse to throw everyone off his scent?

*   *   *

Back at home she saw that the lights were still on in the book-shop. Her father was doing his weekly inventory.

'It's been a good week,' he said as she entered, barely lifting his head from the thick ledger on his counter. The shop was empty. 'The new Sartre is flying off the shelves.'

Sam rarely worked himself up to excitement over a new item in the store, but she knew that he'd been anticipating a strong reception to the third volume in Jean-Paul Sartre's *Roads to Freedom* trilogy. The book, *La mort dans l'âme*, had finally reached India, translated into English as *Troubled Sleep*. Her father had a waiting list of customers.

'Papa, do you have a book in here about architects of the Raj?'

He set down his pen and fixed her with a look. His balding head shone in the light from the electric light fixture above. A fan on the counter ruffled his heavy grey moustache. 'A hello would be nice.'

She smiled and walked over to kiss his cheek. 'How are you feeling? I wish you'd let Uncle Aziz give you a proper physical.'

'I'd rather jump under a bus than let that quack poke around inside me.'

'He's a very able doctor.'

'The only thing he's able to do is drink. Copiously. The starch in his collar is the only thing holding him upright.'

'He's not the only one who needs to watch his drinking.' She looked pointedly down at the tumbler sat beside his ledger.

'A nightcap,' he said. 'Care to join me?'

She shook her head. 'The book?'

He directed her to the rear of the shop.

Stuffed in between *Horology* and *African Anthropology*, she found a small section housing architectural digests and books about architecture.

She pulled out some of the more relevant-looking volumes then went to the old sofa her father kept at the very back of the shop and sat down. The springs creaked alarmingly and continued to rattle as she spread the books across a coffee table, stained and scratched through decades of abuse.

The first book was called *Great British Architects of the 20th Century*. She went through it quickly, noting down those names that had worked in India or had some connection to the country – particularly those who had worked in and around Bombay. She did the same with the remaining volumes and digests, moving back in time, to the beginnings of Britain's colonial adventures on the subcontinent.

By the time she'd finished, her list comprised dozens of names, men from all over the British Isles – architects, draughtsmen, surveyors, town planners, civil engineers. Many had come to India under the auspices of the East India Company, as cadets, eventually taking up rank within the Corps of Bombay Engineers, a military unit stationed in the Bombay Presidency and responsible for numerous civil engineering and architectural projects throughout the region, including the Asiatic Society building.

Men like this had built the infrastructure that had powered the British Empire. Long after they became dust, their work would remain, a living reminder of India's colonial past.

She sat back.

This was useless. Assuming her conjecture was even correct – that she was looking for an architect of the Raj – there was no way to narrow down the list.

She took out her notebook and examined the first sentence of Healy's riddle.

Sundered from Alba's hearth he came.

Who was Alba? Where was his – or her – hearth?

Vaseem Khan

She lingered on her earlier thought, that Healy had left this trail of breadcrumbs to throw his pursuers *off* his scent. Was she wasting her time?

She went back and picked up the last of the digests. An article inside it had caught her eye, detailing the history of an institution known as the Bombay Geographical Society. The Society's members included numerous architects and civil engineers. It had published transactions until 1873, when it had merged with the Asiatic Society. Indeed, the Society had met regularly at the Asiatic Society building.

An idea occurred to her.

Surely that expertise still existed in the city somewhere? Someone who knew all about architects that had worked in Bombay over the years?

She returned the books to their shelves, then sat with her father, watching him work.

'Why don't you go up and have something to eat?' he said, scratching away in his ledger.

'I'm not hungry.'

He sighed and set down his pen again, peering at her over the top of his spectacles. 'You've already had dinner?'

'I – ah – I had a little something.'

'Who with?' His scrutiny seemed to burn right through her. She pretended to look down at her notebook. 'Oh. Just a colleague. It was a work thing.'

'This work thing wouldn't happen to be English, six feet tall, and about as sophisticated as a brick?'

She coloured. A few weeks earlier, Blackfinch had accompanied her home during the investigation into Sir James Herriot's murder. He'd sat through dinner with her father, Aunt Nussie, and Darius. The frosty reception her aunt had given him had gone completely unnoticed. The man seemed to have no feel for

96

such things. Her father had noted the visit but not remarked upon it.

She should have known that he'd sensed something. Sam Wadia had a preternatural ability to sniff out whorls and eddies in the current of her life.

She stood up. 'I think I'll have a shower.'

He continued to gaze at her, then, without another word, went back to his work.

13

'The Bombay Geographical Society?' Neve Forrester, standing beside the statue of former Bombay governor Lord Elphinstone, pursed her lips. 'Well before my time, but yes, you're correct. They were absorbed into the Asiatic Society. What is it you wish to know?'

It was the following morning and Persis had made the Society her first port of call.

Quickly, she explained the reason for her query. Forrester listened intently, her elegant fingers tapping the side of her leg. 'I'm glad to see you're making progress. Though I can't understand why John would leave behind these riddles. If his intention is to lead us to the manuscript, then why steal it in the first place?' Her eyes were troubled. 'I received a call from Delhi yesterday. Some martinet. He had the nerve to ask me how it had been so easy for John to remove the manuscript from our possession. Wanted to know exactly how he'd been vetted to work here. Of course, he hadn't the foggiest idea of who John was or what he did.'

She said no more. Beckoning Persis to follow, she led her back to her office.

Removing a black book from a desk drawer, she riffled through the pages, then picked up her phone and asked for the switchboard.

By the time she returned the receiver to its cradle, she'd made an appointment for Persis to meet with a William Clark, president of the Bombay Architectural Forum, and a lifelong member of the Asiatic Society.

'Rather a grand view, isn't it?'

Persis turned from the window to find a tall, hawkish white man walking towards her across the terrazzo flooring. His sandy hair, flecked with grey, framed an austere face into which had been dropped, like jewels, two blazing blue eyes. He wore a half-sleeved sports shirt with plaid trousers, as if he'd just returned from a round of golf.

She'd arrived at Clark's office fifteen minutes earlier, a seven-storey art deco building on Marine Drive overlooking the Back Bay. The mid-morning sun made prisms on the water as boats bobbed on the chop. Beneath her feet, traffic moved along the road; a steady stream of pedestrians wandered along the curving promenade beside it.

Clark led her from the waiting room into his office, a surprisingly small space, with a desk buried beneath folders and leaning towers of paper. On one wall were photographs of Bombay land-marks – the Eros Cinema, the Taj Palace Hotel, and the Rajabai Tower – modelled on England's Big Ben, and once the tallest structure in the country. On a second wall were pictures of Clark at various building sites, sometimes with a hard hat on, sometimes posing in the foreground as workers clambered up and down bamboo scaffolding behind him.

He noticed her gaze. 'I've been in Bombay a long time, Inspector. Worked on a great many buildings. You could say the city has gotten under my skin.'

He waved her on to a sofa, taking a wing chair opposite. 'Now, please tell me what this is about. Neve was rather cryptic this morning.'

'Have you known her long?'

'I arrived in Bombay thirty-odd years ago, under the auspices of the Asiatic Society. Neve was born here. The Society has a strong geographical tradition and she asked me to chair that aspect of their work. I say asked, but Neve has a way of asking that makes refusal rather difficult. Even then she was a bossy sort. I was a young architect in those days; Bombay wasn't quite virgin territory, but there was plenty of scope for invention. Or reinvention, I should say.' He smiled. 'That's the beauty of this city. In five centuries, it's reinvented itself a dozen times.'

'I'm in need of your assistance. But it's a sensitive matter. Mrs Forrester assured me of your discretion.'

'Ms.'

'I'm sorry?'

'It's *Ms* Forrester, not Mrs. Neve divorced a long time ago. Never remarried. She was always wedded to the Society. Shame, really. She was quite the looker in her day.'

Persis blinked. 'Did you two . . .?'

'Oh, God, no. Not that I'd have minded. In fact, if we're being discreet, I suppose I can tell you that I did make a couple of ham-handed advances. She simply wasn't interested. Between you and me, I think Neve bats for the other side – if you catch my drift. That's why her first marriage failed, I'll wager.'

Persis felt suddenly defensive on behalf of Neve Forrester. This man had no right to discuss her private life in such a cavalier manner. Her expression hardened. 'She assured me of your cooperation. It's a matter of national importance.'

He leaned back, fished a silver case out of his pocket, lit a cigarillo, and blew out a cloud of smoke. 'Please . . . enlighten me.'

Quickly, she brought him up to speed.

'You know, Neve showed me that manuscript once,' he said, when she'd finished. 'Can't say I was impressed. I've never really been one for books. I prefer to get my hands dirty. Stone, clay, marble. That's what makes an empire, Inspector, not dry words on paper.' He bared his teeth. 'But, of course, empire is a thing of the past. It's one of the reasons I stayed on. I suspect India will remake herself, shed her skin and start afresh. I'd like to play some part in that.'

She showed him her notebook, the riddle Healy had left behind. 'I think this refers to an architect of the Raj. For some reason, Healy is directing us towards him.'

'That hardly narrows it down.' He stared at the page. '*Sundered from Alba's hearth he came.* Alba . . .'

'Do you know who Alba is?'

He gave an opaque smile. 'Not *who*, Inspector. What. Alba is the Scottish Gaelic name for Scotland. Historically, Great Britain was called Albion. Later, the name became associated with the Picts of Scotland. Have you ever read Byron's poem *Childe Harold's Pilgrimage*?'

Persis shook her head. She knew most of Byron's oeuvre but couldn't recall that one.

'It describes the travels of a young man, seeking distraction in foreign lands. As you can imagine, it held a certain appeal for me in my younger days. Byron uses the word *Albyn* to refer to Scotland. "And wild and high the 'Cameron's gathering' rose; The war-note of Lochiel, which Albyn's hills; have heard, and heard, too, have her Saxon foes."' He smiled again, displaying a neat row of nicotine-stained teeth. 'I believe you're looking for a *Scottish* architect. That narrows it down, though not considerably. The Scots were wonderful engineers and a great many of them worked in Bombay.' His eyes lingered on the page. 'This is strange. *Enjoined to begg.* I can't immediately think of a British architect in India reduced to beggary.'

'I think that *begg* might be a deliberate misspelling. Healy was a supreme linguist; he wouldn't have made such a mistake.'

Clark's eyes rested on the words, then he got up, walked to his desk, returned with a pen, sat down, and wrote on the page. He turned the notebook to Persis. She saw that the sentence now read: *Enjoined to* Begg, *his labours Empire's pride.*

'John Begg was once the Consulting Architect to Bombay, and later to the Indian government. He, more than anyone, is responsible for the Indo-Saracenic style of architecture you see in the city. He worked on some of the most iconic buildings here: the General Post Office, the Customs House building on Prince's Dock. And something else, of particular relevance to us now . . .'

He set his cigarillo down in an ashtray, then walked to a bookcase and returned with an outsized architectural volume. Laying it down on the desk, he turned back to the notebook. 'This sentence here: *His infernal porta, a King denied. Porta* is Latin for "gate". "Infernal" literally means "relating to hell". So infernal porta can be read as "the gate to hell".' Persis had surmised as much. She hoped Clark had more to offer. '*A King denied* might be read in several ways. Either the king *refused* to build such a gate, or was denied in some way in relation *to* this gate.' He paused. 'I think this sentence is telling us that we're looking for a man who worked on a gate that is held in a negative light, one associated with a king. As it happens, John Begg did indeed work on such a gate.'

He opened the book of architecture and turned it to Persis.

Before her was a full-page photograph of Bombay's Gateway of India, the eighty-foot-tall archway that had been built at Apollo Bunder to commemorate the visit, in 1911, of King-Emperor George V.

'I don't understand.' Persis frowned. 'The Gateway is a celebrated monument. Why would Healy refer to it as the gate to hell?'

'How much of your city's history do you know?' Not bothering to wait for an answer, he plunged on. 'Before the arrival of the

Portuguese in the early 1500s, Bombay was just a collection of marshy islands, home to fisherfolk. The Portuguese built a navy garrison overlooking the harbour, fortifying it with stone walls and cannons. A century after their arrival, they bundled up Bombay as part of the dowry of Catherine of Braganza when she married King Charles II. Charles wasn't overly impressed with this trousseau offering of a bog in the middle of nowhere, and so he promptly leased the islands to the East India Company. The Company silted in the marshes, invested in a countrywide rail network, and began the hard work of transforming Bombay into a bustling trade port.

'So successful were their efforts that, in just a few decades, the city became the "gateway to India", attracting settlers, chancers, and adventurers from all corners of the empire.' Clark paused. 'But the truth is that many of those who came to the subcontinent were swiftly disillusioned. They suffered terribly. Heat, malaria, dysentery, mutinous locals. To the European sensibility, India *was* a kind of hell. Yes, a few men at the top became fabulously wealthy, but for the rest, India was an experience they would rather have avoided.' He picked up his cigarillo and took a deep puff. 'The other key thing about the Gateway to India monument is that, although it was built for the visit of George V, the arch wasn't actually completed by the time he got here. He'd come to India for the Delhi Durbar in 1911, where he was due to be proclaimed Emperor of India in front of every prince and nabob in the country. Bombay was the royal party's official entry point, with the arch built in the king's honour. But instead of a magnificent monument, he was greeted by a plasterboard replica.'

'A king denied!' she breathed. 'Are you saying that the man I'm looking for is John Begg?'

Clark ground the cigarillo out into the ashtray. 'No. Your riddle here says *enjoined to begg*. I take this to mean one of those young architects who arrived in India to work *for* Begg. There were plenty of them, but only one who fits the rest of the riddle. A Scotsman who made his name as a great architect of the Raj. Who worked for John Begg. And who was the principal designer of the Gateway to India monument ... Inspector, I believe you're looking for George Wittet.'

She knew the name. Wittet was the man who had designed Malabar House. When she'd first arrived at the station, she'd been given a tour of the building by an official of the company head-quartered there. The man had made a great deal of the fact that famed architect George Wittet had worked on the building.

'Wittet was fêted during his time in India,' continued Clark. 'But in recent years there has been a backlash against his legacy. Many in India view the monuments of the British as markers of enslavement. Not that much can be done about it. No one is about to pull down these wonderful buildings, though many are being systematically denuded of British artefacts – statues and the like.'

'Where is Wittet buried?'

'At last,' he said, smiling. 'An easy question.'

14

The sun was high overhead by the time she parked the jeep outside the cemetery. She waited for Birla to disembark, then got out of the driver's side and followed him as he walked to the arched iron gate. Embedded in the uppermost arc of the ironwork, the graveyard's name: CHRISTIAN CEMETERY SEWRI.

A man in a dhoti was perched on one of the gate's stone pillars, sanding down the trelliswork. He stopped what he was doing to watch them with curious eyes as they entered through the gate.

The cemetery at Sewri – ten kilometres from Marine Drive – was the largest Christian graveyard in the city. She had picked Birla up on the way. Before leaving William Clark's office, she'd asked the Englishman what he knew of the funeral site.

Clark had dug through his bookshelf again.

The Sewri cemetery had been built in 1865, by the then Municipal Commissioner of Bombay, Arthur Crawford, as a site for European burials. In the eighty-five years since, not only Europeans but many Catholic Indians had also found a final home there. One corner of the cemetery was dedicated to Italian prisoners of war. These luckless soldiers had been captured by the British during the North Africa campaign of World War Two. Brought to India, many had ended up in Bombay. Those that subsequently died were laid to rest in the Sewri cemetery, atop a hill raised in their memory.

The oldest section of the graveyard was reserved for luminaries of the British Empire.

The graves here were larger, more ornate: intricately carved headstones, and flowery epitaphs; statues of angels, cupids, ravens, and anchors. Many of the statues were stained and crumbling, ravaged by time and monsoon, and now neglect.

At the very rear of the section lurked a series of small crypts, hunched in penumbral darkness created by the shade of a banyan tree. Over the years, it had spread and now its creepers curled around the tombs like the tentacles of some fabulous sea creature.

'What's his name again?' sang Birla, as he crunched over crackling leaves.

'Wittet. George Wittet.'

Between them they quickly examined the dozen or so crypts until Birla called her over. 'I think I've found him.'

The tomb was about eight feet on a side, and perhaps ten feet in height, with a domed roof. The stone had blackened over the years and seemed to suck in the little light that filtered through the banyan's branches. Creepers ran down the walls; in places the stone had crumbled beneath the onslaught.

Perched at the apex of the domed roof was a black Cross.

Another jolt of comprehension. *'Neath Cross and dome, his resting place.*

Inscribed on the lintel above the wooden door was an epitaph: *Here lies George Wittet, architect of the Empire, recognised for the greatness of his conceptions.*

Persis glanced at Birla, then pushed at the door. To her surprise, it opened a little, then became stuck. Together, they put their shoulders to the wood; there was an instant crack, and the door flew backwards. She realised that a short wooden stick had been used to hold the door shut from the inside, a sort of makeshift bolt.

Stepping into the darkness, she waited for her eyes to adjust to the gloom.

The first thing that materialised out of the murk was a stone coffin set in the centre of the space. Wittet's final resting place. She moved further in, over unbroken flagstones. She could make out a shape atop the sarcophagus. The only light came from behind her, filtering in through the doorway, and around Birla.

She walked up to the coffin and stopped.

A slow heat rose to engulf her.

There, stretched out on the stone lid like a resting knight, was the body of John Healy.

15

'This isn't going to end well.'

Leaning against the jeep, Birla looked morose.

The mortuary van had just departed. Two hours earlier, Birla had walked from the cemetery to the main road to find an office where he could make the call.

Persis had waited in Wittet's tomb.

Leaning over the body atop the sarcophagus, she had stared at the man's face. There was no doubt. Even without his eyeglasses and robbed of life's essence, it was the same face that had stared out at her from the newspaper cutting at the Asiatic Society.

Healy was fully clothed; a worsted suit, complete with tie. She could not make out any sign of injury. She pushed up the sleeve of his right wrist and checked for a pulse.

Nothing.

What had he died of? How long had he been here?

On the floor, at the base of the coffin, was a leather bag – possibly the same one Pillai had mentioned at the Asiatic Society.

She pulled gloves from her trouser pocket.

The bag's leather was soft and worn. She undid the clasp, and pushed open the top, the two sides moving apart like a yawning mouth. Inside, she found three spiral-bound notebooks, a collection of pens, Healy's spectacles, a sealed envelope, and an empty pill bottle. Tuinal. The same sleep sedatives she'd discovered in his apartment.

But no missing manuscript.

She'd asked Birla to place a second call to Archie Blackfinch.

He arrived thirty minutes later, with a nervous-looking young man in tow, dressed in a lab coat. Blackfinch introduced him as one of his students, Mohammed Akram. He couldn't have been more than twenty-one or twenty-two, Persis thought.

She pulled the Englishman aside. 'This investigation hasn't been made public yet.'

'Not to worry. He's under instruction not to discuss anything he sees here.'

'I don't understand why you brought him along. He has nothing to add.'

'I won't be in India for ever, Persis. It's technicians like Mohammed you'll be relying on. He's the brightest bulb in my class. It's better you get acquainted now, don't you think?'

She glanced at the young man, hovering nervously at the door to the crypt. He was tall, as thin and willowy as a sapling, with a prominent Adam's apple, and ears that stuck out like jug handles. His hair gushed up in Brylcreemed fountains and an ill-advised pencil moustache lingered in embarrassment above his upper lip.

Ignoring the boy, she led Blackfinch into the tomb.

The Englishman had brought a torch, which he now shone over the corpse. 'Mohammed. Set up the camera, please.'

They waited while photographs were taken, the flashbulb exploding brightly into the tomb's semi-darkness. Next, Blackfinch asked them all to wait outside while he and his assistant used Lightning powder to dust for fingerprints. 'Stone is a poor surface for prints,' he called out as Persis waited impatiently by the door. 'But maybe we'll get lucky on the bag or the door.'

By the time he'd finished, the mortuary van had arrived, together with a medic. The man, a dour old soul with sagging eyes and a pugnacious jaw, quickly pronounced death – cause to be determined – then left without a further word.

They followed Healy's body as it was transferred via a stretcher to the van. A family of graveyard visitors turned to watch the strange procession as they moved past. A langur shrieked from the branches of a tree.

As Birla relayed instructions to the van driver, Persis pulled Blackfinch aside.

In her hands were evidence bags containing the notebooks and the envelope she'd found inside Healy's leather bag. 'How soon before you can get me your fingerprint results?'

'I'll make it a priority. I'll also call Raj and ensure that he schedules the post-mortem immediately.' He hesitated. 'I have to say, on the face of it, there seems to be no evidence of foul play. It looks as if Healy came here, broke into the tomb, then swallowed enough sedatives to floor a rhino.'

'And you don't consider that strange? Or the fact that he led us to him by means of a riddle?'

'Who knows what goes through a man's head once he starts thinking about topping himself.'

'There's more to this. There *has* to be. Where's the manuscript? Why would Healy lead us here only for the trail to run cold?'

'Perhaps he'd already disposed of the book? Perhaps his accomplices betrayed him? They took the manuscript, then refused to pay him.'

'That's hardly a reason to kill himself.'

Blackfinch said nothing. He'd seen men die for a lot less. 'Have you checked the envelope?'

She reached inside the evidence bag and took out the sealed envelope. Blackfinch had already dusted the contents of Healy's bag. She looked around, saw Akram hovering. 'Do you have a scalpel?'

He nodded furiously, his gigolo hair bouncing atop his skull, then rummaged in his pockets.

She took the scalpel, set the envelope down on the bonnet of the jeep, and opened it carefully.

Inside was a single sheet of paper. On it, written in Healy's looping hand, were three sentences:

> *Midway upon the journey of our life,*
> *I came to myself, in a dark wood,*
> *For I had wandered from the straight and true.*

Blackfinch looked over her shoulder. 'Another riddle?'

She didn't answer. The words seemed to bear down on her, like a foot pressed against her throat. There was a heavy, exculpatory tone to the verse.

Was Healy reaching out to them from beyond the grave, telling them how to hunt down the manuscript? But then why not just come out and say it?

A burst of frustration flickered through her.

Perhaps Blackfinch was right. Healy couldn't have been thinking logically, not if he was suicidal. Perhaps all of this was nothing but the death spiral of a madman. A dying jest.

She put the letter back into its envelope and cast around for Birla . . . She realised that Blackfinch was staring at her. 'Persis . . . about dinner last night? I – ah – I'm sorry if I said anything untoward.'

'You didn't,' she said automatically, not looking at him.

'I may have gotten my wires crossed,' he mumbled, before falling silent. She knew he was waiting for her to correct him. The words pushed against the inside of her mouth, but her lips wouldn't move.

'Right. Well, then.'

She didn't dare look at him, couldn't bear the thought of it.

'Glad we cleared that up. Mohammed and I had better get back to the lab.'

She watched him walk stiffly away, disappointment spilling from his eaves, knowing that she'd wounded him in a way that neither of them fully understood. A part of her wanted to call out and stop him, but another part of her felt a release of tension.

It was better this way, she thought to herself, as she climbed into the jeep. This was the sensible thing to do.

The only thing to do.

16

A caller awaited her at Malabar House.

She entered the interview room to find a white man standing beneath the ceiling fan. He turned at her approach.

'Mr Ingram?'

'James, please.' He stuck out a hand. He was a tall man, long-limbed and wide-shouldered. The jacket of his black, double-breasted, chalk-stripe suit was buttoned at the waist, his tie securely knotted. Clean-shaven cheeks, a sharp jawline, pale, piercing blue eyes, and blond hair, cut short and smoothed back with such precision it looked as if it had been painted on by a Renaissance master. A side-parting that could have been made using a ruler. There was a severity about him that Persis found both pleasing and mildly disturbing. 'I must apologise for not coming sooner,' he said. 'I didn't get your message until a short while ago. My understanding is that this has something to do with John?'

'How much do you know?'

'Only what I was told. Namely, that he appears to have gone missing.'

She waved at the table. 'Please, take a seat.'

He folded his frame on to a wooden chair, then waited as she poured herself a glass of water. She tilted the jug at him but he declined.

She studied him over the top of her glass as she drank.

His pale eyes were deeply set, hooded, his lips wide and full. There was a stark, unsettling beauty about him.

'How did you know John?'

A hesitation. 'Did?'

She realised her mistake. No point backtracking now. 'I'm afraid that we've just discovered his body.'

His jaw fell. 'John's dead?'

'Yes.'

He seemed stunned. 'How?'

'We're still determining the exact circumstances of his death. But it's in connection with his disappearance that I wish to speak with you.'

For a moment, his focus was elsewhere, and she was forced to repeat herself.

'Yes, of course, anything I can do to help. Perhaps I'll have that glass of water, after all.'

She poured him the glass, then waited until he was ready. 'How did you know him?' she repeated.

'I met him about a month ago, when I came to Bombay. I'm from England, as you can probably tell. I'm a writer. Well, it might be more truthful to say *aspiring* writer. I'm working on a historical novel set in the early period of the East India Company's tenancy on the subcontinent. The Asiatic Society has an excellent collection of Company papers documenting their activities here.'

'Their activities were theft, murder, and political manipulation.'

He seemed unfazed. 'That's what makes that particular period so intriguing. Speaking as an author.'

She bit down on her desire to reorient his viewpoint.

It always amazed her how so few Englishmen could bring themselves to acknowledge the truth of the Raj and the East India Company period prior to that, both constituting little more than a protracted pirate enterprise, a means of taking enormous wealth from the subcontinent while inflicting terrible suffering on the local populace. With independence almost three years in the past, history was being rewritten, or at least, buffed and polished. Men like Ingram would turn the British time in India into an adventure story, the sort of Bigglesian tale of pluck and derring-do aimed at teenage boys that had sold so well over the years in her father's bookshop. 'How did you meet?'

'It was some soirée the Society had organised. He was pointed out to me as a fellow Englishman, and so I went over and said hello.'

'My understanding is that he was Irish.'

'Half Irish. On his mother's side. But he was born in England and grew up there. At any rate, we hit it off. Since then, we've met for a drink a few times. The odd meal.'

'How did he strike you?'

'Well, he was a bit of a loner, if that's what you mean. I can understand that. Company is not always desired or sought, even by those of us with gregarious temperaments. But once he'd had a beer, he'd loosen up.'

'Did he talk to you about what he was doing here?'

'His research? Yes, of course. Translating the Dante manuscript. Fascinating business.'

She hesitated. Should she trust him? He was a writer, and in her experience writers could rarely be relied upon for their discretion. Any number of them had wandered through the Wadia Book Emporium over the years: novice writers seeking inspiration, failed writers in their cups, and renowned authors launching their latest bestsellers. On the whole, she liked them, but *trust* – that was a different matter. 'I must ask you to keep what I now tell you to yourself. At least, for the time being.'

'Yes, of course.'

Quickly, she briefed him on all that had transpired since her summons to the Asiatic Society.

'The manuscript is missing?' His eyes gleamed with interest. 'John told me that volume was priceless.' He paused. 'You know it's going to be impossible for you to keep a lid on this for much longer? Someone's bound to say something.'

She could practically see him penning the story. 'When was the last time you saw Healy?'

He considered the question. 'That would be six days ago, I think. We went for a beer.'

'Did he say anything that hinted at his plans?'

'No. Nothing. If I'd had the slightest inkling he was planning to steal the manuscript . . .'

'Did he speak about anything else, anything that might hint as to his state of mind?'

'No. He seemed his usual self.' He reached out and poured himself another glass of water. 'There's one thing. Possibly irrelevant. I think there was some tension between him and that girlfriend of his. The American.'

'Erin Lockhart?'

'That's the one. Nice-looking, but bossy.'

'What makes you say that?'

'John mentioned it a couple of times. Apparently, Erin was trying to pressure him into convincing the Asiatic Society's managing committee to sell the manuscript to the Smithsonian.'

She frowned. 'I've spoken with Miss Lockhart. She mentioned nothing about an interest in the manuscript. She's here sourcing Indian artefacts for an exhibition about the Quit India movement.'

'That's her cover story. But her real mission is to buy that manuscript. Apparently, the Smithsonian has been after it for years.'

'Why would she not tell me this?'

'Isn't it obvious? The Smithsonian doesn't want it publicly known that they're trying to get their hands on it. Because as soon as *that* comes out, the Italians will have a fit. The mandarins at the Smithsonian would rather whisk it away and *then* let everyone debate the merits of who it should belong to.'

She considered his theory.

Erin Lockhart had seemed a straightforward woman. To discover that the American may have lied to her was disappointing; a note of sourness crept into her belly and curled up there.

'Is there anything else you can tell me?'

'Only that I'd like to be involved. Healy and I may not have known each other long but we were friends. Two Englishmen out in the wilderness together.'

'This is my home,' said Persis. 'Not some wilderness.'

'I didn't mean it like that,' he said, hastily. 'All I'm asking is that you allow me into your inner circle. I could document the whole thing for you. Can you imagine what a story it would make?'

She stood up, her expression hardening. 'Thank you for coming, Mr Ingram. Tell me, will you be in the city for a while?'

He gave her a cool look in turn. 'Wild horses couldn't drag me away.'

After the Englishman's departure, she went to see Roshan Seth, with Birla in tow.

The SP listened intently as she filled him in on the details. When she'd finished, he picked up a wooden carving of a tortoise and shifted it from hand to hand as he spoke. 'This couldn't be worse. Not only is the manuscript still missing, but now the man who stole it is dead.' He sighed. 'At least tell me you have a trail to follow? A scrap of meat I can throw to the rabid dogs up in Delhi.'

She showed him the note Healy had left behind. Seth scanned it quickly. 'What's wrong with this man!'

'He's dead,' said Birla, and then wished he hadn't spoken.

Seth glared at him. 'This isn't normal behaviour. *Normal* criminals steal things and then vanish or do something clumsy and get themselves caught. This man is leaving us riddles. Why?'

'I still think he wants us to find the manuscript,' said Persis.

'Then why the hell doesn't he just tell us where it is!' Seth threw the note on to his desk.

'I think' – Persis began, then hesitated – 'I think he hid it before he died. Somewhere in the city. I believe he wants us to find it. But he wants us to work for it.'

'What makes you so sure he hid it *here*?'

'Because he had very little time between stealing it and killing himself.'

'He could have given it to an accomplice to smuggle out of the city.'

She conceded the point. 'Yes. But Franco Belzoni just confirmed that the manuscript hasn't turned up on the radar of some of the most well-connected international dealers specialising in rare books.'

Haq had picked up the call while she'd been with James Ingram.

Seth pursed his lips. 'Fine. So Healy hid it in Bombay. But again, I ask you: why? Why would he do such a thing?'

That was the question to which she still had no clear answer. Was it some sort of test? Or an elaborate game, a game that would now continue, even in the wake of Healy's death?

'The man was mad,' Seth concluded.

The possibility couldn't be discounted. Persis hoped this *wasn't* the reason. Because if Healy had truly lost his sanity, then his actions would defy logic. Her own belief that the man was operating to some sort of plan was the only glue holding the sequence of his actions together. If that glue melted away, she would be forced to admit that the Englishman might be leading them on a wild goose chase, and that they might all be lost in the labyrinthine workings of a madman's mind.

Following the meeting, she made two phone calls. The first was to Neve Forrester at the Asiatic Society to inform her of Healy's death. The Englishwoman took the news with equanimity. 'I suspected as much,' she muttered. And that was all she had to say on the subject. Her thoughts, like Seth's, had jumped ahead to the matter of true import – the missing manuscript.

Persis told her about Healy's note, reading out the words.

'Simple enough,' she replied. 'They're the opening lines from the first canto of *Inferno*.'

Inferno. The first book in *The Divine Comedy*. 'Can you think of any reason Healy would write those words?'

Seconds ticked away as Forrester thought over the puzzle. 'No.'

Persis asked her for one further piece of information: contact details for Healy's next of kin.

Having put the phone down, she dialled the switchboard at Malabar House and asked for an overseas trunk call to be placed for her, to England.

The phone was picked up on the tenth ring, an instant before she gave up. A deep and distinguished-sounding voice said, 'This is the Healy residence. Peter Healy speaking.'

She hesitated, suddenly overcome by nervousness.

As the lead investigator on the case, it fell to her to carry out this most difficult of duties, but she had little experience in such things and there was no training manual to refer to. Best to plunge straight in. 'Mr Healy, my name is Inspector Persis Wadia. I work for the Indian Police Service in Bombay. I'm afraid I have bad news.' She quickly sketched out the circumstances of John Healy's death, omitting details she felt were irrelevant.

There was a long silence on the line. 'Mr Healy?'

Forrester had told her that Peter Healy was a man of some standing, a successful civil servant. Persis imagined him in late middle age, instantly aged a further ten years by the news. Backing into an old armchair, fumbling behind him as he continued to clutch the phone, falling into it with a *whump*, the air from his lungs expelled at the same time.

Finally, Peter Healy spoke. 'His mother passed away during the war. Emphysema. John was our only child. He was all I had left.'

'Was he in touch with you?'

'No. I mean, *I* would call him regularly, but John was difficult to engage. Getting him to speak at all was a miracle.' She could sense his sadness; it drifted down the line like a fog. 'He wasn't always like that, of course. It was the war that changed him. His mother begged him not to go. There was no reason to put himself in harm's way. With his academic background, he had a job waiting for him in Whitehall if he really wanted to do something for the effort. But John wouldn't hear of it. A man shouldn't say this of his dead son, but John was arrogant, conceited. He'd achieved so much at such a young age that failure was inconceivable to him. He wanted to be able to say that he'd seen action. That he'd fought; not just sat behind a desk fiddling with blotting paper. And then we heard he'd been captured and taken to Italy. It was the worst day of our lives, or so we thought at the time.

'When he came back, he was a different man. A war hero, but it meant nothing to him. He wouldn't talk about it. He couldn't settle.'

'What do *you* think happened to him?'

'I think they tortured him. I think they beat him and did terrible things to him. He was out of touch for so long. He might as well have vanished from the face of the earth. We thought we'd never see him again. His mother mourned him as if he'd already passed; she never lived to see him rise from the dead. I believe John thought he would die in that Italian prison; he never expected to make it out. In a way, he *did* die out there.

'When he finally came to, he tried to pick up where he'd left off but he couldn't stick. And so he left. He spent some time in Egypt at their museum in Cairo, and then he became obsessed with Dante's work. *The Divine Comedy*. And that's when he heard about the copy at the Asiatic Society.'

'When was the last time you spoke with him?'

'A fortnight ago. We didn't say much. We never did.'

She chose her next words with care. 'Mr Healy, before your son died, he behaved in a way that may sound out of character. I wonder if you can help shed some light for me.' She explained about the theft of the manuscript and the clues that Healy had left behind.

A silence floated from the phone, so deep and long that she thought the man might have hung up on her. 'Mr Healy?'

'This makes no sense,' he said, shivering back to life. It was a refrain she was becoming well acquainted with. 'Why would my son do that? He's a respected academic. John's never stolen so much as an apple.'

'I believe you.' The words tumbled out of their own accord. 'But men change. Didn't you just tell me that *John* had changed?'

'There are some things a man knows about his son.' He said nothing further and the call ended on this discordant note.

Birla floated over. 'How did he take it?'

'As well as could be expected.'

'Did he have any bright ideas about Healy's riddle?'

She shook her head.

'Then we're back to square one.' He continued to stare at her. 'Are you getting enough sleep?'

She bucked her head.

'Take my advice: don't hold on so tight. They're just cases. Some we win, some we lose. All you can do is plod on, do your best, and let the coconuts fall where they will.'

But could she do that? She didn't think so. She wasn't built that way. Her whole life, she'd felt the need to prove something – to her father, to the girls at her school, to the world, to herself. She had few friends, perhaps because of this very refusal to bend with the prevailing wind. Prickly. Arrogant. Charmless. These were the labels that had stuck to her over the years. And worse.

The two years at the police academy had been particularly tough, the lone woman in a sea of men, many of them happy to make a pass at her, but unwilling to acknowledge her as their equal, even when staring dazedly up at her after she'd judo-flipped them on to the training-hall mat.

She'd grown gills to breathe the air of male animosity that constantly surrounded her.

She realised Birla was still looking at her. She knew that his concern was genuine.

Birla was one of the few who'd welcomed her arrival at Malabar House. At the least, he hadn't been as scornful as the others. Birla had a daughter just a few years younger than Persis – a forthright woman, by all accounts. He'd long ago seen the sense in giving way to women who seemed to know what they wanted, possibly for fear of being mown down if he stood in their way.

'I want you to do something,' she said, finally. 'Go to the Asiatic Society and find me a modern translation of *The Divine Comedy*.'

'Don't you have one in the bookshop?'

'No. I checked yesterday.'

'What do you think you'll find?'

'Maybe nothing. But Forrester says those lines that Healy wrote came from *Inferno*. I'd like to learn a bit more.'

'What did you make of that Englishman?'

'Ingram? He might turn out to be a nuisance. He's some sort of writer. He's got it into his head that there's a story here.'

Birla raised an eyebrow. 'And you think there isn't?' He scratched at his beard. 'Bhoomi's office called. He's scheduled Healy's autopsy first thing tomorrow, eight a.m.'

She walked to the Godrej steel *almirah* that served as the station's temporary evidence locker and returned with the note-books they'd found in Healy's bag. They were A4 in size, bound in royal-blue stippled leather, and smelled faintly of tobacco.

She opened one. Inside the cover was a note, written in Healy's hand.

IF FOUND, PLEASE RETURN TO JOHN HEALY
C/O ASIATIC SOCIETY BOMBAY.
SUBSTANTIAL REWARD WILL BE PAID.

She turned the page. Her eyes scanned the lines of dense, neat handwriting – Healy had meticulously written out the Italian, line by line, from the copy of *The Divine Comedy* held at the Society, with a translation in English of each line beneath. In the margin were annotations, obscure notes that he had made, actions for himself, his thoughts on other sources to reference.

As she turned more pages, she saw that the entire notebook was similarly crammed, as was the second notebook, while the third was still all but empty.

She spent the next hour going through the books, but her cursory scan threw up nothing that might indicate a connection to the case.

George Fernandes came clattering into the office. He marched to his desk, took off his cap, and collapsed into his seat like a grand piano falling from the third storey.

'Where have you been?'

His expression hovered somewhere between anger and sheepishness. Perspiration stood out on his forehead. 'I – uh—' He began again. 'I went back to Silva as we discussed. His friend in England confirmed that no woman of that age and description had ever worked at RAF Wyton. When I mentioned that she might have been a night worker, he told me about a place called Le Château des Rêves – the Castle of Dreams – over in Nariman Point. I've heard about it before; it keeps a low profile but most people know what goes on there. It's a high-class brothel for westerners, masquerading as a private gentlemen's club. Silva says that during the war it was particularly popular with foreign personnel passing through the city. He had the notion that our mystery woman might have picked up the RAF brooch there.'

Persis knew about the place – it wasn't far from her father's bookshop. She'd never ventured inside. 'You're implying our victim might have worked there?'

He ran a sleeve across his mouth. 'Yes.'

She considered this. 'We should pay the place a visit.'

His shoulders seemed to sag. He couldn't meet her eyes.

Understanding dawned. 'You already went there.'

'I'm the case lead,' he muttered. 'I didn't see the need to wait.'

She counted to five. 'So, what happened?'

'I – uh . . .' He lapsed into silence.

'They gave you the runaround, didn't they?'

He looked up at her sharply, daggers in his eyes. 'I'll try again.'

'No.' Anger constricted her throat. '*I'll* go. Where are the photographs from the morgue?'

With great reluctance, he pulled open a drawer and dug out a brown envelope.

Inside, she found a sheaf of photographs. Most were too macabre to be of any use, except to the coroner, but there was one, a close-up of the face, that would do. The woman looked almost peaceful, as if she were sleeping.

She walked back to her desk, swept up her cap, and stalked out, aware of Fernandes's gaze burning a hole in her back.

17

Her thoughts lingered on Fernandes as she drove to Nariman Point. Her reaction had been disproportionate to his offence, if there was even an offence there. But everything about Fernandes seemed offensive to her these days. Despite Seth's rationalisations, she couldn't bring herself to forgive him. Not just for the betrayal, but for harbouring the attitudes that he did.

Halfway to her destination, she changed her mind.

Fernandes had charged into Le Château des Rêves and attempted to extract information from whoever was in charge there. She could imagine him blundering around like a gorilla at a tea party. But if this was the sort of place where Brits and other foreigners still congregated to play out the fantasy of empire, then *she* might have just as hard a time of it as Fernandes. She was under no illusion that her senior rank would magically open doors for her. And she was loathe to go back to Seth and ask him to pull strings for her. A dead white woman might be a stink on his doorstep that he could do without, but she wasn't important enough for him to beg favours from his former friends on the force. Assuming that he still had any.

She turned the jeep around and headed home.

Back at the bookshop, she found her father chatting to Mrs Farnsworth, a seventy-year-old Englishwoman who'd been frequenting the shop for years. Mrs Farnsworth was one of those who'd stayed behind after independence, weathering the difficult years of the sundering with a belligerence as thick as armour plating. Her husband had been some sort of civil service apparat-chik; he'd died from dysentery in 1942. Mrs Farnsworth had mourned him for precisely two days, then got on with her life. She taught English at a school in Cuffe Parade. Her class ordered books by the dozen from the Wadia Book Emporium. An opin-ionated woman, whose pulpit was anywhere she could find an audience, she remained one of her father's favourite customers.

Persis said a quick hello to the pair, then headed upstairs. It was almost six.

She showered off the day's sweat, then opened her wardrobe. Akbar leaped gracefully on to the bed behind her and settled on to his paws.

It wasn't that she didn't have dresses. Aunt Nussie made it a point to buy her the latest fashions, part of her ongoing mission to trans-form Persis into the woman she felt her only niece could and should be. She wore them sometimes – a family wedding, an unavoidable party. Truth be told, she enjoyed dressing up on occasion.

It was dressing up for *others* that put her off.

She now picked out a knee-length black cocktail dress with short sleeves, floral lace shoulders and a white belt. A pair of black peep-toe heels and a small black hat in the shape of a fitted turban completed the ensemble. As an afterthought, she applied bright red lipstick.

She turned to Akbar. 'How do I look?'

The tomcat slunk off the bed and slipped out of the room.

She took a cab to the nightclub, arriving just after eight. On the door, she discovered a towering Sikh, who nodded at her as she stood there taking in the exterior. Le Château des Rêves. It was nondescript: a white stucco façade and a flat terracotta roof, with a small, lit sign above the door. Nothing to suggest that it deserved its rather grand name or what went on inside.

She passed through a cloakroom where a bored-looking white girl stared sullenly at a landscape on the wall as if assessing its value for the Louvre. She wore round-framed spectacles, was a little too plump for the dress she had squeezed herself into, and had a book open on the counter before her.

With nothing to deposit, Persis moved through the anteroom and arrived at a counter where a slim, officious white gentleman looked at her as if a polar bear had just walked through the door. He was absurdly neat, as if he'd been manufactured by a German doll company, his blond hair glued to his head, his cheeks stropped to a shine. A portrait of Charles de Gaulle hung on the wall behind him. He asked her, in a thick French accent, if she was 'with companion'.

She took out her police ID and held it under his nose. His pasted-on smile crumbled like a Roman arch. 'I shall fetch the owner.'

'No need. I'm just here to spend a quiet evening.'

'But—' he began, then tailed off, as she set down a sum of cash on the counter. 'I'm just here to let off a little steam. We don't need to make a big deal out of it, do we? On the other hand, I could come back in an hour, in uniform, with a team of boys from the local station. How's that going to benefit anyone?'

He stared at her, then scooped the cash under the counter. A nod.

She turned and walked away, and into the club proper.

It was small, a lot smaller than she had supposed, gloomily lit, with two dozen cabaret tables, a bar, and a stage on which a jazz trio was playing a tune she half recognised: 'How Blue Can You Get'. Half of the tables were occupied – almost entirely by white patrons. Scantily clad waitresses in French-maid outfits moved between the tables. A fog of cigarette smoke gave the murk an additional layer of depth.

She hesitated.

An hour earlier, her plan had seemed straightforward. Bursting in here in uniform like George Fernandes would have been pointless. But now . . . she felt strangely naked, out of place.

She walked to the bar and slipped on to a stool.

The bartender, a young white man in a blue tux, smiled at her. 'What can I get you, miss?'

'I'll have a whisky. Black Dog.'

He turned away to fix her drink. She twisted around in her seat to find a woman bearing down on her. Tall, lithe, in a stunning red cocktail dress that ended above her knees, and heralded by a gust of perfume. She had the face of a model: high cheekbones, a wide forehead, and catlike eyes. Raven hair fell in a curtain around her bare shoulders.

She slipped on to the stool beside Persis and beamed at her. 'You're a first-timer.'

It was a statement, not a question.

The woman set a small red leather handbag on to the bar. From this she now produced a silver cigarette case, which she offered to Persis.

'No. Thank you.'

'Suit yourself.' She lit a cigarette, a manoeuvre performed with considerable elegance. 'I don't suppose you'd care to buy a lady a drink?'

Persis hesitated, then nodded. The woman nodded at the barman, who seemed to know what she wanted without her having to utter the words. He returned in short order, with the Black Dog, and an expensive cocktail for her companion.

'My name's Arabella,' said the woman, holding out a manicured hand. Her accent was French, but only vaguely so, as if it had been watered down.

'Persis.'

'Unusual to find a lone woman in here.'

'So I'm discovering.'

'What brings you in?'

'Curiosity.'

'Ah. You're a tourist and we're the local zoo.'

'A very expensive one.'

'Yes. Well, our clientele is quite exclusive.'

'Let me guess: white men with money to burn?'

Arabella ran a finger around the rim of her glass. 'Occasionally, a white *woman*. One with desires that are difficult to satisfy. I'm guessing that's why you're here. It's not my usual ride, but I'll happily oblige if you tell me what you'd like.'

Persis flushed. She sipped at her drink, then set it down. 'I'm here because I'm investigating the murder of a woman. I believe she may have worked here.' She rummaged in her handbag and took out the photograph, setting it down on the counter.

Her companion froze, her gaze locked to the photo. A muscle quivered at her jaw. 'Who are you?'

'My name is Inspector Persis Wadia.'

'You're with that policeman who came in earlier, aren't you?'

'You spoke to him?'

'No. I heard it from Jimmy.' She nodded at the bartender. 'Apparently, your friend spoke with Jules.'

'Jules?'

'Jules Aubert. He runs this place. He probably thought it was just another shakedown.'

Persis imagined that for a place like this to survive undisturbed, money would be exchanging hands. The venality of Bombay's police force was not in question; the only question was how high up the chain the largesse flowed.

'You recognise her, don't you?'

Arabella hesitated. 'I'm sorry. I can't get involved.'

'You *are* involved. You're involved because you knew her. That places an obligation on you.'

'I know what this must look like to you. But this place isn't so bad. The men that come here aren't your garden-variety john. They pay well, and we get to keep most of it.'

'What was her name?'

A silence. 'Francine. Francine Kramer.'

'She was your friend?'

She stubbed out her cigarette and immediately lit another. 'What happened to her?'

'She was strangled and then her body was dumped on to railway lines. A train cut off her legs at the knees.' There had been no need to mention this, but Persis wanted to see the woman's reaction.

Arabella's eyes flickered, and then her head dropped to her chest, as if she were offering up a prayer. 'Oh, Francine.' She sobbed quietly on her stool, before straightening with a shiver. She picked up her drink and slugged it fiercely, then wiped the tears from her cheeks, her expression hardening. 'She was one of the good ones, you know? Some of us do this because we got ourselves into a mess and this is the only way out. Francine wasn't like that. She came to Bombay to find a new life for herself. Tried to make it at a regular job, but she wasn't really cut out for anything. She ended up here one day and somehow Jules convinced her to join his enterprise.'

'He forced her?'

'No. Jules doesn't *force* any of us. He just makes it awfully difficult to get out once you're in.'

'If Francine had wanted to leave, do you think he might have ... ?'

'Jules wouldn't hurt any of us, Inspector. Not physically. He's not that type of man. Besides, he has too much to lose. This place works because he has the best girls in the city. We'll put up with a lot of things, but not brutality.'

A man loomed out of the smoke. He was big, hefty, like a wrestler gone to seed, but dressed like a banker. A beautiful grey suit with a patterned silk tie, a gold tie-pin, gold cufflinks, and a gold watch. His hair was black, shaved to the scalp on either side, and combed flat on top, much like the pictures of Hitler Persis had seen during the war years. The only things missing were the toilet-brush moustache and the eyes like dead flies. A strong aftershave rode ahead of him like Pestilence, the fourth horseman. 'Ladies. May I have the honour of buying you a drink?' The accent was English.

Arabella flicked ash on to the floor. 'No, thank you.'

'Ah. You are already spoken for. I understand. What about your companion?' He turned his lighthouse grin on to Persis. 'You have an exotic look. Are you one of these Anglo-Indians I've been hearing about? I'd be delighted to make your acquaintance.'

'You can't afford her,' snapped Arabella.

His eyebrows rose marginally in amusement. 'I am a man of some means.' His eyes stayed on Persis. 'Name your price.'

Arabella blurted out an astronomical sum. He laughed gently, then realised she wasn't joking. 'That's ludicrous.'

'So is the idea of a man like you pawing at a girl like her. But that didn't stop you, now, did it?'

His features folded into confusion. He raised a finger as if poised to begin an oration, then turned and shambled away.

Arabella picked up her drink. 'Dammit.'

'Will you get into trouble?'

'Jules will huff and puff for a while, but he has a soft spot for me. He doesn't have many French girls left. I remind him of his sister. Apparently.'

'Tell me about Francine.'

'Francine was a sweetheart. I mean, you need a certain temperament to work in a place like this, but Francine – Francine had been through much worse. This place was nothing.'

'What do you mean?'

'I mean that when she came here, she was hollowed out. Something happened to her during the war, something bad enough to send her out here, to India. She was just a kid then. She had this look. The Americans call it the thousand-yard stare.'

'Where was she from?'

'I don't know. Francine never talked about her past. Frankly, most of us don't. But if I had to guess, judging from her accent, somewhere in Eastern Europe.'

Persis realised her tumbler was empty. She ordered another. 'I've been told that you get a lot of military personnel in here.'

'Hardly a revelation. We're a brothel.'

Persis reached into her handbag and took out the RAF brooch. 'Do you recognise this?'

Arabella held the brooch lightly in her palm. Sadness infected her expression. 'Silly girl,' she whispered, then: 'She used to wear this all the time. Some English fly boy working at the Embarkation HQ gave it to her before he rotated back out, told her he was going to come back for her after the war. Beautiful kid. Who knows, maybe he even thought he was telling the truth.' Her hand closed over the brooch. 'I told her to get out. I told her to walk away.'

'Why didn't she?'

'I think she was punishing herself. She wanted to stay here until she was rescued, until someone told her that whatever had happened in her past, whatever she'd done, it was forgiven.'

Persis dwelt on this, trying to imagine the woman whose mutilated corpse they'd found on railway tracks in *this* environment, shimmering through the smoke and music, smiling at strange men, while behind the façade: darkness and secrets.

'Can you think of anyone who might have wanted to harm her?'

'In here? No. Occasionally, a guy will get a little fresh, but Jules has a couple of enforcers to keep the patrons in line.'

'Francine had a burn scar on her breast. And she'd had a child, at some point.'

'She already had the scar when she came here. And no child in tow. Like I said, she never talked about her past.'

'Did she have friends outside the club?'

'Most of the girls tend not to drift too far. No point setting down roots, making friends, that sort of thing. Francine was here a good long while. She had her own place. But she never talked about friends. She kept herself to herself.'

'What about men?'

Arabella smiled. 'Do you know what a lover is for women like us, Inspector? A client who doesn't pay for it.' She drained her glass. 'Before I ended up here, I was a jazz singer. Toured the States for years. I came to Bombay as part of a jazz quartet, played three weeks in this dump. That's when I got myself into hock with Jules. I like to gamble, you see. Terrible habit. Can't seem to shake it.' She lit another cigarette. 'Francine *was* seeing someone on the outside. I don't know who. She wouldn't say. It was relatively recent. There was . . . *something* about it, though. I hadn't seen her so worked up in years.'

'Worked up?'

'It wasn't love. It was . . . something else. She'd been sleepwalking through her life, and then it was as if she'd been given a dose of salts. She was *alive*. I got the idea there was something dangerous about it.' She turned her beautiful eyes on to Persis. 'Jesus, do you think this man might have—?'

'Can you tell me where she lived?'

Arabella continued to stare at her, then nodded. 'Sure. It's not far from here.'

18

The house – a small, neat bungalow on a leafy side street off Madame Cama Road – was silent, a single street lamp casting shadows on to the iron gate. She checked her watch – ten p.m. – then looked up and down the street. Deserted.

She pushed the unlocked gate open with the palm of her hand and walked inside the small front courtyard. A concrete statue of a water nymph frolicked inside a dry fountain. She knocked on the front door – nothing. The bay window by the side of the door was curtained.

She considered her options.

She could call one of her colleagues – but that would mean calling either Birla or Fernandes at home. She dismissed the thought immediately. Hell would freeze over before she called Fernandes, and Birla had mentioned he was busy with a family dinner that evening. Alternatively, she could call one of the nearby police stations and see if anyone was on night duty. She dismissed that idea too.

She had no desire to make herself or Malabar House look helpless.

Her final option was to return tomorrow.

But that wasn't really an option.

Entering the courtyard, she'd noticed a tall wooden gate at the side of the house, presumably fronting an alley leading to the rear. She threw her handbag over the gate, pulled her dress up as high as it would go, and clambered over it. A ripping sound ruptured the night's silence as she hauled herself over the top and fell heavily to the other side.

Cursing, she stood and dusted herself off.

Her dress had caught on something; a long tear had slashed open the front of her skirt to reveal much of her stockings and a hint of underwear.

She picked up her handbag and headed to the back of the house.

The garden was a profusion of greenery. Bushes and flowering trees; a heady scent of jasmine in the air. French windows above a concrete patio. The door was locked.

She looked around, found a half-loose brick skirting the flowerbeds, pulled it out, returned, hesitated, then punched a hole in the glass. Reaching through, she turned the handle and let herself in.

Darkness. She moved around the room and fumbled for the light switch.

She found herself in a living room: a sofa, a gramophone, bookshelves, a sideboard crammed with exotic fauna fashioned from bronze and glass. On the back wall: a large landscape of abstract shapes, a montage of reds and yellows.

She walked through a short corridor, past a grandfather clock, and found three more rooms – a kitchen, a bathroom, and a bedroom. The bathroom was clean, the bedroom comfortable. A mirrored dresser crowded with female creams and more items of make-up than Persis even knew existed. The bed was a double. A sideboard was crammed with more knick-knacks. In fact, every available surface was crowded out with collectibles.

She searched the room.

There was little to find. Francine possessed an excellent collection of dresses, shoes, and nightwear – including an eye-opening selection of satin camiknickers – but little else. A folder was tucked into the dresser containing bills and paperwork, but nothing of any import.

She returned the folder to the dresser, then carried on with her search.

In the kitchen, she found a round walnut table, a well-stocked fridge, and wooden cupboards with a surfeit of plates and cutlery.

Something caught her eye.

She dropped to her knees and peered under the table.

Behind one of the rear legs was a small piece of shattered ceramic. Her finger traced its jagged edge. She scanned the room again, spotted a bin in the corner. Looking inside, she found more shards. Together, the pieces made up a mug.

She looked around the room once more. A small chip on one of the front table legs. An indentation in the lower door of the fridge.

A wave of nausea rode through her. A struggle had taken place here. More than a struggle. There was a quiet fury to the room and now she understood why. This was where Francine Kramer had been murdered, she was suddenly sure of it.

The evening unfolded before her eyes; for an instant, she stepped back in time and floated above the room, a ghostly observer.

Francine had entertained a man that night. Perhaps they'd made love in the bedroom. Then she had dressed – most probably for her shift at Le Château des Rêves. She'd sat down in the kitchen, a mug of something before she left. Her companion had moved up behind her, looped a cord around her throat, and strangled her. She'd been pulled backwards, instinctively lashing out, kicking the table leg, knocking the mug to the floor. The man had fallen back, thudding against the lower half of the fridge, his hands still pulling tight on the cord, Francine flailing at him as her face turned blue. Gradually, her limbs had stilled.

Afterwards, her killer had cleaned up in haste.

And then he'd driven the body to the tracks near Sandhurst Road station, hoping the train would destroy the evidence of his crime.

Her gaze lingered on Francine, eyes bulging, hand outstretched, moments before she succumbed. The image was so real she could reach out and touch it.

She made a decision. There was no point waiting.

She returned to the living room – on a side table by the sofa she'd spotted a phone. Using a handkerchief, she picked up the receiver and dialled Archie Blackfinch.

It was past midnight by the time she headed home. Blackfinch had offered to drop her, but an awkwardness had sprung up between them now that made such a proposition intolerable.

He'd arrived within twenty minutes of her call, with his assistant, Mohammed, in tow. They'd been working late at the lab, and had their equipment to hand.

She'd met them in the street, Blackfinch momentarily stalling, gawping at her. In the heat of the moment, she'd forgotten that she was still wearing a torn dress.

She'd explained quickly, not bothering to hold the front of her dress together. What was the point? Then she'd led them into the house, and left them in the kitchen, stepping back out as they set to work.

Outside, she discovered a neighbour standing in the street.

The woman, in her fifties, by Persis's estimation, was wearing curlers and a silk kimono. She was white, dark-haired, with a sagging jaw and a heavy midriff. Blackfinch's noisy arrival had awoken her; curiosity had driven her from her bed and into the street. Her name was Mabel Hopkins.

'Did you know Francine well?'

'Well enough. She was a nice girl. Kept herself to herself for the most part. But she was always pleasant when we spoke.'

'How long have you lived here?'

'If you mean how long have I known her, that would be about six years. She was here when I moved in, around the beginning of '44. I lost my Ken a couple of months later; she was a great comfort. I was in a complete state. I thought about going back, but I have a good job at the Ambassador Hotel and nothing to go home to, so I stayed.'

'Ken?'

'My husband. He was killed in that big explosion on the docks. Poor bugger was the dock supervisor that day. Five minutes from the end of his shift.'

The Bombay explosion. A British freighter berthed in the Victoria Docks, carrying ammunition and explosives for the war, had caught fire. The resulting explosion had killed eight hundred, give or take, sinking neighbouring vessels and setting fire to the surrounding area.

'When was the last time you saw her?'

'I'm not sure. Maybe four, five days ago. She worked nights. I do day shifts. We'd meet up occasionally for coffee.'

'Can you tell me about her? Where was she from?'

'I don't honestly know. She flat-out refused to talk about her past. I think she was Eastern European, judging by her accent. But she never mentioned her childhood.'

'Why not?'

'I can't tell you. Some people are just very private. Or maybe there was something in her past she didn't want me to know. I learned not to ask questions. Between you and me, I don't think Kramer was her real name. She didn't sound like a Kramer.'

Persis didn't bother to ask the woman what she meant by that. 'Can you tell me about her friends, acquaintances?'

'She hardly ever had visitors. Maybe a couple of girls from that club she worked at.'

'Did she have a gentleman friend?'

'No one regular. I mean, not many ordinary men would put up with that sort of thing.'

'What sort of thing?'

She fumbled a pack of cigarettes and a lighter from a pocket sewn on to her kimono. Lighting one, she took a long pull. 'I'm not the type to judge, Inspector. She did what she did to get by.'

'You can't think of anyone who might have borne her a grudge?'

'Francine was the sweetest little thing imaginable. She wouldn't hurt a fly. But she had this ... sadness about her. Kept it clutched close to her chest. Ken and I never had kids, otherwise I might have known how to get it out of her, how to help.' She flicked cigarette ash on to the road, and shivered, though the night was warm. 'I noticed a gentleman caller outside her home a couple of weeks ago. It was late and I was outside for a smoke. Couldn't sleep. He came out of her gate and headed up the street towards a parked car. Big man, heavy-set. Black hair. Nice suit. I only caught the side of his face, but I thought I saw a scar here.' She waved with her cigarette at her left cheek, tracing a line from the side of her lip to the bottom of her ear. 'I remember it because, as I said, Francine doesn't usually have gentleman callers. She never brings her work home. And, also like I said, there's no one special in her life.'

'How can you be so sure?'

'Because she would have given herself away. A woman in love ... that's a difficult thing to hide, Inspector. Trust me. Francine wasn't in love.' She stared at Persis until the policewoman looked away. Something of her own predicament twisted at her insides and she thought, for an instant, about Blackfinch.

A pack of stray dogs came trotting down the street, yapping mindlessly.

Persis considered what Arabella had told her at the nightclub, that Francine had recently started seeing a man. Not love, but *something*. Something dangerous.

'Did you ask her about this gentleman?'

'I asked. Francine said he was just a friend.'

'What was his name?'

'She wouldn't say. Said he was fanatical about his privacy. She called him Mr Grey. On account of he always wore grey suits, apparently. I suspect he was some married fool besotted with her.' Her eyes became pinpricks. 'You don't think he—?'

Persis made a mental note to speak with Blackfinch's assistant, Mohammed. Apparently, he had let slip to this woman that they'd arrived to investigate Francine's murder.

Ignoring the question, she said, 'Can you remember any details about the car? The licence plate?'

Mabel tugged on her cigarette again. 'A white sedan. Expensive-looking thing. I can't remember the licence plate.'

She arrived home to find her father stretched out on the living room sofa, snoring loud enough to wake the dead. Akbar was curled up on the piano, and shivered to life as she let herself in. She came and sat by Sam, watching his chest rise and fall rhythmically. Occasionally, his breath would hitch and he'd make a sort of choking noise as if a small animal had become trapped in his throat.

Ever since her mother's passing, he'd made it a point to wait until she was asleep before retiring for the night.

Those early years after Sanaz's death had been confusing ones. Persis had always been a loner; her mother her only real confidante. Her relationship with her father had not been close until that moment. He infuriated her, he challenged her, he made it impossible to have a reasonable discussion about anything. The man was incorrigible. And yet, she couldn't imagine life without him.

She reminded herself to check with Dr Aziz on the state of his health. Sam would never tell her the truth. Even stretched out in the Towers of Silence, with vultures pecking at his liver, he'd probably insist he was as fit as a fiddle.

She decided to leave him where he was rather than disturb his rest.

Leaning down, she kissed him on the forehead, then went to her room, showered, and came back into her bedroom wearing a towel. As she dried herself she caught sight of Aunt Nussie's shopping bag, still on the armchair where she had left it. She padded over and took out the black negligee. The silk was undeniably more luxurious than anything she'd ever owned.

She set down the towel and slipped into the garment, then stood and looked at herself in the mirror.

A tremor of shock ran through her.

The woman that looked back at her – tall, dusky, almost naked – was a stranger. Mysterious and dangerous. Like the women in certain risqué magazines her father ordered for his more discerning clients. The only thing missing was a pout.

She had become so used to seeing herself in uniform that it had become difficult to frame herself outside of it.

She thought about Arabella at Francine Kramer's club. Her easy sexuality; her knowledge of what drove men and how easy they were to control once you knew the right buttons to press.

A skill Persis had never had.

If anything, she always seemed to press the *wrong* buttons.

Her thoughts drifted back to the night she'd given herself to the only man she had ever loved. Zubin Dalal. A small, neat presence, with impeccable manners, wit, and the charm of the devil. A fellow Parsee, older and wiser. She'd trusted him; she'd desired him.

That single night of passion blazed darkly in her thoughts.

They'd dined at his apartment, alone, a meal he'd prepared. Afterwards, he'd opened a bottle of Château Margaux, an outstanding 1928. They'd reverted to their favourite subject – literature. It was while they were dissecting Byron's romantic works that he'd leaned over and kissed her. And that was all it had taken.

She still marvelled at how easily she'd fallen into the moment.

Hours later, returned to her own bed, she'd reached out and touched the pillow beside hers, wondering what it would be like to have him there every night. A partner, a companion, a lover . . . Lover. The frisson of that simple word electrified her.

And then . . . the betrayal.

She still couldn't fathom it. The memory of it howled like the rage of angels in her breast, a searing resentment that refused to dim with the passage of time.

She picked up her hairbrush and pulled at her hair furiously.

Another thought crept in, unbidden . . . What would Archie Blackfinch say if he could see her now? What would he *do*? . . . She noticed Akbar watching her.

Foolishness.

She pulled on a set of pyjamas, then wandered back out to the living room to pour herself a whisky. Her father snored on.

Her eyes alighted on a package on the dining table. She recognised Birla's handwriting on the envelope: *The book you asked for.*

She opened the package, lifted out the book, then returned to her bedroom, climbed on to the bed, and opened the translated version of Dante's masterpiece on to her lap.

It was about time she read the work at the centre of all the trouble.

The translation was by Jefferson Butler Fletcher, a printing by the Macmillan Company of New York. The edition contained all three parts of Dante's great poem – *Inferno, Purgatorio,* and *Paradiso* – with an introduction and explanatory notes on each. The book was illustrated with reprints of Italian Renaissance artist Sandro Botticelli's drawings, created for a famed 1485 edition of the work commissioned by Lorenzo di Pierfrancesco de' Medici, a member of Florence's notorious House of Medici.

Quickly, she scanned the introductory text, Fletcher's take on the work's meaning and importance.

Dante Alighieri had been born in 1265 in Florence, part of the Republic of Florence – modern-day Italy – during a time of intense political rivalries, particularly between the Pope and the Holy Roman Emperor. Dante grew up with a love of poetry, works that later influenced his own verse, replete with metaphor, symbolism, and double meanings. At a young age, he fell in love with a girl named Beatrice Portinari – that love would remain unrequited. In time, Dante would marry another, though he continued to adore Beatrice from afar. After Beatrice's early death, Dante remained haunted by her for the remainder of his life, revisiting his love for her in verse, even awarding her a starring role in his masterwork.

Having been dragged into the political quagmire of Florence during middle age, Dante found himself exiled from his home city. It was during this exile that he conceived of and began *The Divine Comedy,* completing it in 1320, a year before his death.

Persis turned to the beginning of *Inferno*, scanning the first canto, the words that Healy had left behind.

> *Midway upon the journey of our life,*
> *I came to myself, in a dark wood,*
> *For I had wandered from the straight and true.*

She continued to read, making notes as she went.

Fifteen minutes later, she had a solid grasp of the contents of the canto: Dante, lost in a forest, meets a ghostly Virgil, who offers to lead him to Heaven – via Hell and Purgatory.

She set down the book.

Why had Healy drawn their attention to this particular canto?

Was there a significance here that she was missing, something that might lead her to the missing manuscript? Unlike Healy's previous clues, there was no riddle to solve here, at least none that she could see.

She read for another half-hour, then, frustrated, set the book aside. Sleep tugged at her eyelids. Beside her, Akbar had already succumbed.

Turning out the light, she fell into a deep slumber in which she dreamed of she-wolves quoting poetry and ghostly visitors speaking in riddles.

19

'Rigor mortis.' Raj Bhoomi looked at her from above the corpse of John Healy, stretched out on the autopsy table before him.

She waited for him to expand, stamping down on her irritation. Why didn't he just tell her? Behind her, Birla yawned like a baboon.

They'd arrived just before eight. Even at that hour the college had been busy, students and faculty stepping briskly through the corridors, the hustle and bustle of a new day.

Her mind lingered on the previous night's events. Standing here, in the autopsy suite, the body of John Healy before her, she was struck by the notion that her life appeared to revolve around the macabre. Murder, death, human perfidy. No doubt Aunt Nussie would have plenty to say on the matter, vindicated in her belief that the role of police officer was no occupation for a woman.

'By my estimation,' continued Bhoomi, 'this man has been dead for well over forty-eight hours. Rigor mortis has come and gone.' He lifted Healy's arm and waved it at her. 'Floppy, as you can see.' He grinned. Persis did not smile back. Bhoomi's smile faltered. 'The body has begun to bloat and there is a bloody foam beginning to leak from the nose. I'd say he's been dead somewhere between three and four days.'

They waited while he removed the victim's clothes, bagged them, then went over the corpse with a fine-tooth comb. 'Oh, hello.' He lifted his head from an examination of Healy's thigh. 'Step closer, Inspector.'

He moved back to give her space, pointing at a small area on Healy's inner right thigh. She moved in, ignoring the stark sight of John Healy's member resting inside a nest of pubic hair. The harsh overhead light had washed out the body, giving it a larval pallor. She immediately saw what it was that Bhoomi had spotted.

Writing – a column of words, followed by a series of numbers – scrawled on the skin.

'A tattoo?'

'I don't think so,' replied the pathologist. He hooked a finger at his assistant, who dragged his camera over and took a photograph. While he was doing this, Bhoomi wrote in his notebook, copying down the mysterious epigraph. When he had finished, he went to a bench of instruments, picked up a bottle, poured some of the liquid into a bowl, stuck his gloved finger in the bowl, then returned to the corpse. Rubbing the tip of his finger on the writing, he held it up to Persis. A smudge now showed on the white glove. 'Not a tattoo. Plain old ink. He's written this on himself. Fairly recently too.'

'How do you know that?' asked Birla.

'Because it would have washed away the last time he took a shower. So, unless he enjoyed smelling like an open sewer, I'd say he scribbled this on himself just prior to his death.'

'Why?'

Bhoomi gave a lopsided smile. 'That's where my job ends and yours begins.'

They waited as he completed his external examination, then moved on to the incision, cutting into the body while humming a tune. Persis thought the man was approaching his work with excessive relish.

'You might be interested to know, Inspector,' said Bhoomi, as he lifted out the heart and carried it to a weighing scale, 'that, later this evening, I will be escorting a young lady to a Prithvi Theatre performance of *Hamlet*. Well, to be accurate, I'll be escorting her whole family, all fourteen of them. A woman of breeding must be properly chaperoned, yes?'

She supposed that he was making conversation, but wished that he would shut up.

When he'd finished, he washed off his hands, then padded over to deliver his report.

Her eyes lingered for a moment on Healy's corpse. The more she discovered about him, the greater an enigma he became. An intelligent man, of that there was no doubt.

And he'd applied that intelligence to creating a puzzle that had followed him into death.

She realised that Bhoomi was smiling up at her. He was shorter than her, a small, scruffy man. 'No defensive wounds,' he began. 'No external injuries that I can find, at all. If this man was murdered, then it wasn't through the use of force.'

'I didn't say that he'd been murdered.'

'No, you didn't.' He pushed his spectacles back up his nose. 'I won't know for sure until we complete the toxicology test, but I suspect, based on the empty bottle of Tuinal you found at the scene, that he killed himself. Suicide by sedative.'

It fitted the facts. She recalled Healy's riddle leading them to Wittet's tomb, the crypt's door locked from the inside with a makeshift wooden bolt.

Together we await in fey embrace.

She knew that 'fey' meant strange, otherworldly. She'd since discovered from Neve Forrester that in Old English 'fey' held another meaning: 'fated to die'.

How long had John Healy felt that way? She recalled his father's words, that Healy had returned from the war a different man.

What had they done to him in that prison?

As to precisely why Healy had killed himself *now*? That was yet another riddle.

And talking of riddles ... She asked for Bhoomi's notebook, then copied out the words and numbers that Healy had written on to his thigh.

AFFECTIONATE
HONOURED
FRIEND
EMBRACES
PRAISED
PERSECUTED
SERVANT

1.3/1.7
1.2/5.8
2.11/52.64.71.72.92.97.102.146.157.158.221
3.14/2.3.63.64
1.7/6.137.139.159.164.168.173.174
26.14/17.30.62
1.21/15.21.24.53

There was no certainty that these held any meaning for her quest, but she was convinced that Healy had led them to his corpse for a reason. Her earlier hypothesis – that he had stolen the Dante manuscript, then hidden it, and was now leading them to it – grew stronger in her mind. This couldn't be the end of the trail.

She continued to puzzle over the strange inscription.

What could it possibly mean? *Affectionate honoured friend embraces praised persecuted servant*. Who was the affectionate friend? Who was the persecuted servant? Was Healy referring to real people? If so, who might they be?

Possibly, he was leading her to someone who might be able to decipher the numerical code written beneath the words.

Disappointment and frustration duelled inside her. There simply wasn't enough information to make any immediate headway.

Back outside, a movement at the corner of her vision turned her head as she was climbing into the jeep.

There, swinging around the corner of the road, was the same Studebaker she'd seen parked outside Malabar House days earlier. And the face in the driver's side window . . .

Her immediate reaction was to pursue, but her hands remained glued to the steering wheel, her limbs unresponsive, her heart thudding in her ears. She realised Birla was talking; his voice came from a long way away.

She calmed herself.

She was seeing things where there was nothing to see – brought on by last night's introspection, no doubt.

Dwelling on the past was never a good idea.

She shook the memories from her mind, and switched on the engine.

She had work to do.

At Malabar House, she found an irate George Fernandes pacing the basement office. The man seemed set to explode, his face volcanic. He looked at her as she imagined a wounded tiger might look at a young nawab out on the hunt. 'You went to Le Château des Rêves last night.' It was a statement, not a question. 'Why didn't you tell me what happened? About Kramer's house.'

'I outrank you. I don't need to tell you anything.'

'It's *my* case!'

'You had your chance.'

'I told you I was going to have another crack at it.'

'Why? So you could embarrass yourself again?'

His face expanded like a bullfrog's. He stepped towards her, hands clenching and unclenching by his sides. Reflexively, her own hand drifted towards the holster at her side.

'In my office. Now. The pair of you.'

She dragged her gaze from Fernandes to find Roshan Seth framed in the doorway to his office.

Once inside, he looked at them both coldly from behind his desk. 'If you're going to piss on each other's legs like pie dogs, at least have the decency to do it in the street.'

Persis's nostrils flared. She'd rarely seen Seth so annoyed.

She watched as he reached into a drawer and slipped out a bottle of Johnnie Walker Black Label, and waved it at them. She shook her head stiffly, as did Fernandes.

'Suit yourselves.' He poured a decent measure, picked up the glass, drained it, then set it down again. 'And you wonder why I keep this bottle here ... I've just got off the line with Shukla. Apparently, the Home Minister almost choked on his toast this morning when he saw the *Indian Chronicle*.'

He rummaged under a pile of red-bound folders and set the newspaper before them.

PRICELESS ITALIAN TREASURE LOOTED FROM BOMBAY'S ASIATIC SOCIETY: CENTRE CLUELESS

'Needless to say, he's now taking a personal interest in the matter. Which means a personal interest in this unit. The last thing I need is my two best officers squabbling like children. Would someone care to explain what was going on out there?'

Neither of them spoke.

'Alright. I'll assume it's to do with the woman you found on the tracks. Where are we up to on the case? And if I don't get a straight answer, I'll kick both cases over to Patnagar's unit and you can sit around here waiting for the next lost cat mystery to wander in.'

It was an empty threat.

Persis knew Seth would never hand any case over to Ravi Patnagar, head of the state CID. He and Patnagar were bitter rivals; Seth's fall from grace, his demotion to Malabar House, had only deepened their enmity. Patnagar was also the man who'd convinced Fernandes to work against her on the Herriot investigation.

She quickly briefed Seth on her visit to Le Château des Rêves, the identification of the victim as Francine Kramer, and the subsequent visit to Kramer's home, setting out her belief that Kramer had been murdered there, before being taken to the railway tracks. She also mentioned the man that the neighbour had seen – Mr Grey – a potential suspect.

'So let me get this straight,' said Seth. 'Fernandes laid the groundwork for everything you discovered last night by leading you to Le Château des Rêves? And *you* then went in and did the rest? Sounds like teamwork to me.'

Persis coloured. Beside her, she heard Fernandes stiffen.

'Contrary to popular opinion, police work isn't a zero-sum game. If you don't learn how to play nicely, neither of you will win.' He evaluated them from over the top of his glass. 'What's next?'

Persis spoke first. She'd been thinking about the problem ever since visiting Kramer's home. 'Two things: firstly, based on the wounds to her body, the pathologist suggested Kramer might have suffered mental and emotional trauma. She may have sought professional help.'

'Excellent,' said Seth. 'Fernandes, why don't you follow up on that? And once you have a lead, might I suggest you involve Persis? She's a woman. She's more likely to understand what went on inside the head of your victim. Do you agree?'

Fernandes stared at him, and then his head creaked forward.

'And you, Persis, will give him the leeway to do this. Because you are taking him under your wing, as the senior officer. And because you have other things to focus on. Do *you* agree?'

Persis stared straight ahead.

'Persis?'

Nothing.

'Inspector Wadia?' Seth allowed a note of harshness to creep into his voice.

Her chin dipped an infinitesimal fraction of an inch.

'Excellent. And the second thing?'

'The Foreigners Registration Office. Francine was here long-term – since at least 1944, according to her neighbour. She would have been required to report to her local registration officer.'

Seth looked at Fernandes. 'You can follow that up too.'

Persis opened her mouth to protest but he cut her off. 'I need you focused on the Healy case. That's not a request.'

He dismissed Fernandes, then slumped back with a sigh. 'There are days I feel as if I'm running a nursery. Now, where are we up to with the Healy investigation? Please tell me the autopsy threw up something.'

She briefed him on the post-mortem, then pulled out her note-book and showed him the series of words and numbers that had been written on Healy's thigh.

'Strange place to scribble anything,' muttered Seth. 'I mean, normal people doodle on their hands, or a wrist, or, heaven forbid, a piece of paper. Any idea what it means?'

'I think it's another clue.'

'You're still convinced he's leading us to the manuscript?'

'Nothing else makes sense.'

'You mean *this* makes sense to you? A renowned academic steals a priceless treasure, leaves behind riddles, and then tops himself?' Seth's expression was one of disgust. 'He's got us chasing our own tails while he laughs at us from whichever hell they've reserved for mad Englishmen.'

She said nothing. Her instincts told her that Healy hadn't lost his mind.

'What next?'

She laid out her plan. She needed to find out more about Healy. Who was he? His father had claimed that his time in a prisoner of war camp in Italy had changed him. Might some motivation for his current actions be found in that experience? Perhaps stealing *The Divine Comedy* was his way of gaining a measure of revenge against the Italians for the torture he'd endured?

'I also need to speak to Erin Lockhart and Franco Belzoni again,' she added. 'Both were less than truthful about their interactions with Healy.'

Seth tapped his fingers on the desk, examining the plan from all angles. 'Good,' he said, finally. 'In the meantime, I'm going to prepare a press statement. I've already fielded a dozen calls this morning. Be prepared for all hell to break loose. Now . . . did you make an appointment to meet those two women from the college? They've been hounding me.'

'Is that still a priority?'

'It is if I want to retain what little sanity I have left. Find an hour for them, Inspector. That's an order.'

Back at her desk, she took out her notebook and focused on the inscription Healy had left behind on his thigh. Could this be related to the lines he'd written down and stuck into an envelope, the opening lines from *Inferno*? She couldn't see how.

A match flared inside her skull.

As a girl, she'd played word games with her father. He'd introduced her to codes and ciphers. They'd fascinated her, especially when she began reading Sherlock Holmes and discovered that Arthur Conan Doyle had employed them extensively. And she already knew that Healy was a fan of riddles . . .

She picked up the phone and dialled her father.

'Wadia's Book Emporium. What do you want?' Her father's curt greeting had no doubt scared away many customers over the years.

'Papa, it's me.'

'Persis? Is something wrong?'

'No. Why would anything be wrong?'

'Because you don't usually call me in the middle of the day, that's why.'

She heard a racket in the background. 'What's going on in the shop?'

'That? I've got a bunch of idiots from the CPI here scouring the shelves for communist poetry.'

The Communist Party of India had fallen from grace the previous year. Stemming out of the socialist movement that had recently set itself against Nehru's ruling Congress Party, the CPI had organised a failed national railway strike the previous spring, followed by several calamitous acts of terrorism. The result: the party had been banned in several states, and now skulked about on the political margins, ridiculed, ignored, and occasionally shot at by government forces. Her father had never liked them.

'Papa, do you have any books about codes and ciphers in the shop?'

'Yes. Why?'

She told him, reading out Healy's mysterious inscription.

'I have no idea what the words mean but read me out those numbers again.'

She did as asked, waiting patiently as he scribbled the sequence down. 'These look like they might be a book cipher,' he said.

'Remind me what that is?'

'A code that uses a particular book or piece of text as its key. The correspondents must possess the exact same book or it's practically impossible to decipher.' He paused. 'Do you know which book Healy used as his codebook?'

She considered this. The obvious thought was that Healy had used *The Divine Comedy* manuscript. But that would have been pointless – in its absence, it would be impossible for her to apply the cipher. 'No,' she said, then, 'Are you certain this couldn't be any other type of code?'

'Of course I'm not certain,' he barked. 'I'm not a professional codebreaker.' He pulled the receiver from his ear so he could shout at one of his customers. 'But I'll wager money I'm on the right track. You'll have to find the book that Healy used. Otherwise, you'll get nowhere.'

'Fine. Can you send me over any books you have on codes and ciphers?'

'I'll send Krishna. Who shall I charge them to?'

'What?'

'The books. Who's paying for them?'

'Papa, are you telling me you're going to charge *me*?'

'Persis, correct me if I'm wrong, but are you not presently engaged in a major investigation for the Indian Police Service? That investigation now requires resources from my bookshop. Am I to provide these out of the goodness of my heart? Or because you happen to be my daughter? What will the IPS ask of me next? Would you like a kidney, perhaps?'

She stifled the urge to laugh. 'Fine. Send me the bill.'

Moments after she put down the phone, it rang.

'Persis, is that you?'

She was momentarily taken aback. 'Jaya?'

'Yes. It's your *friend* Jaya. Not that anyone would know it from the way you ignore my calls.'

'I'm sorry, Jaya. I've just been so . . .'

'Busy? If only that were an acceptable excuse. I'm having a small party at my house at lunchtime today. It's Arun's fifth birthday. Just a few friends. I expect you to be there.'

'Today? Jaya, it's—'

'Too short notice? I've been calling for the past week. I'm sorry, Persis, *you* may have relinquished your responsibilities as a friend, but I haven't. I expect you at one. Don't be late. And bring a present.'

The dial tone sounded in her ear. She returned the receiver gently to its cradle.

Jaya. A wave of guilt washed through her. Jaya was one of the few friends she'd made at school, one of those that had doggedly pursued their friendship, in spite of Persis's own haphazard commitment. It was true that she'd been avoiding Jaya's calls – for no other reason than that she truly had been exceptionally busy, first with the Herriot investigation, and then its aftermath. But explanations of that sort sounded trite, so she'd decided not to bother explaining at all.

Perhaps that had been a mistake. No wonder Jaya had sounded unusually curt.

She looked at the clock on the station wall. Between Jaya and the women from the Margaret Cousins College, she would waste hours, when she *should* be focused on the Healy investigation. But there seemed no way out of either engagement.

Sighing, she picked up the phone and began dialling.

In short order, she made appointments to meet with Erin Lockhart and Franco Belzoni – Belzoni was available later that afternoon, while Lockhart's secretary informed her that she was out of Bombay till the following morning.

She then dialled her father's old friend, military historian Augustus Silva. It was time she found out more about John Healy's past.

20

'There is a common misperception that the British governed India by employing the Roman policy of *divide et impera* – divide and rule. The truth is not quite as dramatic.'

Persis listened with a frown as the Englishman waved them into his office. She followed Augustus Silva inside as their host shut the door behind them.

A shambling, elderly man, almost bald, with a heavy belly, Frank Lindley stank strongly of sweat and cigarette smoke. His shirt, drenched in perspiration, was unbuttoned to his chest, curls of soaking white hair debouching from within. Lindley, like Silva, was a military historian based at Bombay University. She supposed that she should be grateful for his assistance, even if it meant suffering his malodorous presence in the close confines of his office.

'The fact is,' continued Lindley, making his way to the far side of his desk and falling into the chair like a felled tree, 'that, aside from a few notable exceptions – such as Curzon's partitioning of Bengal in 1905 – most of the dividing in India happened with the collusion of local interests, a way for those at the top to maintain their ancient feudal rights. As for Partition . . . Surely, you're not one of these Indians who believes that the British were responsible?'

Persis disliked Lindley's supercilious tone. She'd heard such arguments before. Even if there was some validity to them, it didn't change, for her, the unpalatable facts of colonialism.

Vaseem Khan

Nevertheless, at this moment in time, she needed the man's cooperation. Silva had recommended the Englishman as the best way of finding out about John Healy's past.

Officially, Frank Lindley worked for the British Council in Delhi, preparing a study to complement various post-independence initiatives for the British and Indian armies to work together. In a past life, he had been a soldier – though Persis couldn't imagine him in uniform – and had served extensively around the empire, including in an advisory capacity to Whitehall during World War Two. It was those contacts that he'd now prevailed upon to request the information that Persis needed.

'Did you bring the money?'

Persis reached into the pocket of her trousers and took out an envelope. She watched, with a faint tremor of disgust, as Lindley counted the cash, then put it into a drawer. He grinned at her, displaying stained, yellow teeth, perhaps sensing her thoughts. 'Information is a commodity, Inspector. And there is no such thing as a free commodity.'

He handed her a Manila folder. Inside, she found a sheaf of papers.

'Your man Healy wasn't quite as straightforward to track down as I had anticipated. Luckily, I still have a few friends in the War Office.' He settled on to his elbows and fixed her with his watery grey eyes. 'John Healy served in North Africa, with the British First Army. I say served, but the truth is that almost as soon as he was sent out there, in early '43, he was captured in action and taken to the Italian POW camp in Sulmona – Campo 78, as it was known. At its peak, there were almost three thousand inmates there – British and Commonwealth, both officers and lesser ranks, all captured in North Africa. Records show that, in September 1943, as the Italian government neared collapse, rumours spread

160

among the inmates that the camp was about to be evacuated to Germany. Shortly after, the Italian guards deserted. Hundreds of the inmates took the opportunity to escape into the surrounding hills. Others, unfortunately, chose to tow the official British line – attempt no escapes and wait for rescue. On September 14th, German troops arrived to escort the remaining prisoners northwards. Healy was one of those taken north.'

Persis looked through the folder – Lindley had had the papers faxed over from the British War Office to a Western Union Office near the university, one of the few fax receiving stations in the city. Because of the sensitive nature of the documents, Lindley had had to stand guard over the receiving printer until the papers came through. His attentiveness – and the fact that he'd had to pay a senior contact to get the information out without the red tape that would inevitably have been involved in requesting a British Army service record through official channels – had been reflected in his bill.

Seth had almost fainted dead away when she'd told him the sum.

John Healy's record included basic personal details, the date he'd entered the service, his rank – Captain – his units, and his wounds and hospitalisations – none, as far as she could make out.

A photograph of Healy in uniform showed a rigid face, staring straight ahead, self-assurance in his gaze.

She skimmed through the remainder of the file which also held details of Healy's time in North Africa, and his capture by German forces.

Lindley stood up and opened the casement window behind him, letting some much-needed air into the room. The voices of students drifted in with the midday heat. He lit a cigarette, his figure outlined in a haze of light. 'I suppose the Germans found out that Healy was a bit special,' he continued, eventually. 'Not many star academics out on the front line. He was taken to Campo 12 at Vincigliata. Have you heard of it?'

She shook her head. These names meant nothing to her. She knew little of Italy, and little of what had gone on there during the war, aside from what she'd seen in Pathé news footage.

'It was a particularly notorious *prigioniero di guerra* – "prison of war". Set in a beautiful thirteenth-century castle near Florence, it was used to hold high-rank prisoners. There were only ever about twenty-five there at any one time, including several British generals. The fact that Healy was sent there means that the Germans thought pretty highly of his celebrity status.' He flicked ash out of the window, then returned to his desk.

Persis continued to skim through the file.

She discovered papers describing the prison Healy had ended up in.

Photographs of the place showed a medieval castle standing atop a rocky hill, its most prominent feature a crenellated tower. The former stronghold of a noble Florentine family, it had been requisitioned by the Italian government during the war for use as a prison.

'It wasn't easy getting access to this information,' commented Lindley. 'There seems to be a lack of clarity as to exactly what happened to Healy during his time at Vincigliata.'

'I believe that he was tortured there.'

Lindley stroked his stomach. 'There seems little evidence for that sort of thing at the prison. I'm not saying it couldn't have happened, but these were high-ranking officers. Even the Germans didn't go in for pulling the fingernails off our top knobs.'

'Healy wasn't of a high rank.'

'True. But he was taken to Vincigliata for a reason. I'd be surprised if that reason was simply to abuse him.'

She discovered in the documents a sheet of paper with a sketchy record of Healy's arrival at the Castello di Vincigliata. It was written in Italian, with the Italian repeated in German. Someone had helpfully added an English translation to the text. It merely stated Healy's rank, a summary of his army record, his time at Campo 78, and, notably, a few lines about his pre-war status as a noted academic.

What could have incited the Italians – and their German masters – to torture him? What had Healy done to make them want to break his spirit?

'I need to know more. Is there any way we can track down some of his fellow inmates? Or possibly one of the guards there?'

Lindley scratched at his jowls. 'Fellow inmates might not be difficult to find, but I doubt they'll be keen to talk. As I mentioned, they were mainly high-ranking officers. I can't guarantee any of them will be willing to revisit their experiences as jailbirds in an Italian POW camp. A bit of a dent to the ego, if you catch my drift. As for Italians and Germans . . .' He grimaced. 'If we didn't put them up against a wall and shoot them – as we should have done with every last Nazi, in my opinion – I might be able to trace one or two. But it's a lot more work. I have a contact at the War Office Directorate of Prisoners of War. It's going to cost money.'

She hesitated. Seth had already grumbled at the cost of paying Lindley. To go back and ask for more might give him a mild stroke.

Then again, this was now a national matter. How much was it worth to the authorities to find that manuscript?

'That's fine,' she said, rising to her feet. 'Just do it quickly.'

Lindley grunted and sucked on his cigarette, mentally dismissing her.

21

On the rare occasions that she reflected on her school years, she found herself thinking of the four of them: Jaya, Dinaz, Emily, and Persis herself. Their friendship had been late-blooming – the first few years at the Cathedral Girls School had been largely a trial of hostility.

She'd been told that she was rude, uncooperative, surly. The more they required her to fit in, the less she was inclined to do so. The fact was that she had no real desire to dance like a monkey in the playground in order to earn the dubious badge of popularity. While other girls gossiped about the latest movie stars, she carried a book around, looking for a quiet corner in which to wait before the bell rang for the next class.

But then had come Emily, the daughter of an English couple newly stationed in the city. Emily, who had seen her reading Dostoevsky's *Crime and Punishment* one day and sat down next to her, uninvited. Persis had given her every indication that her presence was unwelcome; to her astonishment, the girl had simply ignored her. She would wonder later if this was another example of the British sense of entitlement her father bemoaned, but, by then, it was too late.

They had become friends.

Emily had brought two of her own friends along, Dinaz and Jaya. Dinaz, Persis had found easy to get along with. She was a fellow Parsee, so there was common ground to work with. But Jaya had been a nightmare. A cultivated snob, she had treated

Persis with aloofness, as one might a familiar servant. Jaya's parents were wealthy – her father had made a fortune producing steel cutlery for the armed forces; her mother was an heiress to a copper mine. Jaya had grown up spoiled, and it showed. She was harsh and supercilious, except around Emily. With her, she was sickeningly ingratiating.

Persis had put up with her needling for about a month – for Emily's sake – until, one day, Jaya stepped on a landmine, muttering something unforgivable about Persis's late mother and her elopement. Persis had promptly punched her in the mouth, knocking out one of her teeth. She could still remember how Jaya had stood there, astonished, staring at her, as if the natural order of the cosmos had inverted itself.

When the fuss had died down, Jaya, to Persis's own astonishment, had returned and sheepishly apologised. Her father, she explained, had told her that she deserved it and wished he had been there to see it himself.

From that moment forth, they'd become the firmest of friends.

The incident had only served to cement Persis's belief that there were few ills in the world that couldn't be cured by a punch in the mouth.

Jaya lived in a three-storey bungalow in Cuffe Parade. It was only when Persis had already rung the bell that she realised she'd forgotten to bring a present. 'Damn.' She jogged back to her jeep and rummaged in the glove compartment.

She stared at the object in her hand. It would have to do.

'You've lost weight.'

Jaya examined her with a critical eye. Persis couldn't help but note that her friend was looking effortlessly glamorous, as ever. Slender, and sporting a sari that had probably cost more than most people's cars, Jaya had always taken pride in her appearance.

It was hard to believe her friend had recently had a second child.

They sat on the new cream-coloured sofas that had just been installed on the rear porch in front of the pool. Children splashed and screamed in the water, mothers watching anxiously from the sides, one or two of the more adventurous ones in bathing suits resembling straitjackets.

'And *you've* gained more hangers-on.'

'Play nicely! These are my friends.' Jaya lowered her voice. 'Or at least, they're the mothers of Arun's friends.'

Persis smiled. 'Motherhood becomes you.'

Jaya sipped at her martini. 'Don't knock it till you've tried it.'

'I can't say that it's on the horizon. Kids, I mean.'

'Ah. Your precious career. Does the police service still not allow married women?'

'No.'

'What about unwed mothers? Since you're so keen on breaking new ground.'

'I was under the impression that a man was needed somewhere along the line. For the purposes of motherhood, I mean.'

Jaya sighed. 'It's not as if you don't have options. I mean, look at you. If we got you out of that uniform and into a decent dress, you'd be quite the catch. Give me the word, and I'll have you married off by the end of the week.'

'You sound like Aunt Nussie.'

'Is she so wrong?'

Persis rolled her eyes. 'I'm not interested in men. Not right now.'

Jaya was staring at her with catlike intensity. 'Hmm.'

'Hmm, what?'

'The lady doth protest too much, methinks. Have you met someone?'

'What? No.'

'You're blushing!'

'I am not!'

'My God! You *have* met someone.' Jaya leaned forward, mischief in her eyes. 'Spill the beans. Who is he?'

Persis gaped at her. Relief washed over her as Jaya's five-year-old son, Arun, waddled over. The boy, Persis couldn't help but notice, was alarmingly overweight, with thick black hair and a heavy, square jaw, like a disgruntled toad.

'When can we cut the cake?' he demanded of his mother.

'Not yet, my darling.'

'I want to cut the cake *now*!'

'Look who it is. Auntie Persis.'

The boy turned to her, looking her up and down as one might a particularly rancid goat. 'Why are you wearing a police uniform? This isn't a fancy-dress party.'

'I'm a policewoman.'

'No, you're not. Women can't be police officers.'

'Why not?'

'Because they're women. Everyone knows that.'

'I assure you, I *am* a policewoman.'

'I don't believe you.' He stared at her belligerently. 'Father says women are only supposed to cook and clean.'

Persis looked at Jaya. 'I don't believe your mother has cooked anything in her whole life.'

'Mommy's different. She's got servants.' He pointed at her hip. 'I bet that isn't even a real gun.'

She took it out and pointed it at him. 'If I pulled this trigger, there wouldn't be much left of you.'

'Persis!' Jaya frowned at her.

But the boy merely looked at her with shining eyes. 'Have you ever shot anyone?'

Persis flashed back to the moment she'd shot the suspect who'd planned the killing of Sir James Herriot. The bullet had also claimed part of Archie Blackfinch's ear. Of course, he *had* been at the mercy of a murderer at the time, which, to her mind, counted as a mitigating factor. 'Yes.'

'Wow! How many people have you killed?'

'Too many,' she said firmly, sliding the weapon back into its holster.

He gave a disappointed look, then said, 'Where's my present? You're supposed to bring a present to a birthday party.'

Jaya rolled her eyes apologetically. Persis was tempted to say that the application of a sandal to her son's ample rump might be a better way of apologising for his rudeness, but held her tongue. She picked up a parcel – hastily wrapped in newspaper – and handed it to the boy. 'Happy birthday.'

He tore away the packaging greedily, then held up the object, eyes glittering. 'Handcuffs!' He stared at her with something approaching adoration. 'I'm going to be a policeman. I'm going to arrest all my friends, then shoot them, just like a real cop.'

'You can't give him handcuffs,' said Jaya, as he waddled off, swinging the cuffs like a slingshot.

'I don't think they work,' said Persis. 'It's an old pair.'

'You forgot to get him a gift, didn't you?' She shook her head, smiling. 'Anyhow, you were talking about a male admirer?'

'No. You were talking about him. *I* was ignoring you.'

Jaya raised an eyebrow and waited.

Persis sighed. Maybe it *would* help to talk the matter through. 'Fine. But don't you go gossiping to anyone.' Quickly, she filled her in on her awkward relationship – if that was the right word – with Archie Blackfinch.

'An Englishman!' whinnied Jaya. 'Well, look at you. Quite the dark horse.' She waved at a passing waiter, accepting another martini. 'Is he handsome? Smart? Accomplished?'

'He's . . . clumsy.'

'That's a good start. Clumsy makes them docile. They're always beleaguered, forever in need of assistance.'

'He's very intelligent.'

'Not *too* bright, I hope. Remember, two positives make a negative.' She examined her old friend over the top of her glass. 'Have you two . . .?'

'No!'

'There's no need to be so prim about it. It's not as if you can mislay your virginity a second time. Anyway, dressed like that, you should thank your lucky stars any man wants to—'

'I have to get back to work,' said Persis, standing up.

Jaya gazed at her, then rose slowly to her feet. 'Look. You're a modern woman. You've already ripped up every convention in the book. If you like him, do something about it. Don't dither around. One thing I can tell you, he won't wait for ever.' She smiled. 'There's another reason I asked you over. Dinaz is going to be in town in a couple of weeks. I thought the three of us might have dinner. Maybe paint the town red.'

Persis grimaced. 'I was never very good at painting the town, red or any other colour.'

'Nonsense. You're a celebrity now. You've got to rub shoulders with the in-crowd.'

She knew Jaya was only teasing. Besides, it would be nice to see Dinaz. She'd been away for the past few years in West Bengal working in the Sundarbans Forest Management Division. Her infrequent telephone calls hinted at an adventurous and sometimes perilous calling, including the occasional encounter with a tiger.

'Fine,' she said. 'Count me in . . . Any word from Emily?' she asked awkwardly.

'No. Dear old Emily seems to have forgotten us.'

Emily St Charles. For years, her best friend and closest confidante. And then the war had come along, and, in its aftermath, the great betrayal. Promises of greater Indian autonomy in return for India's help in the war had proved hollow, and violence towards Brits in the country had escalated, despite Gandhi's calls for restraint. Emily had left for England in 1946 with her family.

She'd written sporadically, for a while, but in the past year, nothing.

Persis had made a half-hearted attempt at writing back, but it simply wasn't in her. Words would wither on the page into meaningless expressions of sentiment. Crumpled balls of paper littered the floor of her bedroom until finally she'd given up.

Sometimes, late at night, she'd feel the past rebuking her, as sharp as a stiff finger poked into the kidneys. Surely, friendship meant making the effort?

'Do you have Emily's number?'

'No. She's moved home. The last time I spoke to her there was mention of an engagement.'

Shock knifed through her. 'She wouldn't marry without inviting us, surely?'

Jaya shrugged. 'People change. Besides, it's not as if we're all disposed to go charging off to London at the drop of a hat.'

Persis walked on in thoughtful silence. It would explain a lot. Emily's wouldn't be the first marriage to dissolve the bonds of childhood friendship.

She remembered that, one day, Emily had convinced her to go to the movies after school, to watch *The Mark of Zorro*. Afterwards, they'd sworn that if either of them married a man half as dashing as Tyrone Power, they'd ensure they didn't behave as soppily as Linda Darnell.

And, of course, they'd be maid of honour at each other's weddings.

Perhaps there was blame on either side for promises that had proven hollow.

At the door, she asked, 'By the way, you haven't heard anything about Zubin being back in town?'

'That serpent? No. Why?'

'No reason.'

'Oh, Persis. You're not still holding out a torch for him, are you?'

'Of course not. I just – I thought I saw him, that's all.'

'Well, if you see him again, take out that revolver and put it to good use.'

22

The guard watched her, smoking a roll-up, as she crossed the street and entered John Healy's home for the third time. He looked like the same man she'd seen on her first visit; she wondered if curiosity would compel him to ask after the missing Englishman.

Inside, she wasted no time, heading straight for the bookcase in the living room.

She took out the six volumes there and set them down on the coffee table. Next to them she set down her notebook and two more volumes, books on codes and ciphers, sent over by her father.

She checked her watch. It was already two and she had a four o'clock appointment at the Margaret Cousins College.

Quickly, she skimmed through her father's books until she found the relevant sections on book ciphers. To her irritation, it appeared that, though relatively well known, book ciphers could be applied with numerous variations. These variations were usually agreed between the correspondents in advance. However, what *was* common to all book ciphers was the use of a single text as a key. Once you knew the codebook or codetext, it was only a matter of working through the various ciphers until you struck upon one that produced a meaningful message.

She picked up *Through the Looking-Glass*. Healy had already used it once in his trail of clues; logically, it was the best place to start.

She began with a simple cipher.

She posited that the first number in Healy's set of numerical clues indicated the page, the next, the line on that page; then the numbers that followed the oblique stroke were either the location of the words to be used from that line or the location of characters. So, taking the first sequence – 1.3/1.7 – she turned to page one of the book, looked at the third line down and picked out the first and seventh words. This gave her 'kitten' and washed'.

Nonsense.

The next sequence was 1.2/5.8. So, again, first page, but this time second line down, then fifth and eighth words. 'Was' and 'kitten'.

With the third sequence – 2.11/52.64.71.72.92.97.102.146. 157.158.221 – she realised that she couldn't possibly be on the right track. The numbers after the stroke couldn't indicate words on the eleventh line of the book's second page because there simply couldn't *be* 221 words on a single line, or even 52, for that matter. Nor could the numbers refer to *characters* on the line, rather than words. She'd been around books long enough to know that no line in any normal book contained over two hundred characters, even if you included the spaces between words.

The answer was simple: she was using the wrong cipher.

She dug back through the reference books her father had sent her and, after some further effort, quickly concluded that none of the book ciphers detailed there would work.

She spent another hour going through the same process with the other books on Healy's bookshelf.

Nothing.

Had Sam guessed wrong? Perhaps Healy hadn't employed a book cipher at all.

Disappointment wrapped itself around her and for a moment she sat back on the sofa, closed her eyes, and allowed the frustration to flow through her.

Having worked it out of her system, she stood, placed Healy's books, and her own, into her bag, then returned to the jeep.

23

'How much do you know about Margaret Cousins?'

Scheherazade Mirza spoke as she walked, keeping up a brisk pace.

She had arrived on the dot of four, parked in the college's courtyard, and made her way into the foyer. The building was smaller than she'd expected – a single, three-storey structure with a broad, art deco façade painted in beige and imperial maroon – calling it a college seemed an exercise in hyperbole. A wooden signboard had been hung by ropes across the front: MARGARET COUSINS COLLEGE OF DOMESTIC SCIENCE. The ropes gave the place a sense of impermanence. It reminded her more of the city's numerous cinemas – the Regal, the Eros – than an educational establishment.

'Not as much as I'm about to be told,' muttered Persis.

'Sorry, I didn't catch that,' sang Mirza over her shoulder, turning sharply into a corner.

'I was just saying I can't wait to find out more.' Persis glanced at her watch. She didn't have time for this.

Voices floated along the corridor. Arriving at a white-painted door, Mirza barrelled headfirst into it, then held it open for her guest.

Persis walked into a large room with whitewashed walls, parquet flooring, and ceiling fans whirring away at regular intervals. Along the walls were portraits of austere-looking women, mainly white, looking down on rows of chairs facing a stage and lectern. The chairs were occupied by perhaps a hundred or so women, chatting, some with cups of tea in hand. All were well dressed, and impeccably groomed: silk saris, dresses, and hats. The odd pair of trousers hinted at the presence of a sexual counterculture.

Her immediate impression was that she'd walked into an aviary, one reserved for rare and exotic birds.

The tall figure of Jenny Pinto turned from another woman and approached her, a smile lighting up her severe features. 'Inspector. We're delighted you could join us.'

'What is this?' hissed Persis. 'I thought I was only here to *talk* about the possibility of giving a talk.'

'That's correct. The annual meeting of the All India Women's Congress will take place in six weeks, right here, in Bombay. And *we* have been chosen to host it. Our hope is that you will speak at the event. But today . . .' She gave a sheepish smile. 'I'm afraid I'm to blame. I couldn't help but mention to one or two of our members that you'd be here today. Before I knew it, they'd decided to gather for an impromptu tea party. I believe they're hoping you might say a few words.'

Persis looked out at the sea of women. She was suddenly acutely aware of the perspiration on her brow, the fact that she was wearing a uniform, that her hair was pulled back, that she looked decidedly out of place in this setting. 'Impossible.'

'We're not asking for a speech,' said Mirza. 'Just a few words of encouragement.'

'I couldn't,' muttered Persis. A hoop of panic tightened around her chest.

'Didn't I read somewhere that you were a debate champion at university?'

Persis gave her a sharp look. Mirza simply beamed at her.

Pinto moved closer. She waved at a portrait on the wall, a white woman with gentle eyes and grey hair. 'That's Margaret Cousins.

A quite remarkable woman. She was a prominent suffragette in Ireland before moving to India in 1915. She spearheaded the fight for women's rights on the subcontinent. We owe her a great deal.' A smile winched up the corners of her mouth. 'But the thing is, Persis ... It's high time we took charge of our own destiny. The plight of Indian women can only be changed *by* Indian women. More importantly, what we really need is *ordinary* women. Many of our colleagues are well meaning, but they've never experienced hardship. For many of them, this is a hobby. What we need is those for whom this is a *cause*. Someone like you, Persis. You, more than any of us, truly understand how the cards are stacked.'

Persis looked out at the audience, now focused on her. The silence in the room was as thick as elephant grass. Her mouth was suddenly dry of saliva. She experienced the bizarre sensation of living through a metaphor made real – from her first day on the force, she'd been held up as some sort of symbol, an emblem of a changing India.

And yet, she'd never asked for that responsibility.

'I'm sorry,' she said, hoarsely. 'I can't help you. Not today. Not ever.'

She turned and walked away.

24

On the drive to the Asiatic Society her thoughts lingered on the meeting.

What had Pinto and Mirza made of her spineless exit?

The tips of her ears burned.

She'd never held herself up as a crusader. She'd chosen to become a policewoman for her own selfish reasons. Inspired by an absent mother, willed on by her own bullheadedness in the face of being told that she wasn't *allowed* to, she'd made it her mission to prove them wrong.

But who *was* this *them* that she was continually seeking to prove herself to?

Sam's face hovered before her. He'd said little when she'd first declared her intention to join the force, merely warning her that she should expect a bumpy ride. Once she'd been accepted into the academy, he'd thrown his weight behind her, though she knew this was partly because Aunt Nussie had taken the contrary position, almost fainting dead away at the notion that her only niece intended to don khaki trousers and patrol the streets like some common *hawaldar*. Persis had patiently explained to her that she had no intention of becoming a constable – there were already one or two token female *hawaldars* around the country. Her sights were set higher.

She intended to qualify as the Indian Police Service's first female *inspector*.

'And what will that get you?' Nussie had asked. 'Do you think any man will want to marry a woman carrying a gun and licensed to shoot him?'

Franco Belzoni was waiting for her in Neve Forrester's office, leafing through a thick volume open on the desk. There was no sign of the Englishwoman.

As Persis entered, he rose to his feet and extended a hand. 'Inspector. It is good to see you again. How can I help?'

Persis waved him back into his seat, then sat down. She took off her cap and wiped a sleeve across her brow.

'I was saddened to hear of John's death,' continued Belzoni, before she could speak. 'I did not know him long, but he seemed a good man. The world has lost an excellent scholar.'

Of course, Forrester would have told him of Healy's death – no doubt it would be headline news by tomorrow. She wondered what else the Italian knew.

He sat forward, eagerness personified. 'Tell me, have you recovered the manuscript?'

'No,' she replied. 'The manuscript is still missing.'

He closed his eyes. *'Questo è un disastro.'* He shook his head. 'John was our principal lead.'

'Our?'

He blinked, as if realising what he'd said. 'Inspector, please understand. This artefact is an Italian treasure. At some point your government will realise this and return the manuscript to its rightful home. You must forgive me if I am taking this matter very personally.'

'You seem to be under some sort of misapprehension,' she said icily. 'I'm not here because I need your help. I'm here because you lied to me.'

His eyebrows lifted in surprise. 'I do not understand.'

'When we met, you forgot to mention that you and Healy had fallen out. That you'd had an argument, over access to the *Divine Comedy* manuscript.'

'But this is untrue!' He waved his hands around agitatedly. 'Yes, John may have turned down my request for more time with the manuscript, but it was only a matter of scheduling. Hardly a falling-out.' His eyes narrowed. 'Who told you this?'

'Does it matter?'

'If I am to be slandered, then I must know who is my accuser, Inspector. This is only fair, *si?*'

'Erin Lockhart. She told me you had a row with Healy just days before his disappearance.'

'I would not call it a row.' He shrugged. 'I am Italian. We express ourselves . . . *appassionatamente.*'

She allowed a silence to pass, then took out her notebook and set it before him. 'Healy left behind another clue. Does this mean anything to you?'

He plucked up the notebook and scanned the words Healy had written on to his thigh.

'*Affectionate honoured friend embraces praised persecuted servant.*' His brow furrowed. 'A riddle? Why would John do this?' His frustration was evident. He glanced at the numbers below the words. 'These sequences look like a cipher.'

'Yes. Do you know which one?'

He shook his head. 'It is not my area of expertise.' He set down the notebook. 'Tell me, did you find anything else with John's body?'

'Such as?'

'Notebooks? A diary, maybe? Letters?'

'Why?'

He seemed to realise that his eagerness had raised an alarm. He sat back. 'Perhaps they might show us the way.'

She debated with herself how much to reveal to the Italian. There was something about Belzoni that bothered her, something about his façade that rang hollow. She was now convinced that, despite his protestations, he and Healy had never been friendly.

'He left behind a note. The first three lines of *Inferno*.'

'"*Midway upon the journey of our life, I came to myself, in a dark wood; for I had wandered from the straight and true.*"'

'Yes. Does it mean anything to you?'

He considered this. 'No. I mean, nothing that sheds light on our problem.' He was silent a moment. 'That is *all* he left behind?' His curiosity was like a hound, snuffling at her heels.

She hesitated. 'We found three notebooks in his bag.'

His eyes lit up. 'What is in them?'

'His translation of the manuscript.'

His brow knitted.

'Were you expecting something else?'

He seemed about to say something, then subsided. 'Perhaps you would permit me to take a look? At the notebooks?'

'Why?'

His mouth flapped for a moment. 'I may be able to see something that you have not.'

'And what might that be?'

He was on the back foot again, taking refuge in silence.

'Why do I get the impression that you haven't been completely honest with me?'

'I assure you, Inspector, my only wish is to help. Our goal is the same.'

But was it?

She found herself wondering, for the first time, at the motivations of those caught in John Healy's web. Neve Forrester. Franco Belzoni. Erin Lockhart. James Ingram. Those he had touched, and who were now left behind to wonder at the secrets he had spun in his wake.

'I think you have been given the wrong impression about me,' Belzoni continued, his face earnest. 'Erin Lockhart is not quite a, how you say, paragon of virtue.'

'In what way?'

'Her interest in John may have had more to do with the manuscript than the man, if you catch my meaning.'

Persis shifted in her seat. So James Ingram had been telling the truth. 'Are you suggesting she knows something about the manuscript? Or Healy's actions? Something she hasn't told me?'

'I suggest nothing, Inspector. I merely point out to you that it is bad form to rely on hearsay.'

25

Back at Malabar House, she called Birla and Haq over.

The pair of sub-inspectors looked haggard.

She knew Haq had been run ragged with the National Games, thankfully now at an end, and she'd kept Birla busy enough with the Healy investigation. The two constables were often feuding, but looked too tired even to grimace at one another.

'I want you two to follow someone around.'

'I've booked the rest of the day off,' said Haq, straightening from his habitual simian slouch. His stomach pushed against the buttons of his shirt. Smears of chutney decorated his collar.

'Cancel it.'

'But—'

'This is important. The Healy case takes precedence over your personal plans.'

Haq subsided with a grumble.

Never a demonstrative man, Sub-Inspector Karim Haq rarely made more than a moment's fuss over anything. Of all her colleagues, he was, perhaps, the most inscrutable. As a Muslim, he and Birla often clashed, mirroring the sectarian hostility that continued to mark relations between the country's two largest religious denominations. Though millions of Muslims had departed – or been forced to depart – for Pakistan and its counterpart territory in the east – the unimaginatively labelled East Pakistan – millions more had chosen to stay.

Whether that was a wise decision remained to be seen.

Despite Nehru's edicts and the centre's efforts to promote unity, the serpent of mistrust had bitten deep. The brutality that had marked Partition was still fresh in the minds of her fellow citizens.

Forgive and forget was a mantra few were keen to embrace.

She looked at him now, a scruffy, heavy-set man, with a head like a lantern, cauliflower ears, a crew cut, and a lugubrious expression. She'd always thought Haq would make an excellent hangman. He'd never mentioned his age, but she guessed he was maybe half a dozen years younger than Birla, who was in his mid-forties. His family circumstances remained a closely guarded secret. He was married; beyond that no one really knew.

She'd once asked Birla how Haq had ended up at Malabar House. Birla himself had been consigned here because his daughter had refused the overtures of a senior officer.

Birla didn't know.

Haq had never said and Seth refused to comment on the matter.

She wrote down Franco Belzoni's name on a sheet of paper and handed it to them. 'Give Neve Forrester a call and find out where he's staying.'

'Why exactly are we following him?' Birla asked.

'He was witnessed arguing with John Healy just days before he vanished. They were fighting over the manuscript. Belzoni's an Italian. He believes, like the Italian government, that the book should be returned to Italy.'

'That's colonialism for you,' said Birla. 'They give themselves licence to take whatever they want, but you hold on to one little book and suddenly all hell breaks loose.' He sighed. 'You think he's mixed up in this? I mean, we know Healy killed himself. Belzoni had nothing to do with that.'

'Maybe not. But I'm convinced Healy couldn't have done this without accomplices. The manuscript is still missing. Belzoni doesn't have it. Maybe he hatched a plan with Healy to steal it and then Healy double-crossed him.'

'Still doesn't explain why Healy's leading us on a merry dance.' He pinched the bridge of his nose. 'Have you got any further with his latest clue?'

She shook her head.

Haq looked pointedly at his watch. 'I'll be back in a minute.'

They watched him wander back to his desk, sweep up his cap, and lumber out of the office.

'It's a good thing he's only as dumb as he looks,' muttered Birla.

'Are you two going to be able to work together?'

He raised his hands in mock surrender, then went back to his own desk to dial Neve Forrester.

Five minutes later, he had the information he needed. 'I'll grab Haq on the way out.' He gave her a wave and left.

Alone in the office now, she closed her eyes.

The only sound came from the ceiling fan. Down in the basement of Malabar House, they were shielded from the traffic rumbling by on John Adams Street. A mouse squeaked somewhere under the jumble of desks and filing cabinets. She'd seen it on several occasions, usually late in the evening, the same one each time, a jet-black little thing with a shortened tail.

She'd named it Stumpy.

The Healy investigation wound itself around her like the coils of a python. The more she knew, the less coherent the picture seemed to be.

What *had* been Healy's purpose in all this?

She opened her notebook, and looked again at the enigmatic inscription he'd left behind.

AFFECTIONATE
HONOURED
FRIEND
EMBRACES
PRAISED
PERSECUTED
SERVANT

Tomorrow, she'd have to ask Seth to help her find a professional codebreaker. Something inside her rebelled at the idea of standing aside while another solved the problem. But she knew that was simply ego, a vice her father often accused her of.

Not ego, she'd told him: ambition.

Fatigue moved over her like an enclosing fog bank. Her eyes became heavy; Healy's words swam on the page. Her eyelids drooped. A moment's rest. Five minutes, before—

Her eyes snapped open. Fernandes was at his desk, fiddling with paper. She glanced at the clock on the wall.

Fifteen minutes had vanished.

She flushed. The idea that Fernandes had caught her napping at her desk . . .

'What did you find out?' Her tone was harsh, even to her own ears, like a cannon-shot signalling the exchange of hostilities.

Fernandes stiffened.

Gradually, he twisted his bulk around in his seat and fixed her with a long look. His thick moustache twitched. She braced herself for an explosion, but then he seemed to take a deep inner breath.

'I went to the FRO. No one named Francine Kramer has ever registered there. This means one of two things: either she registered under a different name when she entered the country or else she never registered at all. In which case, she had a reason for not doing so.'

Persis recalled the statements from both Kramer's friend, Arabella, and, later, her neighbour – namely, that Francine was a woman with a troubled past. Perhaps she'd come to India to forget that past. Perhaps that was why she'd decided not to report to the Foreigners Registration Office. Might she also have adopted a false name to ensure the FRO couldn't track her down?

She wouldn't be the first person to sink without trace into the cosmopolitan soup that was Bombay.

'And the search for Francine's doctor?'

'I spoke to the consultant psychiatrist at the Grant Medical College, a Dr Varun Nayar. He'd never had Kramer as a patient. But he gave me the names of seven other head doctors in the city, those most likely to have treated a foreigner.'

'Show me the list.'

He stared at her, then stood up and walked over to her desk. She was suddenly conscious of how big he was, how he loomed over her. His nostrils flared in the silence as he looked down on her with an inscrutable gaze. Then he reached into the pocket of his trousers, took out a small notebook, thumbed through to a page in the middle, and held it before her face.

A list of seven names and addresses was written there in Fernandes's laboured hand.

She stared at the page, then wondered why she'd even asked to see it.

Fernandes lowered the notebook. 'Do you want me to copy them out for you?'

'No,' she said, looking away. 'How many have you spoken to?'

'Four. The rest were unavailable. I'll get to them tomorrow.'

He made no move to return to his desk. His bulk was like a tree that had erupted from the floor. She could hear his breathing as he continued to gaze down at her.

The moment stretched, became unbearable.

His gaze fell on her open notebook. His brow furrowed. 'Saints,' he murmured.

'What?'

'You have the names of saints written in your notebook. Why?'

She squinted up at him. 'What are you talking about?'

He leaned over and tapped a thick finger on Healy's riddle. 'These are the literal meanings of the names of biblical saints. Or at least biblical characters. We used to learn them as children.'

She knew that Fernandes was a Catholic – a devout one, by all accounts. Bombay's Catholics, the legacy of Portuguese missionaries and forced conversions, were said to be as committed as any living on the doorsteps of the Vatican.

Excitement quickened inside her. She looked again at the inscription. 'You know what these mean?'

'Not all of them. But I recognise some. For instance, "praised" is Jude, one of the "brothers" of Jesus. He wrote the Epistle of Jude. And "persecuted" is Job, the man who was tested by God. His story is told in the Book of Job. "Friend" ... that could be Ruth, though I'm not certain. Ruth married an Israelite, and was known for her kindness. Or something like that. "Affectionate" is definitely Philemon, from the New Testament. Philemon is mentioned in the Epistle to Philemon, a letter written by Saint Paul to him while Paul was in prison. Philemon is generally regarded as a saint. The others I can't recall, though I vaguely remember that there's one whose name means "servant".'

'Do the numbers mean anything to you?'

He peered at the sequences of digits, then shook his head.

She knew that she should thank him, but the words shrivelled in her mouth.

Fernandes waited a moment, then turned, went back to his desk, picked up his cap and a satchel, then left.

Her mind was ablaze.

Could he be correct? If so, what did the remaining three words mean? She remembered reading the Bible as a teenager – it had been a requirement at the Cathedral Girls School. But she was neither a Christian nor a scholar.

A cog turned in her mind, slipping into place with an almost audible clunk.

Bible.

Perhaps John Healy had used a book cipher, after all. And she could now make an educated guess as to which book he'd used as his key.

She walked to the evidence cabinet, picked up the keys atop it, and unlocked the door.

A red register sat on the middle shelf, used to log evidence in and out of the *almirah*, though she knew it was employed haphazardly by her colleagues.

She located the box containing evidence from the Healy investigation and from it removed the book the Englishman had left behind when he had switched it for the Dante manuscript.

A copy of the 1611 King James Bible.

Returning with it to her desk, she opened it and examined the first pages.

The text began with a cover page containing its full title:

THE HOLY BIBLE

Containing the Old Testament, and the New: Newly Translated out of the Original tongues: & with the former Translations diligently compared and revised, by his Majesties special Commandment.

There followed the flyleaf on which Healy had left his first clue: *What's in a name? Akoloutheo Aletheia.* After this was a dedication, a lengthy message to readers from the translators – defending their efforts against possible criticisms – and then a section containing extensive genealogies. The Bible proper began with the first book of the Old Testament, the Book of Genesis, and its opening verse: 'In the beginning God created the heaven and the Earth.'

A quick look told her that the volume contained the thirty-nine books of the Old Testament, the twenty-seven books of the New Testament, and a section containing the fourteen books of the Apocrypha – works of unknown or unclear authorship, filling the gap of time between the period covered by the Hebrew Bible and the period covered by the Christian New Testament.

This was about as much as she recalled from her schooldays.

But one thing she did remember and which she now quickly confirmed: the Bible contained no page numbers. Instead, everything was numbered by reference to chapters and verses.

That was the answer. The solution to Healy's book cipher.

He wasn't using page numbers.

He was using the biblical convention of chapter and verse.

She set her notebook beside the Bible and looked closely at the sequence of numbers from Healy's inscription. Seven sequences, in fact. And above them seven words. The logical conclusion was that each word corresponded to a line.

She rewrote the entire inscription, pairing each word with its corresponding line in the order they had been set out, and adding colons in line with her conjecture about Healy's use of chapter and verse numbers as the basis of his cipher. She also added Fernandes's guesses at the words he had identified with biblical characters:

AFFECTIONATE (PHILEMON) 1:3/1.7

HONOURED (??) 1:2/5.8

FRIEND (RUTH??) 2:11/52.64.71.72.92.97.102.146.157.

158.221

EMBRACES (??) 3:14/2.3.63.64
PRAISED (JUDE) 1:7/6.137.139.159.164.168.173.174
PERSECUTED (JOB) 26:14/17.30.62
SERVANT (??) 1:21/15.21.24.53

She leafed through the Bible to the Book of Philemon in the New Testament. Glancing at the numerical clue – 1:3/1.7 – she found chapter one, verse three.

Now she had a choice.

If Healy was using words rather than characters as his reference point, then she would need the first and seventh words in that verse – 1.7. These were 'Grace' and 'God'.

She frowned. Perhaps he was using characters instead?

She looked up the first and seventh characters in the verse – not counting spaces – and came up with 'G' and 'o'.

Go.

That seemed more promising.

She realised that there was little point in continuing. She needed to find out the biblical names corresponding to *all* the words in the sequence, not just those Fernandes had guessed at. Only then would she know which books in the Bible to look at in order to decipher the message in its entirety.

She needed help.

And she could think of only one person to approach.

She had called ahead. Fortunately, Neve Forrester was also a late worker.

She found her at her desk, forehead cupped in the palm of one hand as she wrote steadily on a sheet of paper. A fan whirred in the silence, gently stirring strands of grey hair that had come loose around her face. The only light in the darkened room came from a desk lamp, focused on the letter. The reflected light lent an uncharacteristic softness to the Englishwoman's features, the impression heightened by the fact that she had shed her usual severe jacket to reveal a short-sleeved white blouse.

She waved Persis into a seat before her, but otherwise did not acknowledge her presence.

Persis waited impatiently. Part of her wanted to shake the woman by the shoulders; having to wait in this manner smacked of a Raj-era mentality, the Indian lackey waiting on her mistress's command.

She held her tongue. Forrester was older, used to working in a particular way. There was little point in trying to change her. She knew, from long experience with her father, that that would be an exercise in futility.

Forrester set down her pen. 'How did John's father take the news?'

It was a curious place to start.

Caught off-balance, Persis blinked before replying. 'He was ... devastated. He told me that his son had changed after his experiences in the war. The time he spent in the Italian POW camp altered him. I'm digging into that, to see if it might have any bearing on his decision to steal the Dante manuscript.'

'To get back at the Italians, you mean?' Forrester considered this. 'It might be one explanation, I suppose.'

'You don't sound convinced.'

'That's because I'm not. To steal a manuscript as a way to get back at a whole nation would seem the act of a disturbed mind. That wasn't my impression of John Healy.'

Persis pressed on. 'I also met with Franco Belzoni. According to Erin Lockhart, he and Healy argued over access to the manuscript.'

'If they did, it's news to me. I saw them together several times. They seemed amicable. Besides, as Curator of Manuscripts, John would have had some say over access, but by no means the last word. The Society's board ruled that Belzoni could view the manuscript. If he and John had a problem, it wasn't brought to my attention.'

'Was Belzoni vetted? Before access was granted?'

'Yes, of course. His credentials are impeccable.'

'What about Erin Lockhart?'

'Erin works for the Smithsonian. Surely, you're not questioning *her* credentials?'

'Not her credentials; just her motives. She told me she's in India to collect artefacts for an exhibition about the independence struggle. But others have claimed that her true motive is to acquire the Dante manuscript. The implication being that she became friendly with Healy in order to convince him to petition the Society to sell the manuscript to the Smithsonian.'

Forrester's expression hardened. 'By "became friendly", I take it you're implying she slept with him. Don't you think you're doing the woman a disservice? Erin Lockhart is highly intelligent and extremely capable. I doubt she'd need to resort to such methods to get her point across. Besides, the Society would hardly hand over its most valuable treasure to the Americans on the say-so of John Healy.'

Persis digested this a moment, then moved on to the real reason she'd come to see the Englishwoman.

Quickly, she brought Forrester up to speed on her attempts at cracking the riddle Healy had left inscribed on his inner thigh. 'I think I'm on the right track. But I need to be sure I've identified the correct biblical books to focus on before applying the rest of the cipher.'

Forrester leaned back in her chair. 'I suppose this explains why he left the Bible behind when he took the manuscript. Did you know that his earliest work was grounded in biblical philology? Interrogating the Bible is one of the oldest applications of the study of ancient languages and our attempts to derive meaning from them. My own doctorate was in such a topic.

'John was a noted scholar in that arena – it's one of the reasons he made such a success of his study of the Tremulous Hand of Worcester. The Tremulous Hand glossed many documents important to Christian doctrine, including the *Historia ecclesiastica gentis Anglorum* – the *Ecclesiastical History of the English People* – by the Venerable Bede, an English Benedictine monk sometimes called the father of English history.' She noticed Persis's expression and said, 'My point, Inspector, is that John spent a lot of time looking at the Bible, its language, its content, and its meaning. I suppose this also explains his later fascination with the Dante manuscript. After all, *The Divine Comedy* attempts to bring to life, in prose, key concepts from Christian theology. Heaven, hell, the rescuing of man's soul from damnation.'

Persis took the King James Bible out of her satchel and set it down before Forrester. She opened her notebook and placed that beside the Bible. 'We think we've identified four of the seven books. An expert opinion would be valuable.'

Forrester's gaze rested on the open notebook. 'Yes. These seem correct. Though, if I remember rightly, the name Ruth might also be interpreted as meaning "companion".'

She abruptly sprang up from her chair and strode to a floor-to-ceiling bookshelf taking up one wall. She looked over the spines, then hopped on a stool and pulled a slim, green-backed volume from the uppermost shelf.

Returning, she showed it to Persis: *Merryweather's Reference Guide to Biblical Characters*.

She settled back in her seat. 'How much do you know about the history of the Bible?'

'Very little. I went to a Catholic school, but I'm not Christian.'

'Zoroastrian?'

'Yes.' She was surprised. Most Britishers would simply have called her a Parsee.

Forrester pushed on. 'The Bible, like most religious texts, came together firstly through oral tradition. The Hebrew Bible – or the Old Testament, as Christians refer to it – was originally written down in Hebrew and its sister language, Aramaic, and first translated into Greek around three hundred years before Christ – this is known as the Old Greek Bible or the Septuagint. The New Testament canon developed over an extended period of time. The term itself arose due to controversy among Christians in the second century as to whether or not the Old Testament should be included in Christian scripture at all. In 382 AD, the Council of Rome set out an authoritative list of books of the Bible and had them translated into Latin – this became the Latin Vulgate Bible, which, to this day, remains the official Bible for the Roman Catholic Church.

'English translations of the Bible began around the 1300s with *Wycliffe's Bible*, a translation into Middle English by a group of pre-Protestant Reformation scholars. A 1525 translation by William Tyndale, an English scholar executed for his part in the Reformation, is generally regarded as the first printed English version of the New Testament.

'Following the English Reformation, the Puritans – a faction of the church unhappy that certain Roman Catholic practices continued to be tolerated – pushed for a new translation. In 1604, King James I of England met with church leaders to formalise a translation that would conform fully to the ecclesiology of the Church of England. The result was the King James Bible.'

Talking about her passion made her seem a different person, Persis thought.

'At any rate, let us see if we can solve your riddle.'

Twenty minutes later, she had updated Persis's notes:

AFFECTIONATE (PHILEMON) 1:3/1.7
HONOURED (TIMOTHY) 1:2/5.8
FRIEND (RUTH) 2:11/52.64.71.72.92.97.102.146.157.
158.221
EMBRACES (HABAKKUK) 3:14/2.3.63.64
PRAISED (JUDE) 1:7/6.137.139.159.164.168.173.174
PERSECUTED (JOB) 26:14/17.30.62
SERVANT (OBADIAH) 1:21/15.21.24.53

'That's as best as I can guess. Now what?'

'Now, I apply the cipher.' Persis walked around the desk, leaning over Forrester, and turned the Bible to the Book of Timothy in the New Testament. 'There's two of them,' she muttered. 'Two books of Timothy.'

'Start with the first,' suggested Forrester.

The numerical sequence that went with the word 'Honoured' – corresponding to the Book of Timothy – was 1:2/5.8. Chapter one, verse two, followed by the fifth and eighth characters in that verse. Applying this to 1 Timothy, she arrived at 'T' and 'o'. *To.*

She applied the same sequence to 2 Timothy but got 'm' and 'h'. She decided to stick with the results of the First Epistle to Timothy.

So the first two words of the riddle were *Go To.*

Excitement churned through her. She could see the far shore.

Fifteen minutes later, she had all seven words written out before her, arranged into a sentence in the order that Healy had written down his clues:

GO TO MOONSTARERS HOME
SPECTARE SUB LUNA

'What does it mean?'

Forrester was silent a moment, then said, 'Look under the moon.'

'What?'

'The last three words are Latin. *Spectare sub luna*. They mean "look under the moon".'

Persis frowned. 'Do you know who *Moonstarer* is?'

'No. It's not a name I'm familiar with.'

'Is it biblical?'

'Definitely not.'

They gazed at the page, before Persis turned away. 'Dammit.'

Forrester watched her pace the room. 'You didn't expect John to make it easy for you, did you?'

Persis stopped. 'I don't know what to expect from him. I just feel . . .'

'You're frustrated. Don't be. For what it's worth, I think you've done an excellent job so far.'

The praise took her by surprise. 'Thank you,' she mumbled. A silence. 'I should probably sleep on it.'

'That sounds like a good idea.'

At the door, she felt an inexplicable urge to turn and say something. 'We've met before, you know.' Forrester gave her a quizzical look. 'I came here with my father a few years ago. His name is Sam Wadia. He runs a bookstore.'

Forrester tilted her chin. 'I remember him. An uncompromising man. He was in a wheelchair. There was no way to get it up the portico steps, so he paid a gang of coolies to carry him – and his chair – to the top. Cursed them out every step of the way, as I recall.'

'That sounds like my father.'

'You looked a lot different then.'

'I wasn't dressed like this,' said Persis, indicating her uniform.

'And how has dressing like *that* been for you?'

'It—' She felt a sudden overwhelming desire to tell Forrester the truth, the plain unvarnished truth. 'It's been a choppy ride.'

'Well, if you wanted easy, then you should have stayed at home and baked biscuits.'

Persis gave a wry smile. 'May I ask you a personal question?'

'I doubt I could stop you, even if I wanted to.'

'Why did you never remarry? Never have a family ...' She tailed off, suddenly unsure of herself.

'You want to know if it was worth it?' Forrester's face had grown still. 'The poet William Blake once wrote: "Some are born to sweet delight, some are born to endless night." I haven't yet worked out which category I fit into.'

'But how do you do it?'

The response was instant. 'Clarity of purpose.'

Persis nodded. 'Do you think Healy had clarity of purpose?'

'Yes. I believe he did.'

'What *was* his purpose?'

Forrester flashed a bloodless grin. 'Now *that*, Inspector, is the question.'

26

The slum kids were in the shop – crowded into the rear, sitting cross-legged on the floor, spread into the surrounding aisles; a few even perched on the shorter bookcases around the battered old sofa where her father was holding court. He was reading to them, his gruff voice rolling sonorously into the shop's corners.

She'd always marvelled at the way he could hold them captive, every head turned towards him, not a murmur in the silence. The fact that such a charitable impulse commanded him at all continued to astonish her.

For the past decade, once a week, he would invite in children from the local slum, and read to them. Word had spread, and what had begun as a trickle had become a flood.

Now, there was barely space to move in the store on such evenings.

He'd kept at it even during the war years.

That had been an odd time. She was not yet eighteen when the British Raj had declared war on Nazi Germany. By the end of the war, two million Indian soldiers had been committed to the effort, though you wouldn't know it, judging by the newsreels.

The country itself had been at odds. Once it became clear that British promises of greater autonomy in return for Indian military assistance were not going to materialise, Gandhi's Congress had launched their Quit India movement. He'd promptly been thrown in prison, along with thousands of his contemporaries.

Others, like Subhash Chandra Bose, had splintered from the Congress, joining the Germans and the Japanese; Bose had gone so far as to raise Indian legions to fight against the Allies.

In Bombay, Persis – along with Emily and Dinaz – but not Jaya, who refused to countenance manual labour – had trained for Air Raid Precaution duties. She'd loved the feeling of being involved in the war effort, not to mention the ARP helmet they were all issued with.

Looking back, she knew she'd behaved childishly, giggling along with Emily at the handsome foreign soldiers that alighted in Bombay in a constant stream, on their way to various theatres of war.

A year into the conflict, the son of her father's friend, a boy named Harish – a boy she'd known – was killed at Libya. Perhaps that was the moment her perceptions had begun to change. Harish was just one of many fighting for an alien power that refused him basic rights in his own homeland, yet asked of him the ultimate sacrifice to protect *their* way of life.

Perhaps that was also the moment a splinter had worked its way into their friendship.

Sam was reading from *The Little Prince* by Antoine de Saint-Exupéry, translating it as he went. One of her own favourites as a child.

Aunt Nussie stood from her seat behind the counter and approached her, signalling her to step outside. Persis knew that Nussie, not to be outdone by her father, had taken to bringing food over for the children. Her aunt didn't do things by halves, so the children ended up taking back their body weight in rice and dhansak.

'They're working you too hard,' said Nussie, examining her face. 'It's past eight. Again.'

'No one is *working* me. I'm choosing to work.'

'When are you going to learn that there's more to life than your career?'

Persis rolled her eyes. She didn't have the strength to go over the same old arguments with her aunt.

'At any rate, there's something I wanted to discuss with you.'

She felt a twinge in the region of her kidneys. Expecting her aunt to present her with another marriage proposal, she began to protest, but Nussie cut her off. 'Reports have reached me that you were spotted at the Wayside Inn two nights ago. In the company of a white man.'

Her mouth flapped open. Her cheeks felt hot. 'Who told you that?'

'It doesn't matter who told me. Is it true?'

It was insufferable to be subjected to this sort of cross-examination. Aunt Nussie had a way of making her feel fifteen. 'Who I have dinner with is no one's business but my own.'

'That's where you're wrong, young lady. Have you any idea how it reflects on the rest of us if you're out gallivanting with a white man?'

'I was not *gallivanting*.'

'Then what were you doing?'

She steeled herself. 'If you must know, it was an official meeting. My companion was Archie Blackfinch.'

Nussie's face darkened. 'The Englishman? The one you brought home with you?'

'I didn't bring him home. He was working with me on a case and it was late and so I invited him in to eat with us.'

'Do the pair of you always end up eating together while working on a case?'

'For God's sake, we're just colleagues! Didn't your spies tell you I was in uniform at the Wayside?'

Nussie was silent a moment. 'Yes. That was mentioned.' She sniffed, somewhat mollified. 'Just remember, Persis, not everyone is as enlightened as I am. I say this for *your* benefit. A woman's reputation can only be lost once.'

The shop's door chimes jangled. An enormous bouquet of flowers wobbled towards them. At the last instant, Krishna's head emerged from around the bouquet.

Her father's manservant grinned at her. 'These arrived for you earlier.' He thrust the flowers at Persis.

Daffodils. Her favourite.

She saw that Aunt Nussie had crossed her arms and fixed her with a *look*.

'They're not from Archie,' she protested. 'He's not the type to send flowers. And besides, we're not . . .' She tailed off as she noticed a small envelope tucked into the centre of the bouquet.

'Hold this.' She handed the flowers back to Krishna, plucked out the envelope, and took out the card inside. There was no name. Only an inscription.

> *So, we'll go no more a roving*
> *So late into the night,*
> *Though the heart be still as loving,*
> *And the moon be still as bright.*

Her heart stopped, performing a complicated somersault inside her ribcage. 'Byron,' she breathed.

'Byron?' Nussie repeated. 'Another Englishman? My God, Persis! What's wrong with you?'

Persis shook her head, unable to explain.

She took the flowers from Krishna and stumbled back inside and upstairs to her bedroom, where she locked the door, threw the flowers on to the bed, sat down at her dresser, and read the card again.

The words were from a poem by Lord Byron: 'So We'll Go No More a Roving'.

Zubin. It could be no one else. The memory lurched out of her, coughed up like a dead bird from a cat's gullet. It was the poem he'd read to her before kissing her that night.

They'd both adored Byron. And through him they'd come to adore each other.

Or so she'd thought.

He'd betrayed her, stolen into the interior spaces of her heart, then broken it in a way she'd never have thought possible.

And now he was back.

What message was he trying to convey by sending her these flowers, this poem?

She sat there, motionless, staring at her reflection in the dresser mirror.

Finally, she stood, took off her uniform, showered, changed into a nightgown, then went into the living room.

Her father and Krishna arrived. Krishna served dinner, as Sam, flushed from his exertions, clattered about the room. His face was drawn, she noted. 'How are you feeling?'

'The next person who asks me that I shall shoot in the foot.'

'You don't have a gun, Papa.'

'I'll buy one.'

Dinner was rice and lamb. 'Nussie tells me someone sent you flowers today.'

She gave a puff of annoyance. 'Are you going to lecture me too?'

'Why would I tell you anything? I mean, it's not as if I'm your father.' He raised an eyebrow. 'You're a grown woman, but that doesn't mean you're not a child.'

'That literally makes no sense!'

'What I mean is that you're not experienced in the ways of the world. In the ways of men.'

'Was Mother when you eloped with *her*?'

He stiffened, his moustache crinkling as his lips bent into a grimace. 'We were in love,' he muttered. 'And we were both Parsees.'

'You caused a scandal.'

'Nothing compared to the scandal of my only daughter carrying on with an Anglo.'

'I'm not carrying on with anyone!' She had the overwhelming urge to thump the table. Instead, she stood, glared at him, then stomped back to her bedroom.

Half an hour later, she heard his wheelchair creak by. It stopped outside the door. She could practically see him contemplating knocking. During her childhood, he'd never been able to sleep without first checking on her; even now, he hated going to bed on an argument.

Truth be told, so did she.

But he'd crossed a line, as had Aunt Nussie . . . She was almost twenty-eight! This was modern India, not the Dark Ages. They had no right to be so overbearing, to – to . . . *interfere*.

She heard him wheel away, headed towards his bedroom.

She distracted herself by picking up *The Divine Comedy* and continuing her reading.

Every so often her eyes were drawn back to the flowers, now dumped headfirst into the waste bin. A fist of anger would rise up through her, rapidly followed by an overwhelming desire to call Archie Blackfinch.

The confusion of her feelings unnerved her. Like a basket of snakes let loose inside her, slithering over one another, impossible to grab hold of.

She focused on Dante's description of Hell. Or rather the nine circles of Hell, each one reserved for a particular type of sinner: the pagans, the lustful, the avaricious. Murderers and thugs; heretics and adulterers.

She paused on two descriptions.

The first was the seventh circle, where those who committed suicide ended up, entombed inside trees and fed upon by harpies through all eternity. Her thoughts returned to John Healy.

Why *had* he killed himself?

He was, by all accounts, a Catholic. She knew that to Catholics, suicide was a mortal sin, a sin that denied them access to heaven. So why?

She spent a moment on the eighth circle, the Malebolge, where fraudsters were consigned to torment. Seducers ended up here, forced to march in circles while lashed at by horned demons.

She imagined Zubin here, the lash in her own hand.

She read on.

Having navigated Hell, Dante now found himself in Heaven, in the company of his beloved Beatrice. Heaven – *Paradiso* – was divided by Dante into nine 'spheres'. Visiting the first sphere, he and Beatrice find themselves on the Moon, home to those souls who had broken their holy vows. Beatrice takes the time to explain why the Moon exhibits dark patches. Dante posits a pseudo-scientific explanation, but Beatrice rebuts this with a metaphysical counterargument, involving the use of divine power that affects the apparent luminosity of heavenly bodies.

Persis smiled. She wondered what modern astronomers would make of Beatrice's explan—

She stopped. For a moment, time stood still.

She slipped out of bed, retrieved her notebook, and examined Healy's last clue.

GO TO MOONSTARERS HOME
SPECTARE SUB LUNA

Moonstarers. Healy, a master of languages, had loved riddles and wordplay. One of the oldest forms of wordplay was also the simplest. She realised now why the word *moonstarers* had seemed so familiar.

With growing excitement, she rewrote the line, making one change.

GO TO ASTRONOMERS HOME
SPECTARE SUB LUNA

Moonstarers. *Astronomers*. A perfect anagram.

And there was only one place in Bombay that could be classed as a home to astronomers.

27

She parked under a peepal tree, then walked the rest of the way, approaching the observatory complex from the coastal road. A warm breeze wound in from the Arabian Sea, through a dense barricade of mangroves, ruffling her hair and the collar of her shirt. The thought passed through her that she should have worn her uniform. Too late now. Instead, she'd chosen a one-piece sleeveless cotton romper, in a muted check pattern, together with tennis shoes.

Around her: the chirrup and whirr of insects, the croak of frogs. It was past midnight and the area was deserted, as she knew it would be.

Above, the sky swarmed with stars.

With the establishment of a new facility at Alibaug in 1906, the Colaba Observatory had relinquished many of its duties. But Persis knew, from visits with her father as a child, that the observatory continued to collaborate with its sister facility, gathering useful measurements. Last year, it had earned a brief news splash by capturing seismographic readings from an earthquake in southern China.

The main gate was locked. There was no night-time security guard.

A crumbling, whitewashed wall ran around the complex, housing a series of outbuildings and the observation tower.

She placed one hand on the wall. Warmth absorbed during the day radiated back into her palm.

She wasn't sure exactly what she was looking for, or even that she was in the right place. Back at the apartment, Healy's directive to *go to astronomers' home* had seemed to clearly point to Bombay's only astronomical observatory. Nothing else made sense. But now, out here, in the starlit silence, doubt gnawed away at her.

Nothing for it but to forge ahead.

She found a section of the wall shielded from the road. Pitted and crumbling, it offered numerous hand and toeholds. Within moments, she had clambered up its seven-foot height and dropped to the far side. She landed awkwardly and rolled on to dry grass, stifling the urge to curse.

Rising to her feet, she winced as her ankle murmured a soft complaint, then plunged onwards, recalling what little she remembered of the place.

The Bombay Observatory – as it had originally been known – had been built by the East India Company back in 1826, primarily as a means of supporting shipping at the Bombay port. Geomagnetic and meteorological observations began shortly afterwards. At the turn of the century, stewardship of the observatory fell to the site's first Indian director, Dr Nanabhoy Framji Moos, who'd studied science in Edinburgh, Scotland, and who also happened to be a Parsee, as her father had taken great delight in pointing out to her.

Almost immediately, Moos was faced with an existential dilemma.

In 1900, Bombay had decided to convert its fleet of horse-drawn trams to electric power. Realising that the electromagnetic noise generated by the trams would ruin the magnetic data collected by the observatory, Moos was forced to petition the government to find an alternate site. This he successfully did, and the Alibaug facility was born, some eighteen miles to the south. Bombay's observatory continued to limp along, though it was, by now, a weary foot-soldier to Alibaug's lead.

She walked through the grounds of the complex, heading towards the observatory proper, a whitewashed tower that stood silhouetted against the sky. She'd brought along a torch, but a bright sliver of moon and a sky sprinkled with stars provided more than enough light, washing out the handful of buildings dotted about the place with a ghostly radiance.

She stopped and looked up at the night sky.

Spectare sub luna. Look under the moon.

What could he have meant by that? She was certain that these three words held the key to whatever it was Healy had sent her here to find. Another clue? Another riddle? Or the manuscript itself? . . . Why not? The trail had to end somewhere. This was as good a place as any. A place that few visited, all but ignored by the bustling ant heap that was Bombay . . . and deserted at night – which is probably when Healy had come here.

She walked past the old magnetic observatories, now disused, and only opened up for the occasional school trip or tourist misadventure. Office buildings glimmered under the moonlight, and then she was at the base of the main observatory.

The door was firmly locked.

She cursed under her breath, then walked around it, looking for an opening.

Nothing.

Spectare sub luna. Frustration welled inside her. What was the point of telling her to *look under the moon*? The whole place was 'under' the moon.

She blew out her cheeks in annoyance, then set off on another traverse of the grounds. If Healy had somehow managed to hide something inside one of the buildings here, she would have to return tomorrow, in uniform, brandishing her police ID. In the meantime, all she could do was—

She stopped.

She had just passed by the old well, located away from the main buildings in a quiet corner of the complex. Beside the well was a moon dial. She remembered her father's friend, a staffer at the observatory, rattling on about it with what she had felt, at the time, was undue enthusiasm.

The moon dial – a circular stone slab on a raised column, with a fin-like 'style' rising from its centre – operated on the same principle as a sundial, only it used the light of the moon to cast a shadow that, notionally, would indicate the time. The problem with moon dials, and the reason they hadn't caught on, was that they were only ever accurate on the night of a full moon. After the full moon, a moon dial 'lost' time – running forty-eight minutes slower every night. This was because the sunlit part of the moon's face became smaller after the full moon, so that, by the new moon, it faced entirely away from the earth, resulting in no moonlight at all.

She approached the moon dial.

Standing beside it, she could make out the markings around its circumference: Roman numerals for the hours, and an engraving of Father Time, complete with hourglass and scythe. And above that, running around the style, were the words 'Sub Luna'. A bolt of electricity shot through her.

This had to be it.

She took out her torch and examined the dial and style closely. Nothing. No new information. No clues. No riddles.

She stood and considered the problem, her mind ticking over in the silence.

Spectare sub luna. Look under the moon.

She dropped to her haunches and shone the torch under the dial. Nothing.

She next ran the torch beam down the stone column holding up the dial, and then around its base— There! It would have been easy to miss. A patch of turned earth.

She set down the torch and began to dig, using her hands as shovels. The soil was loose, and within a few minutes, she'd dug almost a foot into the earth. Her fingers scraped over metal. With growing excitement, she scrabbled away the dirt, worked her fingers around the edge of the object, and pulled it loose.

Standing up, she brushed dirt from it, and set it down on the dial.

What she had before her was a heavy metal box, copper in colour, five inches on a side, and three inches deep. The box was artfully engraved, with what looked like Oriental designs. There appeared to be a discernible upper and lower half, marked by a line that went around the object, jagging up into an odd upside-down isosceles trapezoid shape on either side. There was no keyhole. She tried to open it, but it wouldn't budge.

She resisted the urge to smash the thing against the stone moon dial. She was certain the effort would be futile. The object was so solid, she doubted explosives would make a dent.

Tamping down on her frustration, she headed to the compound wall, scaling it quickly, and dropping back out on to the road.

Back in the jeep, she set the box down on the passenger seat, looked at it a moment, then started the engine.

As she was turning the corner of the narrow road, she heard the sound of an engine behind her. The roar intensified, and then, without warning, she was flung forward as a vehicle rammed into the jeep. Her head smacked the steering wheel. A sudden metallic warmth in her mouth.

Blood.

She braked automatically, lurching her body forward again.

Momentarily stunned, she didn't register the man's presence until he was at the passenger door, flinging it open, hands scrabbling for the box.

No.

She gave a short bellow, reached out, and grabbed it. They tussled with it for a moment, then both lost their grip and it fell into the passenger-side footwell.

The man – clad in black, with a balaclava pulled over his face – swung a fist at her, connecting with her jaw. She fell back, spots floating before her eyes.

He bent to the footwell, scrabbling for the box.

She shook off the pain, focusing on her assailant. She cursed herself for not bringing her revolver with her. She was unarmed, against a larger, more powerful—

Unarmed.

No. Not entirely.

She scrabbled in the glovebox over his head, retrieved the switchblade she kept there, snapped it open, and stabbed downwards.

The man bellowed as the knife sank into his shoulder. He let go of the box and jerked backwards, out of the jeep.

She twisted back around, grabbed the wheel, and slammed the accelerator.

In the mirror, she saw her attacker stagger towards his car, then lean against the vehicle, clutching his shoulder.

Minutes later, she was back out on to the safety of the main road.

28

'I suppose I'll be the one paying to repair the dent in the back of your jeep.'

It was the next morning and she was sitting in Roshan Seth's office, watching the SP stand over his desk and pour out two whiskies. He pushed one across towards her. She considered refusing, then picked it up and took a large swallow. The alcohol burned her mouth where she'd bit into the inside of her cheek when her head had struck the steering wheel.

'Why didn't you call me last night?' Seth continued, gazing at her with a mixture of concern and irritation.

'What would have been the point? I was already home.'

'You're being followed. By a man who doesn't think twice about assaulting you to get what he wants. *That's* the point.' He rattled the ice cubes in his glass. 'Any idea who?'

She'd spent the best part of the night thinking about it, with little success. The darkness, his disguise, the speed with which he'd attacked. There was nothing she could point to, no name she could settle on with any degree of certainty.

'I suppose the real question is *why?*' Seth continued. 'Beyond the obvious, I mean.' He waved at the metal box, sat on the desk between them. Its secrets remained intact, having resisted every attempt to open it.

She recalled something Archie Blackfinch had said, that he thought someone had searched John Healy's home *before* they'd arrived there. The only logical conclusion: someone else was on the trail of the manuscript.

Healy's shadowy collaborators.

If she'd needed evidence of their existence, she now had it.

She explained her theory.

Seth sat down, his expression morose. 'As if the situation wasn't bad enough already. I've been fending off the press since the story broke yesterday; now I've got to worry about *your* safety too.'

She bristled. 'You don't have to worry about me.'

'Don't be so touchy. I'd say the same thing if you weren't a woman . . . So what next?'

'I think there's another clue in here.' She indicated the box.

'Agreed. But how do we get to it?'

'I'm working on it.'

'If all else fails, just take it to a blacksmith. Never underestimate the value of brute force.'

'I'd rather not take the chance of destroying whatever's inside.'

'Fine. Just don't wait too long. I've got so many goons chasing me for progress reports, it's as if I died and they're all calling to collect an unpaid debt.'

Back at her desk, she asked Birla and Haq how they'd got on following Franco Belzoni around.

'He spent the afternoon at Bombay University, lecturing.' Birla squinted at his notes. 'Then he had something to eat. A café near the university. Alone. After that, he went to a bar in Opera House. The Eastern Dragon. A real dump, off the tourist trail. He spent three hours in there.'

'What was he doing?'

'At first nothing. Just waiting. Drinking. And then he was joined by another man. They had a long discussion. It got quite heated at one point.'

'What were they talking about?'

'No idea. They were speaking in Italian. At least, I think it was Italian. There was a lot of hand-waving.'

Haq chimed in. 'The other guy was angry. Looked as if he wanted to rip Belzoni's head off.'

'That's an exaggeration,' said Birla. 'But he certainly wasn't happy.'

'What did he look like?'

'Dark hair. Medium build. Angry features.'

'We followed him too,' added Haq.

'You left Belzoni?'

'We split up. We used our initiative.' He shifted his bulk on the edge of her desk. In the office, Haq seemed incapable of standing upright for more than thirty seconds at a time. She wondered how he'd managed to stay on his feet long enough to follow Belzoni around. 'Our mysterious Italian went to the Italian consulate in Cuffe Parade. I followed him in and asked the receptionist who he was. His name is Enrico Mariconti. Senior military attaché at the embassy in Delhi.'

'Why would Belzoni be meeting with a military attaché? And why meet the man in an out-of-the-way bar? Why not meet at the consulate?'

Questions that none of them could answer.

She thought again of last night's attacker. His build ... No. Everything had happened so quickly that she couldn't be sure of details, but she had the impression her attacker was taller than Franco Belzoni. Besides, Belzoni was a renowned academic. As much as he might wish to get his hands on the Dante manuscript, it was unlikely that he'd resort to violence.

Scholars didn't behave like that.

And then she thought of John Healy and realised that any assumptions she might have harboured had long since crumbled to dust.

29

'It's a puzzle box.' Erin Lockhart looked at the metal box, then back up at Persis. 'John gave me one for my birthday. He used to collect them when he was younger. Or so he told me.'

They were sitting in Lockhart's temporary office at the Asiatic Society, which also served as the home of the Bombay Natural History Society. Lockhart had turned up fifteen minutes late to their agreed meeting, not bothering to explain herself or offer an apology.

Persis wondered if the woman was playing mind games.

The ceiling fan was out. The room was unbearably warm, the walls sweating with humidity. Not that Lockhart appeared to notice. The windows remained shut and she sat there, in another sleeveless blouse, seemingly as cool as ice.

They spoke quickly of John Healy's death. Lockhart had been out of Bombay the day before and hadn't known until that moment.

Persis wondered how long it would be before the English scholar's suicide found its way into the newspapers. At least *that* was one thing that was certain now; Raj Bhoomi had sent over his toxicology report. John Healy had died due to an overdose of Tuinal. There was no evidence of foul play. Suicide was Bhoomi's official verdict.

The news briefly punctured Lockhart's balloon of equanimity. The Olympian self-confidence died from her eyes, and she sat there, wreathed in silence. When she spoke again, she said, 'My father always joked that mortality is like kidney stones. If you have to have them, better to get through it quickly. At least John didn't linger.'

She fell silent again. Persis wondered if tears would be forthcoming, but Lockhart didn't seem the type. Besides, according to Lockhart herself, Healy was a lover not a loved one. Tears would be an extravagance.

Persis decided to push on, quickly detailing her efforts in tracking John Healy's last clue, and recovering the strange box. She decided to leave out that she'd been attacked.

'May I?'

Lockhart picked up the box without waiting for an answer. She attempted to twist the upper half through various directions, then turned it over and tried again.

Nothing.

She pointed with her smallest finger at the trapezoid-shaped 'tooth' on either side of the box, made by the dividing line between the two halves. 'The configuration of the join between the upper and lower half is preventing either half from separating from the other, or from being slid open at a diagonal angle.'

'I gathered that,' said Persis impatiently.

Lockhart set the box on the table, then spun it around like a top. 'Sometimes, with these types of puzzle, there's a metal locking pin inside that can be loosened simply by spinning the whole thing around.'

She picked up the box and tried to open it.

Nothing.

She tried spinning it in multiple directions.

Nothing.

She pushed it back across the table in frustration. 'Why don't you just force it open?'

'No. Healy wanted us to *solve* his clues. He was a man of intellect, not brute force. I still believe he *wants* us to find the manuscript.' Changing tack, she said, 'I spoke to Franco Belzoni. He claims there was no friction between him and Healy. He implied that *you're* the one who hasn't been truthful. I've been led to understand that your real agenda in India is to procure the *Divine Comedy* manuscript.'

Lockhart's dark eyes flashed. A moment of uncomfortable silence passed, and then she spoke. 'Well, there's no point denying it, I suppose. Though that's only half right. The Quit India exhibition is real and part of what I'm doing out here pertains to that. But, yes, the main reason I came here is to try and persuade the Society to part with the Dante manuscript. Let's be honest. It's wasted, sitting out here in the middle of nowhere. The Smithsonian is the world's finest museum. A treasure like that doesn't belong in India.'

Anger flared inside Persis. The unthinking manner with which Lockhart spoke about the country. Her automatic assumption that the rightful place of all things of value was in the west. She impaled the American with a glare. 'India was once the richest nation on earth. The country was systematically looted of some of the world's greatest treasures. *The Divine Comedy* is one of the few items that came in the *opposite* direction.' She stopped, hating herself for allowing Lockhart to goad her into a response. A good detective was a poker player, as Seth had reminded her more than once. 'Why didn't you approach the Society directly?'

'I wanted John as an ally first.'

'Is that why you seduced him?'

'No. That just . . . happened.'

Persis paused. 'And what did Healy think of your attempts to manipulate him?'

She shrugged. 'He wasn't keen on helping. But I was bringing him round.'

Persis leaned in. 'Did you know that the sleeping tablets that killed him were manufactured by an American company? Eli Lilly. They're a new product, very difficult to get hold of in India.'

Lockhart's cheeks tightened. 'What exactly are you asking?'

'Did *you* give him the tablets?'

'Yes. What of it? He needed them, I had a load with me – I sometimes have trouble sleeping when I'm abroad.'

'You don't sound very upset by the fact that *your* tablets killed him.'

'I didn't realise I'd need to put on a performance for you. Should I weep a little? Beat my breasts?'

They stared at each other, neither willing to give ground.

Persis stood, sweeping her cap up from the desk. 'Don't leave town.'

30

Her next appointment, late in the afternoon, was at the Ratan Tata Institute on Hughes Road, in the upmarket area of Kemps Corner. She knew the locale; a thriving Parsee community had long ago settled there. The Institute itself was just a stone's throw from Doongerwadi, the fenced-off tract of forested land on which the Towers of Silence were located. One day, her own corpse would be laid out atop one of the stone towers – known as dakhmas and left for the vultures there.

The Ratan Tata Institute, with its iconic RTI sign perched atop the roof, had been around since the late 1920s, a philanthropic endeavour aimed at helping destitute Parsee women. Now, the Institute ran a soup kitchen famed across the city for its Parsee cuisine.

She found Fernandes waiting for her outside the office of Dr Akash Sharma, Francine Kramer's therapist.

The office, located on the fifth floor, was tastefully decorated, with a comfortable sofa, a marble-topped coffee table, shelves stacked with vases, and a wing chair in which Sharma sat, scribbling on a notepad. A wide man with a comfortable belly, a round face, and curly grey hair, he waved them on to the sofa without looking up.

When he finally turned his attention to them, his gaze was searching. 'I was very sorry to hear of Francine's death. Under normal circumstances, I wouldn't be able to reveal anything about her discussions with me. But, given how her life ended, I'd like to help in any way that I can.'

'How long were you treating her?' asked Fernandes.

'She came to me some four years ago. I run a clinic here pro bono, for women with emotional difficulties. Usually it's domestic violence, abandonment, post-natal depression. Francine's problems were a lot more complicated. To be frank, I don't really know how much help I was to her. It took her a long time to open up. Even then, her attendance was erratic. She'd disappear for long stretches of time, and then return of her own accord.'

'What exactly was she suffering from?' asked Persis.

He rubbed the side of his nose. 'Francine was harbouring dark secrets, and they corroded her from the inside out. Her real name wasn't Francine Kramer. She was born in Latvia, a village called Emburga. Her name was Katya Edelberg, and she was Jewish.' He shifted in his seat. 'At the age of seventeen, she was taken by the Nazis and placed in the Latvian concentration camp at Jungfernhof before being transferred to another concentration camp at Salaspils. This was around late 1941, when Hitler's plan for the conquest and ethnic cleansing of Central and Eastern Europe was in full swing.

'Millions of Slavs were murdered. Mass shootings, starvation, extermination through labour. In the worst incident, twenty-five thousand Jews from Riga were murdered in two days in the Rumbula Forest. I read an article about it last year.' His mouth bent into a grimace of distaste. 'For the next two years, Francine – Katya – was used as a sex slave at Salaspils. At some point, she became pregnant. The child wasn't aborted. When it was born, it was taken from her.' He paused. 'She was told that the child, a boy, was to be cared for at a medical institution. She later discovered that the institution was being run by a Nazi doctor carrying out illegal medical experiments on human subjects. Children, to be precise. She never saw the child again.

'Francine survived the war. But her mind, unfortunately, didn't make it through intact. She suffered trauma that few of us can truly comprehend. That trauma became monsters lurking inside her, climbing up from the darkness whenever she closed her eyes. They chased her all the way out here, to Bombay.' He leaned back, took a cherrywood pipe from his pocket, tamped tobacco into it, then lit it. 'That really is all there is to it.'

Persis absorbed the information. Francine's solitude, the sadness picked up on by those who knew her, now made sense. 'Did she mention anything about a recent man in her life, possibly a lover?'

He frowned. 'Francine found it impossible to develop normal relations with men. Her experience in that Nazi camp warped her ideas of love and sex. She treated her body as an instrument, nothing more. She slept with men for money; just enough to survive.'

Fernandes's broad face crumpled in confusion. 'But why would she continue to allow herself to be abused? The war ended years ago.'

'It's difficult to explain. It's the same reason women who have been abused at home keep returning to their partner. Guilt, self-loathing, a raft of complex emotions at the core of our psyche.' He puffed on his pipe.

Persis lingered on the awful perfection of his logic. Could it be true?

At least Sharma's story explained one thing: the tattoo on Francine's breast that she'd tried to remove through burning. She recalled now reading about female concentration camp inmates who had been branded by the Nazis in that way. 'Is there anything at all you can tell us, anything that might help?'

He thought before answering. 'A few weeks ago, she came to me. There was something different about her. Something had fired her up. She told me about a recurring dream she'd been having. In the dream, a Nazi, a senior man, had walked into the establishment where she worked. She recognised him because he'd once attended the camp where she'd been held in Latvia.

'Of course, he was now masquerading under a new identity – like all the other Nazis on the run, I suppose. In the dream, she seduced him, then convinced him to see her outside of the club, at her home. She wasn't entirely sure, you see. She wanted to keep talking to him, get him to reveal something that would give her some certainty as to his identity.' He stopped.

'And then?'

He shrugged. 'And then nothing.'

Persis blinked. Her stomach had clenched of its own accord. 'You realise she wasn't talking about a dream?'

He pulled the pipe from his mouth, ran a thumb over his lower lip. 'I considered that possibility.'

'Then why didn't you alert the authorities?'

'What would I have said? That my emotionally unwell patient *may* have seen a Nazi in a Nariman Point bar? Besides, it would have violated patient–doctor confidentiality.'

'And instead, Francine is now dead.'

He stared at her with calm eyes, but said nothing.

She reined in her anger. It would do no good. 'Did she describe this man? The Nazi from her "dream"?'

'Yes. Tall, broad, heavy-set. Black hair. And a long scar running across his left cheek.'

Outside, she spoke to Fernandes without looking at him. 'I think she was trying to trap him. Her Nazi.'

'What if she was mistaken?' muttered Fernandes.

'If she was mistaken, would she have ended up dead?' Persis glanced at a woman waiting in reception, unassuming, petite, eyes affixed to the floor. Cowed. That was the word she was looking for.

A drumbeat of anger pounded in her chest.

A world commanded by men, where misogyny was par for the course, where women like Francine Kramer were abused, then murdered on a whim.

It would not stand. It *could* not stand.

She checked her watch. She had an appointment with Frank Lindley in just over an hour.

'Go to Le Château des Rêves. Ask about this mysterious Mr Grey. He should be easy enough to recall. A man with a scar like that.' She locked eyes with him. 'And if they try and run you around, tell them that the full weight of the Indian Police Service will follow unless they cooperate. Tell them this isn't just about Francine's murder any more. Harbouring a Nazi fugitive is an international crime.'

31

Frank Lindley's office had recently been aired and cleaned, which was more than could be said for the man himself. If anything, he looked sweatier and more dishevelled than the last time she'd been here.

The clock on the wall chimed softly. Six o'clock. Where had the day gone?

After the meeting with Sharma, she'd stayed on at the Ratan Tata Institute canteen to eat, the first solid meal she'd had all day.

The hour to herself gave her a chance to compose her thoughts.

The horror of Francine Kramer's death and the past that Sharma had revealed beat away at her like a moth against a windowpane. The Healy investigation may be all that mattered to her seniors, but, for her, Kramer's murder had taken on just as great a significance. Whoever Mr Grey was, he couldn't be permitted to simply murder a resident of the city and walk away unscathed.

And if he was indeed a Nazi, then he was probably a murderer many times over.

Lindley jolted her back to the present. 'I managed to find a German guard who served at Vincigliata from August 1943 through to March 1944. He claims to have been in charge of John Healy's cell.'

Excitement quickened inside her.

She waited as Lindley squinted at a chit before him, then dialled a number with his sausage fingers on the black Stromberg

Carlson. He asked for an outside line, waited to be connected, then spoke briefly in German, before handing the phone to Persis.

'I don't speak German.'

He sniffed. 'I hadn't realised I'd have to act as translator, too. Perhaps I should have charged more.'

Christian Fuchs was a native Berliner who'd managed to avoid the worst of the war thanks to a congenital heart defect that consigned him to less stressful duties than having to weather bombs and bullets on the front line. These duties included serving as a guard in various POW camps. His record showed that he had never served in a concentration camp.

After the war, he'd retired to the beautiful, violin-making town of Füssen in Bavaria, where he now worked as a hospital orderly.

'Yes, I remember Healy,' he said, in response to Persis's question. 'The famous scholar. We used to talk about his work. Or at least, I liked to listen to him. I didn't understand much of what he was talking about. But he spoke beautiful German.'

'When did he arrive?'

'Around September 1943. I remember, because I had only been there a month. We were told to take good care of him, even though he was of a lower rank. All the others there were of a much higher rank.'

'Take care of him? Are you saying that Healy wasn't tortured at Vincigliata?'

'Not to my knowledge. I mean, it could have happened when they took him away.'

Her whirling thoughts stopped. 'What do you mean?'

'Well, Herr Healy was taken away one month after arriving with us.'

Seconds passed. She could hear her own breathing. 'Are you sure you translated that properly?' she asked Lindley.

'Are you questioning my German?' He coughed, nicotine rattling around his lungs.

'Why was he taken away? To where?'

'I don't know,' continued Fuchs. 'A senior Nazi arrived, a Sturmbannführer. He was Waffen-SS, so we didn't ask too many questions. He went into Healy's cell and spoke with him. When he'd finished, he came out and told me he would be taking him.'

'Then why does Healy's prison record at Vincigliata show him as being present there from September 1943 to June 1944? Almost ten months?'

'I don't know. You would have to ask Pepe. Salvatore Pepe. He was the camp's adjutant, the chief administrator. He kept all our records.'

She paused. 'One last question. What was the name of the man who came to take Healy?'

Fuchs ransacked his memory. 'I think his name was Bruner. Sturmbannführer Matthias Bruner.'

The bookstore, to her surprise, was quiet. She glanced at her watch. A quarter to eight. Unusual for her father to retire so early. She hoped he was feeling well.

She considered going straight upstairs, but something had been gnawing away at her on the drive over from Bombay University. Something she'd remembered.

She entered the shop, set her cap on the front counter, then walked towards the rear.

The aisles here were shrouded in a ghostly darkness, the light falling in from the front windows swallowed by the gloom. Not that she needed the light; she could have found her way here in pitch-black.

She reached the sofa at the back of the shop and turned on a single low-watt bulb. It flickered, then shivered to life with a hum.

For a moment, she contemplated falling on to the sofa and simply closing her eyes. A sudden tiredness had infected her; her limbs felt heavy, as if she were walking around in a suit of armour, a medieval knight in search of the Holy Grail.

Not yet. There was still work to do.

She walked along the aisles, towards the section of books her father kept on prominent historical figures. She quickly found what she was looking for.

It was entitled, simply, *Leonardo da Vinci*, a blue-bound edition with gilt lettering on the front board and spine. Inside: hundreds of coloured plates and text illustrations.

She'd thumbed through the edition many times.

Like so many others before her, da Vinci's life fascinated her, the polymath with the mind of a magpie, a genius to rival the greatest thinkers in human history. Painter, sculptor, architect, engineer, astronomer, anatomist, naturalist, mathematician.

But it was in his capacity as inventor that Persis now sought Leonardo's help.

The brilliant Florentine had filled notebook after notebook with his musings for inventions, many of them years ahead of their time, devices ranging from parachutes and flying craft to strange cannons and portable footbridges for use by soldiers on the march. What really interested her were da Vinci's many curios, throwaway designs for artefacts that he had invented simply because it amused him to do so.

Artefacts that included puzzles.

The idea had come to her as she had sat in the Ratan Tata Institute, a memory from childhood that had pierced her with knife-like clarity – reading about da Vinci with her mother. Sanaz had infected her with many of her passions: music, a love of books, and a healthy respect for science and those who practised it.

She flicked through the pages.

To her disappointment, there was nothing in the book resembling the box she now had in her possession.

And then she came across something the author had labelled as the 'da Vinci Ball Bearing Puzzle'. The illustration showed a small boat-shaped block of wood, hollowed out at the top. Two ball bearings had been set into grooves in the hollow. The aim of the puzzle was to somehow juggle the ball bearings into pits on either side of the block. As a puzzle, there really wasn't much to it . . . An idea sent up a flare.

Ball bearings.

She sat down on the sofa and held the puzzle box in the palm of her left hand, staring closely at the enigmatic join between the upper and lower halves.

No keyhole. No way to simply slide it open.

Which meant there was some sort of locking mechanism inside preventing that from happening. If it wasn't metal pins, might it not be ball bearings?

She held the box to her ear and shook it.

Nothing.

She then held it with her right hand, lifted it up, and smacked it hard against the palm of her left hand.

Nothing. She did this three more times, turning it through ninety degrees each time so that she was focusing on another of the four corners.

Nothing.

Frustrated, she considered the problem for a second. Then she turned the box over, and repeated the procedure. On the second thump, she heard a tiny snick.

Her pulse quickened.

She fiddled with the box, pulling the upper half in various directions. Her initial attempts met with resistance, and then, suddenly, as she pulled along its diagonal axis, the top slid away, to reveal a grooved inner section at the centre of which lay a cavity.

A ball bearing was nestled in a small hole in one corner of the box's lower half. In the corresponding corner of the other half was another hole. At the bottom of the hole in the upper half was a tiny strip of metal.

It was now easy to see how the mechanism worked.

Two tiny magnets in the two holes. A single ball bearing. When inside one hole, the ball bearing acted as a lock, ensuring that the two halves were securely fastened together. But give it a good thump in the right place and the ball bearing would drop away from its magnet and fall into the opposite, *deeper* hole, releasing the catch.

Simple, but fiendishly difficult to solve.

She focused on the revealed cavity, just two inches in diameter. Nestled there was a folded piece of paper.

She picked it out, set down the box, then opened the paper.

Written on it, in Healy's hand, were the words:

> *Now was the hour that wakens fond desire*
> *In men at sea, and melts their thoughtful heart,*
> *Who in the morn have bid sweet friends farewell,*
> *And pilgrim newly on his road with love*
> *Thrills, if he hears the vesper bell from far,*
> *That seems to mourn the dying day.*

She'd seen these words before. Recently. In the translation of *The Divine Comedy* she'd just finished skimming. It was one of the many passages that had lodged like splinters in her brain. Dante's vivid prose, his descriptions of what awaited Man, had crept under her defences.

The real question was: *why* had Healy written out another passage from Dante's masterwork . . .?

A noise jerked her head up. Was that the front door? She'd been concentrating so fiercely that she'd blotted out everything else.

She pushed herself off the sofa, walked around the aisle blocking her view of the front of the shop, and padded towards the door. Silence unfurled around her, but there was a quality to it now that prickled the base of her neck.

She stopped yards before her father's counter. The street outside was deserted.

Perhaps it was nothi—

The sound of feet behind her. She turned, just as a figure charged towards her from behind a tall bookshelf, clad in black, a balaclava covering the face.

She reacted without thinking, pulling out her revolver and firing in one fluid movement. The shot cracked loudly in the semi-darkness.

The figure bore her to the floor, knocking the breath from her, the revolver slipping from her grasp. The man – a frantic part of her brain was sure that it *was* a man – sat astride her, his weight bearing down on her. A flash at the corner of her eye, and then a fist connected with the top of her skull. She was momentarily stunned.

Hands scrabbled at her clothing. A thought pierced the haze: was she being *assaulted*?

Ever since she'd put on the uniform, her aunt had told her that she would be raped in the line of duty and begged her to quit before it was too late. Perhaps she'd be pleased that her prediction had finally come to pass.

So easy to quit, to stop struggling. To just lay back and let it happen.

But she'd never quit anything in her life.

The realisation hit her that her assailant *wasn't* assaulting her. He was methodically searching her pockets. Looking for the chit she'd recovered from the puzzle.

The same man who'd attacked her outside the observatory.

No!

Her grasping fingers closed around the revolver. She lifted her arm and fired.

The bullet hit him square in the chest. He rocked back, then lashed out, smashing the gun away. A second swipe and he'd knocked her back into semi-consciousness. She felt his hands close around her throat. Her legs kicked as she pulled at his grip, then flailed her fists at his arms. Might as well have been striking stone.

The sounds of her own choking reached her ears. The room began to revolve around her; her vision clouded . . .

The tinkle of the door chimes, then the sound of rapidly approaching footsteps. Her attacker cried out, then fell away.

She could breathe again. She was pulled into a seated position, where she gulped in great lungfuls of air.

A man crouched on his haunches beside her, staring intently at her with concern.

She focused on him. Shock burned through her.

'Persis!' said Zubin Dalal. 'Are you okay?'

32

'This is becoming a habit. A bad one.' Seth stared at her with a mixture of sympathy and annoyance.

It was eight the next morning, and Persis was sitting in the SP's office, in uniform, with a thumping headache and a bruised throat. Swallowing was difficult, as was talking.

She'd just finished recounting to him the events of the previous night. They remained at the forefront of her thoughts, raw and painful.

Moments after the attack in the shop and the arrival of Zubin Dalal, she'd picked herself off the floor and checked on her attacker.

Zubin had hit him over the head with a cosh.

But the man wasn't just unconscious. He was dead.

So, her eyes *hadn't* deceived her. She knew that she hadn't missed; her second shot had struck her assailant in the chest. Somehow, he'd kept going, powered by adrenalin.

Ultimately, the bullet had done its work.

Breathing deeply, she'd knelt beside the corpse, then reached under the chin and pulled off the balaclava.

A gasp escaped her.

Before her lay the Englishman, James Ingram.

Now, sat before Seth, the questions continued to multiply.

Why had Ingram been following her around? Why had he attacked her?

It made no sense.

Ingram was a writer. No story was worth acting in such a manner. Unless ... Could Ingram have been Healy's accomplice? Had Healy betrayed him? It would explain a lot, including why Ingram had turned up in Bombay a month ago.

She imagined the pair of them plotting to steal the manuscript: Healy, the inside man, Ingram, there to provide support ... But once the deed was done, had Healy charted his own course? Hidden the manuscript, instead of handing it over to Ingram? Why? A change of heart, perhaps? Or something else?

Her head hurt from fruitless speculation. Better to stick to the facts.

'What do we know about this Ingram?' Seth's voice dragged her back to the present.

'Only what he told me. All of which can now be discounted.'

Seth knuckled his temple. The current turn of events had only added to his woes. 'Maybe something in his past can shed some light on where Healy has hidden that blasted manuscript.'

She nodded mechanically.

He continued to stare at her. 'Are you okay?'

She stared at the wall.

'You know, in my entire career, I've never shot anyone. Barely even had to take out my gun in anger. You've now killed two men in the space of a few weeks. I can't claim to know what that feels like, but I *can* say this: they both deserved it.' He unfolded himself from his seat then perched on the edge of the desk before her. 'You have the makings of a fine officer, Persis. If you were a man, they'd be pinning medals on you, grooming you for command. That isn't the world we live in. Instead, they're sharpening their knives. If you don't find that manuscript, they're going to come for us both.'

A bouquet of flowers was waiting on her desk, with a note.

'What's this?' she asked, glaring at Birla. 'I don't need flowers. I'm not in hospital.'

'Don't look at me. I've never given my own wife flowers. Not even at our wedding.'

Haq squashed a chutney sandwich into his mouth. 'Not guilty,' he burped.

There was a note with the flowers.

Can we meet? Z.

The previous night returned with a horrible wrench, like a rogue wave capsizing a rowboat.

Zubin.

In all that had happened, she'd barely had time to register his presence. Seconds after he'd charged into the shop and knocked Ingram cold, her father had arrived, clattering down in his wheelchair with a semi-comatose Krishna at the tiller. The gunshots had awoken them both, dozing in the upstairs living room.

Having ascertained the lay of the land, Sam insisted on waking up Aziz, who lived ten minutes away.

The doctor had given her a quick once-over, despite her insistence that she was fine. Shining a penlight into her eyes and gently palpating her skull, he'd declared that there appeared to be no serious damage.

'You're a lucky young woman,' he'd told her.

Aunt Nussie had turned up moments later, though no one appeared to have called her. She took one look at the scene and launched into a passionate diatribe against the police service, urging Persis, once again, to consider if not her own safety, then the sanity of those around her. What could she gain by persisting in this perverse desire to wander about the city being bludgeoned and shot at by criminals?

'She's the one who did the shooting,' Sam pointed out.

Nussie ignored him.

And ten minutes after *that*, Archie Blackfinch had arrived. He'd come in his official capacity, but once he discovered exactly what had transpired, he'd asked her to step outside.

In the warm night air, he stared down at her from behind his spectacles. 'Are you alright?'

'Why does everyone keep asking me that?'

'Because we're concerned. Because we care.'

She hugged herself, and focused on Akbar, who'd followed them out into the alley and was rubbing himself against her ankles. Less out of sympathy, she thought, and more because it was time for his evening meal.

'You're lucky he wasn't armed. He could have shot first.'

'But he didn't. *I* did.'

Silence. A bicycle came barrelling down the alley, forcing them to step backwards. 'Who was the, ah, gentleman who saved you?'

'He didn't *save* me.'

'That's not the story he's telling in there.'

She turned on him so quickly that he was forced to take a step back. Her face was rigid with anger . . . and then the fire went out of her eyes. It was hardly Blackfinch's fault that Zubin had shown up, that she was now in the insufferable position of being indebted to him.

What the hell was he doing here?

As if invoked by the mere thought, the door behind them opened and Zubin Dalal walked out into the night.

Her heart gave a little bound.

He'd hardly changed. That same insouciant moustache, the merry eyes, the black hair slicked back over a neatly shaped skull. He was a small man, barely the same height as her, but impeccably dressed in a grey double-breasted suit. He moved with the grace of a ballerina, and smiled as if the devil himself had put an arm around his shoulder and told him he could do as he pleased. A black homburg was clutched between the manicured fingers of his right hand.

'It's about time I took my leave,' he said.

Persis said nothing. His eyes stayed on her a moment, then he turned and extended a hand to Blackfinch. 'Zubin Dalal. I'm an old friend of the family.'

'Archimedes Blackfinch. Most people call me Archie. I'm a forensics specialist with the Metropolitan Police Service in London. Currently deputed to work with the IPS.'

They shook hands.

'Pleased to meet you, Archie. Will you be needing anything further from me?'

'No. I think we have the material facts.'

Zubin nodded, then returned his attention to Persis. 'Perhaps you and I could talk tomorrow?'

'We have nothing to talk about.'

He seemed about to reply, then smiled instead. He set his hat on his head, tipped the brim, and bade them goodnight. They watched him walk along the alley and clamber into a black Studebaker. His arm hung out of the window, tapping a rhythm on the driver's side door as the car idled. Moments later, he drove off with a screech of tires.

'Intriguing character,' said Blackfinch. 'How fortunate that he was visiting at just the right time.' The question behind his words lingered in the air.

She knew that Blackfinch was an intelligent man. He could sense something was up. She wondered if it was like alley dogs, some sort of pheromone in the air.

She turned to him. A part of her wanted to embrace him, to feel his warmth against her, to acknowledge the fact that she felt good in his company. That, in the whole shitty business of policing, he was the one man who'd treated her simply as another officer and not a symbol of progress or an unwanted embarrassment. A sudden, perverse desire swelled inside her ... As if sensing her thoughts, Aunt Nussie came barrelling out, breasting the night air like a seahorse. Placing a protective arm around her shoulder, she steered Persis back into the store. 'Let's get you out of uniform and into the shower. And then a nice hot meal.'

Resistance pulsed through her ... and was gone. She surrendered.

Behind them, Archie Blackfinch stuck his hands in his pockets and watched her walk away, the light from the street lamp reflecting dully from his spectacles.

Now, sat at her desk, she wondered if she shouldn't have taken a moment to speak with him.

She could sense the Englishman's increasing bewilderment. Technically, *nothing* had yet happened between them, but her attempts to ensure that nothing *did* happen had sent him spinning into confusion. And the fact that she herself was confused about the confusion that *her* confusion was creating only added to the confusion.

Jaya's words rang in her ears. 'If you like him, do something about it. Don't dither around. One thing I can tell you, he won't wait for ever.'

Persis sighed, then picked up the note she'd found inside the puzzle box.

She needed to focus on the case, take her mind off Zubin Dalal and Archie Blackfinch.

She had confirmed that the passage Healy had written down came from *Purgatorio*, the second part of *The Divine Comedy*, in which Dante climbs Mount Purgatory in the company of Virgil, navigating seven levels of suffering associated with the seven deadly sins.

She set the new verse against the earlier one recovered from Healy's bag.

Was there a link between the two? ... There seemed to be no connection that she could see. The passages were from different books within Dante's masterpiece, focused on different aspects of his journey. Essentially, they were simply different brushstrokes from the same great canvas; there seemed nothing material in their structure or content that set them apart ... She corrected herself. There *was* one minor difference. The second verse was written with spaces between each line, whereas the first was simply three lines bunched together.

A stylistic difference, apropos of nothing.

Disappointment settled in her guts; the ashy taste of failure clogged her throat.

She got up and walked to the interview room, closing the door behind her. She needed a few moments alone, and the room was the only real refuge available.

She slumped into a chair behind the much-abused interview desk. It had been transferred from another station, scratched and dented, one of its four legs inexplicably shorter than the rest, bequeathing it an irritating wobble. On the wall was a portrait of Gandhi, beside it, the tricolour of the new Indian flag.

She closed her eyes and tried to chart a course through the maze.

John Healy was proving to be a harder man to understand than she'd thought. Respected scholars didn't simply wake up one day and decide to steal one of the world's great treasures. The fact that he'd left behind a series of tantalising clues demonstrated the meticulous planning that had gone into the theft. That those plans had ended with him committing suicide was irrelevant.

Or rather, even the suicide held some meaning.

She now knew that the story that had emerged following the war about Healy's imprisonment in Italian POW camps was inaccurate. He hadn't spent any great length of time cooling his heels at Vincigliata. He'd been removed within a month of arriving there.

Where had the Nazis taken him? Why? Did his wartime experiences in Italy hold the key to his actions in India?

A knock on the door. Without waiting for an answer, George Fernandes entered.

'I went to Kramer's workplace last night. Spoke to the man in charge, the Frenchman, Jules Aubert. He tried to give me the runaround again but I told him what you'd said about harbouring a Nazi and that seemed to get his attention. He looked terrified at the idea of someone accusing him of a thing like that.' He grimaced.

Persis was struck by a sudden thought . . . Could Jules Aubert have been a Vichy collaborator? That might explain how he'd ended up in Bombay, and why the mere idea of an investigation into a Nazi at his club would bring him out in a cold sweat.

'I described the man we're looking for,' continued Fernandes. 'Mr Grey. Aubert eventually admitted that he remembered a man like that coming in a few weeks ago. Tall, heavy-set, short black hair, a scar across his left cheek. He called it a' – he checked his notes – 'a *Schmisse*. It's a German word. It means a duelling scar. He said that many German officers, especially upper-class ones, were keen on fencing, and the scar was a sort of badge of honour, a way to signal their status. He mentioned a couple of prominent Nazis who had them, including Rudolf Diels, the founder of the Gestapo.' He flipped a page in the notebook. 'Aubert says he spoke very briefly with Mr Grey. Claims Mr Grey introduced himself as Udo Becker, though he doubts that was his real name. Many of those who frequent his establishment prefer to operate under aliases. Becker claimed he was only in town for a few weeks. He was looking for some entertainment and someone had recommended Le Château des Rêves. Aubert introduced him to Francine Kramer and the pair seemed to hit it off.

'He made a big song and dance about how he never forces his girls on anyone. They're free to *choose*.' Fernandes's contempt made it clear exactly what he thought of Aubert's assertion. 'And that's it. As far as he knows, Francine took Becker upstairs. Another satisfied customer. He never saw him again.' He paused, checked his notes again. 'I spoke to some of his girls. One of them recalled Becker. Remembered the scar. She says he was chatting for a while to another customer, not a regular. Tall man with blond hair. Her description was sketchy. She asked around but it turns out none of the girls had entertained him, though he'd been propositioned, of course. He seems to have come to the club with the sole purpose of meeting Udo Becker – Mr Grey. Unless, of course, they just happened to bump into each other.'

Fernandes's tone suggested that he found *that* highly unlikely.

Persis absorbed the information, as the big sub-inspector waited. 'What next?' he finally prompted her.

It suddenly dawned on her that something was missing from his demeanour. The anger. At the same instant, she realised that her own anger had been relegated to the wings while the problem of uncovering Francine Kramer's murder had taken centre stage.

The undeniable fact was that she and Fernandes had worked well together.

The thought brought a colour to her cheeks. The missing anger returned with a vengeance.

'Can't you think for yourself?' she snapped. 'You wanted to lead this investigation, didn't you?'

He stiffened, his expression momentarily startled, before flattening to a grim stare. He nodded, then turned and walked away.

33

'We must stop meeting like this, Inspector. People will talk.'

Raj Bhoomi grinned at her from behind the autopsy table, his hands buried inside the guts of another of his guests. The joke flopped on to the tiled floor, where it crawled away to curl up and die in a corner.

She watched him pull out the man's intestines, then stride purposefully to a weighing scale on the counter. He spoke to her over his shoulder. 'Give me thirty minutes. I'm running a little late. It wouldn't be right to stop midway.'

She waited impatiently, watching the pathologist at work, her mind flickering over the Healy case, the Kramer case, and the increasing complications of her own life, like a radio hunting across the bands. Every few minutes, Zubin Dalal's face flashed into her thoughts, rattling her heart around inside her chest.

What *had* he been doing at the bookstore last night?

The answer was obvious. He'd been following her around. The thought brought another swell of anger. She cracked her knuckles savagely, causing Bhoomi to look up from his work with a quizzical expression.

She ignored him.

Why? What could Zubin possibly want to talk to her about? Why send her flowers? And those lines from Byron's poem . . . Her brain rebelled at the possibilities. The very thought of it made her want to take out her revolver, hunt him down, and shoot him in the kneecaps. It would be no less than he deserved.

He'd *abandoned* her. Having first ensured that she'd fallen so deeply in love with him that, in some ways, she was still falling. She likened it to diving from a cliff, into waters of unknown depth. She had no idea where the bottom was, but she had run out of breath a long time ago.

Bhoomi vanished through a door, then quickly returned, his round face abloom. The man was in excellent spirits. She noted that both his moustache and his hair had been recently trimmed. A change of pomade too, to something floral, and not entirely unpleasant, though it was hard to tell above the harsh odour of formaldehyde that permeated the autopsy suite. She chalked these improvements down to the young woman he was wooing. Things must be going well.

She couldn't help the sudden resentment that clogged her chest.

Even a man who spent his waking hours elbows-deep inside corpses appeared to have a better grasp of the complex logic of romance than her.

It was a damning indictment.

'I hear that you solved the curious riddle we discovered inked on our last customer,' Bhoomi began. 'Well done.'

He meant Healy. 'The trail's run cold,' she said flatly.

'I'm sure you'll pick it up again. Archie says you're like a terrier when you get your teeth into something.'

Her ears felt hot. She supposed it was a compliment, though hardly the most flattering thing to be called by a man.

She waited while Bhoomi's assistant wheeled in the corpse of James Ingram, and transferred it to the autopsy table, having first removed the previous incumbent. The steel table was barely large enough to accommodate the tall Englishman.

'I suppose we'd better get to it.'

She looked on as he searched Ingram's clothing.

In the inner pocket of his trousers, he found a piece of paper with an address written on it in Hindi, and in Marathi, the state language. She'd seen foreigners not long in the city carry this sort of thing around. Something they could show to taxi drivers.

The address was in Opera House.

She assumed it was where Ingram had been staying.

The paper had been wrapped around a small key – a house key, by the looks of it.

She allowed Bhoomi to log the key, then pocketed it and scribbled down the address in her own notebook.

Next, the pathologist removed the man's clothing, bagged it, and then proceeded to examine the body.

The bullet hole that had killed him made a prominent wound in his chest.

She realised that the thought of his violent end did not bother her as much as she had supposed. Seth had made a point of the fact that she'd already killed two men during her brief time on the force. Should she feel remorse for killing because she was a woman? Was that what was expected of her? A certain feminine *sensitivity*?

Well, to hell with that.

Bhoomi peeled back a bandage on Ingram's right shoulder to reveal a recent stab wound.

Her mind flashed back to the man who'd attacked her outside the observatory. If she'd needed confirmation that it had been Ingram, she now had it.

'Hello!' remarked Bhoomi. 'Inspector, come and look at this.'

She walked forward and loomed over his shoulder. He was examining the inside of Ingram's left arm.

Some twenty centimetres above the crook of the elbow was a small tattoo, less than a centimetre in width, in black ink.

𝔄𝔅

It seemed insignificant, but something about the mark had excited the pathologist. He stared at it, then stepped backwards, passing a sleeve over his brow.

'Does this mean something to you?' she asked.

'I – I'm not sure. I could be mistaken.' His sudden agitation perplexed her. 'I've never come across it before except in the literature.'

'Literature?'

'Medical journals.'

She looked back at the enigmatic tattoo, then turned to Bhoomi. 'Please explain.'

34

Frank Lindley was not in his office. The departmental receptionist informed her that he was out lecturing – one of the duties he'd agreed to in return for a berth at the university.

The woman offered to provide directions, but Persis already knew the way.

Minutes later, she arrived at the Premchand Roychand lecture hall, slipping in the back and taking a wooden seat next to a semi-comatose male student, half asleep on his forearms.

Lindley was on stage, speaking at a lectern, a blackboard behind him. 'In many places, empire ended with a bang, the colonialists expelled, their collaborators rounded up and stood against a wall. In India, independence has become something of a political mine-field. The promise of future economic cooperation holds Britain and her former colony together, even as the tides of history attempt to push them apart. There are even some who view Britain's time here as irrelevant. In the vast patchwork quilt of India's past, the British era represents but a single thread.'

She found his sentiment unexpectedly candid.

Lindley, to her surprise, was an engaging and forceful speaker.

He reminded her of an English lecturer during her own time here, studying political discourse, one of only three female students in her class. That was during the war, of course, when Britain was promising Indians the sun and the moon and everything in between if they would only throw in their lot with the Allies. The rhetoric employed by her lecturer had exhibited a particularly bellicose flavour; he could as well have been a recruiting agent for the war effort.

When the lecture ended, Lindley found himself mobbed by students.

She was astonished. Contrary to all that was holy, the man was *popular*.

In the end, she was forced to wade in and drag him away from his adoring public.

Back in his office, she showed him her notebook – where she'd made a crude effort at reproducing the tattoo found on Ingram – and quickly explained the situation.

He sat back in his chair, and looked at her with a flat expression. 'Is this your idea of a joke?'

'You recognise this?'

He blinked. 'Inspector, are you sure you found this on a dead *Englishman*?'

'Yes. His name was James Ingram. He was a writer.'

'And you've verified his identity?'

She hesitated. 'No. I mean, until he attacked me, I had no reason to doubt what he'd told me.'

He pulled open a drawer, took out a fresh pack of cigarettes, opened it with clumsy fingers, and lit one.

'That tattoo is written in Fraktur, a calligraphic hand of the Latin alphabet. Official Nazi documents and letters employed the font. Or they did until around 1941, when it was replaced by the more modern Antiqua script because of a perceived belief that Fraktur embodied Jewish influences.' He puffed on his cigarette. 'The tattoo on your man Ingram says AB. It's a blood group type. Tell me, how much do you know of the Nazi SS?'

'Only what I've read.'

'The SS, the Schutzstaffel, was the paramilitary organisation that Hitler used to enforce the edicts of his regime, particularly his racial policy. The SS was responsible for the murder of millions of Jews and non-Jews, particularly through its administration of the concentration camps. Heinrich Himmler, one of the chief architects of that murderous campaign, was the Reichsführer-SS for sixteen years, setting up and overseeing the death camps. The Gestapo was a subdivision of the SS, tasked with enforcing Nazi ideology. The military branch of the SS was called the Waffen-SS, primarily combat units. It was common for Waffen-SS officers to have a blood group tattoo – a *Blutgruppentätowierung* – on the inside of their left arms. The purpose of the tattoo was to identify a soldier's blood type in case he was injured and rendered unconscious in battle and a blood transfusion was needed. The tattoo consisted of blood type letters A, B, AB, or O.'

She stared at him. 'Are you trying to tell me that James Ingram was a member of the Waffen-SS?'

'I haven't seen the tattoo, but if it's genuine, then yes. I can't think of another explanation. Those tattoos are a death warrant; no one would willingly put one on their arm. After the war, the Allies have been desperately pursuing Waffen-SS members due to the high volume of war crimes committed by their units. The blood group tattoo has been a principal means of identification. Many Waffen-SS members have been successfully prosecuted for war crimes; a good few have been executed.'

'But if the tattoo is so dangerous, why would Ingram keep it? Why not get rid of it?'

'For many, it's a badge of pride. The only link they have to their shattered Nazi dream.' He waved his cigarette in the air. 'Besides, it's not that easy to get rid of. Surgery, self-inflicted burns. Some have even tried shooting it off, if you can believe that. But the Allies cottoned on to that sort of thing early on. Now, it's the first thing they look for. For a Waffen-SS member, it's just as dangerous trying to disguise it as it is to keep it, so why bother?'

She was stunned. It beggared belief that Ingram could be a Nazi.

'Let me guess. This Ingram spoke impeccable English?' Lindley scraped his tongue over his teeth. 'Following the Treaty of Versailles, the Germans were prohibited from establishing an intelligence organisation, but they did it anyway. The Abwehr became the primary Nazi espionage outfit. For most of its existence, the Abwehr was a bitter rival to the SS, but, having displeased Hitler when the tide began to turn against the Nazis, it was absorbed into the SS in early 1944. Many members of the Waffen-SS ended up serving in the Abwehr. Some of them were trained to infiltrate Britain, especially those who might have spent time in England before the war, or those with excellent language skills. They were provided with plausible cover stories.'

'But why would Ingram be out *here*?' The question was directed more at herself than Lindley, but the Englishman replied anyway. 'It *is* unusual. Most Nazis have been on the run since the end of the war. Many of them fled to South America and the Middle East, enabled by underground escape networks. The Americans code-named one of these back in 1946, calling it Odessa. Whether or not Odessa really exists is irrelevant. The fact is that many Nazis continue to elude the authorities. We know for certain that hundreds ended up in Argentina, with support from Juan Perón, and, allegedly, the Vatican. Another escape organisation we know about is Die Spinne – the Spider – run by the man who acted as the last chief of the Abwehr, one of Hitler's top commandos, a Waffen-SS Obersturmbannführer by the name of Otto Skorzeny.

'Ingram, if he was Waffen-SS, was probably in touch with members of Die Spinne. Though why they'd send him out to India is beyond me. It's not the safest place to lie low for a Nazi in hiding.' The cigarette had burned down to his fingers, and he stubbed it out hurriedly on the desk. 'Look, let me help. I have contacts in the British war crimes investigation team. They're plugged into other Allied and Israeli organisations hunting Nazis. Let me see if I can find any information on your man. All I need is a photograph.'

The offer surprised her. 'How much?'

It was his turn to look surprised. 'No charge, Inspector. Not for this.'

As she left the university, Persis was reminded of a favourite saying of her father's: never judge a book by its cover.

35

The address that Raj Bhoomi had discovered in James Ingram's pocket was just over two miles from the university, barely a mile north of the Bombay Asiatic Society.

She drove past the St George Hospital on Frere Road, and then the remnants of Fort George, a dark, brooding presence facing the sea. The vertical slits in the fort's laterite façade always reminded her of a succession of eyes, peering malevolently out at passers-by.

Ingram lived in a small apartment above a tyre repair shop, accessed by an exterior staircase at the rear of the premises. She wondered why he'd picked such a seemingly low-rent place. It was certainly out of the way, but a tall blond foreigner would have stuck out here like a sore thumb.

The key Bhoomi had found on Ingram's corpse fitted the lock on the door at the top of the iron staircase. She slipped out a pair of gloves from her pocket, then stepped into the flat and took stock of her surroundings.

The place was even smaller on the inside than it looked from the outside. Surely, a man as big as Ingram – if that was, indeed, his name – would have felt confined here?

The place was bare. A sofa, a small table in the kitchen area, a sepia-toned picture of Jesus on the wall, a sideboard. And that was it.

No TV, no gramophone, no radio.

She walked into the bedroom.

The bed was precisely made, as if by a practised hand. In the wardrobe, she found shirts, trousers, three pairs of shoes. A single double-breasted suit. A linen jacket.

She searched the clothing. Nothing in any of the pockets. But, as her hand brushed over the fabric of the linen jacket, she felt . . . something.

She took it out from the wardrobe and laid it down on the bed, then palpated the area just above the lashed hem of the right-side front.

Something was in there. Her fingers traced the outline of the hidden object –rectangular, slim – a piece of card, perhaps?

She took out her pocketknife, opened the jacket, and made an incision on the inner lining, before slashing downwards. Setting down the knife, she poked her fingers inside the slit and extracted the object, then held it up to the light.

A photograph.

Two men, casually dressed, standing in a small boat. In the backdrop, a lake, and a distant shore, dense with tall trees. One of the men was Ingram, smiling handsomely at the camera with his hands on his hips. He wore a pastel pink half-sleeved sports shirt and white golfing trousers. The man beside him was a few inches shorter, but heavier in build, with jet-black hair and a moustache, caught in profile, seemingly addressing Ingram. He wore a plaid sports shirt above green waders. He was holding up a fish by a hook speared through its mouth; she had no idea what type of fish.

There was something ageless about the scene, two men, clearly friends, engaged in the most innocent of pastimes, a male bonding ritual as old as civilisation itself.

And yet . . . here was the man who had attacked her, not once, but twice. Possibly a Nazi, a member of Hitler's murderous Waffen-SS, a man on the run.

She touched Ingram's face.

Who were you?

Why were you here?

She turned the photograph over. There was a date on the reverse: August 1948. But no clue as to who the other man might be.

Her eyes lingered on the bucolic scene. Ingram had felt the need to sew this photograph into the lining of his jacket, presumably to keep it from being discovered by others. The implication was that there was something about it that he didn't want anyone to see, particularly the authorities.

The second man.

Whoever he was, he was important to Ingram, important enough to hold on to a photograph he felt too nervous to display openly.

Her mind made the leap.

Another member of the Waffen-SS.

Lindley had spoken about an escape network, Die Spinne, helping spirit away former Nazis to safe haven. Might Ingram's friend be another to have benefited from the network?

Two Nazis, on the run together.

And then one of them ends up in Bombay, and somehow becomes involved with John Healy and the theft of a priceless manuscript.

But why would a former Nazi care about stealing Dante's *The Divine Comedy*? It was valuable, certainly, but why risk exposure? Why risk capture, trial, and, possibly, execution?

Standing there, in Ingram's bedroom, she felt as if the answers were swirling around her like a flock of birds. All she had to do was hold herself perfectly still and eventually one of them would alight on her shoulder, and tell her everything.

It didn't work.

She stuck the photograph in her pocket and left the apartment.

* * *

Back at Malabar House, she found a message from Frank Lindley awaiting her, in the form of a note taken down by Birla. He squinted at the chit, scratched his head, and eventually worked out what he'd written. 'He wants you to call some Italian. A former administrator at that Italian prison where they kept John Healy.'

Lindley had provided a number.

The man on the other end of the line, Salvatore Pepe, the camp adjutant at Vincigliata during the period that Healy had been there, spoke slowly, carefully, as if vetting every word before allowing it to leave his mouth.

Thankfully, his English was more than serviceable.

'What exactly did you do there?' she asked.

'The commander of Vincigliata was a black-hearted Nazi,' he explained. 'My job was to do whatever he told me to do.' It sounded like a defence plea, though she hadn't accused him of anything.

'Your office kept the records for all the men arriving in and leaving from Vincigliata?'

'*Sì*. Arriving, leaving, dying. Though we didn't see much of that. These were senior officers and we treated them well. Even the Nazis showed restraint and it is not often you can say that about those butchers.'

'Butchers?' Her tone hardened. 'I thought they were your allies.'

'Not *my* allies. Mussolini crawled into bed with Hitler. *Madonna*, it must have been like taking a corpse to bed! I was a bookkeeper before the war. I enlisted because I had little choice. I knew many Italian soldiers on the front line and most were honourable men. They did what they did because that was what the uniform demanded of them. But the Nazis ... they were thugs. Schoolyard bullies whose only answer to every problem was to exterminate it. Tell me, what kind of world is it where men can think like that?'

She ignored the question, not entirely buying his innocent act. 'When did Healy arrive at the prison?'

'September 1943.'

'I've been told that he didn't stay very long. That he was moved out by a Nazi who came to Vincigliata about a month after Healy arrived.'

'It is more complicated than that.' Pepe hesitated.

'Rest assured, whatever you tell me will not be used against you. The war is over.'

'The war may be over, madam, but the Allies have long memories, *si*?'

'Please. It's important.'

A silence drifted down the phone. 'Very well. Yes, it is true that Healy left the prison in October. However, I was instructed to make no record of his leaving.'

'I don't understand.'

'It is very simple. As far as my records were concerned, Healy remained at Vincigliata.'

'Who instructed you?'

'The man who came to collect him. Matthias Bruner.'

'Why would he ask you to do that?'

'I don't know. The Nazis did not like questions.'

Having set down the phone, she continued to stare thoughtfully at it.

John Healy had been removed from the Vincigliata POW camp by the Nazis, who had then gone to great lengths to ensure that no one knew that fact. As far as the world was concerned, Healy remained at the camp until he appeared again halfway through 1944, having escaped captivity.

What had happened to him during the period he'd vanished from Vincigliata, disappearing into an administrative black hole? What had the Germans done to him? Why had they concealed the fact that they'd taken him out of the prison? Most puzzling of all . . . why had Healy himself never spoken of that missing time?

Questions that would have to await answers.

She pulled out the photograph she'd recovered from Ingram's apartment and tucked it into an envelope.

Calling over the office peon, Gopal, she instructed him to deliver it to Frank Lindley at the university, with a short note asking the Englishman to see if he could find out who Ingram's mysterious fishing companion was.

36

She arrived home to find Aunt Nussie preparing a lavish meal.

'It's really not necessary,' said Persis. 'I'm fine.'

'No one can be *fine* a day after they've almost been murdered,' said Nussie, shooing her towards her bedroom. 'Go and change. Dinner will be ready in a bit. And wear something nice.'

She showered, dressed in a pair of silk pyjamas, then returned to the living room.

Nussie stared at the pyjamas. 'Wouldn't you like to dress in something a little more formal?'

'Why?' she said. 'Is the Prime Minister coming to dinner?'

Nussie looked as if she was about to say something, then nodded and turned away.

Sitting at the Steinway, Persis tinkled out a few desultory notes as Akbar watched her, licking his lips. Distracted by thoughts of the case, she hit a wrong note. The cat rose up on his hackles, hissed at her, then leaped off the piano and scooted from the room.

'Everyone's a critic,' she muttered.

By the time dinner was on the table, her father had arrived from downstairs. He'd closed the shop early. She hoped it wasn't on her account.

They'd hardly sat down when the bell rang.

Nussie, her face glowing from the heat in the kitchen, bounced towards the door. Swinging it aside, she said, 'Oh. Hello.'

Persis couldn't see who it was. The caller was not tall; Nussie's body shielded him – or her – from view.

And then her aunt moved aside.

Zubin Dalal stepped into the apartment, slipping off his homburg.

'I apologise if I'm interrupting,' he said. 'Perhaps I should come back another time?'

'Absolutely not,' said Nussie. 'You'll sit and eat dinner with us.'

Persis began to rise from her seat. 'Aunt N—'

'Sit down, Persis,' said Nussie, cutting off her incipient protest. 'This gentleman saved your life last night. We shall not turn him away at our door.'

'But—'

Directing herself to Zubin, Nussie said, 'Please take a seat.'

Words piled up in her throat until Persis felt she would choke. But her aunt merely flashed her a look and gestured for her to retake her seat.

She could only watch, helplessly, as Zubin sat directly opposite her, nodding at her father, who stared at him in stony silence. She'd never told Sam precisely what had happened between them, but he knew enough. Nevertheless, even Sam Wadia wouldn't send away a man who'd saved his daughter's life.

Nussie had made sautéed chicken with lemon rice. The fragrance of the food wafted around the room. Persis ignored it. Her appetite had vanished, to be replaced by a ringing sense of alarm.

'Why are you here?' The words were forced out, as if at gunpoint.

Zubin affected a complaisant smile. 'I was in the area and thought I might see how you were feeling.'

'And *I* thought I made it clear I had no wish to see you.'

He smiled again, and lapsed into an infuriating silence. Her heart swelled with fury. The past barked in her chest like a rabid dog, a holy frenzy that threatened to overwhelm her. What right did he have to turn up here, to act as if all had been forgiven, if not forgotten?

'So, Zubin . . . how is your wife?' asked Nussie, brightly.

He set down his fork, looked directly at Persis. 'We're no longer together. Divorce. Four months ago. My marriage, I'm afraid, proved to be an unfortunate wrong turn.'

The word resounded inside her skull.

Divorce.

'And do you still live in Delhi?' Nussie continued.

'No. I returned to Bombay a few weeks ago. I've been getting reacquainted. The city has changed so much in just a few short years.'

'But its heart remains the same,' sang Nussie.

Persis shot her a look. Her aunt was acting oddly. Like her father, she knew only the outlines of Persis's brief relationship with Zubin . . . If only she knew the whole of it!

Persis lowered her head, seeking to control her rage before it spewed out of her. Hacking savagely at a piece of chicken with her fork, she said, 'You're not welcome here.'

'Persis!' Nussie frowned at her.

'Why don't you ask him *how* he just happened to be passing when I was attacked.'

Nussie turned to Zubin in confusion.

The man had the decency to look embarrassed. 'Very well. Cards on the table. I *have* been following you around. I was summoning up the nerve to approach you. I admit, I tried on several occasions, but at the last, my courage failed me.'

'Like the spineless coward you are.'

He spread his hands. 'All I want to do is talk.'

Her look could have felled a charging rhino. 'There's nothing you have to say that I want to hear.'

He subsided. An uncomfortable silence fell over the table. Sam ate noisily, glaring at his guest with a whisky-drinker's aggressiveness.

'Don't you want to know *why* my marriage ended?' said Zubin finally.

'I suppose she found out what sort of man she'd married.'

He sighed. 'Persis—'

She stood up, so abruptly that they all froze. 'I need some air.'

She left him staring after her, his mouth hanging foolishly open.

Downstairs in the shop, she sat at her father's counter, steadying herself.

She'd imagined the encounter for so long, the day that Zubin would make the mistake of crossing her path again. In gleeful dreams, she'd pictured herself taking out her revolver and forcing him to his knees, watching him squirm as he begged her not to shoot him. She'd imagined humiliating him in a thousand and one ways, taking from him every iota of self-respect, just as he had all but taken hers.

But now that the moment had arrived . . . she had failed. Failed to deliver the speech she'd rehearsed so often it was burned on to the insides of her eyelids. A grand diatribe in which she dissected every flaw in his character, reducing him to a wreck, a husk, a parody of the man he believed himself to be.

She'd failed, and in that failure, she'd lost the opportunity to undo years of hurt.

Zubin's presence had simply rekindled the very grass fires of the heart she'd long thought extinguished. Distance had allowed her to heap the memory of his charms on to the bonfire of her hatred; but now, up close, she saw that he had lost none of the tigerish magnetism that had so enthralled her, that sense of swashbuckling gasconade that had once sent swarms of bees buzzing around her heart— No!

She swatted the counter in anger.

The man was a despicable toad, deserving of her contempt . . . God, she needed a drink!

She rummaged through the drawers below the counter. Her father usually had a bottle of something in here . . .

A rattle at the door jerked her head up. She peered through the glass, at the outline of a woman . . .

Moments later, Jaya, impeccably dressed in a beautiful evening gown and heels, was looking around the shop. 'My God, this place is still a dump.'

'I'll be sure to let my father know,' said Persis. 'What are you doing here?'

'A little bird tells me you were almost strangled to death last night.'

'That little bird wouldn't happen to be Aunt Nussie, would it?'

Jaya smiled. 'I thought it might be some sort of sexual fetish, but then I remembered it was *you* we were talking about.' Her face became serious. 'Look, I know you're a hotshot policewoman now and risks have to be taken, but isn't this a bit much? I mean, you don't have to prove your point by actually getting yourself killed.'

Persis dismissed her friend's concerns with a wave of the hand. She was too tired to argue.

'Stubborn as ever . . . I also hear Zubin materialised out of thin air to save your life.'

'He didn't save my life! I had the situation under control.'

Jaya smiled infuriatingly. 'What was he after, do you think?'

'It's the case I'm working on—'

'Not your attacker. I meant Zubin.'

She blinked. 'I don't know. What's more, I don't care.'

Jaya seemed about to say something, then shrugged. 'No. Of course not. A louse is a louse even if he does prevent your imminent death.' She raised a hand before Persis could protest further. 'Anyway, dinner with Dinaz is confirmed. No excuses. And talking of dinner . . . I'm off to a soirée with some friends. I don't suppose you'd care to join us?'

Persis could imagine the sort of friends Jaya was having dinner with dressed like *that*.

'No.'

'Suit yourself.' She turned at the door. 'By the way, your hand-cuffs have proved to be a big hit with my son. I've had to release my maid from captivity three times already. Heaven knows what would have happened if you'd given him a revolver.'

After Jaya had left, Persis sat in the semi-darkness. Her friend's visit had, perversely, depressed her. Jaya had a way of pulling things apart that forced Persis to confront realities she would rather have ignored.

Zubin. Would she never be rid of him?

She picked up the phone. It was answered on the fifth ring. 'Does your offer still stand?' A pause. 'Very well. Do you know the Eastern Dragon? It's in Opera House.'

Half an hour later, she was standing outside the bar that Birla and Haq had followed Franco Belzoni to. On first impression, it was exactly as they had described it: a dump. A darkened façade, with a red dragon painted over the lintel, much of the paint cracked and faded. One of the dragon's taloned legs had been effaced by monsoon rain. A desultory Chinese lantern hung from a hook above the door, unlit.

Inside, she found a dimly lit, smoke-filled mugginess, and a bar behind which a fat Oriental gentleman was leaning on his elbows talking to another man in a suit. About a dozen round, unclothed tables were scattered about the place, with a series of booths at the rear.

She made her way to the booths.

In the third one along, she found Archie Blackfinch nursing a beer.

He sprang to his feet as she arrived, an uncertain smile lighting up his features. The smile faltered as he saw that she was wearing what looked like a pair of silk pyjamas. Refraining from comment, he waited as she slipped on to the cracked red leather of the booth, and leaned back.

'How are you feel—' He began, then stopped, perhaps recalling the last time he'd asked her that. He tapped the side of his glass. 'You look like you could use one of these.'

She asked for a whisky.

The waitress stared at her when she arrived with the drink. It was either the pyjamas or the fact that the bar was one of those where someone like her rarely set foot. A small slice of home for Bombay's Chinese community, an oasis in the Indian desert . . . So what had Franco Belzoni been doing here, meeting with a military attaché?

The stray question swept across her bows like a freak wave. She'd picked the bar precisely because Birla had said it was off the beaten track, somewhere no one would recognise her or Archie Blackfinch and report back to her aunt. Somewhere she might have a few moments where her life was completely her own.

But she realised now that even in this seemingly instinctive choice, her underlying desire to work the case had shown itself.

She forced her mind to a deliberate stillness.

'Rough day?' asked Blackfinch.

She blinked. 'The man you met yesterday, the one who . . . He turned up for dinner. Uninvited.'

'Ah. You mean the "old friend of the family",' said Blackfinch, quoting Zubin's description of himself.

She looked directly at him. 'He was the first man I ... was intimate with. I was in love with him. I adored him.' She didn't add that he was the *only* man she'd been with. 'I thought we would spend our lives together. And then he vanished. Ran away to Delhi to marry someone else.'

'It could have been worse.' He sipped at his beer. 'He could have married *you*.'

She flashed him a dark look.

'A man's character rarely changes, Persis. Once a cad, always a cad.'

'You don't think we evolve? Outgrow our mistakes, the defects in our personality?'

'To a certain extent. But you can't change who you are. A man who'd betray a woman as incredible as you ... A fool like that doesn't deserve a second chance.'

Embarrassment forced the glass to her mouth. She couldn't remember the last time a man had praised her.

'I met my wife at a cocktail party,' he continued. 'She was a singer. Frankly, her voice wasn't great, and I told her so. She stared at me, then threw a drink in my face. Later, when I went to apologise, she grabbed my face in both hands and kissed me. I'd never been kissed like that before, and certainly not by such an attractive woman. It made me feel eight feet tall. We married within a month. She was impetuous, flighty, easily bored. I thought that side of her would settle down in time, but it didn't. A tiger doesn't stop being a tiger just because you put it in a cage.'

Blackfinch had turned up in a taxi and so she offered to drive him home.

Parked in the narrow alley outside his apartment complex near the Sassoon Docks, she listened to a stray dog barking. The three whiskies she'd had had left her with an inner warmth that rose gently like a cloud of steam to envelop her thoughts. 'Thank you,' she mumbled.

'The pleasure was all mine,' said Blackfinch, slipping off his spectacles to wipe them on his trouser leg.

She twisted in her seat and locked eyes with him. In the half-light, he seemed even handsomer than usual. Something unspoken pulsed between them. He leaned in and kissed her. For an instant, she froze ... and then pressed back. Time passed, she became lost to the sensation, and then she felt his hands on her, on her thighs, her waist, moving up the front of her silk blouse. Excitement shivered along her spine. It had been so long ...

The dog barked again, and the spell was broken. She pushed him away, turned towards the wheel, gripping it like a drowning woman grabbing at a lifebelt. 'It's late,' she stumbled out.

He stared at her stupidly, then slowly returned his spectacles to his nose. 'Yes. Of course.'

He opened his mouth, then closed it again.

She heard the door open. 'Goodnight, Persis.'

She didn't dare look at him. 'Goodnight, Archie.'

The sound of footsteps, moving away. She glanced around, saw him vanish inside the gate of his compound.

She swore, then lowered her head to the steering wheel.

Her father was waiting up for her, hunkered in his wheelchair, reading. She slumped on to the living room sofa, and held her head in her hands. He looked at her from over the top of his half-moon spectacles.

'May I give you a word of advice?'

'No.'

'Matters of the heart are never simple. The heart wants what it wants. Unfortunately, it rarely knows *what* it wants for very long.

The only way to navigate the minefield is to charge right through it and hope the explosions don't catch up with you.'

She stared at him glumly.

'And now, I bid you goodnight.'

Unable to sleep, she took out her notebook and returned herself to her work. It seemed the only safe port in the current storm threatening to capsize her neatly ordered life.

Briefly, she wondered how Fernandes had got on with the Kramer investigation. The truth was that they had run into a dead end and her own mind was too full with the unfolding mysteries of the Healy case.

She took out the two notes the Englishman had left behind. Two passages from two separate books in Dante's magnum opus.

What connected them? What did they mean? More importantly, how did they point the way forward?

She stared at the words until she felt the letters would fall off.

Glancing at Akbar dozing beside her, she muttered, 'Maybe he *was* crazy.'

There was nothing about these riddles that pointed anywhere. Just two verses plucked, seemingly at random, from the manuscript. The only difference between them was that one was spaced out—

She paused.

Why *had* Healy done that? He'd left a trail of breadcrumbs, each just obscure enough that it would take time and effort to unravel. But these two were not clues at all. They were simply verses taken from *The Divine Comedy*. If he intended them to serve as clues, then there had to be something else here, something she wasn't seeing, something between the lines—

She froze.

The thought stood out like a steeple on a flat landscape.

She slipped out of bed, and padded to the kitchen. Turning on the gas hob, she held the second of the two notes above the flame. Moments later, characters began to form in the spaces between the lines of text.

Invisible ink. It was so simple, so *childish*, that she almost let out a shout.

She wondered what agent Healy had used. Vinegar? Lemon juice? A honey solution? She knew that even cola worked well. Such agents oxidised at a lower temperature than the surrounding paper, turning the words written with them a brown colour.

When all the hidden lines were revealed, she tried the other note, just in case. There were no spaced lines, but she wanted to be sure.

Nothing.

She sat at the dining table, set the first note aside, and focused on the second one, examining the newly revealed words. Together they formed another riddle.

The road to salvation has many gates,
That which you seek in Cutters embrace awaits,
'Neath Sun and Moon and unchanging skies,
Watched over by God, in litteral disguise,
'Twixt Jerusalem and Mecca, it lies.

37

'Curious fellow, this Italian of yours.'

Birla had wandered over and perched himself on the edge of her desk. 'Haq and I took the liberty of following him again yesterday while you were recovering from your fracas.'

Recovering? That was hardly a fair description of how she had spent the previous day. She bristled, but he cut off her incipient protest by raising a hand.

It was mid-morning and Malabar House was relatively quiet. Fernandes was busy typing at his desk, Haq was out, and Seth had barely made his presence known.

'Belzoni went to Healy's home,' continued Birla. 'Marched in, spent an hour in there. When we checked afterwards, he'd pretty much torn the place apart. Cut up the sofas, moved the fridge.'

What was he looking for? The manuscript? No. That would be pointless. Surely, he didn't think they were *that* incompetent?

She realised that she now had good cause to bring Belzoni in and haul him over the coals. Rattle him around to see if anything shook loose.

But what would that achieve?

Belzoni would simply plead desperation. He'd made it clear that he would not leave the country until the manuscript was recovered. The man was Italian *and* a scholar; clearly, the book meant a great deal to him.

'What else did he do?'

'He followed some white woman around,' continued Birla. 'Blonde. Small. Angry-looking.'

She sat straighter in her seat. 'Do you mean Erin Lockhart?'

'I don't know. I didn't catch her name. I figured you would know.'

There was only one reason for Belzoni to follow the American around. He must be hoping she'd lead him to wherever Healy had hidden the manuscript.

Which meant that he suspected Lockhart.

Did that mean that Belzoni himself couldn't have been in league with John Healy? Or was there something else going on here that she hadn't grasped?

She pondered the pieces of the puzzle, but couldn't make them fit.

Birla wandered away.

Her eyes strayed to Fernandes, hunched at his desk. She considered asking him what he'd been up to on the Kramer case, but the words died in her throat.

Ten minutes later, she was saved from having to do so.

Seth looked at them both sternly. A copy of the *Indian Chronicle* was open on his desk. On the second page was a piece about Francine Kramer, including a ghoulish photograph taken at the morgue. In the space of a few paragraphs, the article managed to skirt decency, accuracy, and good taste.

'Can either of you explain this?'

'What's there to explain?' said Persis. 'That's a morgue photo. You should be talking to Raj Bhoomi.'

'I've already spoken to him. He claims to know nothing of it. He suggested that one of the morgue orderlies might have been bribed to let Channa and his photographer in the back door.'

Aalam Channa. The man behind the article. Bombay's most notorious hack and the same man who'd painted such an unflattering portrait of her own efforts on the Herriot investigation after she'd refused to play ball with him. The same man to whom Fernandes had leaked information.

Seth turned his attention to Fernandes. 'Have you been up to your old tricks?'

Fernandes stiffened, a shocked puff of breath escaping him. As he squirmed under the SP's gaze, Persis discovered, to her surprise, that she didn't enjoy the man's humiliation.

Strange.

'He didn't get anything from me,' Fernandes finally ground out.

Seth continued to scrutinise him. 'Very well. Then perhaps one of you can explain exactly where we've got to on the investigation? No doubt someone will come knocking on my door soon enough, someone I can't throw back out into the street.'

Fernandes remained silent, waiting for her to speak. She found words in her mouth, words that, minutes earlier, she wouldn't have dreamed of uttering. 'Fernandes has taken the lead while I've focused on the Healy investigation.'

She could feel him staring at her in astonishment.

When he finally turned back to Seth, waiting impatiently, he spoke quickly. 'Our only real lead is the suspect identified as Mr Grey aka Udo Becker.'

'The man with the scar?'

'Yes. I've been trying to find him. I did a tour of the major railway stations and spoke to the porters. I spoke to the staff at the aerodrome. Then I spoke to the concierges at some of the bigger hotels, the sort foreigners usually stay at.'

Seth waited. 'And?'

'And nothing. The man hasn't been seen. Whoever he is, he seems to know how to keep a low profile.'

'And yet he *was* present at Le Château des Rêves. Why? What was he doing there? Who was the man he met with?'

But neither of them had an answer to this. Seth sighed. 'What next?'

'I keep looking.'

After Fernandes had returned to his desk, Seth looked at her thoughtfully. 'Could it be that you two have learned how to play nicely?'

She frowned. 'I've been too busy to monitor his every step.'

'It's called delegation, Persis. Fernandes is a good policeman.'

'So you keep telling me.'

'He has a two-year-old son.'

'I know.'

'Did you know that his son has a congenital liver disease? That it costs Fernandes a small fortune in medical fees just to keep the boy alive? That he often picks up extra work on his off days as a dock labourer just to make ends meet?'

Her jaw tightened. She stared at him.

'No. I didn't think so,' said Seth. 'He's not the type to talk about it and you're not the type to ask.'

'What's your point?'

'My point is that before you judge others, you should at least have all the facts to hand. What Fernandes did was wrong. But he did it for the right reasons. *His* reasons. For what it's worth, I consider him a man of integrity.'

She chewed on this silently, before Seth turned his focus to the Healy investigation. 'What next?'

She quickly brought him up to speed on the discovery that James Ingram might have been a Nazi.

'Nazis!' He collapsed spinelessly back into his seat. 'They'll tear the clothes from my back if this gets out.'

She wasn't sure if he was talking about the press or the marionettes in Delhi.

He recovered sufficiently to open a drawer and pour himself a drink. Having settled his nerves, he asked, 'Why would the damned Nazis want a copy of *The Divine Comedy*? Last I heard, they were all running to South America with their tails on fire.'

A question to which she could offer no answer.

'As if we didn't have enough madmen of our own,' he muttered, shaking his head. 'You know why I hate the Nazis so much?' He put down his glass, picked up a pen, and scribbled on the back of a sheet of paper, then turned it towards her.

On it was a symbol now recognised around the world.

The Nazi swastika.

Seth observed her reaction, then put his pen to the paper again, adding four dots, in between the four arms of the swastika. He then turned the paper so that the base was flat, instead of at an angle, as the Nazi logo had been.

Persis recognised the new symbol – everyone on the subcontinent did.

'Symbols have great meaning, Persis. The word "swastika" comes from the Sanskrit for "well-being". For thousands of years we Hindus have used the swastika as a symbol of good luck, something benign. But in two decades those bloodthirsty murderers have turned it into an image of hate. Every nation has had its madmen; every society is carnivorous to some extent. The difference is that the Nazis managed to turn mass murder into an ideological enterprise. And now you're telling me one of them has been running around Bombay, up to God only knows what mischief.'

'Once we know Ingram's real identity, we may be able to understand his motives. For what it's worth, I don't think he was working alone.'

'What makes you say that?'

'Common sense. What would a lone Nazi gain by exposing himself out here? There has to be something bigger going on that we haven't yet understood.'

'Don't go inventing conspiracies,' warned Seth, waving his glass at her. 'It's the surest way to put us in the firing line.'

'We're already in the firing line,' she shot back. 'It's just that the shooting hasn't started yet.' She took out her notebook and showed him Healy's latest riddle.

Seth examined it glumly. 'Well, I can't make any sense of it.'

'The good news is that I think it might be the last one.'

'What makes you say that?'

'The second line. *That which you seek in Cutters embrace awaits.* I think this time Healy intends to lead us to the manuscript itself.'

'You still believe he wants us to find it?' His scepticism was obvious.

'I do.'

'Then why this ridiculous runaround?' Frustration boiled from him.

She considered, perhaps for the first time, the enormous pressure he must be under.

Seth had once been an excellent policeman. But with independence, he'd found himself on the wrong side of history, accused of aggressively enforcing the whims of his former masters, the sort of silent, insidious accusation against which there was no defence. With the reorganisation of the imperial police force into national and state services, he had found himself sidelined, a noose slung around his career and the stool kicked out from under it.

For Roshan Seth, Malabar House represented the last chance saloon. Another failure and he'd be shoved back out into the coldness of the civilian world.

She couldn't imagine him slaving away at a managing agency,

or standing behind a department-store counter selling fridges to housewives.

'It's his funeral later today,' she said.

He frowned. 'Whose?'

'Healy's. His father has given instructions that his son should be buried locally.'

'He doesn't want him shipped back home?'

'No.'

Seth considered this. 'I suppose they weren't close. Fathers and sons rarely are, in my experience.'

'On the contrary, I think he loved him very much. But Healy became a stranger to him after the war. I think he feels that his son came out to find peace in India and he wants to believe that he did just that.'

A strange half-smile took over the SP's lips. 'Did you ever read Rumi? That passage about the lion jumping at his own reflection in the water. It was his way of telling us that the evil we see in the world is really just the potential that lives inside us all.'

Dipping back into her notebook, she threw out another name. 'Enrico Mariconti. He's an Italian military attaché. I need you to call your friends in Delhi and find out a bit more about him.'

'I don't have any friends in Delhi,' he snapped. 'Just a bunch of bureaucrats who enjoy pulling the wings off people like me.' He pouted in self-pity, then knocked back his whisky, and said, 'Why do you want to know about this Mariconti?'

'Because I want to rattle someone's cage.'

38

Two hours later, she arrived outside a grand home at the southern tip of Marine Drive, in Nariman Point, Franco Belzoni's place of work. The bungalow, an art deco affair – recently painted, by the look of it, in pastel shades of pink and yellow – sat serenely in the afternoon sun, surrounded on three sides by the Back Bay, where boats bobbed on the water.

She was led inside by a uniformed house servant.

In an office at the rear, she found Belzoni working at a desk. The office was vast, more of an audience chamber, complete with chandeliers, tapestries, and the sort of heavy furniture that looked as if it could survive a direct hit by V2 rockets.

Belzoni stood as she approached, greeted her, then asked her to take a seat.

'How can I help you, Inspector?'

'You can start by telling me the truth.'

He raised a quizzical eyebrow. Leaning back in his chair, framed by sunlight falling in from the window behind him, he held a pen, caught between the tips of the index fingers of each hand. 'I do not understand.'

'Why are you really here?'

'I have already explained this.'

'I had a couple of my officers follow you around. You met with an Italian military attaché named Enrico Mariconti. Why?'

The pen slipped from his fingers. He sat up straighter. 'You had me *followed*?' He seemed astonished, more than upset, yet she was satisfied that she had scored a palpable hit. 'But this is an invasion of my privacy!'

'You can write to my boss with a complaint,' she said. 'Why were you meeting with Mariconti?'

His expression hardened. 'A personal meeting. It is no concern of yours.'

'I disagree.' She took out her notebook. 'The Indian Home Office has taken a keen interest in my investigation. They're very concerned that we recover the manuscript. They were most helpful when we made enquiries about your friend. It appears that Mr Mariconti is more than simply a military attaché.

'For many years, he worked as a senior operator in the SIM, the Servizio Informazioni Militare, the Italian Military Information Service. This was the military intelligence outfit of the Italian Royal Army. There are also reports that he worked for OVRA, the Organization for Vigilance and Repression of Anti-Fascism – Mussolini's secret police, and the outfit that Hitler's Gestapo was modelled on. The OVRA was employed by Mussolini to control those opposed to his regime, and to bring others into line, including the Vatican – OVRA maintained a regiment of spies inside the Holy See whose sole task was to dig up dirt on Vatican priests so that Mussolini could bend the Pope to his will.

'After the war, both OVRA and the SIM were disbanded, to be replaced, in part, by SIFAR, the Armed Forces Information Service. Mariconti works for SIFAR.' She paused, waiting for a reaction, but Belzoni's normally animated face had settled into a stone mask. 'So my question is this: why is a senior Italian military intelligence officer meeting with an Italian academic who just happens to be in town when a priceless Italian treasure goes missing?'

The silence that followed was broken by the sound of a bell ringing somewhere in the house.

Belzoni, who seemed to have slipped into a trance, stirred. 'This house belongs to an Italian financier who settled in India many years ago. He is a member of the Board of Governors of the University of Bologna and allows us to use the property. I grew up in a fishing village on the Tuscan coast – the sound of the sea is, how you say, *familiare*.' He paused. 'Whatever you think you know, you are wrong. I cannot tell you anything more.'

'What I know is that you're not here for the reasons you say you are. What I know is that I've been attacked twice by a man who, it now turns out, might be a former Nazi. And here you are, running around town with a man who worked for Mussolini's very own Gestapo.'

Alarm spread over his dark features. 'What do you mean? What Nazi?'

She hesitated. Perhaps she'd made a mistake. The circumstances of James Ingram's death and the fact that he might be a Nazi had, so far, stayed within the investigation – to tell Belzoni would be to risk releasing those details into the wild. She would swiftly lose control of the situation if that information ended up as tomorrow's headlines.

Belzoni spoke. 'I understand that it must be difficult for you to trust me. Please understand, I am here only to help. Our interests are the same.'

'What interests *are* those exactly?'

He seemed on the verge of saying something, but then pulled back. 'I'm sorry, Inspector. I cannot tell you more. Not at this time.'

She stood. 'In that case, tomorrow, your name, and the name of your good friend Signor Mariconti, will be splashed across the front pages of every major newspaper in this country. I will personally see to it. "Italian interference in the investigation of the missing Dante manuscript." I wonder what your paymasters, whoever they are, will think of that?'

'You would not!'

'Try me.'

He stared at her in mild horror. Finally, he sat back. 'Give me three hours. I will speak to Mariconti. I make no promises, but I will try my best to convince him that we should share our information with you.'

'What information?'

'Information about what really happened to John Healy during the war.'

39

John Healy's funeral took place in a church in Sewri near the Sewri Christian cemetery. The irony didn't escape her. Healy had hidden himself in the same cemetery and would now end up buried there.

It was a small service, presided over by a native priest, Mervyn Alvares, a bald, regal-looking man of indeterminate age, whose white cassock dragged over the warm flagstones of the nave. Passing beyond the communion rail, he ascended the altar, turned, and looked down over his gathered audience.

There were few mourners.

Neve Forrester and a handful of Healy's colleagues from the Asiatic Society shuffled noisily among the pews towards the front; two rows behind them, Erin Lockhart sat, stony-faced, on her own. At the very rear were a trio of journalists, admitted after much protest and under strict orders not to cause disruption. The news of Healy's death had filtered out, though it had yet to make the papers. That would soon change.

Persis supposed that she would have to brace herself for the onslaught, particularly if the full circumstances of Healy's disappearance and death also came to light.

An inevitability. Keeping a secret in Bombay was as difficult as trying to hold down a shadow.

She slipped into the pew behind Lockhart, forcing the American to twist around on the wooden bench. She stared at the policewoman, then dipped her head fractionally in greeting. Behind her, the priest launched into his eulogy.

Alvares had a theatrical style, and the picture he painted of Healy was both sympathetic and bombastic: an intelligent, talented young scholar, a man who had suffered the iniquities of war, and whose life had ended too soon.

John Healy: a Greek tragic hero.

Minutes later, Neve Forrester took the stand to offer a few words in eulogy.

Persis leaned forward and whispered into Lockhart's ear. 'Shouldn't it be you up there?'

'I don't do eulogies,' said the American, curtly, without looking around. 'Once you're dead, people will say everything about you except the truth.'

A noise turned them around. Persis saw Archie Blackfinch clatter into the church. He spotted her, gave an uncertain wave, then fell on to a pew near the door.

Forrester looked down on the small gathering, her expression unreadable. 'Whatever the circumstances that drove John to act as he did in his final days, the fact remains that a young man of immense talent has been taken from us. I did not know John well; none of us did. He was a committed scholar, a man who valued history and the way that it might be used to illuminate our present. In his short time on earth, he achieved more than most of us do in a lifetime. He was a complex man, a thoughtful man. But some shadow had fallen over his soul, and I believe he found it impossible to find his way out from under it.

'Sub specie aeternitatis, we are all dust, our lives inconsequential. Nevertheless, wherever John ends up, I hope that he is now in the light.'

Persis found the words strangely moving.

An hour later, she looked on as the soil was patted down over Healy's grave.

She waited as a carved slab was laid over the soil and set into place. A stone Cross served as a simple tombstone.

The group gathered around the grave began to shuffle and look at their watches. A crow cawed from a nearby tree, setting off its neighbours, the cacophony raucous in the silence. The sound seemed to serve as a starting pistol, and the mourners dispersed quickly, racing for the cemetery gates.

Neve Forrester hung back. 'I'm glad you came, Inspector,' she said. 'I would appreciate an update.'

Persis quickly brought the Englishwoman up to speed.

Taking out her notebook, she showed her Healy's last riddle.

Forrester stared intently at the page, as if she might force meaning from the words with the fierceness of her gaze. Finally, she sighed. 'No. It means nothing to me.' She patted Persis on the arm, a gesture of intimacy that surprised her. 'Well done. I have every faith you'll see this through.'

She turned and walked briskly away.

Stepping back towards the grave, Persis saw that Erin Lockhart was still there, Blackfinch with an arm around her shoulders.

A splinter stabbed its way under her skin.

Lockhart was silently weeping. Persis found the display of emotion jarring. She wouldn't have believed the hard-nosed American capable of such sentimentality.

She waited in silence.

Sunlight gilded the tombstones around Healy's plot; the air danced in the heat.

Finally, Lockhart reached into a pocket for a handkerchief and dabbed at her tears. 'Forgive me. I never cry at funerals. It's just . . . such a damned waste!' She seemed to get hold of herself. Turning to face Persis, she asked, 'Archie tells me you're one step closer to finding the manuscript?'

Archie?

Persis blinked, momentarily nonplussed. The woman was all business again.

She glanced at Blackfinch who, having withdrawn his arm from the American, was now standing there like a lost sheep. A wave of heat prickled her skin as she recalled the taste of his lips, the feel of his hands on her—

'Inspector?' Lockhart was staring at her, waiting for an answer.

She coughed to hide her embarrassment, then told her about her recent findings. She had decided that taking Lockhart into her confidence was worth the risk – the American was probably the one person in Bombay who had known Healy's mind or as much of it as he was willing to reveal.

But Lockhart could make nothing of the latest riddle. Nevertheless, the idea that Nazis were running around the city chasing the manuscript seemed to enrage her. 'Three years ago, the Smithsonian sent me to Poland to look at their concentration camps in preparation for an exhibition. Auschwitz. Sobibor. Treblinka. I have a strong stomach, but the revulsion I experienced walking around those places, knowing what the Nazis did to millions of civilians, to women and children ...' Her jaw clenched. 'I don't suppose until that moment I understood what depravity *really* means. We've been programmed to believe that humanity is better than it is. That we're somehow fashioned in God's image. Well, if this is what God looks like, then I really don't ever want to meet him.'

'Did Healy ever mention them? The Nazis?'

'No. As I said before, he refused to talk about his time in the war. He hated them, that much I know. Whatever they did to him over there, it left its mark.'

'Can you think of any reason they would transfer him out of the prison in Vincigliata, but then doctor the records to show that he was still there?'

She shook her head, her golden hair bouncing around her shoulders. 'It's strange. They must not have wanted anyone to know they'd taken John somewhere else. I suppose if you're going to torture a man as relatively well known as he was, you take precautions. The propaganda war was just as important as the physical one.'

But Persis didn't think the explanation fit the facts.

Lockhart looked at her watch. 'I've got to be going,' she said. Her usual brisk demeanour appeared to have reasserted itself, the uncharacteristic display of emotion no more than a passing aberration. 'Look, I know this is asking a lot, but can you keep me informed?'

Persis flashed a humourless smile. 'You still think you can procure the manuscript for the Smithsonian?'

Lockhart refused to back down. 'The world must go on, Inspector. I have a job to do.' She turned to Blackfinch. 'Perhaps we can meet up for lunch, sometime? I'd love to know a bit more about your work out here.' She held out a card. Blackfinch looked at it stupidly, then accepted it as if it were a live grenade, glancing guiltily at Persis as he slipped it into the pocket of his jacket.

They watched her walk briskly away.

'I wonder why Healy's father didn't ask for the body to be returned to England?' remarked Blackfinch in an overloud voice. She got the impression he was filling the sudden void to prevent her from commenting on the lunch invitation.

Not that *that* mattered to her. In any way. Why should it?

'I think he said goodbye to his son a long time ago. Whoever Healy was now, he wasn't the same man that left to go to war.'

Her eyes lingered on Healy's grave. Words had been carved on the slab.

Father in thy gracious keeping
Leave we now thy servant sleeping

The clipped epitaph brought a lump to her throat. The strangest sensation overcame her then, that John Healy's life had somehow become superimposed on her own; that his emotions, his thoughts, the tortured mystery of his final days, had become invested in *her*.

On the heels of this feeling came a quiet desolation, temporarily stilling her thoughts.

'Are you alright, Persis?'

Blackfinch, looking down at her with concern.

She grimaced, embarrassed that he had seen her overcome by . . . what? A vision? A momentary empathy with a man she had never known?

'I should be getting back.'

'Persis.' He hesitated. 'Do you want to talk about last night?'

She risked a glance and saw that a high colour had risen to his cheeks.

'There's nothing to talk about.'

'I disagree. Something happened. It would be silly to den—'

'I must be getting back,' she said, cutting him off. She turned and began to walk away, her feet seemingly encased in cement. Unbidden, her mind kept replaying their encounter in the jeep, the closeness of his face, his breath on her lips, the feel of his hands moving over her body.

He followed, his long strides easily keeping pace.

'Is it because of *him*?'

'No.'

'He wants you back, doesn't he?'

'No.'

'You're still in love with him, aren't you?'

'No.'

She flew through the gates and scrabbled into her jeep, slamming the door shut behind her.

He stared at her through the window like a boy outside a sweet shop without the money to venture inside.

She felt her heart twist and bend. Why did she feel as if she'd walked out on to a branch that was about to crack under her? . . . No!

She had vowed never again to allow any man to have control over her emotions.

If the price for that was loneliness, then so be it.

She switched on the engine, put the jeep into gear, and screeched out into traffic.

40

It was almost four before she returned to Franco Belzoni's residence. The sun had moved across the sky, but the air was still stiflingly hot. Her shirt stuck to her back as she drove the jeep through the gate, parked, then crunched over the gravel forecourt to the front door.

A different house servant answered, a small, bookish man in white livery. He led her through the house, this time out into a rear garden. Here Belzoni was standing, sipping lemonade as he conversed with another man, smaller, with thick shoulders, a ruthless grey buzz cut, and a hard stare. A terrier in human form.

The man wore a suit that looked about as comfortable on him as a cocktail dress on a rhino.

Belzoni dipped his head as she approached. 'Inspector, may I introduce il Signor Enrico Mariconti?'

Mariconti did a strange shuffle while standing on the spot, a sort of semi-bow while clicking his heels together, then held out his hand. She looked at it, then shook it quickly.

Moist fingertips.

Belzoni ushered them towards a set of cane garden furniture. They sat and ordered more drinks from the house servant, who was hanging around them like a nervous bat.

'How much has Franco told you?' asked Mariconti, once the pleasantries were out of the way. His English was excellent.

'Not nearly as much as I need to know.'

His jaw worked silently. He had small eyes, but his gaze was hard and penetrating. 'Very well. What I will tell you now must be kept in the strictest confidence until such time that I deem fit. Agreed?'

'No,' she said. 'Whatever you tell me must be the truth. No conditions attached. I will use it as *I* see fit to further my investigation.'

His face opened in surprise. A look of pure wonder crossed his rustic features. She supposed that he wasn't used to hearing the word 'no', let alone from a woman. A sort of half smile, half grimace moved the edges of his mouth.

A silence passed between them, until, eventually, he nodded.

'Very well. But may I ask that you operate with discretion?'

'Yes. You may ask.'

He lifted a glass of chilled water and sipped at it before setting it down. 'John Healy is no hero. Yes, he went to war to fight the Nazis, but at Vincigliata he quickly learned what it means to be a real soldier. He was a scholar, a soft man. Once the Nazis discovered who he was, they came for him. They demanded his cooperation. Help them or face torture, even death.'

'What cooperation did the Nazis need from him? He was an academic, not a spy or a politician.'

Mariconti flashed a superior smile. 'Perhaps you are not aware, but Hitler – along with many of his senior officers – was obsessed with art. They looted priceless treasures from across Europe: paintings, statues, jewellery. How do you suppose they knew what was worth stealing, what was worth keeping?'

She waited for him to explain.

'Himmler, in particular, was obsessed with the occult. For this reason, the acquisition of old manuscripts became a passion with him. But there were so few men who understood what he wanted, or could make sense of the treasures he amassed. The SS murdered much of the intelligentsia during their purges; the ones they didn't murder were forced to flee overseas.' He tapped the top of his glass with a thick index finger. 'That is where Healy came in.'

'Are you telling me that Healy worked for the Nazis?' Her tone was sceptical.

'Yes. To be more accurate, he was a collaborator.'

The word sat between them, as heavy as a cannonball.

'He must have had no choice,' she said.

He wagged an admonitory finger at her. 'He was a soldier. A soldier has only two choices if he is captured. To suffer or to die. A soldier who chooses to help the enemy is a collaborator. A traitor.'

She shifted in her seat, processing the idea. Healy – the renowned scholar, the fêted war hero – a traitor. 'Why does no one know of this? What I mean is, if you're correct, then why isn't this common knowledge?'

A hard edge entered his eyes. 'It took a long time for the facts to come to light. Healy had been very clever, you see. He made a deal with the Germans, tried to cover every eventuality. If the Nazis lost the war, and he made it back to England, he did not wish for his reputation to be destroyed. He did not wish to be treated as a collaborator.

'So he asked his new masters to alter the records at Vincigliata. This way, anyone checking after the war would think he had remained imprisoned there. No one would look too closely – and no one did.

'At some point, he found his way out of Italy. We don't know if he escaped or was released, though the latter is unlikely. What matters is that he returned to England, where they called him a hero and gave him a medal.' The sneer in his voice was audible. 'When the truth came to light, only the Allied intelligence services knew. And they decided to keep it to themselves. This, at least, I can understand. After all, the British government did not want anyone to know that they had fêted a Nazi collaborator. What is that saying? Let sleeping dogs lie? Healy was their sleeping dog.

'The only reason that we are talking about it now is because six months ago, my own organisation, SIFAR, stumbled across the truth. My superiors decided they could use this information. You see, the Italian government has made it clear that they wish to recover as much of the lost treasure that the Nazis stole from Italy as possible. Healy helped the Nazis to loot many rare books and manuscripts from my country. Monasteries, museums, university libraries, private collections. Nothing was safe from those vultures.'

She tried to imagine John Healy in league with the Nazis. No doubt, he had agreed only to preserve his own life, to save himself from torture or worse.

But was that cause enough to justify his actions?

How would *she* have acted in the same situation? Sitting here, in this walled garden, with sunlight gilding the trees, it was easy for harsh judgements to prevail; but the moral arbitration of any act depended on the circumstances. She had only to look at her own mother's death. Who, ultimately, was responsible? The British? Her father? Or her mother, for insisting on travelling to that rally?

Yet, by the same token, the facts couldn't be ignored.

For there *was* such a thing as evil, a line that should never be crossed, at least by anyone who wished to return to the light unscathed. John Healy had chosen to collaborate with a regime of unprecedented evil – and hardly anyone *knew*.

She took a long gulp of her iced tea, buying herself a moment to think, then looked at Belzoni. 'Is that why *you're* here?'

He nodded. 'My job was to convince Healy to work with us voluntarily.'

'You gave him another option?'

He shrugged. 'You can guess, no?'

'You would expose him,' she said flatly. 'Do you think that's what drove him to do what he did?'

A crease appeared between his eyebrows. 'I did not make him steal the Dante manuscript. I did not drive him to suicide.'

'Then why did he kill himself? Why *now*?'

'Guilt,' he replied. 'He must have carried it with him since the war. It is no easy thing, to betray one's country.'

It was possible. Erin Lockhart had stated that Healy had been sleeping badly. Nightmares. Guilt could do that. How many times had Persis seen Sam thrashing in his sleep, recalling the fateful day that he'd taken her mother to the rally? Sanaz Wadia's death had cast a shadow that remained to this day.

'None of this explains Healy's actions *now*,' she said, finally. 'Why steal the manuscript in the first place? I mean, if his aim was to help you recover lost manuscripts? Unless ...' She looked squarely at Mariconti. 'Did you order Healy to steal the Dante manuscript so that you could take it back to Italy?'

His head snapped back. 'No.'

'That would explain a lot.'

'I tell you no.'

'What would be the sense in that?' Belzoni cut in. 'We would never be able to exhibit it publicly in Italy if it was stolen. It would cause a diplomatic nightmare.'

'Since when has that ever bothered anyone? Possession is the only thing that matters, right?'

The two men exchanged a glance that she couldn't fathom. She wondered if she'd hit closer to the mark than she'd thought.

Certainly, it would make sense.

Force Healy to steal the manuscript. Smuggle it back to Italy. Then deny any knowledge of his actions. Let the arguments roll on for ever.

Even now, the Indian government was making representations to its British counterpart for the return of priceless treasures such as the Kohinoor diamond. The British, for their part, had all but ignored the requests. There was about as much chance of the stolen loot being returned as there was of her father giving up drinking and taking up a life of piety.

'What do you intend to do if we find the manuscript?'

'We will continue to petition the Indian government for its return to Italy,' said Mariconti. 'Through official channels.' It had the sound of a rehearsed line.

She debated with herself, unsure whether to believe him.

'Believe me, Inspector, our only purpose is to ensure that the Dante is safe,' said Belzoni gently. 'It is part of our history. It means a lot to us.'

She pulled out her notebook. Turning it to Healy's final riddle, she set it down on the table. 'Healy has been leaving clues behind. I think he *wants* us to find the manuscript.'

They examined the riddle. Mariconti's lower lip curled downwards like a camel's. 'I do not understand.'

'That's the point,' she said. 'I think he wanted to make his trail difficult enough so that not just anyone could work it out.'

'*You* worked it out,' said Belzoni. He stared at her with undisguised admiration.

She coloured. 'I had help.'

Mariconti slapped the table in frustration. '*Merda!*'

The house servant materialised, bearing an envelope on a silver tray. 'Madam. A peon has arrived with a message for you.'

She stood, took the envelope, and opened it.

It was from Frank Lindley at the university.

Must speak now. Meet me at my office.

She checked her watch. It had just turned five.

41

Clearly, Frank Lindley had discovered something.

She watched him as he paced his office, jowls trembling with excitement. Every few seconds, he would stop and mutter, 'This is incredible.'

She waited until he was ready to speak. He handed her a sheaf of papers from a Manila folder on his desk. 'This is your friend, James Ingram.'

The top sheet was a fax of a military service record. At the top was the Reichsadler, the Nazi Imperial Eagle, wings outstretched, clutching a swastika in its talons. She'd read somewhere that the symbol was corrupted from the aquila, the heraldic eagle used as a standard by Roman legions.

Immediately below the eagle were the words *Personal Bericht*.

Next, there was a headshot of James Ingram, staring straight ahead. He was wearing a Nazi cap and uniform. His hair was dark, not the blond she recalled. Below the photograph were his personal details – height, age, address, followed by what she presumed were the particulars of his service record.

And his name.

Matthias Bruner.

'What does it say?' The text was in German.

'Ingram was a Nazi, of that there's no doubt. But he wasn't just any Nazi.' Lindley's eyes shone. 'He served in the Waffen-SS. He made his name in Ukraine, following the German invasion of the Soviet Union in 1941, where he was given charge of an

Einsatzkommando, a unit of the Einsatzgruppen, Hitler's mobile death squads. These were the SS units whose mission was to exterminate Jews, Polish intellectuals, and communists in captured territories, usually behind the advancing German front. Many operated in the aftermath of Operation Barbarossa, the Axis invasion of the Soviet Union, murdering countless Jews. We managed to track down most of the commanders of these units after the war, but many of the ranking officers escaped justice. Bruner – Ingram – was one of those officers.'

She turned to the other pages, appended to the top sheet.

The text was accompanied by disturbing photographs – corpses in pits, corpses piled against a wall before what looked like a Nazi firing squad.

'Units like Bruner's were responsible for mass murder,' Lindley continued, 'often using mobile gas vans. They'd bundle Jews into the van, and drive out into the forest. By the time they got there, the van would have done its work, and bodies would tumble out of the rear doors. They'd then have other Jews bury the dead in pits.'

Her insides shuddered. Such inhumanity! Truly, the horrors of the Nazi regime couldn't be logged on any normal scale of evil.

She stared at Bruner's photograph . . . And to think, this man had sat just a few feet away from her! Had tried to kill her.

A vicious sense of satisfaction pulsed through her.

She was glad she'd shot him dead.

'How did he end up in India?'

'That's where it gets complicated.' Lindley rocked back and forth on his feet. 'Towards the latter half of the war, Bruner found himself working for the Abwehr. Do you remember I told you about that?'

She nodded. 'You said it was an intelligence and espionage outfit.'

'Correct. The Abwehr recruited members of the Waffen-SS, especially those with the sort of track record Bruner had. Men who would follow orders to the letter, no matter how unpalatable. The Abwehr was involved in several daring raids, led by its last commander, Otto Skorzeny.

'Skorzeny, as I mentioned before, is thought to have run a Nazi escape network called the Spider. My guess is that *that* is how Bruner escaped the Allies. Disguised as James Ingram. Skorzeny is also the man from the photograph you sent me.'

He handed her the picture she had had delivered to him, the one she had found in Ingram's jacket. She had been right. Ingram's mysterious fishing companion *had* been another high-ranking Nazi.

'None of this explains what Ingram – Bruner – was doing in India and his apparent interest in the Dante manuscript.'

'Bruner was never given high command. That's saying a lot in the Nazi structure, where the bigger a sociopath you were, the more likely you were to be promoted. He was, however, the perfect adjutant. Intelligent, ruthless, capable. He finished his last years as Skorzeny's right-hand man. I can only surmise that he's still following orders.'

'If that's true, then who's giving the orders to him now?'

'I don't know. Though, if I might indulge in wild speculation . . . Skorzeny himself is on the run. Has been since he escaped in 1948. That's the same year as that photo of yours is dated. I think it proves that Bruner and Skorzeny were in contact.'

'Escaped?'

'From an internment camp in Darmstadt, Germany. After escaping he hid out in a farm in Bavaria, but fled after a tip-off that the authorities had found him. He was later spotted in Paris. That was three months ago. He's a slippery customer, by all accounts. Not your run-of-the-mill Nazi.'

'In what way?'

'He's a charismatic man. An old-school soldier, unlike a lot of the Nazi high command, who were basically civilians who saw which way the winds were blowing and clambered aboard Hitler's National Socialist German Workers' Party bus. Skorzeny was a civil engineer by background. He tried to join the Luftwaffe, but, at six four, was deemed too tall. He ended up in Hitler's bodyguard regiment, the Liebstandarte SS Adolf Hitler. He subsequently distinguished himself in the invasion of the Soviet Union, where he ran a technical section tasked to seize Communist Party infrastructure.

'He received an Iron Cross, and was posted to a desk in Berlin, where he developed some fairly ingenious proposals for unconventional commando warfare. This led to him being appointed to set up and command an SS school to train operatives in sabotage, espionage, and paramilitary techniques.' He paused to pick up a second set of papers from the folder on his desk. Flicking through them, he continued: 'Skorzeny practised what he preached. He was never the type to be happy sitting in an office. He led a number of notorious raids. For one of them, Operation Greif, in which his men wore Allied uniforms, he was later tried for breaching the 1907 Hague Convention, but was acquitted.'

'As I said, none of this explains why he or Bruner would be interested in the Dante manuscript.'

'You're correct. To be honest, I have no idea why they would care about a copy of *The Divine Comedy*, no matter how old. My point is that if Bruner was out here, it may be that your investigation can lead us to Skorzeny too. Skorzeny is a fugitive. He was never convicted of the sort of slaughter that many in the Nazi command were deemed guilty of – and there is little evidence to say that he was ever involved in mass murder – nevertheless, it would be quite a coup if we could find out where he's holed up.'

Persis did not share his obvious excitement. But she understood now why Lindley had seemed so agitated. Helping track down a military criminal as notorious as Otto Skorzeny would undoubtedly offer its own rewards to a man in his field.

Perhaps sensing her lack of enthusiasm, Lindley subsided. He stuffed the papers back into the folder, and thrust it at her. She added Bruner's papers, then tucked the folder under her arm. 'Thank you for your help.'

'Think nothing of it. I lost good friends in the war. In my opinion, the only good Nazi is a dead Nazi.'

42

A cold shower usually helped to clear her mind. But, having showered and sat down for dinner with her father, she found her thoughts mired in quicksand.

Each revelation in the investigation only seemed to raise more questions. Lindley's findings had verified the fact that James Ingram was a Nazi, but had offered no further clarity as to his interest in the Dante manuscript. As the case sat, several suspects remained in her crosshairs, as potential conspirators in the theft of Dante's masterpiece.

Franco Belzoni.

Enrico Mariconti.

Erin Lockhart.

Sam stared at her over his plate. 'Am I boring you?'

She gave a guilty start. She'd tuned out his latest tirade, this time against the nuns of the Order of Carmel.

The nuns, cloistered in a three-acre monastery in the western suburbs, rarely left the premises. Over the years, they had become steady clients of the bookshop, ordering both religious texts and wider reading material. Their habit of haggling over the price infuriated Sam. The nuns tended to pay for most of their commodities with blessings, something for which her father had little use. Their latest crime? The head of the order, Sister Clara, had asked Sam to source for her an early edition of *Wuthering Heights*. Having done so, she now told him the cover was too dog-eared for her liking, and refused to pay.

'Why don't you give it to her as a gift?'

He glared at her as if she'd asked him to hand over a lung. She held his gaze until he looked back down at his plate. 'It's the principle of the thing,' he muttered. 'Just because they're nuns doesn't mean they're holier than thou.'

She left him, still grumbling, and went downstairs into the bookshop.

Here she searched the shelves for a book she'd come across a month ago, an account of Nazi Germany.

Sinking into the sofa at the shop's rear, she began flicking through the pages.

It was a dry rendition of facts, the rise of Hitler and National Socialism during the interwar years, the battles and major fronts of the war. The book glossed over the horrors of the concentration camps, the mass killings.

She snapped the book shut and stared at the ceiling.

A fly crawled along a crack.

She walked to the front counter and picked up the phone.

Blackfinch sounded as if he'd been drinking. His voice was a little too bright, a little too cheerful. 'Persis. How can I help?'

She hesitated, suddenly unsure of herself. 'When we first met, you said that you'd spent time looking at mass graves. After the war.'

A pause. He probably hadn't expected her to lead with that. Not after the way she'd run from him earlier in the day. 'Yes. I was working for a Ministry of Defence mission digging up such graves across Europe. They needed a crime scene expert on the team. Why do you ask?'

The words seemed to unfurl of their own accord.

She told him about James Ingram's real identity, about the Einsatzkommando units and their mission to suppress the threat of native resistance behind the German Army's fighting front via a campaign of mass murder.

'Did you follow the Nuremberg trials?'

She remembered seeing coverage in the newspapers, snatches of the trials covered on Pathé News. There had been too much going on in her own country – those last years of the independence movement, the horrors of Partition, Gandhi's assassination, the tumultuous first years of Nehru's government – for her to take an overt interest.

'Nuremberg marked the first time we put men on trial for crimes against humanity,' said Blackfinch. 'A Polish lawyer, Raphael Lemkin, coined the term "genocide" to describe the Nazis' extermination of Jews – Hitler's "Final Solution". The word is an amalgam of "genos" – the Greek word for "tribe" – and "-cide", Latin for "killings".' He paused. 'The Nazis were a horror the like of which we'd never seen. It's still incomprehensible to me, the things they did. I've never bought the "I was only following orders" defence. I can't imagine a situation where any decent man could follow such orders.'

Persis wasn't so sure. She'd witnessed the Partition rioting up close, how quickly men could become something less than human, more than monsters. Two million had died in an unthinking wave of violence that had left no part of the country unscathed.

As he spoke, she began to flick through the folder Lindley had given her.

She quickly stopped, held by a photograph attached to Matthias Bruner's war record.

A group of prisoners digging. Behind them, nonchalantly smoking a cigarette as he chatted to a comrade, was a German soldier. His colleague was smiling, as if they'd just shared a joke. It occurred to her that the German soldiers knew that, in just a short while, they would murder these men, women, and children in cold blood. They were standing there joking as they forced their victims to dig their own graves. There was no solemnity to their bearing.

It was simply routine; they gave no more thought to the matter than stubbing out a cigarette.

More photographs followed.

The same prisoners kneeling before a firing squad. A Nazi standing behind a young woman, a gun placed to the back of her head. The angle of the photograph made it impossible to see her expression.

And finally, a shot of the pit, corpses piled inside it like rag dolls.

Darkness welled inside her, a great tide of loathing and horror. How could human beings behave in this way? How could any morality justify such unthinking evil? Why hadn't *they* done something? The victims. Why hadn't they fought? Didn't they realise what was about to happen?

'Persis, are you alright?'

She stopped turning the pages. Nausea swirled around her insides.

'I – I'm sorry about last night.'

A beat of silence. 'Why are you sorry?'

She took a deep breath. 'Archie, I think you're a wonderful man—' She stopped.

'But?'

'But . . . we're colleagues. And soon, you'll return to England.' She grasped for the words. 'We're from two different worlds.' She realised that she sounded like a hackneyed scene from a Hollywood potboiler. She plunged on. 'It simply wouldn't work.'

'Do I get any say in this?'

Be firm, she told herself. 'No. I'm afraid my mind's made up.'

'Do you mean that others have made up your mind for you?'

The accusation wasn't without merit. Unconsciously, she began to flick through the sheets again, struggling to frame her next words. 'You don't understand.'

'So why don't you explain?'

The words rushed out of her in a torrent. 'Have you any idea what it's like? Being me? Fighting the battles I fight each day? My life is a public spectacle, fair game for every hack in the country. For no other reason than because I'm a woman.'

Her fingers continued to turn the sheets, moving on to the papers Lindley had collected pertaining to Otto Skorzeny, Bruner's former commander.

'Can you imagine the field day they'd have if you and I ...' She froze.

The sheet beneath her fingers was the first page of Skorzeny's service record. It included a photograph.

Shock rolled through her.

It couldn't be.

'Persis?'

'I'm sorry,' she breathed. 'I have to go.'

She put down the phone, snuffing out his incipient protest.

Picking up the sheet, she stared at the page. A prickling sensation crawled over her scalp.

This was it.

The missing link.

Call it serendipity, call it blind luck. But the answer had fallen into her lap. Or at least, the shape of an answer.

She glanced at the clock on the wall. Almost ten.

Not too late.

43

The building was rundown, seemingly held up by the two towers on either side of it, like a drunk. A maze of black cables criss-crossed the narrow spaces between the towers, some employed as washing lines. The front façade was weather-beaten, cracked by sun, pitted by rain, and marred by torn and faded Bollywood posters, stretching all the way to the top floor.

Many of the balconies had grills over them. On the second floor an elderly woman stared glumly down at her through the mesh.

There was no guard at the entrance, and no elevator. She hadn't expected either.

She climbed five flights. A young woman in the stairwell on the fourth floor nursed a baby at her breast. Persis wondered why she didn't do it in her apartment. And then the woman – no more than a girl, really – shifted on the concrete steps and Persis saw the swollen right cheek, and understood.

Standing before Flat 503, she hesitated.

What if she was wrong?

She knocked on the door.

Moments later, it swung back to reveal a small woman, in her twenties, dark-skinned and beautiful. She wore a sleeveless cotton nightgown, patterned with butterflies.

'Yes?'

'I'm sorry to disturb you but I need to speak with your husband.'

The woman stared at her, suspicion gathering in her eyes.

Perhaps she should have worn her uniform.

'My name's Persis.'

Understanding dawned. And with it rage. Her jaw tightened. 'You – you have the nerve to come here?' She thrust a finger at her, stepping forward, forcing Persis to back-pedal. 'Get out! Get out of here before I—'

'Martha!'

The woman froze. Behind her appeared the towering figure of George Fernandes, clad in vest and shorts, with an infant asleep on his shoulder. The infant twitched but did not wake. Fernandes's eyes widened as he caught sight of Persis. 'What are *you* doing here?'

'We need to talk.'

Martha seemed about to erupt again, but Fernandes cut her off with a look. He handed her the child. 'Put him to bed.'

'But—'

'Martha. Please.'

She glared daggers at Persis, then retreated to a bedroom, slamming the door behind her.

Fernandes ushered Persis in and waved at a sofa that had seen better days. The room was small, a third the size of her own living room. Fernandes seemed even larger in the space, a bear trapped in a cage.

She took the folder from under her arm, looked for a space on the cluttered coffee table to set it down. Fernandes pushed plates and toys to one side.

She lifted out Otto Skorzeny's personnel sheet and set it on the table. Beside it, she laid down the photograph she'd found sewn into Ingram/Bruner's jacket – Bruner fishing with Skorzeny.

The two photographs – of Skorzeny in his personnel file and Skorzeny fishing – were clearly of the same man, the only difference being that in the personnel photo the left side of the man's face was visible – including the prominent scar running from the corner of his mouth to his ear.

'This is Otto Skorzeny. A Waffen-SS Obersturmbannführer – one of Hitler's senior commandos. He ran a German intelligence agency called Abwehr. After the war, he supposedly ran an escape network for Nazis called the Spider.'

'They call them ratlines,' muttered Fernandes.

'What?'

'Nazi escape networks. I read that somewhere.'

She stared at him, wondering why people of her class so often underestimated those born into lesser circumstances. She'd never pegged Fernandes for a reader. 'During the war, he was the commanding officer of the man who attacked me. James Ingram, real name: Matthias Bruner, a Nazi on the run. Skorzeny himself escaped from an internment camp two years ago.

'On the way here, I stopped at Le Château des Rêves. I showed Jules Aubert the photograph and he confirmed that Skorzeny was the man they'd seen in there – Udo Becker – our Mr Grey. And Ingram was the "tall blond man" Skorzeny met with that evening.'

Fernandes sat back, realisation hitting him like an express train. 'Are you saying that our investigations have led us to the same place? That we're both looking for the same man?'

She nodded. 'Bruner and Skorzeny came to Bombay for a reason. I believe they came here to steal the Dante manuscript. I think they convinced John Healy to help them. Or coerced him.'

'How?' asked Fernandes. 'Healy was a famous man.'

'I think they used the truth about Healy's time in Italy against him.'

Quickly, she explained about John Healy's falsified prisoner of war record and Belzoni's allegations that the Englishman had been a collaborator during the war. 'Matthias Bruner was the man who took Healy out of Vincigliata prison. I think that's why Skorzeny asked him to take on this mission. I think Bruner supervised Healy during his time working for the Nazis.'

Fernandes allowed the new information to sink in. 'But why? *Why* would they want to steal the manuscript?'

'I don't know. Whatever the reason, somewhere along the line, Healy had a change of heart. He hid the manuscript after stealing it, instead of handing it over to Bruner and Skorzeny. And then he left behind clues so that we could find it again. I think he hoped the delay – the time it would take us to unravel his clues and locate the manuscript – would be enough to scare the Germans away. They wouldn't want to hang around in the light of such scrutiny.'

'Why not just *not* steal it in the first place? If it mattered so much to him to keep it safe, why not just tell us there were Nazis out here trying to steal the damn thing?'

'I guess he didn't want to risk the truth about his own past coming to light. Being labelled a collaborator. I think he might also have worried that the Nazis would simply find someone else to do their dirty work if he refused them. He wanted to keep the manuscript out of their hands at any cost.' She paused to organise her own thoughts, then pressed on. 'This was a form of atonement, for helping them steal so many valuable manuscripts during the war. This one became a symbol. If he could just save Dante's masterwork, perhaps he could go to his death absolved. In his own eyes, at least.'

Fernandes seemed to turn this over, inspecting it from all angles, then nodded. 'And Francine Kramer?'

'As her doctor told us, she thought she recognised Skorzeny when he came to the nightclub. He must have visited the camp where she was imprisoned. Perhaps he even abused her while she was there. It doesn't matter. He was a Nazi and for Francine that was enough. She invited him to her home to confirm his identity. Or perhaps she'd already made up her mind and just wanted revenge.'

'You think she was planning to kill him?'

'It's possible. But she made a mistake. He saw through her and killed her.'

A sombre silence. 'Skorzeny is still in the city, isn't he?' Fernandes said.

'I don't think he'll leave without the manuscript.'

'Which means *you're* still in danger.'

She hadn't thought of it in those terms, but Fernandes was right. Healy's final clue was in her possession. If anyone was going to solve it, it was her.

Skorzeny would stay close, waiting for her to unravel the mystery.

Which meant that it was a good bet that he was following her, as Bruner had done.

And *that* meant that she – and she alone – had the chance to finish what Francine Kramer had begun.

When looked at it that way, she really had no choice at all.

44

The hammering on the door pulled her blearily from sleep. Akbar made a soft protest at the back of his throat, then rolled spinelessly away, twisting the cotton sheet around himself.

It was her father. He glared at her from his wheelchair. 'It's a phone call. He says it's urgent.'

She stumbled into the living room, rubbing sleep from her eyes. The carriage clock said six-fifteen a.m.

The phone sat on a sideboard, beneath a photograph of her late mother, the receiver off its cradle. She picked it up.

'Are you awake?' It was Seth. Surprise moved through her. It was highly unusual for the SP to be alert and active this early in the day.

'Is everything alright, sir?'

'No,' he replied stonily. 'Everything is *not* alright. It's about as far from bloody alright as it could be. The man you've been following around – the Italian, Belzoni ... He's turned up dead.'

Belzoni lived on the ground floor of a three-storey building just yards from Electric House, the former headquarters of the city's electric supply, located near the Colaba Causeway. As a child, Persis remembered wandering around a showroom that had once been housed there, marvelling at a range of modern appliances while the sweating salesman tried to convince her sceptical father that electrical gadgets were the 'wave of the future'.

Belzoni's building was located on a side street, a narrow alley made narrower by trees and overhanging cable lines, blotting out the sun.

A police jeep was parked outside.

Beside it, she recognised Blackfinch's latest transport.

The guard at the gate salaamed nervously as she walked past.

She found Seth and the Englishman in the bedroom, together with Blackfinch's assistant, Mohammed Akram. Blackfinch was kneeling beside the bed, looking under it, while Seth's attention was focused on Franco Belzoni's corpse.

The Italian was trussed securely to a wooden chair in the corner of the room, head lolling forward on his chest. He wore only a pair of undershorts. His disarrayed hair flopped over his forehead. Blood smears ranged over his body; blood had also pooled at his feet, soaking into a thin rug.

Strange triangular marks, painfully red and raw, marred his chest. There was one on his right cheek, she saw.

Seth lifted his eyes. She saw that he'd lit a cigarette. It jittered in his fingers.

'He was tortured. They used an iron on him.'

Her stomach inverted itself.

She looked back at the dead man, her thoughts returning to their last meeting. She realised that, despite Belzoni not having been entirely truthful with her, she'd come to like the Italian. The idea that he'd suffered such a torturous death, that anyone could have done . . . *this* to him . . . She exhaled deeply. 'What killed him?'

Blackfinch stood up. He approached and handed her a pair of gloves. 'Lift up his head.'

She pulled on the gloves, then did as he'd suggested, gently raising the Italian's head.

Belzoni had been shot through the right eye. The socket was a pulped mess. Blood matted the back of his skull.

She lowered his face back on to his chest, took a deep breath, and stepped back.

Beside her, Seth made a coughing noise in his throat. She knew he rarely ventured out of Malabar House these days. He seemed naked without an office around his shoulders. Or a drink in his hand. The truth was she could use a stiff whisky herself about now.

'Skorzeny,' she breathed.

Seth looked at her curiously.

She brought him up to speed on developments, glad of something else to focus on. Blackfinch listened in, intently. The uncomfortable conversation from the night before kept intruding into her thoughts, but she pushed it away.

He was a big boy. He would have to deal with it.

When she'd finished, Seth sat down gingerly on the edge of the bed. He seemed to have shrunk. 'It was bad enough having one Nazi running around the city, now you tell me there's another one? And God only knows how many more, ready to crawl out of the woodwork.' He waved his cigarette at Belzoni. 'They tortured that poor bastard for a reason. What was it?'

'I think Skorzeny's been following me around. If that's the case, he'll know I've been meeting with Belzoni. He might even know Belzoni's working for the Italian government. Perhaps he thought I told him somethi—' She stopped as the implications of what she was saying hit her.

Was *she* responsible for Franco Belzoni's death? Had she inadvertently given Skorzeny a reason to torture and murder the Italian?

A shudder moved through her.

'You're not to blame for this,' murmured Blackfinch.

She looked up at him. His features were softened by the early light filtering in from the windows. If he was still upset about yesterday, he didn't show it. There seemed only concern in his eyes.

Her expression hardened.

She didn't need his pity. Or any man's. 'How was he able to walk in here, do this, and then walk out again without anyone realising?'

'The guard at the gate says a man turned up late last night, claimed he was a friend of Belzoni's. He was tall, dark-haired, scar on his cheek. Had a bottle of whisky with him. He left a couple of hours later. Gave the half-finished bottle to the guard.'

'Such arrogance!' Seth had risen from the bed, his face swollen with fury. 'These – these *animals* think they can walk around *my* city, doing just as they please!'

'This Skorzeny seems like a man of unusual boldness,' observed Blackfinch. 'I mean, a man that recognisable, on the run from any number of authorities, parading around as if he's at the beach.'

'I think that's part of his persona,' Persis said. 'He's managed to evade justice for so long, he actually believes himself to be invulnerable.'

'Then that,' said Blackfinch, 'is how we'll catch him.'

45

Birla was asleep on his forearms at his desk. Beside him, Haq was chewing on a samosa. It was an article of faith at the station that Haq would always be eating, no matter the time. The man had the appetite of a bear.

She saw that George Fernandes was typing at his desk.

He nodded as she walked in and sat down heavily at her desk.

She sent Gopal scurrying for a glass of lime water.

Closing her eyes, she meditated on the case.

Things were coming to a head. It was anyone's guess how the Italian government would react to the murder of Franco Belzoni. The man was an academic, a respected scholar. By rights, he should have been tucked away in a leafy university setting far from murderous Nazis. But he'd clearly agreed to work with Enrico Mariconti's intelligence agency, SIFAR. He'd put himself in harm's way, for a cause he believed in.

Why? Were old manuscripts really worth a man's life?

Belzoni had clearly thought so. He'd seen something noble in his mission, aiding in the recovery of stolen treasures for the Italian people. His people. He couldn't have anticipated that his life would be cut short in the pursuit of that cause.

Murdered at the hands of a hardened killer.

She knew in her gut that Skorzeny wouldn't flee the city. Not without the manuscript.

A thought occurred to her, and she sat up straight.

She'd shared Healy's final clue with Belzoni. She had no doubt that the Italian would have told Skorzeny everything – it was only in the movies that men laughed at their torturers, daring them to do their worst. No man – or woman – could have endured the pain Belzoni had undoubtedly suffered.

Which meant that, in all probability, Skorzeny now had the riddle . . . What if he worked it out before she did?

Panic fluttered in her throat like a trapped moth.

She stood and called over the rest of the team. Haq nudged Birla awake. The pair, together with Fernandes, gathered around her desk.

She told them about Belzoni's murder, and the connection to Otto Skorzeny, impressing on them the need to find the escaped Nazi.

Birla clicked his tongue in disgust. 'Torture.' He shook his head sadly. He walked back to his desk, returned with a copy of the *Times of India*, threw it on to her desk. 'Healy's death is all over the front pages. Everyone seems to have their own theory, the crazier the better. When they get hold of Belzoni's murder and connect the dots, all hell is going to break loose.'

They stared glumly at the newspaper. It was early in the day, but they could imagine the hordes descending on them soon enough.

'Then we don't have much time to solve the puzzle, do we?' she said, eventually.

Birla sighed. 'How hard can it be to find one white man with a scar like that?'

'Harder than you think. Skorzeny was an expert in espionage.'

'It's not as if he's lying low,' observed Haq.

'I think he keeps himself out of sight until he has to act. And then he does it boldly. I think he relies on that façade of self-confidence. It was something Hitler used, a tactic of war. Besides, few people will challenge a man who presents himself with authority.'

'So what do we do?' said Haq.

'We should get his description out there,' offered Fernandes. 'In the newspapers, on the radio. Make it impossible for him to show his face.'

'No,' she said. 'That might drive him away. Do that and we'll never catch him.'

'We can't just let him wander around the city killing innocent people.'

'There's only one more person he might need to kill,' she said, softly.

It took them a moment to understand what she meant.

A hiss of breath escaped Birla. 'You intend to use yourself as bait? Did you wake up in a suicidal mood this morning?'

'Does Seth know about this?' Haq asked.

Only George Fernandes remained silent, his expression thoughtful.

They were interrupted by Gopal. 'Madam, there's a man here to see you.'

She frowned, then looked behind him ... and froze in astonishment.

Zubin Dalal nodded at her, his hands tucked into the pockets of his jacket. 'Do you have a moment? I'd like to speak with you.'

She closed the door to the interview room – and the curious faces of her colleagues – then turned to face him.

'What are you doing here?' Anger tightened her voice.

'I'll be leaving Bombay for a while. I'm going south, to Bangalore. I have an old friend who's asked me to come in with him on a business venture. He's supplying the capital; I'll be the face of the business.'

'I expect he'll be penniless soon.'

He gave a pained smile. 'I suppose I deserve that.' He lowered his head, assuming the posture of the damned. 'I came back to

Bombay for you, Persis. I know that I disappointed you. Hurt you deeply. But that's in the past. I can't do anything to change that. All I ask is that you find it within your heart to forgive me.' He stepped towards her. 'I chose her over you because I was penniless, not because I loved her. My father made some bad investments. What kind of life would I have been able to give you? I reasoned that it was the best thing for both of us. I was wrong.' Another step forward. 'I never stopped thinking about you. You could say it poisoned my marriage.' Another step, and now she could smell his cologne, see the small mole on his left earlobe, the way his dark eyes caught the light. His words seemed to whisper along the inside of her ear. 'Won't you give me another chance? Have you forgotten how in love we were? How it felt when we held each other? When we . . .?' He stopped, gazing at her with an intensity she found unbearable.

Feelings that she'd long suppressed came rushing to the fore. She wanted to deny them, but couldn't. She had loved this man, his charm, his intelligence, his charisma. She'd given him every-thing. And, in return, he'd wounded her more deeply than she would ever allow anyone to know.

She turned away. 'There's nothing for you here.'

A silence like the ringing aftermath of an explosion.

He stood there a moment, then said, 'I understand.'

Time passed and then she heard him walking away. It took every ounce of self-control to stop herself from turning around.

'Persis.' He'd paused by the door. 'I'll be waiting at the Café Eden. My train is at ten-twenty. I hope you'll come.'

She slumped back into her chair, anger bubbling from her like molten lava.

What right did he have to do this? To say those things? How could he expect her to – to simply *forget*?

She grabbed her glass and drained the lime water, then thought about throwing the glass at the wall.

She needed to take her mind off Zubin Dalal.

She picked up the folder Lindley had given her and went through it again, focusing on Otto Skorzeny.

It was on the second look that something snagged.

A covert operation, conducted back in July 1943.

A few weeks after the Allies invaded Sicily, the Italian Grand Council of Fascism voted a motion of no confidence against Benito Mussolini. The Italian king immediately ordered his arrest. Mussolini was taken to the Hotel Campo Imperatore, a ski resort in Italy's Gran Sasso massif, high in the Apennine Mountains.

Hitler sent Otto Skorzeny to rescue the embattled Italian dictator.

On 12 September, Skorzeny, together with sixteen SS troopers, set out on a high-risk glider mission, landing ten DFS 230 gliders on the mountain near the hotel. Skorzeny's crack troops, together with Luftwaffe paratroopers, overwhelmed Mussolini's captors without a shot being fired.

Ten minutes after the beginning of the raid, Mussolini left the hotel, accompanied by German soldiers. He was subsequently flown to Pratica di Mare, and then to Vienna, where Mussolini and Skorzeny stayed overnight at the Hotel Imperial.

The next day Skorzeny escorted Mussolini to Munich, and on 14 September, they met a triumphant Hitler at the Führer's Wolf's Lair headquarters near Rastenburg.

Something about this curious incident bounced around her mind.

This was the missing piece of the puzzle, she was suddenly sure of it, at least insofar as Skorzeny's involvement in the theft of the Dante manuscript was concerned. She didn't know exactly how the jigsaw fit together, but she felt certain the answer lay in Skorzeny's encounter with Benito Mussolini, the man who had once offered a king's ransom for Dante's masterwork.

All she had to do now was find out *where* John Healy had hidden the manuscript.

She took out her notebook, and looked once again at the Englishman's final riddle.

> *The road to salvation has many gates,*
> *That which you seek in Cutters embrace awaits,*
> *'Neath Sun and Moon and unchanging skies,*
> *Watched over by God, in litteral disguise.*
> *'Twixt Jerusalem and Mecca, it lies.*

Between Jerusalem and Mecca? Had Healy somehow managed to smuggle the manuscript out of Bombay?

She knew, from poring over atlases as a girl, that there were any number of small towns between the two great centres of worship – the reference to the manuscript being *watched over by God* and *the road to salvation* would make sense in this context. And the desert skies above the region were usually dry and cloudless; in that sense, they were *unchanging*.

But why would Healy send the manuscript so far away? Who had he entrusted to get it out of Bombay?

She returned to her notebook, focusing on the first line. *The road to salvation* ... Could that be a reference to the contents of the manuscript? *The Divine Comedy* was, quite literally, a story about how man might achieve salvation. And that salvation was possible in a variety of ways – through *many gates* – depending on the nature of the sin.

She went to the next line. *That which you seek in Cutters embrace awaits.* Cutter's embrace. Who was Cutter? It certainly wasn't a common name and no one of prominence in Bombay's history possessing that name sprang to mind.

She quickly confirmed this by calling Neve Forrester, followed by an equally fruitless call to a prominent Bombay historian that Forrester had recommended.

The historian did, however, send her thoughts spinning in a different direction.

'Perhaps *Cutter* isn't a name?' he'd suggested. 'For instance, a cutter is also the word for a small sailboat.'

Could Healy have hidden the manuscript inside an old boat?

A call to the Royal Bombay Yacht Club, and the club's 'commodore', Captain Homi Daruwalla, threw up nothing.

She all but slammed the phone down.

Seeking to clear her head, she decided to take a walk, stopping at the corner of the road for a glass of chai from Afzal's tea stall. In his characteristic white dhoti, the reedy old man had run a brisk trade from that spot for as long as anyone could remember. He kept his ear to the ground and was a source of both scurrilous gossip and, occasionally, useful information. Rumour had it that, in a former life, he'd acted as an informer for the British; counter-rumours suggested that he'd been a double-agent for the revolution.

The only thing that could be said with any certainty was that he made the best cup of tea in the city.

She ran the problem by him. He considered it from all sides, then said, 'You're trying too hard to find hidden meanings. Perhaps you should simply take the facts at face value.'

What did he mean? But he'd already turned away to his next customer.

She walked back to the office, sipping on her tea.

Cutters embrace. What if she took Healy's words at face value? *Cutters* embrace.

A pair of cutters? Could Healy have meant a pair of bolt cutters? Or scissors? Scissors' embrace?

No. That was patently ridiculous.

What about those who performed the *act* of cutting?

Leather workers, for instance? Or carpenters? Butchers? She shook her head. The list could go on endlessl—

A boulder crashed through her thoughts.

She stood on the spot, allowing the idea to unfurl itself, like the wings of a newly hatched butterfly . . . Yes! That could be it.

Immediately, doubt assailed her. Was it too bold a leap?

There was someone who would know, someone she could ask. Someone she trusted implicitly.

She turned on her heel and headed for her jeep.

46

'Must you take so long over *every* move?'

'Chess is a game of patience, my friend. It cannot be rushed.'

'I've seen more animated corpses.'

'A man of your vintage should be less concerned with haste.'

Her father was in the bookshop, sat at his counter, playing chess with Dr Aziz.

He looked up as she entered. 'Persis. What are you doing here?'

'You're looking well, dear,' said Aziz. 'Which is more than I can say for your father. If he doesn't want to fall flat on his face, he really should adhere to the dietary regimen I've prescribed him.'

'Your dietary regimen consists of bitter gourd juice and lentils. I may as well be dead.'

'You soon will be, if you don't listen.'

'I'll outlive you, you deranged old quack.'

'Not according to my rectal thermometer, you won't.'

'Be quiet, the pair of you. I have something important to ask.' She looked around. There was only one other person in the shop, an elderly white woman at the very rear, in the *Botanicals* section.

She lowered her voice. 'When I was young, a couple of years after Mama died, I walked in on the pair of you playing dress up.'

They stared at her, her father examining her over the top of his half-moons with an expression that could have curdled milk.

'What I mean is that you were both dressed in outlandish costumes. You told me they were for some fancy-dress ball you were going to, and shooed me out of the room. You never spoke of it again.' She took a deep breath. 'I want the truth. Why were you dressed like that?'

'Why the sudden interest?' asked Aziz. He seemed unperturbed by her accusation.

She hesitated, then plunged on and explained everything she had learned about Healy's final riddle. 'The word *Cutters* could refer to a profession. And it occurred to me that it could mean *stone*cutters. In other words, stonemasons.' She looked squarely at them. 'Are you both members of the Freemasons?'

They glanced at each other. Aziz shrugged. 'Yes.'

'In that case, there's something I'd like to ask you.'

The building, despite its central location near Victoria Terminus station, had always remained invisible, hidden in plain sight, in keeping with the tenets of its builders.

Freemason's Hall was situated on the corner of Murzban Road. Evening traffic roared past as she parked the jeep and made her way to the front entrance where she was met by a tall, slightly stooped elderly man in a plain white shirt and dark trousers. His name was Tariq Shah and he was the Grand Secretary of the District Grand Lodge of Bombay.

'The hall is actually closed at present for renovations,' he said, shuffling under the sandstone porch towards the front door. 'But your father and I have been friends for a long time.' He took out a set of keys and unlocked the door, then ushered her inside.

They entered a grand entrance hall.

Shah waved a hand expansively around. 'Sam said you wished for a guided tour. We don't usually do this sort of thing for the uninitiated, but your father would never let me hear the end of it.' His eyes wobbled behind bottle-bottom glasses. 'That' – he pointed to the corner of the room – 'is the foundation stone, located at the north-east corner of the building, in line with the edicts of Freemasonry. How much do you know about us?'

'Not a great deal,' she said, more to keep his curiosity at bay. Sam had brought her up to speed with all she really needed to know.

Shah immediately launched into a rendition of the history of Freemasonry on the subcontinent. 'The Masons in India go back to the early 1700s, when officers of the East India Company began to meet in Calcutta's Fort William. The first Indian lodge was constituted in 1729. Within two decades, lodges had appeared in Madras and Bombay. Bombay's first Grand Master was Brother James Todd.' He nodded at an austere portrait of a red-faced white man who seemed to be suffering from severe constipation. 'In 1775, the first Indian Mason was initiated, but it wasn't until 1872, when the first *Hindu* Freemason was initiated – a P.C. Dutt – that the doors were flung open to native members.' He swept a hand over the portraits and statues crammed around the entrance hall, historically some of the country's most accomplished men. 'As you can see, the Masons have always attracted men of high worth.'

But no women, she couldn't help but notice. An enlightened institution? Not so enlightened, after all.

A carpeted staircase led in both directions. 'Downstairs, we have our banquet hall and offices,' said Shah, noting her gaze. 'Upstairs is the main temple.'

'The basement,' she said. 'I'd like to see the basement.'

He seemed confused, then shrugged. As they padded down, she couldn't help but say, 'Isn't it true that the British used Freemasonry to strengthen imperial rule in India?'

His cheek twitched. 'It's true that the British employed the bonds of Masonry to bind networks of influential Indians to their cause. But Indians benefited too by such association.'

She decided against probing further. She hadn't come here to debate the rights and wrongs of Freemasonry. Her focus had to be on John Healy and his last act before he had killed himself. And she now believed that some part of that final curtain had taken place here, at Freemason's Hall.

The basement proved to be a warren of rooms.

They walked along a low-ceilinged, carpeted corridor, Shah flicking on light switches as they went. At the end of the corridor they entered a banquet hall – a large, open space with oak panelling and wooden cross-beams, lined with sturdy oak trestle tables. More portraits decorated the walls; a legion of unsmiling busts sat on sideboards. Chandeliers hung overhead, interspersed with ceiling fans. Cast-iron sconces held Gothic candles.

It was a distinctly male redoubt, she couldn't help but think; an excess of pageantry and a dearth of good taste.

On one side of the room was a stage with a lectern. Red curtains covered what she presumed was a screen.

She walked to the stage, climbed a short flight of steps, and made her way to the lectern. Bending down, she swung open a small door built into its base, then took out a wrapped bundle.

Shah looked at her quizzically. 'What's that?'

'An artefact of immense value. This manuscript was stolen from the Asiatic Society and hidden here.'

A hiss of breath escaped his teeth. 'You're talking of the Dante manuscript? The one that's been in the newspapers?'

'I am.'

He seemed astonished. 'What would it be doing *here*?'

'It's my belief that John Healy, the man who stole it, was a Freemason. I believe he couldn't think of any better place to hide it.'

'May the Grand Architect be praised,' murmured Shah.

'Thank you for your help,' she said. 'I have what I came for.'

He nodded and turned to limp back towards the door, stopping short as a shadow detached itself from the darkness beyond and entered the room.

Otto Skorzeny, dressed in a sharp black suit, pointed a pistol at the old man.

'What is this?' said Shah. 'Who are you?'

'Forgive the intrusion,' replied Skorzeny mildly. He waved the pistol at Persis. 'I'll take that, Inspector.'

She stared coldly at him. 'You followed me here?'

'Persis – may I call you Persis? – I must commend you. You have been magnificent! But that is *my* prize, not yours.' His English was impeccable.

'You expect me to just hand it over to you?'

He moved forward. 'I really don't want to hurt you. I didn't want to hurt anyone. It was supposed to be a simple operation.'

'Tell that to Franco Belzoni. To John Healy. To Francine Kramer.' The names arrowed out of her.

'I had nothing to do with John Healy's death,' he said. 'As for the others: regrettable. Especially Francine. I really did like her. But she couldn't let go of the past.'

'You mean her own rape and torture? The murder of her countrymen?'

A hard edge entered his eyes. 'A regime is a powerful locomotive, Inspector. Once it begins to move, you either hop aboard or it cuts you down. For the record, I was never *that* type of Naz— *Stop*!' He aimed the gun at her hand which had drifted towards her holster. 'I really don't want to shoot you, Fräulein. Please don't make me.'

He moved towards Shah, stuck the pistol in his stomach, and pushed him back on to a dining chair.

The speechless old man fell back with a whump.

'I would appreciate it if you did not move.' Turning back to Persis, Skorzeny said, 'The manuscript. *Bitte*.'

Her jaw writhed. She had no doubt that Skorzeny was not only an excellent shot but more than willing to demonstrate his resolve. And there was Shah to consider.

Too many had died already, caught up in Healy's strange game.

She stepped down from the stage, and walked over to him. He was a tall man, broad and heavy-set. He loomed over her in the hall, a giant in a fairy tale. The scar on his cheek seemed to glow.

'First, your revolver. *Slowly*.'

She slid out her revolver and gave it to him. He stuck it into the pocket of his suit.

'And now the manuscript.'

She looked down at the wrapped package in her hands. For a moment, time stood still ... So many had died for this book, words penned almost seven centuries ago. And now it would all be for nought ...

She took a deep breath and handed the manuscript to him. He tucked it under his arm, then held her with an evaluating gaze. 'You really are a remarkable woman. In another life, if we had met, just ordinary citizens of the world...'He grinned. '*Auf Wiedersehen*, Inspector.'

'Wait.' She took a step forward. 'Why? Why did you do this? What could you possibly want with that manuscript?'

He appeared to consider the question. 'I suppose you deserve to know. You've certainly earned it. Very well ... In 1943, I helped to rescue Italy's rightful leader, Benito Mussolini, from imprisonment by disloyal factions in his own country. While escorting him to Munich, we stayed together at the Hotel Imperial in Vienna. I'd never had much time for him before, but that night we drank together and I discovered that he was my twin. We shared a love of the same things; he believed in everything I believed in.

'Mussolini was not like Hitler. Mussolini was a fascist in name only. He believed, like a father, that children must sometimes be beaten for their own good, but he never believed in murdering non-combatants. Hitler had the type of courage that rarely hesitated to volunteer others for death, but Mussolini was a real soldier. He was ... Il Duce.' Skorzeny's voice filled out the room; there was a sense of heavy music to it that made her think of Wagner. 'When I asked him what he desired most, do you know what he told me? A sympathetic woman, a good bottle of wine, a fine cigar ... and peace in Italy.

'I suppose you could say we poured our sins into each other's ears that night. He revealed to me an obsession that had ruled him for many years. A copy of *La Divina Commedia*, here in Bombay. He was an acolyte of Herr Dante Alighieri and it was his dream to collect together all the oldest versions of the manuscript, to put them on display in a new museum in Rome, one he would build after the war.

'That night we got drunk and swore eternal friendship. He made me promise that I would help him recover the Bombay manuscript. He offered me a fortune. We slashed our palms and made a blood oath.

'Six months ago, after fleeing Bavaria, I was given shelter by a wealthy Italian living in France, an old friend of Mussolini. We got to talking and I mentioned the vow I had made. He became animated. A day later, he came to me with a proposition. If I would fulfil my pledge, if I would steal the manuscript and give it to him, he would ensure that I'd receive the sum Mussolini had promised me.' He smiled. 'For a man in my position, it was an offer I could hardly refuse. The mission did not seem overly difficult or dangerous, and the money would allow me to stay out of sight for a very long time without having to rely on the goodwill of others.'

He stood there, wreathed in the room's dimmed lighting, a man blinded by his own glory.

'And Bruner?'

'Matthias and I have been in touch since the end of the war. I helped smuggle him out of Germany, helped him settle in Brazil. Three years later, he repaid the favour by helping me escape from Darmstadt.' An arrogant smile crept around his mouth. 'It was incredible. He walked in with two SS officers dressed in US Military Police uniforms and told the fools there that they were under orders to take me to Nuremberg for a legal hearing. I still find it hard to believe that such a simple ruse worked. Truly, I cannot understand how we lost the war to such dolts.

'Eighteen months later, I was in Paris, sitting in a café, and I saw an article in *Le Monde* about John Healy, the famous English scholar and war hero, now based at the Asiatic Society of Bombay – this was just a few days before my Italian benefactor made me his offer; in fact, it was the article that touched off our conversation. The article stated that Healy was the Curator of Manuscripts at the Asiatic Society and detailed his efforts at producing a new translation of Dante's masterwork.

'I remembered Healy. You see, it was the Abwehr that had been tasked to secure his cooperation during the war. Himmler wanted an expert in ancient manuscripts and Healy practically fell into our laps. When we found out that he was being held at Vincigliata, I sent Matthias along to talk to him.'

'Talk? You mean to threaten him.'

He flashed a lopsided grin. 'I'm afraid Healy didn't put up much of a fight. He was a coward, Inspector. Matthias hardly had to apply any pressure at all. He agreed to help us readily enough. In return, all he asked was that we keep his involvement a secret.'

'That's why you had the documents pertaining to his stay at Vincigliata forged.'

'It was a small price to pay for his willing cooperation. I believe in doing things the easy way, Inspector. Torturing a man into cooperating is a means of last resort.' He bared his teeth. 'We doctored the records and gave Healy a false ID, a nom de guerre. Of course, the alias wasn't much good once he came face to face with some of those he helped us track down; old colleagues, men who knew him or knew of him . . . Not that it mattered. Himmler was never the type to steal a man's possessions and leave him alive to complain about it afterwards.'

Her jaw tightened. 'How did Healy escape?'

'A momentary lapse. Healy had been so docile during the time he'd been working for us that his escort – including Matthias – let their guard down. They'd been raiding a home near the French-Italian border. Things had gone well and they'd decided to celebrate in the local brothel; naturally, they all ended up blind drunk. By the time they regained their senses, Healy was gone. He made it over the border and managed to get to Monaco. He'd stolen a few items of value that helped pay his way on a fishing trawler that took him across the Med to the Tunisian port city of Bizerte – the Allies took it back from us in 1943.'

'Why didn't you expose him?'

'You've never worked in intelligence, have you, Fräulein? One never burns an asset unless there's something to be gained. Healy was being fêted as a hero in England. We knew he hadn't told them the truth. For an intelligence officer, that's the perfect scenario. A man in the enemy fold who might easily be compromised.

'Of course, I had no idea I'd ever need Healy again. But fate has its own plans for us all, yes?'

'So you came to Bombay and threatened to expose him unless he stole the manuscript for you.'

'We did what was necessary.'

'But if he *voluntarily* agreed to cooperate . . . what went wrong? Once he'd taken the manuscript from the Society, why did he hide it? Why did he kill himself?'

The big man shrugged. 'The truth? I don't know. I suspect he had a change of heart. Even the rat looks in the mirror one day and hates what it sees.'

They stood there, allowing a moment of silence for the man at the centre of it all, a man who'd taken his secrets to the grave.

Skorzeny lowered his pistol and began to back away.

A noise darted his head upwards.

George Fernandes emerged from behind the curtains at the rear of the stage. He held a revolver, trained on Skorzeny. 'Take another step and I'll put a hole through you.'

The German's face slackened in astonishment. Then his eyes shifted to Persis. 'Very clever.'

'I knew you'd be following me, now that Bruner was gone, and armed with the information you'd gotten from Belzoni – namely, that I was tracking the final clue Healy had left behind. Once I'd solved the riddle, I sent Fernandes here in advance, to wait for me. To wait for us both.'

'What if I hadn't shown myself?'

'Then I would have set the trap elsewhere. I don't believe you're the type of man to shy away from a challenge.' She grimaced. 'Put the guns on the table. *Slowly*.'

She watched him closely as he placed the weapons on the nearest trestle table.

Fernandes moved down from the stage. On the bottom step, his foot caught, and he stumbled.

Quicker than Persis would have thought possible, Skorzeny grabbed his pistol and fired. Fernandes went down with a grunt.

Persis lashed out, kicking the gun out of the German's hand. She whipped around, swept up her own revolver, and fired.

The retort was extraordinarily loud in the basement room. Skorzeny bellowed in pain, clutching at a spot just below his right shoulder where it met the upper chest; and then his eyes narrowed and he leaped at her.

They went down together, him on top of her, clutching with his left hand at her wrist as she fired off two more shots. She screamed as his weight bore down on her; spots wavered before her eyes.

No!

She gritted her teeth, then reached out with her free arm and stuck a thumb into the wound on his upper chest.

He roared in agony, let go of her gun arm, then smacked back-handedly at her wrist. The blow was powerful enough to dislodge the gun from her hand and send it spinning under the table. He reached back with the same hand and punched her in the jaw.

Her head cracked against the tiled flooring, and she momentarily forgot about the world.

She felt his weight lift from her.

Groggily, she raised her head and saw him limping away, clutching at his shoulder, the manuscript tucked under his arm.

'No!' she breathed, but the room began to spin again. She lay back and closed her eyes.

Eventually, she was able to scrabble to her feet.

Her every instinct screamed at her to hurry after Skorzeny, but, instead, she turned and went to Fernandes.

He lay there like a beached whale, his face pale, eyelids fluttering. She saw that he'd taken a bullet to the stomach. A stain darkened the front of his uniform.

Kneeling beside him, she clutched his hand.

It pulsed warmly.

'Breathe steadily. Don't close your eyes.' She looked up at Shah, still sitting in his chair, clutching at himself in terror. 'Call an ambulance.' She waited. 'Now!'

47

'How far can he get? In that state?' Roshan Seth paced the checker-tiled floor of the Freemason's Hall foyer, wheeling in a tight arc and almost bumping into Archie Blackfinch, standing silently beside a bust of Swami Vivekananda, the famed spiritualist. 'His picture will be everywhere by the morning.'

'Are you sure you want to do that?' asked Persis.

'Things have gone too far,' he said. 'We have no choice.' He stared at her. 'What the hell were you *thinking*?'

She stiffened. 'I was sure he was following me. So I made it easy for him. I guessed that if he thought I'd tracked the manuscript down, and that it was only me here, he'd show himself. I was right.'

'You were reckless! All you did was get Fernandes shot *and* lose the manuscript.'

Her lips pursed, but she held her tongue, allowing Seth's fury to wash over her, then: 'How is he?'

Blackfinch shivered to life. 'The doctors say it's touch-and-go. We won't know if he'll survive until they get him out of the operating theatre.'

She rubbed the back of her neck, stifling the urge to curse. Her jaw throbbed where Skorzeny had struck her . . . *They'd had him!*

How had it gone so wrong?

She remembered George Fernandes's tiny apartment; the incongruous image of the hulking policeman with an infant on his shoulder. She remembered his wife's fury. What would *she* say when she found out?

Seth shook his head in disgust. 'Get yourself cleaned up. Get a good night's rest. There'll be a debriefing at eight a.m. tomorrow.' He exhaled dramatically. 'They're going to nail you to the Cross, Persis.'

After he'd left, Blackfinch said, 'I'd ask you how you were feeling except I suspect you'd bite my head off.'

He moved closer and she was suddenly glad of his presence.

'They'll catch him,' he said. 'They'll get the manuscript back.'

She shook her head. 'No. They won't. Skorzeny has spent years learning how to evade the authorities.'

He shrugged. 'I know it's an important artefact but it *is* only a book. It's not as important as your life.'

She met his eyes. For a moment, they just stood there, staring at each other. And then she turned to Tariq Shah, splayed on a sofa in the foyer, still recovering from his ordeal. 'Could you come with me, please?'

Shah stared at her, then turned to Blackfinch, who was looking at her curiously. 'I'd do as she says,' he finally said.

She led them up the carpeted staircase to the first floor, where they stopped at a set of double doors. 'Is this the main temple?'

'Yes,' said Shah.

She waited as the old man unlocked the door.

They walked into the temple.

At first glance, it resembled an enormous courtroom. There were three high chairs positioned at the east, west, and south of the room, like the chairs of judges. A letter G, fashioned from metal and about two feet in height, hung from a chain attached to the ceiling.

Persis reached into her notebook. She turned to the page containing the final riddle, then handed it to Blackfinch, who scanned the inscription:

> *The road to salvation has many gates,*
> *That which you seek in Cutters embrace awaits,*
> *'Neath Sun and Moon and unchanging skies,*
> *Watched over by God, in litteral disguise.*
> *'Twixt Jerusalem and Mecca, it lies.*

'*The road to salvation has many gates* refers, I believe, to the central idea of *The Divine Comedy*, namely, man's journey to Paradise via Hell and Purgatory. At each stage, for each sinner, there are different ways to repent and achieve salvation. Many gates.' She waved a hand at the room. 'The line about *Cutters embrace* led me here, to Freemason's Hall, the Bombay home of the Masons – the guild that originated with ancient stonemasons, or stone*cutters*.'

'Persis, I don't understand. Skorzeny already *has* the manuscript.'

She allowed herself a grim smile. 'Skorzeny has a wrapped package that he *thinks* contains the manuscript.'

Astonishment spread over the Englishman's face.

She turned back to the room. 'Mr Shah, what do those chairs represent?'

Shah cleared his throat. 'Well, the three chairs are for the sun, moon, and Grand Master of the Lodge.'

She pointed upwards. The ceiling was painted with a map of stars.

'*'Neath Sun and Moon and unchanging skies*,' breathed Blackfinch. He stared at her. 'The manuscript is here, isn't it?'

She next pointed to the hanging G, then looked again at Shah.

'The G signifies that the Grand Architect is always watching over us.'

'The Grand Architect being God?'

'Yes. But we don't call Him that.'

She tapped the line in the notebook in Blackfinch's hands. 'The word *litteral* threw me at first. Did he mean *literal* disguise? But I knew Healy wouldn't have made such a mistake. Besides, he'd used this trick before. Playing with words. So I called Neve Forrester.

'It turns out that *littera* is an ancient Latin word meaning "a letter of the alphabet". It didn't become clear to me what he could have meant until my father described this temple. *Watched over by God, in litteral disguise.* God disguised as a letter of the alphabet.'

Blackfinch looked up again at the metal G suspended high above their heads. 'And the final line? Between Jerusalem and Mecca? What could that possibly mean?'

She smiled. 'Look around you.'

He glanced around the room, not, at first, seeing. And then it sank in.

Against the walls of the temple were book cabinets, stretching from floor to elevated ceiling. The books were kept behind glass, and there were thousands of them.

She asked Shah to explain. 'Well, yes, our collection has built up over the past seventy years, ever since the Bombay Lodge was initiated.'

'Are the books regularly used?'

He shook his head. 'No. We keep them as a repository of our history. They are rarely taken out of the cabinets.'

Persis turned to Blackfinch. 'John Healy was a Mason.'

'How do you know?'

'I spoke with his father. *He* was a Mason too.'

She swept her arm over the book cabinets. 'What better place to hide the manuscript than in plain sight?' She stepped across the tiled floor to the nearest cabinet. 'What we're looking for are religious books.'

'In that case, you're looking in the wrong place,' said Shah. 'That's engineering.' He led them across the room, to another set of towering cabinets. 'All the religious books are here.'

'There must be thousands of them,' said Blackfinch, surveying the shelves.

'There'd be no use hiding a needle in a haystack containing only a handful of straws,' she said.

Dropping to her haunches, she peered at the lowest shelf. 'Unless I miss my guess, Healy hid the manuscript between a copy of the Tanakh – or the Torah – or possibly even the Bible – and a copy of the Koran.'

'*Twixt Jerusalem and Mecca*,' said Blackfinch.

'Precisely.'

They set to work with a will.

Fifteen minutes later, Blackfinch shouted from atop a stepladder. He clambered down with a book wrapped in velvet cloth. 'Right between the Tanakh and the Koran.' He handed her the volume.

She walked to the lectern in front of the Grand Master's chair and set the book down. Behind her, a clock struck ten.

Ten.

There was something she was supposed to do at ten.

Zubin. *I'll be waiting at the Café Eden. My train is at ten-twenty. I hope you'll come.*'

If she left now, she might still catch him.

She looked up at Blackfinch. His face glowed with admiration.

Zubin could wait.

With shaking fingers, she untied the string, and removed the velvet wrapping.

48

'Father Alvares will see you now.' The young curate ushered them forward, past the church's magnificent organ, and through a door behind it.

Inside, the parish priest, Mervyn Alvares, rose from a seat behind a cluttered desk and greeted them warmly. He herded them on to a small sofa, then took a wing chair opposite.

Up close, she saw that he was possibly in his early fifties, bald, dark-skinned, with handsome cheekbones and a narrow moustache.

'How may I help?'

Persis glanced at Erin Lockhart. The American nodded. She had arranged the meeting – she knew Alvares, having made his acquaintance through her former lover.

'Erin tells me that you were John Healy's priest?'

'Yes. He came to me. A very troubled young man.'

'What was troubling him?'

Alvares shifted uncomfortably. 'I'm afraid that much of what John discussed with me was done so within the sanctity of the confessional.'

'Healy is dead,' she replied. 'Surely, it's more important that the truth now be told?'

He remained silent, wrestling with his conscience.

'John Healy made a mistake,' she continued. 'The world will soon discover that he collaborated with the Nazis. That error of judgement cost him everything, including his moral centre. He spent his final years running from himself. If we're to salvage anything of his life, then I must know the truth.'

'What exactly is it that you *think* you know?'

'Healy was blackmailed into stealing the Dante manuscript. But I don't believe he ever intended to hand it to the Nazis. His aim was to *protect* it from them. He removed the manuscript from the Asiatic Society and then hid it, where he thought they wouldn't find it. Having done so, he took his own life. In his mind, he had obtained absolution. This was his great act of atonement.' She paused. 'Either that, or he just didn't want to give them the chance to torture the truth out of him. They'd cowed him with fear once; he wasn't about to let them do it a second time.'

'Suicide is a mortal sin,' Alvares reminded her.

'Yes,' she said. 'But my understanding is that there are three conditions that must be met for a sin to be deemed "mortal". First, the sin must be grave; second, the sin must be committed with full knowledge of its seriousness; and, finally, the sin must be committed freely. I believe the first two conditions are satisfied in Healy's case – certainly, as a biblical scholar, a Catholic, and a man who had studied *The Divine Comedy* extensively, he knew that suicide was a grave sin. But the third . . . I think Healy believed that he had no choice but to end his own life in order to protect the manuscript. He was prepared to endure Purgatory, as penance for his "sin", the sin of collaborating with the Nazis during the war.' She stopped, marshalling the arguments she had rehearsed before the meeting. 'In *The Divine Comedy*, though Dante clearly states that suicide is a mortal sin, he also paves the way for debate. In Canto XIII, he is led through the forest of suicides, and speaks with the soul of a man named Pietro della Vigna, once the chancellor to Holy Roman Emperor Frederick II. Dante portrays della Vigna as a "heroic suicide", a man who killed himself as a means of protesting injustice. The episode discusses the morality of suicide, and I think this gave Healy the courage to decide that taking his life for what he believed was a just cause would ultimately be forgiven.'

'Your reasoning is sound,' said Alvares, nodding. 'Though ultimately flawed. I don't believe we can interpret God's diktats to suit our circumstances.'

'Why don't you just tell us what he spoke to you about?' snapped Lockhart. 'All that time he spent here. Sticking Crosses on his bedroom wall. Maybe *you're* the reason he killed himself. Filling his head with pious guff.'

Persis put a hand on her arm and the American subsided.

Alvares looked shocked. A silence passed, and then he sighed. 'Very well. May God forgive me ... Yes, John came to me. He confessed everything, everything that had happened during the war. He told me that he'd chosen to work with the Nazis rather than suffer their brutality. They'd threatened to torture him; to hang him in his cell at Vincigliata and make it look like suicide. He couldn't stand the idea of it. Of pain. Of death. He was a coward – that's how *he* described himself.

'He travelled around Italy with a team from the Gestapo, looking for old manuscripts. He helped them identify and track down scholars who possessed such items. He stood by as men – and sometimes their families too – were murdered. Stood by while their houses were ransacked. And then he sat down and examined the plunder they'd taken.

'He told me of one instance when he was forced to look through a manuscript while an old Italian colleague, his wife, and their three children lay dead against the wall in the same room. He'd led the Nazis to them. Without him, they'd still be alive.'

Lockhart groaned beside her.

'John hadn't expected to survive the war, but somewhere along the way he gave his captors the slip and returned to England. To a hero's welcome.

'In time, the shades of all those who'd died because of him returned. He began to see them, first in his sleep, and then in broad daylight. He couldn't escape them. Wherever he went, they were there.

'That was when the idea of salvation began to seep into him. He'd studied the Bible – now he began to study Dante. He ended up in Bombay so that he could examine Dante's great work about human salvation.'

'But why Bombay?' asked Persis.

'Because he wanted peace. He wanted to be where few people knew him. He was looking for the answer to his troubles. How could a man who'd done the things he'd done find a way to Paradise?'

'Why not just use a recent translation?' Persis persisted. 'Why *this* manuscript?'

'He'd already looked at every translation he could find. He wanted to return to the source. To see if Dante's many translators had overlooked something. Something that would free his mind.' He sighed. 'John wasn't thinking clearly.'

Those words stayed with her.

An hour later, sitting at her desk, typing up an addendum to the report she'd submitted four days earlier, she couldn't help but think of John Healy's suffering. He'd shown weakness, and that weakness had cost lives. Both during the war, and now, in Bombay.

She had little doubt that if he'd immediately alerted the authorities to Otto Skorzeny's plot to steal *The Divine Comedy*, Franco Belzoni – and possibly Francine Kramer – would still be alive.

She would never be able to find it within herself to forgive such weakness.

And yet ... John Healy was a victim, too, of a war that had revealed, over and again, the true ugliness of the human condition.

She remembered now the envelope he'd left in his bag before taking his own life. The lines from *Inferno* that he'd written on the note she'd found inside. '*Midway upon the journey of our life, I came to myself, in a dark wood, For I had wandered from the straight and true.*'

She felt certain that those lines had been specifically chosen; that, in Dante's words, John Healy had seen his own predicament.

He had lost his way and had never really been able to find it again.

Perhaps that explained why he'd ultimately taken his own life. For a Catholic, suicide *was* a mortal sin. But by sacrificing himself for a higher cause, perhaps he'd hoped to balance the scales, to recover what he'd lost.

His soul.

In some ways, she felt sure Healy identified with Dante, lost in the forest of his own moral abasement, gradually finding a way to Heaven – via Hell and Purgatory. Perhaps, that's why saving *The Divine Comedy* had meant so much to him.

She glanced at the clock. She'd agreed to meet Blackfinch for lunch in less than thirty minutes. A Chinese hole in the wall, the Dancing Stomach represented a sort of neutral ground. A setting to throw cold water over anyone's romantic aspirations.

They'd simply be two colleagues celebrating the successful conclusion to a case over a plate of noodles. Prawn crackers, the kind that disintegrated as soon as you looked at them. Maybe dumplings too. And if the conversation should veer around to a possible trip to the Elephanta Caves, then who was to say she might not find the idea worth considering? It had been a while since she'd visited Elephanta Island.

If Blackfinch tagged along, well, that was up to him . . .

Her thoughts oscillated between Zubin and Blackfinch, two men who couldn't be more different if they tried. Where was Zubin now? What was he doing?

And Archie Blackfinch, an enigma wrapped up in a riddle wrapped up in the most awkward, middle-aged Englishman she'd ever met . . . Yet, the man seemed to turn up whenever she needed him, with his badly knotted ties, his frayed elbows, his expression of a bemused cocker spaniel—

A newspaper slapped on to her desk. A copy of the morning's *Indian Chronicle*. Birla loomed over her. 'Channa's been up to his old tricks.'

She glanced at the article, a round-up of the events leading to the recovery of the Dante manuscript. A photograph showed the manuscript being handed over by a glum-looking Neve Forrester to the head of the State Bank of India to be stored, henceforth, in the vaults of the bank's Bombay headquarters.

Persis's contribution to the manuscript's successful return had been all but erased.

Instead, credit for the investigation's positive outcome had been given to Roshan Seth, to the wounded George Fernandes, to ADC Amit Shukla, to Archie Blackfinch. The men peripherally involved in the case.

For the woman who had solved it, who'd risked her life for it, no more than a minor mention.

A geyser of anger roared through her.

Her thoughts whipped about like a kite in a high wind, eventually latching on to something Jaya had said, about her being a *modern* woman . . . Weren't they *all* modern women? Hadn't they earned that right? They'd stood shoulder to shoulder with the men of this country during the Quit India years. They'd shed blood and tears. Sacrifices had been made, and for what?

She thought ahead to the reunion with Dinaz. Another woman who'd slashed and burned her way through the jungle of male ego. It would be interesting to compare scars. But for now . . .

'Are you okay?' Birla was looking at her with concern.

She ignored him, her insides seething.

Her eyes alighted on a card on her desk. The card given to her by Jenny Pinto.

She picked it up and stared at it.

Snatching up the phone, she dialled the number.

On the fourth ring, the call was answered.

'Jenny Pinto?' She waited for a reply. 'It's Persis Wadia. I've changed my mind. I'll be delighted to do that talk. But be warned. I won't be holding back.'

THE END

Author's Note

Although this is a work of fiction, many of the ingredients have been culled from fact:

- The copy of *The Divine Comedy* held at the Asiatic Society of Bombay for almost two centuries is thought to date back to the 14th century, though one historian has suggested that it dates from the 15th century. Either way it is considered a national treasure, so much so that it is now held in a bank, and only brought out for special occasions.
- The manuscript was gifted to the society in the 19th Century by Mountstuart Elphinstone, Governor of Bombay.
- Mussolini tried to buy the manuscript in the 1930s but was rebuffed by the Indian government.
- Mussolini was rescued from an Italian prison by Otto Skorzeny, a top commando and *Obersturmbannführer* in the Waffen-SS, and the last chief of the Abwehr, the Nazi intelligence agency.
- Skorzeny was arrested after the war but escaped from the internment camp at Darmstadt, Germany in 1948. His escape was engineered as I have described in the book.
- Skorzeny later turned up in Egypt where he worked as a military advisor for Gamal Abdel Nasser. He later spent time in Argentina, as an advisor to President Juan Perón and acted as a bodyguard for Eva Perón. He died in 1975, aged 67.
- George Wittet was the principal architect behind the Gateway

to India monument. He is buried in the Sewri Christian Cemetery in Bombay.

- The POW camp at Vincigliata (the Castello di Vincigliata Campo P.G) housed many senior British prisoners.
- The book cipher clues in the novel were all created from the 1611 *King James Bible* – which can be found online.
- Freemason's Hall is a prominent building in Mumbai, over a century old, and largely as I have described. The Freemasons have been in India since the 1700s. They are still going strong.
- Byron's poem *So We'll Go No More A Roving* reads as follows:

So, we'll go no more a roving
So late into the night,
Though the heart be still as loving,
And the moon be still as bright.

For the sword outwears its sheath,
And the soul wears out the breast,
And the heart must pause to breathe,
And love itself have rest.

Though the night was made for loving,
And the day returns too soon,
Yet we'll go no more a roving
By the light of the moon.

Newport Community
Learning & Libraries

Acknowledgements

A follow-up novel is, in some respects, as difficult as the beginning of a new series. If this book works at all it is thanks to the efforts of many.

So, thank you to my agent Euan Thorneycroft at A.M. Heath, my editor Jo Dickinson, and my publicity team of Steven Cooper and Maddy Marshall.

I would also like to thank the rest of the team at Hodder, Sorcha Rose in editorial, Amanda Mackie in production and Dom Gribben in audiobooks. Similar thanks go to Euan's assistant Jessica Lee. And thank you once again to Jack Smyth for another terrific cover.

My gratitude also to Dominick Donald, crime author and military historian, whose eagle eye has been invaluable in fact-checking some of my wilder flights of military fancy; and to my friends and UCL colleagues, Enrico Mariconti and Hervé Borrion, who straightened out my mangled, Google-translator Italian and French respectively.

Finally, a heartfelt thank you to the Red Hot Chilli Writers, Abir Mukherjee, Ayisha Malik, Amit Dhand, Imran Mahmood and Alex Caan, not just for your work on the Red Hot Chilli Writers podcast (tune in if you haven't yet heard us!) but for being the best literary companions anyone could ask for.

Acknowledgements

DISCOVER
VASEEM KHAN'S
charming Baby Ganesh Agency series,
combining murder, Mumbai and
a baby elephant.

And the fun never stops . . . Listen to bestselling crime
authors Vaseem Khan and Abir Mukherjee on the
Red Hot Chilli Writers podcast

A podcast that discusses books and writing, as well as the
creative arts, pop culture, risqué humour and Big Fat Asian
weddings. The podcast features big name interviews, alongside
offering advice, on-air therapy and lashings of cultural
anarchy. Listen in on iTunes, Spotify, Spreaker or visit
WWW.REDHOTCHILLIWRITERS.COM

You can also keep up to date with Vaseem's work by joining his
newsletter. It goes out quarterly and includes:

*Extracts from Vaseem's next book *Exclusive short stories and articles
*News of forthcoming events and signings *Competitions – win signed
copies of books *Writing advice *Latest forensic and crime science articles
*Vaseem's reading recommendations

You can join the newsletter in just a few seconds at Vaseem's website:

WWW. VASEEMKHAN.COM

Order the next book in The Malabar House series . . .

THE LOST MAN OF DEHRA DUN

Bombay, 1950

The monsoon has started and as Bombay grapples with rain-induced chaos, a new case arrives at Malabar House. A man has been found frozen in the foothills of the Himalayas, near the town of Dehra Dun, his face crushed. The case is handed to the unflappable Inspector Persis Wadia and the man is christened 'The Ice Man' by the national media. *Who is he? How long has he been there? Why was he killed?*

As Persis and Metropolitan Police criminalist Archie Blackfinch investigate the case, they uncover a trail left by the enigmatic Ice Man that leads directly into a decades-old conspiracy. Meanwhile, two new murders send ripples of fear through Bombay. Is there a serial killer on the loose?

Order now.

HODDER &
STOUGHTON

THRILLINGLY GOOD BOOKS
FROM CRIMINALLY
GOOD WRITERS

CRIME FILES BRINGS YOU THE LATEST RELEASES FROM
TOP CRIME AND THRILLER AUTHORS.

SIGN UP ONLINE FOR OUR MONTHLY NEWSLETTER AND BE THE FIRST
TO KNOW ABOUT OUR COMPETITIONS, NEW BOOKS AND MORE.

VISIT OUR WEBSITE: WWW.CRIMEFILES.CO.UK
LIKE US ON FACEBOOK: FACEBOOK.COM/CRIMEFILES
FOLLOW US ON TWITTER: @CRIMEFILESBOOKS